"I don't want to be a bother…"

"You won't be a bother. That's why I'm going to hang out with you. I miss you." Wade didn't realize how much he meant it until he said it.

"I'll be boring to be around, anyhow. I've taken napping to a whole new level." Kit flashed him a half-hearted smile and averted her eyes.

She was lying. He knew her too well.

"You're sleeping pretty good, then?"

He'd been right to take the time off. Kit wasn't sleeping. Her mind was probably racing circles around the baby's health troubles. Or she was mourning Cam. Both, most likely.

Kit needed a friend. And, frankly, so did he.

It was only for a week. Nothing to worry about. Then they'd go back to being long-distance friends. The way it should be.

Why didn't the thought fill him with relief?

Jill Kemerer writes novels with love, humor and faith. Besides spoiling her minidachshund and keeping up with her busy kids, Jill reads stacks of books, lives for her morning coffee and gushes over fluffy animals. She resides in Ohio with her husband and two children. Jill loves connecting with readers, so please visit her website, jillkemerer.com, or contact her at PO Box 2802, Whitehouse, OH 43571.

Tina Radcliffe has been dreaming and scribbling for years. Originally from Western New York, she left home for a tour of duty with the US Army Security Agency stationed in Augsburg, Germany, and ended up in Tulsa, Oklahoma. Her past careers include certified oncology RN, library cataloger and pharmacy clerk. She recently moved from Denver, Colorado, to the Phoenix, Arizona, area, where she writes heartwarming and fun inspirational romance.

His Wyoming
Baby Blessing

Jill Kemerer

&

Her Last Chance
Cowboy

Tina Radcliffe

LOVE INSPIRED
INSPIRATIONAL ROMANCE

LOVE INSPIRED®

INSPIRATIONAL ROMANCE

Recycling programs for this product may not exist in your area.

ISBN-13: 978-1-335-46126-1

His Wyoming Baby Blessing and Her Last Chance Cowboy

Copyright © 2021 by Harlequin Books S.A.

His Wyoming Baby Blessing
First published in 2019. This edition published in 2021.
Copyright © 2019 by Ripple Effect Press, LLC

Her Last Chance Cowboy
First published in 2019. This edition published in 2021.
Copyright © 2019 by Tina M. Radcliffe

This edition published by arrangement with Harlequin Books S.A.

For questions and comments about the quality of this book, please contact us at CustomerService@Harlequin.com.

Love Inspired
22 Adelaide St. West, 40th Floor
Toronto, Ontario M5H 4E3, Canada
www.Harlequin.com

Printed in U.S.A.

CONTENTS

HIS WYOMING BABY BLESSING

Jill Kemerer

To the AW baseball moms!
Sandi Hood and Kerri Penrod—you've taken the
brunt of my plotting nonsense and iced-coffee
addiction—thank you! Special thanks to Amy, Jill,
Rhonda, Kim W., Kim K., Marla, Dawn, Michelle,
Dreama, Katie, Heather, Amber, Brooke and Jessica
for your encouragement, pictures and smiles.
My sincere apologies to anyone I might have missed!

Thank you to Shana, Melissa and Elizabeth,
the editors who helped shape this book.
You make me a better writer.

And finally, thank you to my agent, Rachel Kent,
for all you do.

Now the God of hope fill you with all joy and peace in believing, that ye may abound in hope, through the power of the Holy Ghost.
—*Romans* 15:13

Chapter One

She should have been here by now.

Wade Croft paced the front porch of the sprawling log cabin he called home. Late May wildflowers and blue skies spread as far as he could see, pausing only at the white-capped Bighorn Mountains. Unfortunately, the peaceful scene did nothing to slow his rapid heartbeat. Kit McAllistor would be here any minute, and the last time he'd seen her had been at her husband's funeral four months ago. The experience had unsettled him.

Kit's stricken, drawn face as she'd cried over the casket had picked off the scab on emotions he'd gotten used to pretending didn't exist, and, as much as he sympathized with her loss, he'd avoided contacting her since then. The little girl he'd met in foster care all those years ago—his childhood best friend, the one who always believed the best in him—had grown into a very special, very beautiful woman.

Her husband passing away complicated things.

A dust cloud formed in the distance. It must be Kit's car. He propped his hand against one of the posts. His land stretched for miles. Land he'd been blessed with.

He'd taken it for granted in his quest to expand. Look where it had gotten him. On the brink of losing it all. Why had he overextended himself last year to buy Dudley Farms, a massive farm east of here? If he didn't find a buyer for Dudley Farms soon, he'd lose everything, including his home, JPX Ranch.

Somehow, he'd find a way to get out of this financial hole, and until he did, no one needed to know about the trouble he was in.

Right now he had to focus on Kit.

The compact silver car stopped in front of the garage. He had the oddest sensation that if he moved even a muscle, his life would change forever.

Nonsense. Get over there like the barn is on fire!

He took off toward the driveway as the car door shut with a thud. Kit walked his way. A perfectly rounded belly jutted out from her long sundress.

His feet refused to move another inch.

She was pregnant.

Why the concept floored him, he couldn't say, maybe because the thought of her having a baby hadn't occurred to him, with Cam's death and all.

If he thought her husband dying complicated things...

"Wade." The word sounded scratchy, defeated. Her skin was drawn, dark crescents shadowed her pale green eyes and weariness burdened her shoulders. The woman standing before him barely resembled his vibrant friend.

"Kitty Cat." The old nickname fell off his tongue before he could worry about the consequences.

Something sparked in her eyes, and she closed the distance between them, wrapping her arms around his waist. He held her lightly, trying to ignore the sensations crowding his brain. Soft skin. Long silky hair with a hint of coconut shampoo. A pregnant tummy separating them. She seemed thinner, not taking into account the baby. There was a frailness to her that didn't mesh with any version of the Kit he knew. At least the freckles on her nose were still there.

"I didn't know where else to go." She stepped back and let out the most pitiful sigh he'd ever heard.

"What have I always told you?" He tried to capture the teasing tone he saved especially for her, but he didn't quite nail it.

"If I ever need anything, you're here for me." She didn't crack a smile. In fact, her face was as devoid of expression as it was of makeup.

"Exactly." He straightened, locking his jaw. The fragile, pregnant woman standing here wasn't the feisty, optimistic girl he'd bonded with as a kid. Life had beaten her down. It had beaten him down enough, too, but he hated that it hadn't spared her.

"Come inside." He held the door open, then he led the way to the great room, a large open space with plenty of windows, hardwood floors, leather furniture and area rugs to keep the chill out. Visible signs of the wealth he'd accumulated and, in his greed, put in jeopardy.

"You really did it, didn't you?" She looked around, lowering her body onto one of the couches. "You always said you were going to own the biggest ranch in Wyoming someday. Your house alone is massive."

A surge of shame filled him. If he hadn't bought Dudley Farms, he'd have been financially set for a lifetime. All attempts at trying to salvage his mistake hadn't worked. Last year the farm's old irrigation equipment had failed, and the drought had polished off any hopes of growing enough crops to be profitable. On both properties—here on JPX Ranch and on Dudley Farms—he'd downsized all his employees to the bare minimum. Sold as many calves, heifers and horses as he could, except for his favorite stud horse, Del Poncho. He'd sell Del Poncho only if absolutely necessary. But the way the bills were coming in, he'd have to sooner rather than later.

"I didn't realize you were…having a baby." He waved in her general direction as he sat in a chair opposite her. "I mean, it was hard enough Cam died." Heat licked up his neck, and he averted his gaze. What was wrong with him? He wasn't shy. Didn't get squeamish. And here he was acting like a pimply kid instead of a grown man.

She tucked her hair behind her ear and averted her own eyes. It brought him back to their younger days. She'd been eight and he'd been ten when they'd met at a foster home. They'd been best buds the three years they'd lived there. He could still see the freckles on her nose as she swung her legs high in the air, brown hair flying in the wind. Her eyes had danced with delight as she begged him to push her higher, higher. When her swing would finally come to a stop, he'd sit on the one next to hers, and, with their legs dangling, they'd talk about the future.

He'd been set on owning the biggest ranch in Wyoming. He'd have so much money no one could ever again tell him what to do. She was going to be a teacher and get married to the best husband in the world and have two boys, one girl, a dog, a cat and a nice house. They both had been on their way to achieving those dreams. And though they still shared a childhood bond,

Kit's marriage to Cam had strained their friendship. Wade understood. Marriage changed things.

"I guess the perfect family you always wanted isn't turning out the way you'd hoped," he said, as gently as possible.

"Yeah, well, it was a stupid dream, anyhow." She gazed out the wall of windows. Sadness and something else was etched into her face. Bitterness?

Not Kit. Sunny, kind, spitfire Kit never let anything get her down.

He didn't like to think of her spirit broken, but maybe he was overanalyzing things.

"When are you due?"

"October second." Her shrug gave him the impression she was nervous. "Depending."

Depending on what? He scuffed his foot against the floor.

"Thanks for letting me stay here. It will only be for a week. The extended-stay hotel should have a room for me by then."

She hadn't given him much information when she called last night. Just said she needed a place to stay for a week and did he have a spare room for her? He'd offered her one of several renovated cabins on his property. They'd been remodeled a few years ago for his friends to use for getaways, hunting, fishing…whatever. She was welcome to hunker down in any of them.

But last night she hadn't mentioned an extended-stay hotel.

She also hadn't mentioned she was having a baby.

"Why are you going to some roadhouse?" He needed more information from her. Nothing was adding up, and he didn't exactly consider himself slow.

One of her shoulders lifted. "I'm moving to Casper."

"Did you get a new job or something?" He couldn't picture her accepting a different position. She loved teaching second grade in Fort Laramie. But maybe the memories with Cam made it too hard for her to continue working there.

"No." Her hands covered her tummy.

Her short answers, air of gloom and lack of animation kicked up his stomach acid.

"Kit, this is me. You don't have to hide anything." He leaned forward, immediately recognizing the hypocrisy of his words. He was hiding his problems from her and everyone else he was close to. "What is going on?"

"I need a new start."

Normally, he'd buy what she was saying. She'd lost the love of her life. She was alone. Pregnant. But…she was keeping secrets. He narrowed his eyes. "You're not telling me everything."

"Look, I need a place to crash for a few days, and then I'll be on my way. Don't ask me to tell you my life story in the meantime."

"I already know your life story." He knew most of it. The important stuff, anyhow.

"That was the old me."

"I liked the old you."

"Well, she's gone, so don't bother looking for her. Why don't you show me the cabin where I can put my stuff? Then you can go back to work." She braced both hands against the couch cushions in an attempt to get up. He sprang to his feet, offering her his hand.

"Why the hotel? Why Casper?" He kept her hand in his and searched her face for clues about whatever she wrestled with. Had Cam's death destroyed the best part of her?

Her eyes welled with tears.

Great, he'd made her cry. Why had he badgered her? Of course she wanted to move. She was alone and pregnant and grieving the sudden death of her husband. No wonder she was shattered and prickly. He'd always tried to fix anything bothering her, but this was beyond him.

Maybe he should do as she asked. Take her to the cabin and leave her alone to work things out.

"It's the baby," she whispered.

"What do you mean?" He gently clasped her forearms and bent to look into her eyes.

"He has a large hole in his heart."

"What?"

"A few weeks ago, I had a routine ultrasound. I figured I'd be finding out if it was a boy or girl, and everything would be fine. Unfortunately, they suspected there was a hole in his heart, but they told me not to worry and to come back in a few weeks for a fetal echocardiogram. Well, I did, and the hole was confirmed, which led to another ultrasound with a specialist last Wednesday. Since the heart defect may be caused by chromosome abnormalities, I had an amniocentesis done on Friday. They're using the cells to do a chromosomal microarray test to check for Down syndrome, DiGeorge syndrome and a few other things. The results won't be in for about three weeks."

He let go of her arms. Friday. And today was Tuesday. Chromosomes, tests, a hole in the baby's heart… *his* heart, she'd said.

The baby was a boy.

An image came to mind of a little tyke with Kit's

freckles holding Wade's hand as the child stared up at him with excitement at the thought of riding around the ranch.

"This amnio-cent-whats-is and chromosome thing— what does all of it mean?"

"Amniocentesis is a test to determine the likelihood of genetic problems. It was offered in my first trimester, but I opted not to have it at that time because I'm young and healthy. And chromosome abnormalities are just a fancy way of saying my baby might have special needs." Her inhalation was long and shaky.

"Okay, we'll deal with it." The earlier image of a little boy morphed from one who looked like Kit to one with Down syndrome. The image appealed to him as much as the first one had.

"The hole could heal on its own." A tear dropped onto her cheek, and she swiped it away. "But if not, the baby will require heart surgery. And if he has DiGeorge syndrome, there's a strong chance he won't make it to his first birthday. The doctor told me not to worry about DiGeorge too much and that heart defects are common, but I don't know what to think at this point. I'll know more after the test results come back. In the meantime, I'm praying he doesn't die in the womb."

Die? He tried to process it. No wonder she'd become a shadow of her former self. She'd lost her husband, and now she might lose her baby, too.

"I'm scared, Wade." The faint words spun him out of his thoughts.

He understood scared. Too many sleepless nights trying to come up with a solution to his lack of cash flow had taken their toll.

"You're staying here until the baby is born. Not in

a hotel." He straightened, widening his stance. "I want you to rest. You won't move a muscle. I'll take care of you."

Why had he promised the last part? Him? Taking care of her? He could barely keep up with the mortgage on his land. He didn't trust himself to take care of a stray dog at this point.

"No." She clutched her hands, wringing them together.

"If he does have special needs, would you still want him?" he asked.

"Of course! I just want him to live. I don't care what problems he might have. I love this baby so much. I can't bear to think of him dying."

He wasn't surprised. She'd love any child fiercely, but her declaration reminded him of those complications from earlier.

Kit wasn't his. Never had been, never would be.

And that's the way it would stay. She deserved someone who would treat her right and take care of her financially and emotionally. He'd never been good at the emotional stuff, and, frankly, he had little to give in the finance department, either.

He'd just have to do his best to support her, regardless.

"Stay here in the main house. I have three guest rooms. That way if you need me—"

"No. I need space." She shook her head rapidly, her long brown hair swishing behind her. "I appreciate the offer, but I can't. One of your cabins will be fine."

"You can take your pick. Stay in one of them until the baby is born."

"That's kind of you, but I'll just stay the week." She

ducked her chin. "I'm only crashing here until the hotel has a vacancy."

He should be relieved. It wasn't as if he could offer her anything more than a temporary place to stay. As much as he'd like to see her taken care of long-term, it wasn't his place.

"If you'll point me in the right direction…"

He gave her a curt nod. "I'll take you over there right now."

JPX Ranch truly was her last resort. On the long drive here, Kit had dreaded having to rely on Wade. She'd messed up her life, and he'd always been able to see right through her. But as she followed his truck down a dirt driveway behind his house, relief replaced the dread. He was the one person—the only one—she'd ever been able to count on for anything.

And here he was, coming through for her again.

If he had any idea what a disaster her life had been for the past three years, would he view her the same?

She had no intention of finding out.

Wade stopped in front of a large log cabin. She could see four other smaller structures spaced out farther down the lane. As she got out of her car, she was glad the blooming wildflowers had spread to surround the guest homes. Silver lupine and little yellow castles waved in the breeze, and she couldn't help but enjoy their beauty. For a moment, anyway. Nothing good in her life ever stuck around for long.

"I think you'll like this one the best." Strength oozed from him as he strode up the covered porch, then swung open the door and waited for her to join him.

She tried not to stare. In form-fitting jeans, cow-

boy boots and a short-sleeved Western shirt, he looked
every bit the cowboy most women only dreamed about.
His blue eyes crinkled at the corners—a side effect of
his sense of humor. He kept his dark blond hair short.
The bone structure of his face was perfectly symmet-
rical, and she'd often thought he could model for one
of those rodeo calendars she'd hung on her wall as a
teen. Not that she'd ever tell him that. Most days his
head was too big for his cowboy hat without her swelling it even more.

What woman wasn't attracted to Wade Croft? Even
one on her deathbed would likely revive if it meant
catching a glimpse of the prime Wyoming cowboy.

The cabin was anything but the dusty old hunting
lodge she'd expected. Freshly renovated with big windows, gleaming wood floors and comfortable furniture,
it was nicer than any place she'd lived. And, better yet, it
held none of the bad memories or mistakes she'd made
in her other homes.

"It's so light and open." The high wooden ceilings
cast a pretty glow on the room.

"The kitchen's back here. Should meet your needs."

She followed him and stopped, her mouth dropping
open.

"You're kidding, right?" She trailed her fingertips
along the marble—or was it quartz? It certainly wasn't
the chipped counters she was used to. This was hands
down the best kitchen she'd ever seen. With stainless
steel appliances, tall cabinets and a pretty backsplash,
it was her ideal kitchen.

From the window above the sink, a carpet of wildflowers came into view. A reprieve for her weary soul.

"Kidding? What do you mean?" His defensive tone

would have made her laugh if she still had a shred of joy left, which she didn't. Not by a long shot. "What's wrong with the cabin?"

"Not a single thing." She could at least attempt to set him at ease. He'd been kind today. But then, he'd always been kind to her. "Except your boots are leaving dirt all over the floor."

He kicked up the bottom of his boot, then shot her a teasing glare. "My boots are as clean as the day I took them out of the box."

"You sure about that?"

"As sure as I am a hotel won't do you a lick of good."

The hotel. Right.

She massaged her belly. Until recently, she'd been dealing with Cam's death as best as she could, but finding out about the hole in the baby's heart and learning it might be caused by special needs… As much as she hoped the hole would heal on its own, the fact the doctor was running all those tests didn't reassure her. Nor did the online research she'd done on her own.

"Does this place have a bedroom?" She forced a tight smile. The sooner Wade concluded the tour, the sooner she could sit and think. Well, worry and fret about the baby was more like it.

His forehead furrowed as if he wanted to press the issue. "Down the hall. I'll show you."

The bedroom had log walls, traditional furniture, a neutral area rug and a puffy white comforter on top of a king-size bed.

"The television works. Bathroom is attached." He paused in the doorway with one hand planted on the frame. His long body filled the space. "Tell me what you need."

What did she need?

A healthy baby. Well, that wasn't entirely true. Even if the child *wasn't* healthy, she still wanted him. She could handle the hole in the heart, the special needs. What she really needed was a *living* baby. She just wanted a chance to raise him. No matter what complications were involved.

Her life had been one big complication for years. For her entire life, really. With each change, she'd dug her feet in, disciplined herself to be good, to meet other people's needs in the hopes they'd keep her around.

And every single time, she hadn't been good enough.

The sincerity radiating from Wade's expression tempted her to confess the truth about why Cam had died, but she hadn't survived an abusive aunt, four foster homes and a cheating husband for nothing.

"I'm pretty tired." She sat on the edge of the bed. If Wade wasn't here, she'd crawl under the covers and sleep for a month. Try to, at least.

"Stretch out and rest. I'll get your bags." He knocked on the door frame and left.

She was too tired to protest. Besides, Wade was a strapping cowboy. He'd never let her haul her suitcases and bags inside. She had nothing to prove by overexerting herself and everything to lose if she let her pride override her common sense.

This baby needed a healthy mama.

Her idea of a perfect family had been shattered long ago. She'd give about anything to have any family— perfect or not. A family of two suited her fine. Her and her boy.

Please, God, let my baby live.

The front door creaked, and Wade's footsteps

clomped closer. He set two suitcases in the bedroom. The muscles in his arms and chest strained as he straightened. Even pregnant, she couldn't help but notice. Unfortunately, her pulse did, too.

"Be right back with the rest." He waved his fingers toward the bed. "Why aren't you lying down?"

"I don't need to lie down. Now scoot." She was surprised how easily she fell into their familiar sassing, but it left a bittersweet tang on her tongue.

His lips curved into a cocky smile as he exited the room.

She wished she could be the same Kit McAllistor she was before Cam had announced he wanted a divorce. The one who could banter with her old friend Wade, the one who believed love conquered all and if she just tried hard enough, her husband would want her and not other women.

The old Kit wouldn't have screamed at Cam the night he had a heart attack and died.

She might not have killed him, but it was her fault he was dead. If she hadn't yelled those terrible things, he wouldn't have had the heart attack. He still would have divorced her, though.

The old Kit was gone, along with her dreams and her husband.

No matter what happened, she was on her own. Deluding herself into thinking Cam would provide the security she'd craved had been her biggest mistake. She couldn't afford to make the same one twice.

"That's everything." Wade deposited the bags and wiped his hands down his jeans. "You hungry?"

She almost said no, but her stomach growled.

"Guess that answers my question." He hitched his

chin for her to follow him. "Come on. I'll take you back to my place and feed you."

Why tears sprang to her eyes, she didn't know. Maybe because with all the uncertainties she faced— no job, no husband, a baby with serious health problems—she could still count on Wade.

"What are we having?" She stood, pressing her palm into her lower back. The drive had tightened every muscle in her poor body.

"Steak." He rolled his eyes. "Du-uh."

"Grilled?" Her mouth started watering. The man had always been able to grill a mean steak. "With melted butter on top?"

"As if I'd cook it any other way."

A steak. Warm bed. Gourmet kitchen. And wildflowers as far as the eye could see.

She didn't deserve this.

One week.

Then back to the real world.

She'd build a new life. In Casper. With her sweet baby. If he lived…

For now, she'd do her best to get through the next seven days. "Lead the way."

Chapter Two

If he could find a way back to the easy friendship he'd enjoyed with Kit over the years, their first supper together wouldn't be awkward. Well, not as awkward as it was at the moment. It was hard to believe she was actually sitting across from him at his dining table.

The top of her rounded stomach was barely visible from where he sat. Why her being pregnant messed with his head so much, he couldn't say, but it brought out weird feelings. Protectiveness and worry and…never mind about the rest.

He'd practically grown up with her, they'd been friends for so long. They relied on each other, but not in a romantic way. She'd always viewed him as a big brother, and he'd considered her a…

He took another bite of steak and chewed a little too aggressively.

So he'd had a crush on her and lived for her emails and calls all through high school, even though they'd been apart.

And big deal, he'd visited her every chance he could get when she was at college.

The day she'd called and told him she'd gotten engaged had been like a big cow patty to the face for him. But he'd congratulated her, hung up, dusted off his chaps, gotten back in the saddle and ridden out to the section of fence he'd been about to replace. He may have chopped an old post into tiny bits that afternoon, but by the next morning, he'd been fine.

"Is Casper temporary? Are you moving back to Fort Laramie after the baby is born?" He sprinkled pepper on his baked potato.

"No." Her eyelashes fluttered. "I canceled the lease on our house. I tried to finish out the school year, but it was difficult. I ended up using the rest of my vacation time before giving my notice. Now that there's so much uncertainty with the baby, I'm taking life one day at a time."

Made sense. Continuing her day-to-day existence after losing Cam must have been hard.

"Casper is permanent, then?"

She pushed the meat around her plate. "I don't think in terms of *permanent* anymore."

He didn't, either.

Jackson Poff would turn over in his grave if he knew how poorly Wade had managed his inheritance. Wade never should have mortgaged JPX Ranch as collateral for the loan on Dudley Farms. If he sold the new property soon, even at a loss, he'd be able to pay off the loan and have his nest egg back in his bank account where it belonged. If he couldn't sell it…he'd have to put JPX Ranch up for sale, too.

Why had he been so careless with the land he loved? It had been pure arrogance to think he could add to his profits by buying a big farm when he only had experience growing hay.

"Do you have anyone who can help you?" he asked. "Cam's parents?"

"His mom died, and his dad and I aren't close." She patted her mouth with a napkin, but tension lines edged her lips.

"Friends?" He tried to think of who she'd had in her wedding, who she'd hung out with, but he drew a blank.

"Letting women into my life has never been my strong suit, Wade." She nudged her plate to the side and leaned back in the chair. "My life revolved around Cam and my job. I'm not like you. I don't even have to ask to know you're still best friends with Clint, Nash and Marshall."

It was true. They'd been his brothers since the day they'd met at Yearling Group Home for teen boys. He was blessed that two of them, at least, had settled into homes not far from his ranch. He could see them anytime he wanted.

Kit, for all appearances, was alone. He didn't like it. Who would take her to doctor's appointments? Who would make sure she got to the hospital when she went into labor? Who would hold her hand during the birth?

"You're not seriously thinking about having this baby all by yourself, are you?" The words tumbled out before he'd thought them through. "I mean, you need help. There's got to be someone who can take you to the hospital when you go into labor."

She flashed him a surprised glance, then averted her eyes. "Don't worry about it. I've got it covered."

"What does that mean?" He set his fork down. He'd lost his appetite, anyhow. "Do you have someone to be there with you or not?"

Her hands balled into fists, and she pulled them onto her lap.

"Kit?" He used his you'd-better-tell-me voice.

"I found an apartment two blocks away from the hospital. It will be available in a month or so. And the extended-stay hotel is nearby, too. Like I said, I've got it covered."

That was her idea of having it covered? He wanted to wipe his hands down his cheeks in frustration.

"But what if—"

"My whole life is one big *what-if* right now, so please don't lecture me."

He clenched his jaw. Lecture her? He'd hound her until she talked sense. What did she think? That she could walk a few blocks to the hospital when she got contractions? Of all the foolish ideas…

"I'm doing what's best for me and the baby. Wyoming Medical Center has a level two neonatal intensive care unit, and, if necessary, they'll transfer the baby to a level three or level four NICU. I'm better off in Casper."

He couldn't argue with that. But more worries, more questions came to mind.

"You quit your job. What's your medical insurance situation?"

"I'm paying for an extension of the insurance I had through work."

"Can you afford it?"

"I have Cam's life insurance."

"Will it last?"

She glared at him. Wade didn't care. He needed to know she'd be all right.

"Honestly, I don't know. Specialists and hospitals tend to be expensive, even with insurance."

"If you need help…" He had no idea where he'd get the money, but if Kit was broke, he'd figure out something. Selling Del Poncho came to mind.

"I don't."

"Are you sure?" Why was he pressing her, when he wasn't in a position to help? Old habits died hard, he guessed.

She stared at him dead on. The muscle in her cheek flickered. "I'm not taking one red cent from you. This is my life, my baby and I'm a grown woman. I'll handle it. It's bad enough I had to ask you to let me stay here for the week."

What was that supposed to mean? Didn't she want his help? His friendship?

"You might want to sheath those claws. I thought we were friends."

"You're right. I'm sorry." She pinched the bridge of her nose. "I'm not good company lately. Thanks for dinner and everything. I think it's best if I get out of your hair." Pushing her chair back, she started to rise, and winced.

He was at her side in a heartbeat. "What's wrong? You okay? Is it the baby? Should I call the doctor?" Who was her doctor? Was there a baby doctor around here? He had no clue. His ranch was over thirty minutes to Sweet Dreams, not exactly ideal in an emergency, and Sweet Dreams didn't have a hospital.

"It's nothing." She patted his arm. "I get aches and pains now and then. They go away."

"I don't think you should be running around."

She let out a long-suffering sigh. "Do I look like I'm running around? I got up from a chair."

"Why don't you sit on the couch? Kick those legs up. I'll put a movie on. Whatever you'd like."

With a sad smile, she shook her head. "Thanks, but I'm really tired. I think I'll go to bed. Don't feel like

you have to cook for me and entertain me this week.
I'll get along on my own just fine."

What if he didn't want her to get along on her own?

He'd done everything wrong tonight. He should do
as she said and give her the space she needed. Tomorrow he had a meeting with Ray Simon, his real estate
agent. The stack of bills he'd been hoarding in his home
office meant he needed to come up with a plan.

He glanced at Kit. He'd try one more time.

"It's early," he said. "Stay."

"Like I said, I'm real tired."

He'd tried. It would have to be good enough.

"Then I guess I'll take you back."

Ten minutes later, Kit warred with her conscience as
Wade parked his truck in front of her cabin. He'd been
nothing but sweet and nice and caring since she'd arrived, and he'd offered to help with medical bills. Who
did that? Only Wade. But she couldn't accept his money.
Money always had strings attached, and she'd been tied
up pretty tightly in the past. Never again.

Still…this was Wade, and she'd hurt his feelings, and
he was the one person who knew her history. She could
count on him, and she'd treated him poorly.

She needed—and wanted—to make it up to him.

"Wait, don't move a muscle. I'll come around and
help you." Wade held his finger up, then got out and
jogged over to her. His rough hand in her palm made
her heart do a flip.

Strong, hardworking hands for a strong, hardworking man.

What would her life be like if she'd married someone like Wade instead of Cam?

What did it matter? No sense wasting energy on stupid thoughts like that. She'd made her bed and had to live with the consequences.

"Do you want to sit with me on the porch for a spell?" She gestured to the two rocking chairs angled to face the mountains.

"You sure?"

"Yeah, I'm sure."

The sun glowed low on the horizon as they settled into the chairs. A herd of cattle grazed in the distance. The rocking motion soothed her, and she wrapped her arms around her stomach. *Can you feel it, too, sweet one?* This might be the only time she got to rock her little boy.

Really, she had to stop being so morbid.

She'd enjoy the baby now and not think about the future.

Nagging at the back of her mind were the key moments that had triggered the losses in her life. Getting the belt on a daily basis before being sent to the first foster home as a five-year-old. Not being docile enough for the second family and moving to the next foster home. The third home was where she'd met Wade. Happiest days of her life. Until the family moved out of state, scattering the foster kids. The next place she'd earned her keep, tucked away her needs and emotions to ensure she had a place to live.

Being her real self never felt safe. Whenever her true feelings came out, bad things happened. Just look at Cam.

"Tell me about this place," she said. "I remember when you lived south of here. I'm assuming you still own that property. Is the little house still there?"

"The shack?" He clasped the ends of the rocker arms and slung one ankle over his knee. "I do still own it.

That hundred acres was my first slice of owning a ranch. And, yeah, the shack is still there."

"It was hardly a shack. I liked it. It was cozy, cute."

"And infested with mice, lacking in insulation and tiny."

"It suited you." Her mood lightened at the memory of visiting him during one summer break. When she'd arrived, he'd been sweeping the floor, muttering about rodent droppings. He'd been younger, full of energy and ambition.

She peeked at his profile. Some things never changed. He was still full of energy and ambition.

When she was younger, she'd considered Wade her knight in shining armor. Still did. But he was all wrong for her. She'd known it then. She knew it now.

He was into building a ranch empire.

She was into raising a family.

The two concepts didn't gel where he was concerned. Ranching would always be his love, his priority. Kit had closed the door on any fantasy of being with him. Then she'd locked it, thrown away the key and bricked it over for good measure.

Wade was too attractive inside and out for her to revisit youthful fantasies.

How many times over the years had he told her he didn't see himself ever getting married?

Looking out over the land, she realized it had been years since she and Wade had really talked. After her wedding day, she'd felt it was inappropriate to keep texting and calling him, so they'd drifted apart, exchanging birthday cards and not much else.

She'd missed him. His friendship had been her lifeline until marrying Cam. And here Wade was extending his friendship again.

"I'm sorry, you know." She kept rocking.

"For what?"

"For not keeping in touch better."

He waved his hand dismissively. "Don't worry about that. Would have been weird with you being married and all."

Her chest grew tight. He understood. Most guys wouldn't have.

"Well, I'm sorry just the same. Why don't you fill me in on all I've missed? You were pretty tight-lipped about how you came to own this land. Do you own more, too? What have you been doing for the past couple of years?"

A shadow crossed his face and he narrowed his eyes as he stared off into the distance. "I always had my sights on this acreage, mainly because the man who owned it, Jackson Poff, didn't have kids to pass it down to. I figured it gave me a chance to negotiate, so I struck up a friendship with him."

"Wade!" She widened her eyes, tilting her head. "You used him?"

He flashed a grin. "No, Kitty Cat. I was up front with him from day one. I rolled up in my truck, introduced myself, told him I loved his land and planned on buying a portion of it someday. Then I offered to help him feed his cattle. He spat on the ground and told me to take a hike, but not in such friendly language."

She couldn't help it—she laughed.

"The next morning, I showed up again and told him how I admired his pastures." He pointed to the right. "That section there to be precise. I asked him what his plans were for the day, and he told me he was checking fence and for me to take a hike—once more, not in such friendly language. I ignored him and helped him fix fence. For six months I came over every day after

I'd taken care of my small cattle operation. And we became good friends. I told Jackson I wanted to buy some of the land when he retired."

"And he obviously retired." Her head rested against the back of the chair, and she relaxed for the first time in a long while. Wade's low, mellow voice soothed the rough places inside.

"No." He dropped his head. "I wish that's how it had gone."

"What happened?"

"He died. It was sudden."

Poor Wade. It sounded like he'd really enjoyed Jackson's company.

"And you bought this after he passed?"

He shook his head. "I would have. But I didn't have to. He gave it to me. All of it. Almost eight thousand acres. The house, the cabins, the outbuildings, the cattle—everything. Even his substantial savings. I still can't believe it."

"Wow." She couldn't imagine anyone doing something so generous. "No one contested it?"

"Nope. Jackson didn't have any next of kin." His eyebrows furrowed. "He made everything possible for me. I likely never would have been able to afford to purchase this entire ranch. I'd hoped I could buy a slice of it—and I had no illusions about the fact I'd need a huge mortgage—but his generosity made it a moot point."

"So how much land do you own altogether, then?"

He told her about Dudley Farms, as well as a few smaller properties in the southern part of the state he rented out for pasture.

"I'm impressed." She savored a deep breath of the fresh air. The fact Wade's dream had come true warmed her soul. "You made it. You did everything you said you were going to do."

"I haven't made it." He flashed her a confused glance. "Not by a long shot."

"What do you mean? You own thousands upon thousands of acres and run your own cow-calf operation here, as well." Wasn't all this enough for him? The thought of being responsible for so much land gave her a headache.

"Yeah, well, I put Dudley Farms up for sale."

"Why?"

"Doesn't matter." From his tone, she'd say he wasn't happy about it. "I hope it sells soon."

"If it doesn't?" The warmth of the air and the rocking motion made her eyelids heavy.

"It will."

"When will you have made it?" she asked lightly.

"What do you mean?"

"Well, I told you you'd made it, and you said not by a long shot. How do you define making it?"

He didn't answer.

She yawned. He'd probably never be done acquiring properties. And since he hadn't married, she could confidently assume his conviction to stay single still held true. Exactly why she'd been wise to brick that wall over her heart all those years ago.

His priority was ranching. Her priority was her unborn child.

Exhaustion took over. She'd never been this tired in her life. She couldn't fight it any longer. She gave in to sleep.

Wade flipped pancakes the next morning in his kitchen. Tendrils of steam rose from his mug of coffee next to the griddle. The floor felt cool beneath his bare feet. Wearing athletic shorts and an old rodeo T-shirt from his friend Nash's bull-riding days, he inhaled the smell of batter and told himself for the eighteenth time that morning he'd done the right thing.

Earlier, he'd called his real estate agent and canceled his appointment. Ray had sounded shocked, and Wade didn't blame him. He couldn't remember the last time he'd backed out of an appointment.

When will you have made it?

Kit's question last night had caught him off guard. Then when she'd fallen asleep with her dark eyelashes fanned across her cheeks, he'd watched the gentle rise and fall of her chest, her hands still cradling her stomach as if she could keep the baby safe, and something had tumbled inside him.

She'd looked like the girl who'd grabbed his hand the day he'd arrived at the foster home where she'd been living. Full of excitement, she'd said, "Come on! I have something to show you!" And she'd dragged him through the never-ending backyard, past the sheds, beyond the horse pasture to a sliver of a creek. She'd crouched down, pointing at the water gurgling over the stones. "See them?"

"See what?" He'd crouched, too, somewhat mesmerized by her pretty green eyes and long brown hair pulled back in a ponytail. She was younger than him, but he'd instantly bonded with her. Probably because she was so full of life.

"There! The tadpoles. They're swimming!"

Black dots with skinny tails swirled in the water. The coolest thing he'd ever seen. Mostly because she'd been the one to show him.

What had happened to those days? Tadpoles and secrets and lemonade in Mrs. Bradley's kitchen.

The timer beeped. He flipped the pancakes. Browned to perfection. It was all in the timing.

The truth was he *had* made it. And, unfortunately, he was on the verge of losing it. But the appointment with Ray would have taken all morning, and he didn't want to leave Kit here on her own. Not yet. She'd barely touched her food last night. She was clearly exhausted. And there was a sharp edge to her he'd never seen. He didn't like thinking of her jaded about Cam dying and the baby's health problems. If he could soften that edge a bit, take care of her, make sure she ate and slept and relaxed, well, he'd cancel everything until she left next week.

His ranch manager could call in a few local teens to help out with the chores.

Just for the week, though.

Even thinking about not hustling out to check cattle tightened his chest uncomfortably.

It would be fine. Everyone took a vacation now and then.

Except him.

The smell of burning caught his attention. He lifted a pancake—black on one side. *Well, giddyap.* This was what happened when his mind wandered to unwelcome places. Perfectly good pancakes turned into hockey pucks. He tossed the ruined flapjacks in the trash and started a new batch.

Fifteen minutes later, he loaded the foil-covered platter of pancakes, a dish full of cooked bacon, strawberries, maple syrup, milk and orange juice into the back seat of his truck. Then he drove into the bright sunshine and headed to Kit's cabin.

After knocking several times, he contemplated his next move. Knock harder? Let her sleep?

Her pinched face when she'd gotten up from the table last night came to mind. What if something was wrong? She could be unconscious on the floor right this minute.

Pounding on the door, he yelled her name. If she didn't get out here in ten seconds, he was letting himself in.

He heard movement inside, and the relief almost buckled his knees. She opened the door, her hair mussed, eyes half-closed, and wearing a short-sleeved pajama top with matching shorts.

"What's wrong?" she asked.

A wave of embarrassment washed away his worry. What was wrong with him? He never overreacted. Why was he so worked up? He was worse than a nervous mama with a freshly born calf.

"Nothing." He tried to act cool. "I brought breakfast. Figured you were hungry."

"Really? Why all the noise?" She let him inside. "I'll be right back. Let me brush my teeth and get dressed."

As she walked away, he blew out a long exhalation. He had to stop fussing. By the time he'd brought in the food and set the table, he'd returned to normal.

"You made all this?" Kit appeared in a sundress. Her hair had been combed to fall over her shoulders, and her face, though pale, had more life to it than yesterday.

"I did." He hitched his thumb to the coffeemaker. "Should be done in a few minutes."

"Decaf?"

"Decaf? Why in the world would you want that? Might as well grind up the dirt out back to brew." He tore off two paper towels to use for napkins.

"The baby. I'm not supposed to have caffeine." She

lifted the foil off the pancakes. "Oh, wow, this looks so delicious."

"I didn't realize about the coffee." He rubbed his chin. "I'll go into town later and get you some decaf."

"No, thanks. I can get my own food."

Stubborn as they came. But he knew how to work around her determination. He'd picked up a few secret weapons over the years.

"I'm going into town, anyway. You can either let me get you what you need or you can come with me. Your choice."

He held his breath, hoping she'd let him go alone and hoping even more she'd join him.

"We'll figure it out later."

And that was one of her secret weapons against him. The delay tactic.

"I'm surprised you aren't riding around the ranch. Or did you already check the cattle and do all your cowboy stuff?"

"Cowboy stuff?" He chuckled. "I figured I haven't seen you in a long while. I'll take a few days off."

She choked on her bacon, coughing. "You don't have to."

"I know."

"Seriously, Wade. I don't want to be a bother." She took a drink of milk. "Just do what you normally do."

"You won't be a bother. That's why I'm going to hang out with you. I miss you."

He didn't realize how much he meant it until he said it.

"Well, I'll ride into town with you then. But I insist you stick to your routine. I'll be boring to be around, anyhow. I've taken napping to a whole new level." She flashed him a half-hearted smile and averted her eyes.

She was lying. He knew her too well.

"You're sleeping pretty good, then?"

She nodded, shoving a big bite of pancake into her mouth.

He'd been right to take the time off. Kit wasn't sleeping. Her mind was probably racing in circles around the baby's health troubles. Or she was mourning Cam. Both, most likely.

He bit into a piece of bacon. Cam was gone, the baby had a hole in his heart and Wade might not be able to fix any of it. But he could be present.

Kit needed a friend.

And, frankly, so did he.

It was only for a week. Nothing to worry about.

Then they'd go back to being long-distance friends. The way it should be.

Why didn't the thought fill him with relief?

Until he sold Dudley Farms and got his financial life back in order, he had to tread carefully.

Chapter Three

A girl could live in a place like this forever. Kit sipped a glass of water on the porch of her cabin late Friday morning. The rocking chair had quickly become her favorite spot. She'd spent hours watching butterflies flit around and hawks circle overhead. The mountains added serenity to the scene. For the first time in years, she'd found space to breathe again. The anxieties of life didn't choke her here, and she'd been sleeping well, too.

She wouldn't get the results of the chromosome microarray tests for almost two more weeks, but she'd begun to make peace with whatever they might reveal. Every morning she prayed for her baby boy. Every evening, too.

Her cell phone rang. Probably Wade. Ever since she'd arrived three days ago, he insisted they eat most meals together. Afterward, she'd excuse herself to rest, and he'd wait precisely two hours to call and check on her. With anyone else it would be overbearing, but not with him.

He cared about her. Plain and simple.

The phone rang again, but she didn't recognize the number. "Hello?"

"Is this Kit McAllistor?"

"Speaking."

"This is Jambalaya Suites. A room opened up. You can check in after three this afternoon."

The extended-stay hotel. It would have been welcome news when she'd been driving to Wade's ranch, but after spending a few days here, she didn't immediately jump for joy at the chance to move on.

"Do you still want it?" The man sounded exasperated.

"Yes, thank you. I'll take it. I'll be there this afternoon."

After she hung up, she sighed, continuing to rock on the porch. She really didn't want to leave yet. But the longer she stayed, the harder it would be to go. She'd forgotten how calming the wide-open prairie could be.

Heaving herself to her feet, she cast a longing look at the countryside, then turned and went back into the cabin. She had to pack up her stuff. She'd stop in at the main house on her way out to thank Wade.

He'd be mad, of course, and maybe a little hurt she was leaving like this, but she couldn't face an argument right now. It was bad enough she'd be living in a hotel for weeks. The thought of being in a strange town and not knowing anyone didn't exactly sweeten the deal. Under no circumstances would the hotel room have a porch and butterflies and wildflowers and silence.

But she'd be close to the hospital. She could start looking into job options for after the baby was born. Maybe she'd teach online classes. She'd figure out something.

After hoisting one of her suitcases onto the bed, she

gathered her things. It didn't take long. A knock on the door came as she zipped her smallest bag. Her stomach clenched, and it wasn't because of the baby.

Wade wasn't going to be happy about her leaving like this.

"Come in," she hollered, rolling the luggage down the hall.

"What. Is. Going. On?" He stood in the living room, hands on his hips, legs wide and eyebrows furrowed.

"The hotel had an opening. I'm headed there in a little bit."

"No, you're not."

"Yes, I am."

"Nope." Embers licked to flames in his eyes. He pointed to her suitcase. "Roll that right back into the bedroom. You're staying here."

"I'm going to Casper. Today."

He pursed his lips, shaking his head. "I don't think that's a good idea."

"Well, I do." As much as she'd like to stay here indefinitely, she couldn't. She'd set her plans in motion, and if she changed them now, she might do something stupid. Like stay here and get too comfortable with the one man she could count on. The incredibly gorgeous, caring one who wasn't into love or marriage. She'd made many poor emotional decisions over the years, and she couldn't afford to make another one now. The baby had to come first.

His jaw could crack a walnut, and he opened his mouth, but she raised her hand. "You're not going to convince me, so don't bother trying." She resumed rolling the suitcase to the front door, but he blocked her path. Being within two feet of the strapping man rattled her. She glared at him. "Move."

"Make me."

Move that tall beam of solid steel? If she pushed him, she'd have to touch him, and touching him would merely remind her how appealing his strength was.

"Wade!" She almost stamped her foot.

"I don't like this. Casper is too far away, and you don't know anyone, and the hotel might have nasty bacteria and drifters."

Bacteria and drifters? Like she needed more to worry about at this point. "You're not my boss."

His expression softened. "No one's ever been the boss of you. I wouldn't want to be, and I'd never try."

Closing her eyes, she couldn't decide if it was an insult or a compliment. Either way, it solidified the truth—he viewed her as a friend. Same as she did him. And if she stayed, she'd be in danger of putting on those rose-colored glasses from her youth. She needed to concentrate on herself and the baby.

"Good," she said a little too briskly. "Then kindly put this suitcase in my trunk while I get the rest of my stuff."

A strained moment passed with neither of them speaking.

"Won't you consider it, at least?" He shrugged helplessly. "I think you should stay."

"This is best. For me. For the baby. And for you— you can get back to work. I know you've taken off a lot of time on account of me being here."

He exuded frustration. "Well, if you're dead set on going today, I'll drive you."

"No, I can't ask you to do that."

"You didn't. I offered."

Hours in the car with him? Her senses might not be able to take it.

"How would you get back?"

"I'd rent a car when we got there."

"Seems awfully complicated." She chewed her bottom lip. It would be nice not to have to drive, though.

"Really? Seems simple to me. Besides, I want to make sure this hotel is in a decent area. I don't want to worry about you getting mugged."

"I'm sure the location will be fine. I doubt I'd be in any kind of danger."

"You don't know that." He crossed his arms over his chest. "Either I drive you or you stay here. Those are the options."

"Or you move out of my way and I drive myself. I'm a big girl."

He had the grace to look sorry. "I know. It's not that I think you're incapable. It's just…well… I wouldn't be able to live with myself if something happened to you on the way there. Your car could break down. You could get a flat. Or what if you get pains or something?" He waved helplessly at her abdomen.

Why did he have to say the perfect thing? Her eyes prickled with emotion. Cam had barely spoken to her for months before he died. And the only reason she was pregnant was because of a last-ditch effort to save their marriage. Even if Cam had lived, her marriage would have ended. He'd been adamant about it.

To have a man care about her well-being like this was strange territory.

And she liked it.

But it was a mirage.

Wade cared about ranching and having lots of land. And he cared about her, too, because they were friends. That was all. She wasn't fooling herself into thinking he'd ever want more.

She didn't, either. But he had the power to tempt her.

Which meant she needed to get to Casper soon. Like today.

"Okay," she said. "You can drive me, but I'm staying in the hotel whether you find bacteria or drifters or not."

"We'll see about that."

Wade kept Kit's car below the speed limit. He wasn't in a hurry to deliver her. How could he keep an eye on her when she'd be living so far away? A honky-tonk song played on the radio. She was staring out her window. While they'd spent the first leg of the trip remembering old times, the past hour had been mostly quiet. As buildings dotted the side of the road more frequently, a sense of unease tightened his muscles. They were almost there.

And he wasn't ready for this time with her to end.

His phone's navigation system directed him through town. The closer they got to the address, the more danger signals flashed in his mind. It wasn't the older homes he minded, it was the fact they were run-down. He stopped at a traffic light and assessed the area. Graffiti marked a warehouse on the corner. A skinny dog without a collar ran by, and a group of three teen boys who spelled trouble sauntered down the sidewalk.

The light changed and he drove ahead, taking a left and pulling into the parking lot of Jambalaya Suites. The neighborhood around it clearly had taken a downturn in recent times. The exterior of the hotel was dated, and weeds poked through the lawn.

Kit didn't say a word. She got out of the car and slung her purse over her shoulder.

He fell in beside her as they strolled toward the entrance. A train whistle blared, practically deafening him, and Kit jumped, slapping her hand against her chest. He met her shocked gaze. "Wasn't expecting that."

"Me, neither." She raised her eyebrows. "Home sweet home."

Over his dead body...

They entered the lobby, and Wade forced himself to keep his cool. The forest green carpeting had stains and worn patches. Striped wallpaper peeled in several places. As they approached the front desk, he clenched and unclenched his hands and did everything in his power to stay quiet. The counter had deep scratch marks. Had someone knifed it? And what, for the love of Wyoming, was that smell?

Breathe through your mouth.

The clerk behind the desk didn't look up.

They waited.

And waited.

As much as he wanted to scoop Kit into his arms and run out of here, he remained silent. If he said one wrong thing, she'd dig her heels in. He *would* convince her not to stay here, but in order to do that, he needed a level of patience he might not possess.

"Excuse me." Kit's pleasant voice didn't fit here. *She* didn't belong here.

"Just a sec." The clerk continued to stare at the computer screen.

Just a sec? Wade was *this* close to grabbing the guy by the collar and informing him what good service entailed.

"Yeah?" Bored eyes looked up at them.

"Kit McAllistor." She lifted her chin. "You have a room for me."

"Oh, right."

"She'd like to see the room before she puts down a deposit." Wade leaned forward.

"Whatever you say." The clerk ignored them as he typed. Then he held out a key card to her. "Your room is on the second floor. End of the hall, Kate."

"It's Kit," Wade practically growled.

"Okay, *Kit*."

Don't beat the twerp up. Keep your eyes on the prize.

He'd have Kit in and out of here in ten minutes. Tops.

"Where are the elevators?" she asked the clerk.

"Don't have them. Stairs are to the left."

Wade held his arm out to her and gave the jerk the most lethal glare he could muster, but the kid had already resumed staring at the computer screen.

The smell of wet dog, mold, and what he could only describe as liver and onions filled the hall. Surely, the scent alone would send Kit running back to her car. She couldn't seriously be considering living here, could she?

They climbed the stairs and turned left. This hall smelled marginally better than the one downstairs. Kit stopped in front of the door. It looked like she was praying, but he couldn't be sure. Then she slid the card into the slot. Red light. She swiped it again. Red light.

He took it from her and quickly swiped it twice, getting a green light. She opened the door and walked in, with him on her heels.

The train whistle blew again, and the rumble of the cars moving on the tracks was so loud they could have been right outside the building. Wade crossed over to the window. The train *was* right outside the building. The railroad tracks butted up to the property. He swiped the curtains shut.

He could stay silent no longer.

He was getting her out of here.

Turning, he opened his mouth to let her know in no uncertain terms that this place was a dump and there was no way he was leaving her, but he didn't have a chance to speak.

With her hands over her face and her shoulders shaking, Kit sobbed.

Stupid Jambalaya Suites. Muttering under his breath, he took three strides and pulled her into his arms.

"It's okay, Kitty Cat," he said softly. "You're not staying here."

She lowered her hands, tears streaming down her face.

"I'm sorry, Wade, I don't mean to be like this. But the thought of spending the next month or so here… I'm already nauseous from the smell—and I can't take the noise and the carpet and the awful bedspread…"

"I know. I think someone heated up liver and onions, and that's unacceptable."

"I could handle the smell. I think I could, at least, but it's so loud, and there's no front porch with a rocker. And the bathroom tile freaks me out. Where are the butterflies? I can't do this!"

He didn't know what she was talking about, but if it meant she was coming home with him, he liked it. Keeping his arms around her, he stroked her hair. Soft, lush hair. "Shh… I know. This is no place for you."

"I agree." She stepped out of his embrace, tilting her chin up. "I'm finding another hotel."

"What?" Didn't she get it? She wasn't staying in Casper in a hotel. She was coming back to JPX Ranch, where she'd have rest and fresh air and good food. And him.

He needed to keep an eye on her…as long as possible.

"Come on." She hurried to the door. "I'm serious. We have to find another hotel. Today."

The familiar no-budging tone had him gritting his teeth. Just when he thought he'd won, she threw down a new gauntlet. He couldn't argue with that tone. No one could.

"Fine." He'd take her to other hotels, but he wasn't going to leave her at any of them.

He hadn't been in the habit of praying for a long time. But he needed help. This was a situation he couldn't control on his own. Would God even listen to a guy like him? He knew he was saved. Believed Jesus had died and risen for him. But he hadn't been to church in years. And he kept a Bible in his nightstand only because when he left it on top all it did was gather dust.

Look, God, I know we're not exactly tight, but Kit's a praying woman. She might think she's better off here in Casper, but I need You to convince her to come back with me. I don't want her alone in her condition.

Wade followed Kit out of the room. He clearly needed to work on his praying skills.

In the meantime, maybe if he gave her more reasons to come back with him, she'd cave. He'd think of them while they drove.

She hadn't felt this low in, well, a week, but today had been extra discouraging. Kit slid into the booth of the restaurant Wade had picked out. Her carefully constructed plan had fallen apart.

The best hotel with long-term vacancy was three times the price of Jambalaya Suites. She couldn't afford it, and even if she could, the room had been small, and she hadn't liked the location.

None of the rooms she'd toured today had a view

of meadows. None of them had a big comfy bed and a gourmet kitchen. She'd felt claustrophobic in them. All the anxieties she'd been fighting a week ago had flooded back to her as she'd stood in the confined spaces.

If she stayed in any of the hotels, she'd spend every waking minute worrying about the baby. At Wade's she'd been able to rest, to think, to clear her head. And while she hadn't exactly been happy, she'd felt more like herself than she had in years. Which in itself unsettled her. Who was she if not Kit McAllistor?

"What are you hungry for?" Wade peered over his menu. "I'm starving. Let's get an appetizer."

She realized how hungry she was. "Yeah, I'm famished."

"I'll get us a sampler platter."

Sounded delicious. But food wasn't the main issue on her mind.

She wanted to go back to Wade's ranch. Just until the apartment opened up.

How could she ask that of him when he'd already driven her all the way here and she'd forced him to trek to hotel after hotel? He might not even want her staying in his cabin anymore. She was too much trouble for him. Just like she'd been for Cam.

She let out a loud sigh.

"What's wrong?" He folded the menu and placed it on the table.

"Nothing."

"I know better. That sound was not nothing."

"I guess I'm disappointed." She set her menu on top of his. "I thought this would be the perfect solution."

His eyebrows formed a V as he nodded.

"And the only hotel I'm considering is the last one we visited."

"The room was small."

"I don't need much space." It was true. She didn't. But it didn't have the porch and the view she'd enjoyed all week.

"Listen, I've been thinking." He leaned forward, clasping his hands and resting his forearms on the table. His baby blues captured hers. A girl could get lost for days in those eyes. "I know you want to be close to the hospital. But you're not due for months. Sweet Dreams has a medical clinic. I'm sure they have a baby doctor. And if they don't, any of the other neighboring towns must have at least one among them."

She could see where he was going with this, and the gesture was so wonderful, she almost started to cry again.

"I think you should put the hotel idea on hold for now. Just stay in my cabin. You liked it there. I could tell. You look more rested, and your color's back. It's good for the baby."

A lump grew in her throat, and she ducked her chin to keep a lid on her emotions.

"You want what's best for the little guy. The air, the rest, the peace of my land does you good. And if it does you good, then it's surely doing the baby good, too."

Her thoughts exactly. The fact he was being so tender with her when she knew he'd itched to take charge all day made her feel small. He'd been amazing from the minute she arrived on his ranch, and here he was, sacrificing his time to give her the support she needed.

"I don't know what to say, Wade. Thank you. I was trying to figure out how to tell you I wanted to come back with you, but I feel so bad about wasting your time."

"You aren't wasting my time. I needed to be here."

Kit regarded him thoughtfully. She'd never forgotten what he'd told her about his mother disappearing years ago. Maybe he was worried the same thing would happen to Kit.

"I will be all right on my own, you know," she said gently. "I would have been alone no matter what. The day I found out I was pregnant was the day Cam died."

"Oh." He blinked.

"He wanted a divorce, and I thought the baby would change his mind. When it didn't, I screamed things at him, terrible, awful things."

The way his mouth dropped open, she guessed he was trying to process everything.

"I'm the reason Cam is dead."

"That's crazy," he said. "He had a heart attack."

"Because of me. I've never lost control like that. I yelled the most hateful things… He slammed out the door. And had a heart attack a few hours later."

"Kit…you weren't responsible—"

"Yes, I was. He would not have had the heart attack if I hadn't been so angry. I would take back every horrible thing I said if I could."

"We all get angry. We all yell nasty things."

"I shouldn't have done it. I knew better." She felt steady now. She could see it all clearly. "The girl you grew up with doesn't exist anymore. She might not have ever existed."

"The Kit I grew up with is sitting right in front of me." His eyes blazed with intensity. "You didn't kill your husband."

"Only you would say that. You always saw the best in me. But I'm asking you not to. See the real me. No illusions."

"I see the real you. I wonder if you do." The words were quiet, sincere. "I'm taking you home."

Home. The word swamped her with relief. Maybe Wade didn't get it, but right now she didn't care.

"You'll see things more clearly when you've had some time to rest and move forward. And I don't care what you say or how you try to convince me you're some horrible person. You're not."

Some of the bricks she'd mortared over her heart tumbled down, but there wasn't much she could do about it now. The man sitting before her would be terribly easy to fall in love with.

And then she'd be right back to square one.

Every time she gave her heart away, eventually it was tossed back to her, bloody and damaged.

"And before we head back, we're driving to the apartment of yours to make sure it's in a safe location." He picked his menu back up. "Don't argue with me. It's nonnegotiable."

She'd just have to get another pile of bricks.

Living on his ranch for another month would be worth it.

Chapter Four

Score one for team Croft. He'd gotten Kit to give up on her foolish notion of staying in some stinky, sketchy hotel. Wade zipped Kit's car through the streets of Casper to check out the apartment before they headed back to the ranch. If the place wasn't up to his standards, he'd get her to give up on that, too.

And then what?

He couldn't ask her to stay on his ranch forever. He might not even have a ranch in the near future.

He had to stop thinking in worst-case scenarios. There was no way he was losing JPX Ranch. Not after Jackson had entrusted him with it. He'd find a way to keep it going one way or another.

But none of that mattered at the moment. He was here for Kit. He still didn't get why she blamed herself for Cam's heart attack. Couldn't she see how irrational she was being?

The navigation system alerted him to take a left. He drove slowly until they found the apartment's address. The neighborhood left a lot to be desired. He ground his teeth together. Had she deliberately chosen the worst possible housing options? He pulled up to the curb in front of the building and kept the engine idling.

From the looks of it, the old brick building contained eight apartments, four in the front and four in the back. A metal set of stairs led to a narrow balcony with entrances to two apartments on the second floor. A ripped trash bag spilled its contents on the cement near one of the first-floor doors. Loud music could be heard thumping even from inside Kit's car. An unshaven man smoked as he sat on top of an overturned five-gallon bucket. A slim woman with a toddler on her hip stood in an open doorway as she shouted at someone inside. Then she slammed the door shut, shifted the child to her other hip and kicked a canister of chewing tobacco out of the way. It rolled off the landing and fell to the grass.

"Well, this isn't what I expected." Kit's weak voice was so unlike her, he glanced her way. Yep, she looked green. Funny, since the scene before him made him see only red. The area looked eerily similar to the one where he'd lived with his mother as a small child.

"No big deal," he said gruffly. "You can keep on looking."

"The pictures online were much nicer."

"I don't doubt it."

"I should have known it was too good to be true. Cheap rent. Close to the hospital. Two bedrooms. Furnished." She gazed up momentarily. "It's okay. I'll make it work."

"You're kidding, right? This isn't the place for you. You tried, but you couldn't have known the apartment would be…" A pit. A cesspool. He didn't know how to finish the sentence without offending her.

"Go ahead and say it. It's a dive." She rubbed her temples.

And now he felt like a jerk. It wasn't like he wanted her to be miserable. He just couldn't wrap his head around her living here. The dude smoking on the overturned bucket didn't exactly look like the helpful, neighborly type.

Wade could just make out the pulse in the vein in her forehead. The only way he could in good conscience be okay with her moving to Casper alone was if she was in a safe, clean apartment. With a bodyguard posted out front at all times. Okay, the bodyguard was over the top, but, considering how his mother's life had ended, justified.

"Why don't we drive around and look at some other areas? Do an online search for a few other apartments, and we'll see if they look respectable."

"No. This will be fine."

"It's not fine. You living here isn't happening." Shifting into Drive, he checked his mirrors and merged back onto the road.

"I already put down the first and last months' rent. Most landlords won't rent to me since I don't have a job."

As her situation sank in, he couldn't help but press harder on the accelerator. A year ago, he would have paid the rent himself. He'd had more financial assets than he'd ever thought possible. And now he could only sit by and watch helplessly as Kit slogged through a bad situation.

"Stay on my ranch until the baby is born."

"You mean it, don't you?"

"Of course, Kitty Cat." He scoffed. "We're family."

Her head dipped too quickly. Had he made her cry again?

"I have to be close to the hospital, or I'd be tempted to take you up on your offer."

"Call the landlord and see if you can get your deposit back. We'll find you another place."

"I don't think he'll give me my deposit back."

"You can try. And right now I think we should look at a few other apartments in the area. Just in case."

"It's pointless. Like I said, without a job, no one is willing to rent to me."

"It won't hurt to look." If he sold Dudley Farms for close to what he was asking for it, he'd be in a position to help Kit out with the rent.

"Not tonight."

"It's almost dark, anyhow. We can head back. Why don't you try to rest?" He turned around to get to the main drag.

"Okay." Her shoulders sagged, and her head dropped back to the headrest. "Thanks, Wade."

"Don't mention it."

"I mean it. I appreciate everything you did today. Driving me here, carting me around to all the hotels, buying me dinner and helping me check out the apartment. I haven't had someone to rely on in a long time."

While his masculine pride swelled, his mind tripped over the last part. What about Cam? Hadn't she relied on him? Part of him wanted to ask, but the other part figured it was better not to know.

He'd spent years assuming Cam was the man of her dreams, that Cam was taking care of her and loving her and being the husband Wade could never be.

Maybe he'd been wrong.

Why had Cam wanted a divorce?

Wade peeked at Kit. Her eyelids had closed, but he could tell she wasn't sleeping. Just resting. She looked peaceful. The most content she'd appeared all day.

His questions could wait. If he started digging into her past, he might not like what he'd find. And the feelings he'd destroyed the day she'd gotten engaged could come back to bite him.

He had nothing to offer Kit at this point. She needed someone who could support her and her baby boy. He'd never supported anyone but himself. Even if he got his finances back on track, he wasn't in a position to offer Kit much emotionally.

Sometimes loved ones disappeared, like his mother had, leaving despair and questions behind. And later he'd found out his worst fears had been realized. His mother had been kidnapped. Murdered.

It was better not to get too attached to anyone.

As the car drew farther away from civilization, he tried to brush off his anxieties.

If he could get his finances back in order, he'd be able to make sure Kit lived in a safe area and had the medical care the baby needed.

It was time to put JPX Ranch up for sale. He just had to make sure Kit and his friends didn't know about it.

He might have to give up his properties, but he wasn't about to give up his pride.

Kit woke to sunshine streaming in her room and the white comforter cocooning her in its soft nest. She glanced at the clock. After eleven. She couldn't remember the last time she'd slept so hard and for so long. Must be the country air.

Propping another pillow under her head, she luxuri-
ated in the sensation of lingering in bed. A few hours
of doing nothing sounded great. Especially now that
she knew she'd be staying here longer—at least a few
weeks. Maybe more.

She mentally came up with a plan for the day. She really should make sure there was a clinic nearby in case
complications cropped up while she was here. She'd
already been referred to a cardiologist and an obstetrician in Casper, but her appointments with them weren't
until next month.

She was almost twenty-three weeks pregnant, and
she still hadn't felt the baby kick.

Was the baby still alive?

Her lungs clenched. What if his little heart had given
out? She could be sitting here making all these plans,
hoping for her son to live...

Lunging for her phone, she ignored the notifications
and went straight to the internet to check the pregnancy
websites she'd bookmarked. Her nerves ratcheted as
her finger swiped through the ones about miscarriage.

Cramping, bleeding, dizziness, fever—she had none
of the symptoms.

Lord, thank You.

She had to believe her son was growing. Every day—
every minute—felt precious.

Resting against the pillows, she let her mind wander. Would the baby look like Cam? She wouldn't mind.
She'd loved her husband once upon a time, but she
wasn't mourning him. In some ways, she'd mourned
him during their marriage. He'd disconnected from her
long ago, and, after the funeral, she'd quickly adjusted
to the concept that the marriage was truly over. He

hadn't been around much while they were married, any-how. She'd liked to stay home, and he'd made it clear that his nights with the boys were not to be missed.

Only those nights with the boys had turned into nights with the girls, too.

She'd been devastated when she found out about the first affair. He'd promised he'd made a mistake and that he would change. She'd believed him. But he'd contin-ued to go out constantly, shutting her out of his life. After the second affair, her heart had started the process of mourning her dreams of happy-ever-after.

She'd accepted it. Put up with it.

Finding out about the baby had sparked hope in her, and she'd taken the pregnancy as a sign their marriage could be saved. She hadn't known he'd grown so close to a new girlfriend, close enough to want a divorce so he could marry the woman.

It did hurt that he'd never know his child. He'd been adamant he wasn't going to be in the baby's life, but if Cam had lived, he might have changed his mind.

Are you really deluding yourself into thinking Cam would have embraced this baby?

She could handle special needs and a hole in the heart and whatever complications got thrown her child's way. What about the rest of the world? If her baby did have Down syndrome, would they treat him differently as he grew older? Would she have to protect him from mean kids? Would she have to take care of him as an adult?

A fiery burst of heartburn hit her hard.

She was better off not dwelling on what-ifs and could-have-would-have-should-haves. She'd spent enough time doing that after moving to each new foster home. It changed nothing.

Swinging her legs over the bed, she stood, cradling her belly with one hand. Her phone showed two missed calls and a text. Sandra Bixby, one of the teachers she used to work with, had called and left a voice mail. The other number was probably a telemarketer. Her finger hovered over the voice mail button, but she decided to wait. She couldn't take a sympathetic message asking how she was doing, even if Sandra had always been kind to her.

Kit had never opened up about her personal life with her coworkers. How many times in high school had she confided something to a girlfriend, only to have her pain gossiped about and mocked? It had been bad enough not having a real family to live with. By the time she got to college, she'd learned to keep her private life close to her heart.

Kit hadn't told anyone except Wade about the baby's health problems. He was also the only one who knew she'd been having marriage issues—well, besides the two women Cam had cheated with, as well as the one he'd claimed he was going to marry.

Wade texted her. He was riding out with his ranch manager and wouldn't be back until supper. Which reminded her…she was starving.

Listening to Sandra's phone message could wait. Breakfast—scratch that, lunch—could not.

If Wade was out working, maybe she could repay him in a tiny way for all he'd done for her this week. She'd cook him a hearty meal even a cowboy couldn't turn down. But her supplies were slim here.

She texted him. I'll cook supper. Do you mind if I raid your cupboards?

Her phone rang. Well, that was quick.

"Hello?"

"Kit?"

Sandra. Her stomach grew twirly. Why hadn't she checked the caller? "Yes?"

"It's Sandra. How are you holding up?"

Like four-week-old celery in the hot sun. "I'm okay."

"I stopped by your house the other day to drop off some baby supplies, but there was a For Rent sign out front and no one answered. Did you move?"

Here we go. Questions I don't want to answer.

"I'm staying with a friend for a while."

"But you'll be coming back?"

Closing her eyes, she fought for the right words. What was the appropriate response? She'd never been good at this. Didn't want to open her mouth and have every skeleton in her closet topple out.

"Um, no. I'm moving to Casper."

"Casper? Did you get a new job or something?"

Emotion pressed against the backs of her eyes. How she wished she was moving for something as hopeful as a new job.

"Not exactly. Life's been…well, it's been rough lately."

"I can't imagine what you're going through." Sandra's voice filled with sympathy. "Losing Cam. You two always seemed like the perfect couple. And the baby… he would have loved your child. I'm so sorry you'll have to raise the baby without him. If there's anything I can do to help…"

And this was why she should have checked her phone

before answering it. Everything inside her wanted to scream that they weren't the perfect couple and that precious Cam hadn't even wanted the baby and wouldn't have loved it and how dare Sandra presume to make him out to be a good guy.

"Thanks, Sandra. I appreciate it." She tried not to choke on the words.

"If you give me an address, I'll send the baby things to you."

The kind gesture shrank Kit down to the size of a mouse. Sandra always had a pleasant word for her when they passed each other in the halls, and she'd organized funeral flowers from the school staff as well as dropped off casseroles twice. Maybe Kit had been wrong to lump her in with the girls who'd turned on her in the past.

"You don't have to do that."

"I want to. Don't tell me you already have everything for the baby. Trust me. You always need more."

Have everything for the baby?

She had nothing. Not one thing.

"I haven't exactly started shopping for infant items yet."

"Well, I figured as much, with all you've been through. The other teachers contributed, too. I'll box all this up and ship it first thing."

Kit didn't know if she could handle opening a box of baby delights. It would make it all the more devastating if her son died.

She just wouldn't open the box.

"I'll send you the address."

"Be sure you do, or I'll hound you for it."

"I promise. I'll text it to you as soon as we hang up."

"Okay. Take care of yourself, you hear? I'm praying for you."

Praying for her... Kit closed her eyes. Sadness and gratitude clogged her throat. "I need those prayers. Thank you."

She hung up. Before Kit could change her mind, she quickly texted Sandra the address of Wade's ranch. Then she headed to the kitchen to fix herself some food.

At some point she needed to buy baby supplies.

If the sweet child would just kick, make his presence known somehow, it would be easier to move forward. The days were ticking down until she'd find out if he'd be dealing with more than a hole in his heart.

Her phone chimed. Wade texted her. Raid away. My cupboards are your cupboards if you're cooking.

One kind deed deserved another. She'd make a good meal for Wade. And she'd come up with a way to thank Sandra for all she'd done. And maybe, just maybe, she'd forget about the baby's problems and enjoy the moment for once.

He had to stop fretting about Kit. Wade pulled on a clean pair of jeans after showering. The aroma of garlic and cheese hit him hard. When he'd walked into his house twenty minutes ago after a long day of riding the ranch, the first thing he'd seen was Kit tossing a salad. She'd cheerfully announced the lasagna would be done in half an hour. The scene had affected him a little too much. He'd practically sprinted down the hall to his master suite.

How was he supposed to concentrate on the ranch, the bills and Dudley Farms languishing away when his brain was filled with concern for Kit's future?

And then, to walk into his home—which normally was silent, dark and smelled like leather—and have every one of his senses flame to life because of her?

It wouldn't do.

As much as he pooh-poohed his friends' domesticity, he could easily be sucked into fantasies about it if it meant piping hot lasagna and Kit smiling away.

He yanked the T-shirt over his head and shoved his arms into it. This was ridiculous. He'd ridden around the ranch for hours, helped move cattle and left a message for Ray earlier. He'd done what he needed to do.

So why was he so keyed up to eat dinner?

He braced his hands on the edge of the bathroom counter and stared at his reflection in the mirror. *Get yourself together, man. You're too old to act like this. And don't go out there being all weird. Treat her like you normally do.*

After taking a deep breath and running the towel over his damp hair one more time, he padded into the kitchen. Kit was pulling the lasagna out of the oven. His heart skipped two beats.

Act normal.

"All this for me? I hope you're not hungry." He winked at her and noticed the table had been set. "What's left for me to do?"

"Well, I plan on eating, too." She smiled. "You can sit down. It's ready."

"Here, let me." He took the oven mitts from her and carried the steaming dish to the table while she brought over the salad. "So what did you do all day while I worked my fingers to the bone on the ranch?"

That brought a smile. Her cheeks grew pink. "Your

fingers look fine to me. In fact, they look mighty delicate. Not a callus to be seen."

"I'll have you know these are hardworking hands." He held them up and wiggled his fingers.

"Uh-huh." She slid a large slice of lasagna onto his plate. The cheese oozed down the sides. "Well, while you were doing your cowboy things, one of the teachers I used to work with called."

Cowboy things. Her phrase made him smile. "Oh, yeah?"

"She's sending me some baby supplies. I gave her your address. If a box comes for me, you'll know why."

Speaking of baby supplies... "Do you have what you need for the little guy?"

She averted her gaze, shaking her head.

"When are you supposed to start shopping for that stuff?" He cut off a bite of lasagna with his fork. Looked hot enough to melt iron. He'd let it cool a minute. His mind began swimming with items babies needed. Diapers. Bottles. A bed. Clothes. And more. Lots more. But what? He wouldn't know where to begin. "What do babies need?"

She finished chewing a bite of bread. "I'm not sure, but I've got time to figure it out."

Early October, she'd said. It gave her—he mentally ticked off weeks—right around four months. Plenty of time. Or was it?

"I guess you can see what your friend sends and go from there."

"I guess."

He glanced at her. "Don't sound so enthusiastic."

Guilt flashed across her face. "It might be better if

I shop after I get settled in Casper. Easier than moving it all, you know."

"I've got a big truck. Shop away. We'll get it there."

She didn't reply, just took a bite of her salad. Why wasn't she jumping all over buying the baby items? Did she think she could bring the baby home without having a crib and diapers and whatnot?

"Don't you want to be prepared?" he asked.

She stretched her neck to the side, looking like she'd rather be anywhere but here. Maybe she didn't know what to purchase.

He tore off a hunk of garlic bread. "Lexi went out and bought the entire baby department of a store last month when she and Clint found out they were expecting. She could tell you what you need if you're not sure."

Her forehead wrinkled. "Who's Lexi?"

"Clint's wife. You remember Clint Romine?"

"I remember Clint. I didn't realize he'd gotten married and is expecting…" The words trailed off.

"Trust me, I was shocked when he told me he'd fallen in love. I mean, we're talking about Clint. You know how quiet he is. But he's taken to married life. So has Nash. He's raising his little sister—and when I say little, I'm talking five years old—and he got hitched, too."

"Sounds like love is in the air for your friends."

He nodded. "Even Marshall is taking the plunge. Next month. In three weeks, to be precise. I'm one of the groomsmen."

Her fork clattered to the table, and she swiped it up, keeping her gaze on the food. Had he said something wrong?

"Okay, what's going on? You're acting funny." He

leaned back in his chair and watched her. Her eyes wouldn't meet his.

"I'm happy for your friends. It's just hard knowing…" Her jaw shifted.

Well, he'd gone and put his foot in his mouth big-time. Here he was, jabbering on about his happily married friends and their families, while she had no husband and a baby with health issues. *Great going, Croft.*

"I'm sorry," he said. "Me and my big mouth."

"Don't say that." She swallowed. "It's just…well, I've been thinking I should have felt the baby kick by now."

The food in his stomach congealed. If the baby wasn't kicking… A wave of sadness at the thought of the boy not making it crashed over him.

"What are you saying? Do you think…?"

Her eyes were filled with anguish, but she gave her head a little shake. "I think he's okay."

"How do you know?"

"I don't have the signs of a miscarriage. I'm not cramping or bleeding or anything."

He pushed his chair back. "Maybe I should take you to the hospital. You know, to be sure."

"The nearest hospital is too far away. I'm fine. Really. The baby was alive when I had all the testing. I just think too much. And thinking leads to worrying. I keep trying to leave it in God's hands where it belongs, but five seconds later, the anxieties mount."

Leaving it in God's hands sounded good, but how could she know if He'd come through for her? God hadn't come through for his mother.

"In fact, I know what I need. Tomorrow's Sunday. I'm going to church."

He'd officially lost his appetite. The last time he'd gone to church had been for Nash's wedding. Wade hadn't attended a regular service in years.

It was on the tip of his tongue to offer to take her. But church? Him?

His cell phone rang. Ray Simons, his real estate agent. *Please let this be good news.*

He lurched to his feet and answered it, padding away from the table down the hallway to his home office. "What have you got?"

"I heard through the grapevine there's a couple looking for a ranch with a lot of acreage. I already talked to their agent about Dudley Farms. Should I mention JPX Ranch as a possibility, too?"

His chest hurt. All the hours spent with Jackson, getting to know every rock, every gully, every inch of pasture had been like spending time with the father he'd never had. And then, when the lawyer called him after Jackson died, he'd found out he'd been given the ranch outright. All of it his! Along with Jackson's savings and other assets…

He'd squandered it. Hadn't treated it like the precious gem it was. His greed had put it and his future in jeopardy.

"Go ahead, but don't advertise it yet. We can discuss it more on Monday if you're free."

"Good. And, yeah, I'm free." His cheeriness sounded through the line loud and clear. "Don't change your mind, now. Buyers are in short supply. From the sound of it, your ranch is exactly what this couple is looking for."

His chest squeezed even more tightly. What if they

bought JPX Ranch? Would he have to move to Dudley Farms?

He wasn't a farmer. He was a rancher.

Why had he risked everything he loved to try something he didn't know much about?

"I understand."

"I'll call you if I hear anything," Ray said. "See you Monday."

"See you then." He tapped his index finger against the back of the phone as he returned to the table.

"Is everything all right?" Kit's clear gaze kicked him right in the chest.

Less than two minutes. That's all it had taken for him to forget she was there.

He'd never considered himself husband material, and it didn't take a genius to see he'd been right. Over the years he'd done a good job of not getting too close to a woman. When he thought about his mother…well, he wasn't going through that again.

This anxiety about Kit felt familiar.

He slid back into his chair. "Everything's fine."

"Nice try." She arched her eyebrows. "I know when something is bothering you."

Why her words comforted him, he couldn't say. Maybe it was just nice to have someone know him well enough to care. He didn't want to shut her out. He also didn't want to tell her how he'd messed up.

"That was my real estate agent." He cut a bite of the lasagna, which, thankfully, was no longer burning a hole through his plate.

"Good news?" She smiled, then sipped her water.

"It might be. A couple is looking for acreage. I'm heading into town Monday afternoon to talk to him."

"I thought you were obsessed with buying land, not getting rid of it."

"Obsessed?" He glanced up and wished he hadn't. She was giving him the watchful probe. "Nah. I'm making some business decisions."

Time to change the subject. It wouldn't kill him to offer to take her to church. Chances were she'd insist on driving herself, anyhow. "Why don't I take you to church tomorrow?"

A few seconds ticked by as she continued to stare. Then her expression cleared. "I'd like that. What time should I be ready?"

He had no clue. A part of him hoped she'd tell him not to bother. "I'll find out."

"Thanks." She cocked her head to the side. "If you want to talk about whatever is going on, I'm here."

Nothing like a sharp poke to the ol' conscience. He couldn't talk to her about this—couldn't talk to anyone about it. Maybe someday, after he'd fixed the mess, he'd be able to share it as a life lesson. But until then…he was changing the subject.

"So today, I was out riding and I came across this mean mama cow. I've been tired of that broad for months. But she always has healthy calves, so I put up with her, you know?" He told her about the cattle on the ranch and how a section of fence needed to be replaced soon.

She laughed at the right places, but he had the feeling he'd disappointed her.

Well, she could join the club. He disappointed himself, too.

As the sun set, Kit rocked on her porch. Wade had dropped her off a few minutes ago. The lasagna had been a success. The dinner itself, though, had been disconcerting. Ever since she'd driven into JPX Ranch, she'd been lapping up the attention Wade lavished on her. When he'd taken the phone call right in the middle of their meal, it had been a wake-up call.

How many meals had she finished alone because Cam had gotten a call from one of his buddies during it?

The interruption she could forgive, but something was bothering Wade, and he'd refused to confide in her.

That's what hurt.

She tried to focus on the orange and purple streaks feathering across the sky. Her heart wasn't in the sunset.

Maybe it was time to face facts. As a girl, she'd been tossed aside again and again. The message had been received—she was unimportant. In her marriage, she had been, too.

But she'd never felt unimportant with Wade.

Until tonight.

Oh, she wasn't being fair. When she needed him, he was her rock. Didn't change the facts, though.

Her home wasn't here.

After church tomorrow, she was looking into other apartments, and if she found a better one that would lease to her without her having a job, she'd call the landlord in Casper about getting her deposit back. If not, she'd have to suck it up and live there until she had the baby and went back to work.

Don't worry, baby. I'm going to be the best mom you could have. I'm putting you first. No one ever put me first, and I don't want that for you. I want you to know how loved you are. I'll do anything for you.

Gently rubbing her tummy, she continued to rock.

God, do You have a plan for me? I know You love me.

Thank You for that, but is there more? If the baby dies, what do I do? What am I here for? Do I even matter?

Everyone had a reason for being here. She trusted God would let her know her purpose in His time. She wasn't content with being unimportant anymore. She hadn't been content there in a long time.

Chapter Five

Tempted to loosen his collar, Wade shifted in his seat on the pew the next morning. He'd been doing life on his own just fine since the day he legally became an adult. Sitting here, singing hymns and listening to the service—or trying to, anyway—reminded him he was no longer doing life fine on his own. He'd always tried to make the most of what he'd been given, which, admittedly, he'd failed at recently, but ever since last night, his conscience had been niggling him. Did he have his priorities all wrong?

He glanced Kit's way. Her sundress and long brown hair pulled into a braid made her appear younger than she was. She stared intently at the pulpit, and she looked peaceful, like she was soaking in the sermon.

Unlike him.

He stretched his neck from side to side. How could she sit there and hang on every word? The only words he could hang on to right now would be *Congratulations, you got an offer on Dudley Farms.*

That's what he'd been hoping to hear last night when he'd taken Ray's call in the middle of a meal with Kit.

That had been a jerk move.

He should have waited until they finished the meal and called Ray back. He could sense her distancing herself from him. Part of him was glad. Her seeing his true colors kept him safe. But the other part of him...didn't like those true colors as much as he used to. Sometimes he wanted to be a better man.

A better man? Get ahold of yourself. This is what happens when you go to church.

Another hymn started playing, and Kit's voice rang off-key. What she lacked in musical talent she made up for with enthusiasm. He began to sing, too. The words were familiar, and as he started into the second verse, he remembered all the times he'd come to this very building as a teen with Dottie and Big Bob Lavert. They'd been in charge of Yearling Group Home, and they'd given him a real education. Taught him how to be a moral, upright citizen.

Was he a moral, upright citizen?

The words to the hymn stuck in his throat. How could he sing about needing God's strength when he relied solely on his own?

This was why he should have stayed home. He wouldn't be thinking about things he was better off leaving alone.

Kit's arm brushed his as they stood for the final prayer. A tingling sensation rushed over his skin. He tried not to let it affect him. He could see why she would need God's strength. There wasn't a thing she could do about the condition of the baby growing inside her.

But why would she find comfort in God? Why wasn't she mad at Him? Her husband had been ready to divorce her. Then the idiot had died, leaving her pregnant and alone. And the baby, who had a hole in his heart, might have special needs or might not even live.

Why wasn't she mad at God?

Wade would be.

Thankfully, the service ended and he escorted her from the pew. He hoped Kit was comforted by the service. If anyone deserved a happy ending, it was her.

He followed her out of the church and onto the lawn. A hand on his shoulder made him turn.

"Are you terminal or something? Since when do you go to church?" Nash Bolton stood next to him with his typical cocky grin. Then he turned to Kit and pretended to clutch his heart. "Say it isn't so—Kit? Is that you?"

She smiled, revealing a row of pretty white teeth. "It's good to see you, Nash."

Nash's wife, Amy, sidled up next to him as their little girl, Ruby, ran to Wade and lifted her arms for him to pick her up. "Uncle Wade!"

"My favorite cowgirl!" Wade hugged the tiny blonde close. She kissed his cheek before wriggling to be set back on her feet.

"You have to come over and see me ride Chantilly." Her eyes lit up.

"Name the time. I'll be there." He winked. He'd bought her the horse last year as a welcome home present when Nash took custody of her. Best gift he'd given to anyone in years. He loved spending time with Ruby. Although not related by blood, he considered himself her uncle, and she, his niece.

"Promise?"

"Would I lie to my favorite cowgirl?" That brought a smile to her face.

"Congratulations, I hear you got married." Kit smiled at Nash.

"I had to beg, but I got this incredible lady to agree." Nash put his arm around Amy's shoulders. "Amy, this is Kit McAllistor. She and Wade go way back. Kit, this is my wife, Amy, and our daughter, Ruby."

"It's nice to meet you." Kit shook Amy's hand and addressed Ruby. "Are you going to school yet?"

Ruby lifted wide blue-green eyes to her. "I'm all done with preschool. The teacher gave me a paper with my name on it and everything."

"That's wonderful."

"Mommy says real school will be fun." She bit her lower lip. "I don't know. It's awfully big."

"It might seem big now, but you'll know your way around in no time," Kit said. "And you're going to learn all kinds of neat stuff. I'm a teacher."

"Can I be in your class?" She clasped her hands together and stared up with hope.

Kit laughed, caressing her tummy. "I would love to have you in my class, but I'm taking a break from teaching so I can have a baby."

"A baby!" She looked about to burst, then she solemnly nodded. "Aunt Lexi is having a baby, too."

"Speaking of…" Clint and Lexi joined the group. "Howdy, Kit. This is my wife, Lexi. Lexi, Kit."

They exchanged hellos, but before they could continue the conversation, Nash raised his hand. "Let's take this to Dottie's Diner and catch up over some breakfast."

Wade leaned in to Kit. "Are you okay with that?"

"Fine with me." She turned to him, her face glowing.

"We'll meet you guys over there." Taking Kit's arm, he guided her toward the parking lot. He loved his friends. He loved breakfast. He really loved Dottie. But joining the gang with Kit felt an awful lot like getting initiated into a club he had no intention of becoming a member of.

The marriage club.

Marriage club. He scoffed. This was just a breakfast. Nothing more.

The diner's exuberant atmosphere infected Kit as platters of eggs, bacon and waffles arrived. She sat next to Wade. Lexi and Amy chatted next to each other across from her, and Ruby had claimed the chair beside Kit's. The men talked calves and bull riding on the other side of Wade. Church earlier had soothed her troubles, making her believe she'd be okay no matter what happened with the baby. And she hadn't had time to fret about meeting Clint's and Nash's wives, since it had happened naturally. Both Amy and Lexi seemed nice and accepting.

Would they be so accepting if they knew the truth about her marriage? And what about the reality of her baby's health? She couldn't handle a Q and A session about him right now. She didn't have it in her to tell them about the hole in his heart. But smiling and nodding had never been her style, either.

She thought of Sandra Bixby. The woman had gone out of her way to be nice to her. Kit was getting tired of keeping people at a distance. But she also didn't want to scare them away by burdening them with her problems.

Nash clanged a butter knife against his mug. "While we're all together, Amy and I have an announcement."

The rest of the diner continued to buzz with laughter and conversation, while everyone at their table looked expectantly at Nash. Kit sneaked a peek at Amy. Her cheeks glowed pink, and her brown eyes sparkled.

"We found out we're having a baby." Nash glanced over at Amy with a look full of tenderness. He positively beamed. The table erupted in a round of congratulations. Lexi actually started to cry.

Kit's heart squeezed at the obvious connection everyone felt. The love flowing between Nash and Amy had been what she'd hoped to have with Cam. He never would have announced their pregnancy to friends, but then, they didn't have many friends. She'd give about anything for a relationship like Nash and Amy's or Clint and Lexi's.

"I thought it was a secret, Daddy!" Ruby scolded.

"It was, RuRu. Just until today."

Ruby tugged on Kit's hand. "Is my mommy's tummy going to get round like yours?"

"Yes, it will." Her voice cracked. She sipped her orange juice and tried to appear as happy as everyone else.

"I hope Mommy has a girl. I want a sister."

"Well, I'm having a little boy." She smiled down at Ruby. The girl was too cute.

"You are? How can you tell?"

"The doctor has a special wand to take pictures of the baby. Some people like it to be a surprise, but I wanted to know what I'm having."

"I'm telling Mommy to go get pictures tomorrow. I want a special wand, too!"

Kit laughed. "She'll have to wait a few months before the doctor can tell if it's a boy or a girl, and only doctors can use the wand."

Ruby's face fell.

"Ruby, remember what we told you?" Amy prodded gently. "We'll take whatever God gives us."

"Well, I'm praying for a sister." She hopped off her chair, went to Nash and climbed onto his lap.

"I'm a little anxious." Amy looked at Kit, then Lexi. "I'll feel better after the three-month mark. I've wanted a baby for so long. What if something goes wrong?"

Kit's throat felt scratchy. She wanted to reassure her, but how could she? It would be cruel to burden her or Lexi, who was just starting to show with her own baby bump, with news about her son.

"I felt the same way, Amy." Lexi put her arm around her and leaned in for a side hug. "I still worry. What if I get in a car accident? What if the cord wraps around the baby's neck? What if… I have to tell myself to stop worrying."

Amy nodded. "I know you're right. From the minute we found out, though, I've flip-flopped between pure joy and pure fear."

Kit hadn't worried much about the baby before finding out about the hole in his heart. She'd resided in pure bliss at the thought of having a child. Dealing with Cam's final words as well as his death had made her heart numb. The baby had been a welcome reprieve from reality. She'd done what she always had. Made the best of a bad situation.

That was what she was doing now, too, she supposed.

"When are you due, Kit?" Lexi asked.

"Beginning of October." Kit shook her thoughts away. "What about you?"

"My official date is December 4. My clothes already feel tight." Lexi puffed out her cheeks and widened her eyes. Then she turned to Amy. "When are you due?"

"End of January. Can you believe it? Our kids will practically be siblings."

Siblings. Kit's heart pinched. If her baby lived, he wouldn't have siblings.

Wade touched her hand. "Are you okay?"

His eyes swam with concern and questions.

"Yeah." Trying to smile, she nodded quickly. "I'm fine. Excuse me a minute." She set her napkin down and pushed her chair back. Then she weaved through the packed diner toward the restroom.

Why did a simple breakfast have to be so complicated? She locked herself in a stall and realized her hands were shaking. Her emotions had been colliding ever since Nash announced Amy's pregnancy. And then Lexi's and Amy's honesty about their fears had made her want to join in and tell them the truth—she was terrified she'd lose her baby.

Tears welled in her eyes. Their babies would have fathers who adored them. Lexi and Amy had strong men who would comfort them and support them throughout the pregnancy. Neither woman had to worry about going into labor alone. Neither had to worry about her baby having special needs. Or living in a horrible apartment in a strange town.

One tear fell to her cheek, then another. She swiped both away and patted her cheeks with toilet paper.

Pulling herself together, she splashed water on her face and left the bathroom. She took two steps and felt a hand on her shoulder.

"You feeling okay, sunshine?" Dottie Lavert pulled her aside.

"I'm fine, Dottie, thanks for asking." She'd met Dottie several times over the years and always smiled at

Dottie's nickname for her. Sunshine. Lately, all she felt was gloom.

"You need to get off your feet and have one of my ooey-gooey cinnamon rolls. I'll bring one over to you in a jiffy. I sure am glad you're staying out at Wade's."

She was, too. "Thanks."

Dottie winked and sauntered toward the kitchen. Kit returned to the table as Lexi was speaking to Amy. "Dr. Landor used to work with high-risk pregnancies in Chicago. I'm so glad she started a practice here."

"Can you give me her number?" Amy asked.

"Of course. She's taking new patients, too. She's a newlywed, and her husband grew up in Sweet Dreams, so they decided to relocate."

An obstetrician who had experience with high-risk pregnancies? At least there was help nearby if anything were to go wrong before she moved to Casper.

In the midst of suffering, God always provided mercy.

Thank You, Lord.

She'd take the good with the bad. And be thankful for any crumb of hope.

Wade hiked back from the stables to his house. After breakfast, he'd dropped Kit off at her cabin, saddled up his favorite quarter horse, Thunder, and ridden around the ranch. The ground was dry and hard, and wisps of clouds streaked overhead. He'd come across a prairie dog family, a doe with twin fawns and three elk. He loved the rugged land and all its occupants—well, except for rattlers. He could do without those. There was something about this slice of Wyoming that cleared his head and made him feel like he belonged in the world.

But being out here hammered home the fact he might lose it. It was time to tally the stack of bills he'd been avoiding.

Taking long strides, he cast a quick glance at the cabins down the lane. Kit wasn't on her porch. She must be resting.

This morning at the diner Kit had seemed to enjoy breakfast with his friends. But then he'd noticed she'd grown quiet. And pale. And just like that, his gut had clenched and his mind had raced with worries.

Was she all right? Really all right? And would she tell him if she wasn't?

He'd been blindsided so many times as a kid. Zipping along, thinking everything was stable, and then he'd get moved to another home. When he and Kit had been separated, he'd changed. Grown resentful. His mood had hardened. It was a good thing he'd been placed at Yearling. Big Bob and Dottie had helped smooth him out again.

He still feared getting ripped away from loved ones. He could admit it. But it was hard not to notice that all the creatures he'd encountered today, including his friends, had someone to share life with.

He entered through the sliding doors off the patio and headed straight to his bedroom to change. After slipping into fresh jeans and a T-shirt, he walked to the other side of his home where his office was located. On the way down the hall he glanced into the guest rooms. The room across from the office made him pause. It would make a nice nursery—a guest nursery—for Kit and the baby if they wanted to visit.

A text dinged. Would you be mad if I used your supplies to bake cookies?

Cookies? Who got mad about those? He texted her back. Not if you let me have some of the dough.

Two seconds passed. One bite. That's all. I know you.

He laughed and replied, When do you want me to come get you?

A knock from the patio door had him hurrying to the living room. Kit stood outside. She still wore the simple sundress from earlier. She grinned.

"I would have picked you up." He slid open the door and escorted her inside. "You shouldn't be walking so far."

"It's not far. Exercise is good for me and the baby."

He followed her to the kitchen. "What if you turn your ankle or something?"

"I'm not going to turn an ankle." She bent to poke through his cupboards.

"I don't like you traipsing about."

"Traipsing?" Her laugh tinkled. "I can handle the walk."

He studied her through narrowed eyes. She looked better than she had at the diner. There was a glow about her, and he was happy to see her cheeks weren't as sunken as they'd been when she'd arrived. Maybe it was due to her smile.

"What can I do?" He thumped his knuckles on the countertop.

"Thaw out some butter. I need two sticks."

He opened his fridge and found the butter. "It's going to take a long time to thaw."

"Pop them in a bowl in the microwave for twenty seconds."

He tossed both sticks in a bowl. "Won't they blow up?"

"You have to take the paper off first, you goofball,

and no, they won't blow up. Unless you put them in for several minutes or something."

"Well, now you tell me." He winked at her. Then he unpeeled the wax paper from each stick and put them in the microwave. The bills had waited this long. They could wait a few hours more.

Kit found the sugar and flour. She started pouring ingredients in a large bowl.

"Can you grab two eggs for me?" she called over her shoulder as he removed the butter from the microwave.

"Sure thing." He set them next to the bowl. Then he rounded the counter, sat on a stool and watched her mix everything together. She was starting to spoon the dough onto the baking sheet when she frowned. Then her face cleared. She kept placing dough on the sheet.

"Oh." She blinked and met his eyes.

"What is it?" He stood up. "You hurt? Going to be sick? What?"

A look of wonder crossed her face. "I think I felt the baby move."

"What? Right now? Where?" He was at her side in an instant. He inspected her from head to toe, his gaze lingering on her stomach, but nothing looked different.

She turned to him. "Yes, I felt him."

He got lost in the green pools of her eyes. Everything he needed to know was in there. Relief. Amazement. And gratitude.

"How do you know?" His voice was low, gravelly.

She took his hand. Her soft touch nearly undid him. Then she placed it to the side of her belly.

"Just wait."

He held his breath, not because of the baby, but because her warmth, her light touch, her floral perfume, all locked him in a trance.

And then he felt it. The tiniest flutter.

He jerked his hand back, his eyes opening wide.

He'd just felt her baby. A baby really was kicking in there!

He couldn't stop his mouth from curving into the biggest grin, and he tenderly placed his hand on her stomach again.

He waited.

And waited.

And there it was. The slightest of movements.

"Kit…your baby. He's there. Moving around." The awe of it overwhelmed him.

Her lips trembled, but joy streamed from her gaze. He wrapped her in his arms and held her close. She took a deep, wobbly breath, and relaxed her head against his shoulder. He held her for the longest time and it still wasn't long enough.

She leaned back, bringing her palms together in front of her lips, and shook her head as if she couldn't believe her good fortune.

"He's strong, Kitty Cat."

"I hope so."

"He is. Just like you."

Her eyes grew wide. "You think I'm strong?"

"I know you are."

She flung her arms around his neck and hugged him tightly. All he could think to do was keep her in his embrace. The proximity of her overloaded his senses, made him reflect on what he'd been thinking earlier— everyone had someone except him.

She's your family.

It was true, but this felt different. She'd been part of his family for many years, and he wasn't thinking of her as a sister. He certainly hoped she didn't think of him as a brother.

He was a man.

She was a woman.

And there was a baby between them.

Reality crushed his temples. The bills in the other room. The baby's heart problem. For Sale signs and hospitals and a seedy apartment. Loving someone and never getting to say goodbye.

"I guess we'd better get these cookies in the oven." He stepped back and wiped his hand down his cheek.

Her lips curved into a wide smile. "I couldn't agree more."

Well, maybe it would be better for them both if she did view him as a brother. It would help him get over some of the emotional stuff her being here kicked up.

But…he still would prefer it if she'd see him as a man.

Chapter Six

The following Friday, Kit enjoyed a grape Popsicle as she rocked on the front porch of her cabin. Wade had been gone most of the week. On Monday, he'd been busy on the ranch and then had an appointment in town with the real estate agent. He'd been tight-lipped about it when she'd asked that night. On Tuesday, he'd said he had business to catch up on and had holed up in his house most of the afternoon. Then on Wednesday, he'd left to move cattle for a few days. He was due back late tonight. While she missed his company, the days alone had given her precious time to get her bearings.

Now that she could feel the baby moving, her resolve to keep him alive and healthy had grown to borderline obsessive. Had she spent too much time searching the internet for pregnancy advice? Absolutely. She'd pored over forums of parents who'd had babies with the same diagnosis as hers until her eyes had glazed over. The testimonies simultaneously terrified her and filled her with hope.

What if the test results came back and her baby *did* have special needs? What if the hole in the heart was one of many health problems? What if— Oh, she had to stop this!

If only there was something she could do, a medicine to take, a diet that would cure his little heart…but her options were to be patient and wait, eat well, exercise, and get plenty of rest. Check. Check. And check.

All week she'd spent hours calling landlords about different apartments but hadn't found anyone willing to lease to her without her being employed. It looked as though she was stuck with the one she had. The thought depressed her more than she wanted to admit.

A drop of purple Popsicle fell onto her hand. She licked it off and finished the final bite. The sound of a vehicle rumbled closer.

A truck stopped at Wade's house. He'd had two deliveries this week already. The only other people who came around were Clint or Nash, to stop in and check on her. They'd brought supper for her while Wade had been gone. Lexi had come with Clint yesterday, and Kit had enjoyed her company. It still felt strange to have people go out of their way to help her, although she knew Wade had put them all up to it. She didn't mind. Being cared for was a nice change from life with Cam. And in a few short weeks, she'd be all alone again. Doing life on her own.

Her phone dinged. A text from Sandra came through. The package should arrive today. Enjoy!

The package—she'd forgotten about the baby items. She dialed Sandra's number.

"Hi, Kit, did you get the box?" Sandra sounded out of breath.

"Something was dropped off to the main house of the ranch where I'm staying. I'll head over in a few minutes. I just wanted to thank you for going to all the trouble to get it here."

"It was no trouble. I hope you enjoy all the goodies."

The goodies. She wouldn't think about them yet. "How is your summer going?"

"Busy. Now that Greta graduated, it's all I can do to keep on top of her college plans. Orientation is next week already. How did that happen? When your baby is born, try not to blink. It goes so quickly. Anyway, how are you feeling? I miss you. It was always nice seeing your smiling face at the school."

"I miss you, too." And, surprisingly, she did. She hadn't made much effort with the teachers, but since she'd been away for a few weeks, she missed the interaction with them, however small it had been. "What is Greta studying?"

"She has no clue. She talks about getting a business degree, then claims she's going to be a doctor. Honestly, I don't care at this point. Just pick something, you know? It's a shame she didn't get the teaching bug."

Kit chuckled. "I had that particular bug since I was a little girl."

"Me, too, Kit. For as long as I can remember." A voice shouted in the background. "Frank's calling. I've got to go. Sorry to cut this short. You take care now, you hear?"

"You, too, and congratulations about Greta graduating."

They hung up, and she rested the phone on the arm of the rocking chair. Sandra's package was probably sitting on Wade's front porch right now. She might as well go up there and see for herself.

Pushing herself to a standing position, she assessed

her body. Everything seemed fine. The baby hadn't kicked in hours, but his kicks were sporadic at best. Her flip-flops probably weren't the best option to walk up the gravel drive; she'd better change.

She slipped into her favorite cowboy boots and meandered up the drive to Wade's house. New wildflowers had popped up—crimson flames of Indian paintbrush, delicate periwinkle of blue flax and splashes of yellow from balsamroot. A hawk circled overhead.

Peace.

This place radiated peace.

How she'd longed for peace her entire life.

It wouldn't last. Never did. But she wished she could scoop up this feeling and put it in a jar to sprinkle out whenever the hard times hit.

She skirted Wade's garage and climbed the two steps to the porch. A large box stood near the door. Bending slightly and pushing her hair over her shoulder, she read the label. It was addressed to Kit McAllistor.

Now what?

She hadn't expected such a large package. She couldn't carry it to her cabin. And she didn't feel like walking back to get her car. Wade wouldn't care if she opened the box in his house and came back for it later.

Back at the garage, she typed in the key code and strode to the door leading to the kitchen. Then she continued through the living room and hallway to the front entrance. After dragging the package inside, she pushed it to the living room near one of the couches.

She remembered seeing scissors in a kitchen drawer. A few moments later, she was on her knees near the box with the scissors poised to cut through the packing tape. But she held back.

Was she ready for this?

Her hopes had already been soaring since the very first fluttery kick. Was it wise to open this box of delights and sink into the delicious sensation of actually being able to use the contents?

Maybe she should wait until the microarray test results came back. Then she wouldn't get wrapped into dreams, only to be crushed by them later.

She set the scissors on the package and slowly made her way back to the garage. She shut the door and plodded back to her cabin. The sun didn't seem as bright as it had earlier.

At some point in her life, she'd look forward to something without worrying about it being snatched from her. Until then, protecting herself from the pain was the best way forward. Which meant it was high time she sealed up her heart. Wade's sweet reaction at feeling the baby kick had allowed longing to shimmy in where the shards of her broken dreams with Cam still lay.

She'd be leaving this ranch in a few weeks. Wade would be here. And she'd be going through life on her own. Again.

Yawning, Wade headed out to the kitchen as the sun rose Saturday morning. The past three days had been exhilarating and exhausting. Moving cattle to their summer pasture made him feel alive. Riding with the other cowboys, taking a good look at the entire outfit, watching for cows acting out of the ordinary and making sure they were all healthy, gave him a purpose. Reminded him his dream had always revolved around ranching in Wyoming. It had also given him clarity about the bills he'd finally tallied.

JPX Ranch was on the market, but, for now, it wasn't being advertised. He'd told Ray not to put the sign up, and if anyone wanted to come tour the property, Wade would make sure Kit wasn't around.

All week his mind kept tripping back to her. Wondering how she was doing. Marveling at feeling her baby kick. Chastising himself for caring so much.

At least his friends had checked on her while he was gone. He'd actually grown panicky at the thought of her getting cramps or falling and being in pain for days without anyone around to help. Asking Clint and Nash to check on her had been the only way he'd been able to keep his anxiety under control.

He poured water into the coffee maker, dumped scoops of grounds into the filter and flipped on the switch. Light began streaming in through the windows, and his gaze fell on a big box next to the couch. He hadn't noticed it last night when he'd arrived. He'd driven in around two in the morning, and he'd been so bleary-eyed it was a wonder he'd found his bed.

With a yawn, he inspected the package. Addressed to Kit. Must be the baby things she'd mentioned. Weird she hadn't opened it.

He rubbed his chin. Had she gotten bad news and hadn't told him? Doubtful. Then why would she have gone to the trouble of lugging it in here and getting the scissors? She must be scared. He really didn't blame her.

He was scared, too. And it wasn't even his baby.

Maybe she needed a distraction from her troubles. He'd take her…where? Town didn't excite him. Too many people. From the looks of it outside, the weather would be fine. What about a picnic at the river later? She'd always liked being outdoors. Wade returned to the kitchen and poured a large mug of coffee. He took it out to the front porch and sat on one of the chairs. The land splayed before him in ridges and valleys. The riot of meadow colors would be gone soon, leaving behind dry grass, sage and patches of red earth.

Would he have to say goodbye to all this? Even considering the prospect made Wade's palms clammy. He'd spent a small fortune renovating the house and all the outbuildings. This was his home. His life was here.

If someone bought JPX Ranch, he would have to move. Dudley Farms would mean a huge life change. He didn't want to say goodbye to cattle ranching. And he hated the thought of being hours away from his friends.

Sorrow made him bow his head. *God, I don't want to lose this ranch. I don't think I've ever appreciated it the way I do right this minute.*

For a moment, his entire being filled with gratitude, which didn't make sense. Why would he be grateful when he likely would have to sell it?

God, what's going on? Am I cracking up?

Dottie's voice from back in his Yearling days ran through his mind. He'd been going through a tough time the year after he and Kit were separated, and Dottie had slid a plate of cookies his way. *God created everything, champ. I figure He's got your life under control. We can praise Him through sunshine and storms.*

Sunshine and storms. Most of his adult life had been sunshine. His childhood had been storms. Both had brought him where he was today. Without overthinking it, he simply bowed his head and thanked the Lord. For these quiet moments. For today.

He sipped the rich coffee and let his mind wander. He'd been introduced to church and God by Dottie and

Big Bob. He remembered the warmth in his heart as he read the Bible with her. He'd gotten baptized. For a long time, he'd made prayer a priority in his life. When had he stopped?

Probably when he stopped going to church.

Avoiding church hadn't been a conscious decision. Life had called. Ambition had driven out any leisure hours as he'd scrimped and saved to buy his first tiny ranch, where the shack still stood. Success upon success had allowed him to expand, and Jackson's ranch had driven him to financial gain he'd never thought possible at his age.

Had he ever thanked God for any of it?

The coffee tasted like vinegar as it slid down his throat.

I know it's late, but I'm truly grateful for all You've blessed me with, Lord. Don't take it away from me.

He stayed on the porch a long time, letting the uncertainties and anxieties dissipate. Finally, he checked the time. Almost eight thirty. Maybe Ray would have an update for him.

He went inside, found his cell phone and returned to the front porch. Pressed Ray's number and waited. Two rings. He took a drink. Three rings. Man, he needed a shower. Four rings.

"Ray Simon speaking." His crisp voice was all business.

"What's the scoop on the couple looking for a ranch?" Wade asked. "Good news, I hope."

"Sorry, no news here. I've talked to their real estate agent. They plan on touring both your properties. They haven't been out to see Dudley Farms yet."

"Yet, huh? That means there's still hope."

"I wouldn't count on them wanting Dudley Farms. They're young and ambitious. Looking for land with multiple guest cottages on it. In addition to ranching, they want to host high-end corporate bonding retreats."

He let the news sink in. "Obviously, my ranch is better suited for that. Dudley Farms only has the house and outbuildings. Nothing livable besides the main house."

"Right," Ray said. "And the location isn't ideal, either. They have family over in Cody. They'd like to be closer to them."

"Sweet Dreams would be an easy drive." A pit grew in his stomach. "Do they have the money to purchase either of my properties?"

"Yeah. They're newlyweds. It's my understanding he inherited a lot of money from his late grandfather."

"Does he even know how to ranch?" The thought of nonranchers coming in and ruining this operation made him sick.

"I'm not sure about him. He owns a corporate retreat business. He's very successful at it. The wife grew up on a cattle ranch in Oklahoma."

Well, at least one of them would know what they were doing.

"Are there any other potential buyers for Dudley Farms?" He knew the answer, but had to ask anyway.

"A big game hunter is still looking at properties. Another couple has been eyeing land near Montana. Other than that, no new buyers that I've heard of."

"Okay."

"I'm doing everything I can, Wade. I created new flyers to appeal to the corporate retreat angle of JPX Ranch."

"You know the minimum amount I need."

"I know." Papers rustled in the background. "Would you still want to sell Dudley Farms if JPX sells?"

He really didn't want to start over there. His life was here.

Why had he ever bought that property? If he could go back and do it all over...

"I'm not sure."

"Think about it and let me know."

"Thanks, Ray."

He could always move back to the shack and the hundred acres that started it all. Then his failure would be complete.

He needed a distraction as much as Kit did. He'd drag her out for a picnic if she even hinted at saying no.

"Thank you for suggesting this." Kit tucked a rolled quilt under her arm, while Wade carried a cooler in one hand and a large tote bag in the other. They walked through green grass toward the river—more a stream— on the east end of Wade's ranch. A wooden bridge arched over the river, and trees full of green leaves crowded the banks. Cottonwoods, aspen and lodgepole pines provided cover for the singing birds flitting about.

"I figured you could use a change in scenery." A heather-gray T-shirt stretched across his chest. "This is one of my favorite spots."

"You come here often?"

"Not as often as I'd like."

"Busy, busy." She kept her pace slow. She wasn't in a hurry and hadn't been in a few weeks, which was a huge contrast from when she'd been working.

Every day had been like running a marathon. As soon as the alarm went off, she'd jump out of bed, get ready, pack a lunch, slurp down coffee on the drive to the school, prep her lessons, try to engage the children, grade papers, take calls, make lesson plans, come home and crash. Evenings were spent making dinner, eating it in silence—sometimes alone, sometimes with Cam—telling herself she should exercise but not actually finding the energy to do so, and either binge-watching television shows or surfing the internet until falling into bed, to do it all over again the next day.

How had she managed to live for years in such an unfulfilling routine?

The routine had been comfortable. She'd known what to expect. This new life was unpredictable, scary and forcing her to rely on God in ways she hadn't since she was a child.

"What do you think? Is this a good spot?" Wade pointed to a flat stretch of lawn on the bank. The view of the river was unobstructed. Gurgling water added to the peaceful scene.

"Perfect." She unrolled the quilt, and he took an end from her hands. Together, they spread it on the ground.

"Take a seat. I'll dish out the food."

She lowered herself to the quilt before easing back to a seated position. He poked around in the cooler and tote bag. A few minutes later, he handed her a plate.

After thanking him, she took a bite of a sandwich. Delicious. The air was hot, but a gentle breeze from the river kept it from being oppressive.

"This reminds me of the picnics we'd take down at the Bradleys' creek." She kicked off her sandals and wiggled her toes on the quilt.

He finished chewing a potato chip. "We'd sneak soda crackers and those cheese slices wrapped in plastic."

"I'd hardly call that cheese."

"Back then you did." He grinned. "You'd break the slices into quarters and layer them between the crackers. What did you call them?"

"Finger sandwiches. I'd read about fancy luncheons in a book. I thought they were high society."

"They were." He popped a red grape in his mouth.

She thought back to the one picnic that had seared itself into her mind. It was the day they'd swapped their growing-up stories. Neither of them had liked to talk about their past, and they'd decided to come clean with each other on the promise they would never discuss them again.

"Remember the day we told each other our stories?" she asked.

"Yeah." He grew pensive.

"Does the promise still hold?" She could practically see him all those years ago, handsome in a baby-faced way, and, boy, had he been scrappy. He'd sat next to her on a torn blanket. They'd both had their knees tucked up and their arms around their legs. Neither had looked at the other while they spoke.

This scene felt the same as all those years ago.

"A promise is a promise," he said quietly.

Fair enough. She'd memorized his tale, anyhow. He'd been born to a teenage unwed mother who'd waited tables at a truck stop to support them. He'd been four years old when she vanished. Police had speculated she'd run off with someone. Shortly after, he was placed in a foster home. A year later, her remains were found in Utah. She hadn't run off; she'd been kidnapped and murdered. Wade had lived in two other homes before ending up at the Bradleys' with Kit.

"Well, I kept one story to myself that day." She sat up, trying to tuck her knees to her chest, but the baby was in the way. She kept her legs straight out before her instead.

"Good story or bad story?" He turned to her, his eyes full of compassion.

She'd always told him the good stories, embellishing if necessary. Making him happy had made her happy back then. She still wanted to bring him joy, but the truth was more important now.

"Bad."

He bent his knees and wrapped his arms around them, sitting next to her, the same as he had long ago. "Go ahead. You can tell me."

"Remember how I told you about Aunt Martha?"

"Yeah." He flicked a glance her way.

"I lied about her."

"Which part?"

"The her-being-nice part. She beat me, screamed at me. Told me she'd whip the bad out of me. Every single day."

He blinked, his jaw shifting.

"Deep down, I believed she was right. Why else would my birth mom leave me there as a baby? I thought I deserved the belt."

"The belt?" He stared ahead, his jaw clenching. "How long? How long were you there?" His voice was low, gruff.

"Until I was five, almost six. My teacher saw the bruises. The belt marks. I was removed from her home shortly after."

"I liked your original story better."

"The one where she died peacefully in her sleep after

loving me like I was her own little girl?" Kit attempted a smile.

"Yeah." He put his arm over her shoulders and gave her a sideways hug. "I'm sorry. Physical and emotional abuse is never okay."

"I agree. Looking back, I think she may have had mental issues. She'd be nice one minute and a terror the next. I lived in a constant state of fear and didn't even know it. I came to expect hot and cold behavior from everyone around me."

"You shouldn't have gone through that. You didn't deserve it. No one does."

Her throat tightened. Hearing him say those words was like a healing balm on a long-festering wound.

"It affected me. I never felt wanted. I thought there was something wrong with me." Why had she said that out loud?

He nodded, swallowing. "I didn't, either."

"You didn't?" She couldn't imagine this confident, successful man ever feeling unworthy.

"I may have left out a story from my past, too." He shifted to face her. His blue eyes shone bright with intensity. "My second foster home was abusive."

She reached over and squeezed his hand. He held it tightly. She wanted to take the pain from him, to go back in time and give whoever did that to him a piece of her mind. "I'm sorry. I hate that you went through it."

"I hate the same for you," he said. "The day I met you was the best day of my life. You're going to get it right. You know, with your baby. He won't know the cruelty we faced."

Meeting her was the best day of his life? The words filled a hole in her soul she hadn't known was there.

Meeting him had taken her life from lonely and gray to bright and exciting. Wade had always been the best thing that had ever happened to her.

She rubbed her belly. "I'll do everything I can to protect him, but if he has special needs, he could face a different type of cruelty."

Wade sighed, letting go of her hand. "I know. I don't like it. I guess you could homeschool if things got bad. You're the teacher, right?"

"I'm trying not to put too much thought into the future until I have more information."

"Information is good." He leaned back on his elbows, extending his legs out. "I've been thinking about that property I mentioned a while back, Dudley Farms."

"Oh, yeah?"

"If Ray doesn't find a buyer for it, I might move."

"I thought your dreams were wrapped up here. Don't you like ranching anymore?"

"I love ranching. It's in my blood."

"Then what would happen to this ranch? It's yours. It was meant to be yours."

Pain flashed across his face so quickly she thought she imagined it. Had she said something to upset him?

"Maybe I need something new. I could try farming." His teasing tone didn't fool her. Something wasn't right, but if he didn't want to tell her, she wouldn't drag it out of him.

"Should I start calling you Farmer Croft?"

"Yep." He chuckled. "By the way, why didn't you open the package in the middle of my living room? Did you expect me to do the honors or something?"

Her face grew warm. "No, I... Well, this sounds pathetic, but I chickened out."

"Diapers scare you that much?"

"Very funny." She swatted his arm. "No, it's my warped way of thinking. If I get my hopes up, they'll come crashing down. I don't know if I can handle any more bad news at this point in my life."

He lay back, his head resting in his palms, elbows wide. "You'll be fine. Just open it. I'll help you. A few baby bottles won't give you a breakdown."

She drew her eyebrows together and mindlessly plucked a stem of wild blue flax. Maybe he was right. Was she overthinking the baby supplies? A part of her shouted, *"No, don't do it!"* But the logical side scolded her for being a ninny.

Trying to anticipate her reaction to opening the package was giving her a headache. Her original plan of opening the box *after* finding out the results of the tests seemed the best choice. They would be in soon. Sure, she feared the worst, but shouldn't she at least be preparing for the baby's arrival? Why was she dragging her feet?

Because I can't bear to have this baby ripped from me.

A butterfly caught her attention as it flitted to a flower, then flew haphazardly away. This picnic spot was an oasis. No more worrying about the baby.

She glanced over at Wade. His eyes were closed, and his chest expanded and relaxed in regular intervals. He looked at peace. Still a big hunk of muscular man. But beneath it all, she could see the young boy she'd bonded with.

Who took care of him out on this secluded ranch? Was he lonely? Was that why he was talking about selling it? And what was this talk about farming?

She couldn't picture him on anything but a horse.

Who did he have to comfort him on the bad days?

Did he even have bad days?

She sighed. Everyone had bad days. She and Wade had just gotten used to hiding them. They'd gotten used to hiding a lot of things because of their childhoods.

Did he suppress his emotions the way she did? Keep the most important stuff to himself?

She wanted to know his most important stuff. She'd wanted to know it from the minute she'd met him.

But she wasn't an optimistic little girl anymore. She came with issues. Problems. And she wouldn't burden him with those, too.

She kissed the tips of two of her fingers and placed them on his forehead. *Rest up. You earned it.*

Chapter Seven

He was going to get her to open the box even if it meant bribing and cajoling. The woman needed to face reality—she was having a baby. And that meant she had to start preparing for it. No more of this protecting-herself-from-the-pain-of-possibly-losing-the-child nonsense. Did she really think avoiding the box would somehow prevent her from being devastated if the baby didn't make it?

Wade washed his hands in the kitchen sink. Supper was almost ready. He'd set the table earlier. He'd drive to the cabin to get her in a minute.

This morning at church, he'd actually listened to half the sermon before his mind started wandering. He hadn't liked where it had traveled. Right up there to the front of the church where his buddies had gotten married. The look of love on their brides' faces when they'd said their vows had etched into his memory.

All the tuxedos he'd had to rent recently must have rubbed romance dust off on him or something. Couldn't have happened at a worse time, either. His life was collapsing around him.

What did he have to offer a woman?

A woman? Like there was anyone besides Kit he'd even consider spending his days with. But after all she'd been through in life, she deserved someone who would protect her from problems, not someone who would add to them.

They'd skipped the group breakfast at the diner when Kit complained of feeling a bit low. What did "a bit low" mean? He had no clue, but he'd sure spent enough time trying to figure it out today. Worrying hadn't been his style until recently. He'd finally gotten sick of himself and had prayed for a clear head. He was tired of feeling strung out. Tired enough to ask God for help.

Two knocks on the glass of the patio door and a sliding sound drew his attention to the dining area.

"It smells so good in here." Kit's cheeks were pink, but worry clouded her eyes. "Whatcha cookin'?"

"A slab of beef. Brisket, to be precise. Been in there for hours. Why didn't you wait for me to pick you up?"

"Yum. What can I do?"

It didn't escape his notice that she ignored his question. It was on the tip of his tongue to say, *"First of all, you can stay off your feet and let me drive you, and second, you can open that big box in my living room,"* but he didn't. "Grab a seat. I'll bring the food over."

He carried a platter of sliced brisket with potatoes and carrots to the table. After Kit said grace, they both dug in.

"What did you do this afternoon?" she asked.

"Rode Thunder."

"It's been forever and a day since I rode a horse."

He scooped a bite of potato on his fork. "You miss it?"

"Yeah. I always enjoyed riding. It seemed like all my friends had their own horses."

"Any time you get an itch to ride, let me know." He frowned, growing tense. "After you have the baby, of course. Don't want anything happening to you or the little guy."

"Don't worry." She smiled, shaking salt on the vegetables. "I have no desire to ride one now."

The tension in his neck eased.

"Maybe after the baby is born I can come visit." The words sounded choked. "I'll be moving in a few weeks."

It didn't seem like nearly enough time with her.

"You found a different apartment?" He dug into the brisket.

"I'm meeting with the heart specialist in a few weeks. I'll need to be in Casper by then."

"You didn't answer my question." He knew he sounded testy, but he hadn't realized she still planned to move to that nasty apartment. A roach-infested hovel if he ever saw one.

"I meet with the cardiologist three weeks from Tuesday, and I have an appointment with an obstetrician the following Thursday."

He lunged for the glass of water. Three weeks? They'd fly by faster than a hawk with a field mouse. Man, he was jumpy.

"Let me know when you want to check out apartments. I'll drive you there."

"Wade, I'm moving in to the one I put the deposit on."

"No way." He leaned in. "I want you and the baby safe."

"We'll be safe. God always watches over me." The gleam in her eye as she nodded just about did him in. She looked like she was trying to convince herself as much as she was trying to convince him.

"It's not the place for you—"

"It is." Her quiet words were harder than steel. "I told you, I don't have a lot of options. I have no job and I need to be near the hospital."

"I'll cover the deposit for a better apartment and the difference in rent. You can't live there." And she couldn't. He knew it down to the bottom of his toes.

He *had* to sell one of his properties soon. It wasn't too much to ask, was it? He still had a few weeks before Kit moved. And selling Del Poncho would free up some cash.

She blinked several times. "It's kind of you, Wade, but I can't accept it."

"You can't accept it?" His chest hollowed out. Was he some stranger she couldn't trust? Didn't friends help each other? "Oh, that's right. You don't accept help from anyone, including me."

"I'm here, aren't I?" Her eyes flashed.

"As a last resort." He leaned back and cocked his head toward the living room. "What about the package over there? Someone took the time to buy those gifts and send them here, but opening it would be accepting help, wouldn't it? And we both know you don't take charity."

"That's not it—"

"Prove it, then. Open the box."

"I don't think this is the right time. I'll take it back to my cabin and—"

"Kit."

She hated when he used that tone. He was wrong. She could accept help. She could.

Then why was it so hard to open this package?

Presents she'd unwrapped over the years rushed

back. Gifts that had been stolen by other kids or lost when she'd been forced to move. If she opened this package, would her dream of becoming a mother be stolen, too? Would she get her hopes up, only to lose the baby?

It's just a box. You're giving it too much power. It's cardboard, Kit. Come on.

"Fine. I'll do it now." She marched to the kitchen, snatched the scissors out of the drawer and headed to the living room.

She knelt next to the box. Carefully cut through the packing tape. When the flaps were free, she sat back on her heels for a moment. She was going to love every item in here, and if the baby died, each gift would hurt that much more.

God, I'm scared. Please help me see this for what it is, not for what I think it represents.

"What are you waiting for?"

"Nothing." She lifted one flap. Then the other. And, taking a deep breath, peered into the box.

A crocheted white baby blanket covered the top. She tenderly lifted it and brought it to her chin. It was so soft. Beautiful. Tears pricked her eyes. Someone had made this for her child. The hours it must have taken. The generosity.

Wade let out a low whistle. "Someone was feeling confident. White? With a baby? I don't think it will stay clean for long."

She let out a shaky laugh, not trusting herself to reply.

"Is that it?" He made a production of craning his neck to peek inside. "Seems like an awfully big box for one blanket."

She gave him a fake glare. "Don't rush me." She

could do this. Now that the first item was out, she could handle the rest.

She reached in again and pulled out a package of bottles. One by one, she brought out the treasures. Newborn-sized diapers, a pack of onesies, rattles, bibs, a mobile, a sleeper with yellow duckies, a floppy stuffed dog, pacifiers and, at the bottom, a card in a purple envelope. She'd wait to read it at the cabin. If she opened it now and saw all the signatures of the people she'd worked with for years and hadn't truly appreciated, she'd lose it.

Wade was right. She'd never been able to accept help. What had she lost out on over the years because of it?

"What do you do with this?" Wade held the box with the mobile. His grimace was priceless.

"It attaches to the baby's crib. The little fish dangle from it as it turns. I think it makes music, too."

He squinted at the back of the box. "Yep. It needs two AA batteries."

Carefully, she placed everything back inside, then pressed the blanket to her chest once more.

"If the baby doesn't make it, I'm keeping this no matter what." She rubbed the soft material against her cheek. "Then I won't forget."

"You won't forget. You'd never forget."

She lowered her lashes, nodding. He was right, of course.

"But you should keep it. It's real nice." He cleared his throat. "And don't even think along those lines. He'll make it."

She wasn't sure. Women had stillborn babies on a regular basis, and her baby already had been diagnosed with problems. The idea of losing her son and having to give birth to his lifeless body had kept her up many nights.

"I'm becoming grim and pessimistic, Wade," she said quietly. "I try not to think of all the things that could go wrong, but there they are. In my head, waiting to pounce. And then I can't stop thinking about them. And I try to get answers on the internet, and…"

"Well, there's your problem. Don't go on the internet. You'll only find a million more reasons to be scared. I had a pain in my abdomen, and I went on one of those doctor websites, thinking it might be my appendix. Two hours later, I was convinced I had either intestinal worms or cancer. Worst night I've had in a while. Stay off the internet."

"I know you're right, but…"

"Can't you just enjoy this? I mean, a baby is growing inside you. Doesn't it count for something? If the worst happens, you *will* be devastated. Period. You can't prevent the pain by worrying about it beforehand."

She hadn't thought of it in those terms. "So you're saying whether I enjoy the pregnancy or worry my way through it, the outcome will be the same? And I should be thankful for each moment?"

"Yeah."

"What if you're wrong?"

"I'm never wrong. You know that." His white teeth gleamed through his smile.

She'd let that one slide. "I hate feeling so…helpless. There's nothing I can do to fix this."

"Well, there is one thing." He grew serious. "I mean, besides eating healthy and getting rest."

"What?"

"I know you have a strong faith. I know you pray. When I was at Yearling, Dottie told me over and over that God hears our prayers."

"But I don't always like His answer."

"This morning the preacher said you can take everything to God in prayer."

"Do you?" She watched him carefully. He'd never been overtly religious. He'd even admitted to her he hadn't regularly attended church in years. But it didn't mean he lacked faith.

"No, I don't." He looked toward the windows.

"Why not?" Her knees started burning, so she lugged herself up and sat on the couch, keeping the crocheted baby blanket folded on her lap.

"I don't know." He rubbed his chin. "I guess I rely on myself."

It made sense in a way. Wade had everything he'd ever wanted. A big house, huge ranch, oodles of property, freedom, friends—maybe he didn't feel the need to pray.

"What about when something is out of your power to handle or fix?"

He shrugged. "Doesn't happen very often."

Hmm…was he missing the point? He wasn't in control of his life. No one was. "Well, God isn't just here for our problems. I used to only rely on Him in times of trouble, but I realized I was missing out."

He frowned. "Missing out on what?"

"When things started going south with Cam, I relied on God more and more. I started seeing His everyday mercies. Eventually, I realized I finally had the dad I'd always wanted."

"Dad, huh?" The confusion on Wade's face lingered.

"Yeah, He's my loving Father."

"If you're convinced He's so loving, why are you worried?"

The question made her pause. "Life doesn't always turn out the way we want."

"Sometimes it does, though."

"I know." He didn't get it. The rules were different for her than they were for other people. Her dreams had been crushed on a regular basis for as long as she could remember. And after the way she yelled at Cam? Well, there were consequences for her sins. "I don't deserve it."

"That's silly. You do deserve it."

"What if I'm being punished?"

"For what?"

"The things I screamed at Cam." She choked on the last words. Why was it so hard to admit her mistakes?

"You're not being punished. Don't you believe in forgiveness?"

"Of course I believe in forgiveness. Jesus died on the cross and rose again for my sins. I'm forgiven."

"Then why are you holding on to this guilt?"

"Because a sin is a sin. And I'm not holding on to guilt." The last line didn't come out very strong. Was that what she was doing? "I'm not. Let's drop it."

He stared at her thoughtfully a moment, then gestured to the box. "What else do you need for the baby?"

"I'm not sure. I'll think about it another time." She placed the blanket back on top of the items and closed the flaps. "Can we just sit on your patio and watch the countryside?"

"If that's what you want."

She did. She was tired of thinking and talking. Tired of it all.

Chapter Eight

Babies sure needed an awful lot of stuff.

Wade tucked the list of supplies he'd jotted last night into his pocket as he strode down the lane toward Kit's cabin Monday afternoon. She might not be fired up about shopping for the tyke, but Wade didn't want her waiting until the last minute and bringing the baby home to nothing. If he could convince her to go shopping with him, he'd sleep easier.

And sleep had been a tricky minx last night. Why he couldn't get Kit's words about praying and seeing the everyday mercies out of his mind, he couldn't say. One thing he did know? He'd taken his blessings for granted. All night his conscience had weighed heavily. Finally, he'd gotten up, stared out the window at the full moon and thanked God for his health and friends. He'd also prayed for Dudley Farms to sell so he wouldn't have to give up the ranch. He wished he could say he felt peace—that God would surely provide the buyer he'd asked for—but he didn't.

A morning of ranch work had given him a reprieve

from his thoughts. At this point, he needed the distraction of baby shopping more than Kit did.

He closed the distance to her cabin. Usually at this time in the afternoon she'd be rocking on her porch. But she wasn't out there. He didn't want to wake her if she was napping. Wanted her to get as much rest as possible. He loped up the porch steps and knocked quietly on her door.

A few moments later, she opened it, beckoning him to come inside. She held her cell phone to her ear. He entered, closing the door behind him as quietly as possible. Then he took a seat on her couch, trying not to eavesdrop on her conversation and failing miserably.

"And what does that mean?" Her voice sounded strained. "Uh-huh. Okay. And you're sure about the numbers?"

She hurried to the dining table and wrote something on a sticky pad. He narrowed his eyes. What was going on? Her hair was pulled back in a messy bun, and she wore khaki shorts with a billowy bubblegum-pink shirt.

"Do I need to send everything over?" She straightened, biting her lower lip. "You will? Thank you. And thanks for calling."

A few seconds later, she ended the call and whirled to face him. She opened her arms wide, her face shining. "The baby doesn't have special needs!"

No special needs! The implications hit him one by one like a lighted pathway up to his heart.

He hustled over to her and hauled her into his arms. Lifting her, he twirled her off her toes as she laughed and wrapped her arms around his neck. Then he set her down. Her eyes darkened, and the hope within them exploded to life the emotions he'd dammed. She radiated relief and joy and all the things he wanted her to have. Without thinking, he got down on his knees.

Gently, he placed his hands on the sides of her belly and planted a kiss in the middle.

"Junior, you keep growing, you hear me? You're going to be strong. This hole you've got in your heart won't slow you down. You're made with your mama's steel, and trust me, she's something."

Still on his knees, he lifted his gaze. Kit's smile was full of tenderness as she lightly brushed her fingers over his hair. Compassion, understanding and happiness— all for him. He could feel it as sure as he could feel the hardwood floor beneath his knees.

He stood up and hugged her again.

"I'm starting to believe the baby might actually be okay." The words were tentative, as if she feared saying them aloud would bring down thunder and lightning.

"Does this mean the hole has a better chance of healing on its own?"

"No, I wish it did. But at least I don't have to worry about Down syndrome or, worse, DiGeorge syndrome."

"Whatever happens, I'm here for you."

Her face flushed as she gave him a quick smile.

"Let's sit and you can tell me everything." Taking a seat on the couch, he rested his elbows on his knees while she sat in the chair kitty-corner to him.

"There's not much to tell. The chromosomal microarray test didn't indicate any genetic mutations. I'm so relieved. The hole in the heart might simply be an abnormality." She averted her eyes. "Sorry, all of this gets me choked up."

"Hey, no need to apologize. I know how worried you've been. I worry, too. This is big news. Good news."

"It is." She beamed, nodding.

He remembered the list in his pocket. What better time to bring up shopping than now, while she was optimistic?

"I hope you're ready to get serious about having this baby." He pretended to be stern.

"Get serious?" She huffed. "I couldn't be any more serious."

"Well, then you're going to have to prove it." He unfolded the paper and snapped it open, holding it out to her. "I did a little investigating, and the box of baby things? Not even close to what you need. It's time to go shopping."

Her mouth dropped open. "You came up with a list of baby items I need?"

"I did." He nodded firmly.

"You're telling me you went online and searched for what parents should have on hand for newborns."

"Yes. Why is that so hard for you to grasp?"

Her eyebrows soared to her forehead. "It's just... you're a bachelor. I don't remember the last time you mentioned a girlfriend, and I didn't picture you being interested in domestic stuff. How many times did you say you didn't see yourself married?"

Domestic stuff. For years, he'd shut out all thoughts of domesticity, focusing instead on expanding his ranching empire.

But tucked beneath all those layers, a part of him cried out to have what his friends had—love, marriage, a partner, babies.

His mother had barely been out of her teens when she'd been kidnapped and murdered. If she'd had someone looking out for her—someone financially supporting her—she wouldn't have had to work in a dive restaurant at the truck stop or live in a sketchy apartment on the wrong side of town.

Kit's apartment in Casper was no better. No safer.

"I might not be Mr. Domestic, but it doesn't mean I can't help you out."

"If you wanted to be Mr. Domestic, you could be. You'd make a great daddy."

Him? *Make a great daddy?* He needed to beat down the desire those words were puffing up before he started believing them.

His cell phone rang. He whipped it out of his pocket and checked the caller. Ray. Maybe it was a day for good news. Mr. Domestic wouldn't be possible until Mr. Overextended's circumstances changed. And even then he doubted he could embrace the vulnerability inherent in loving a woman.

"Hello?" Lifting one finger to indicate he'd be back in a minute, he went out onto the porch, where he could talk in private.

"The young couple I mentioned wants to see both your ranch and Dudley Farms."

Music to his ears. And yet his stomach dropped. It meant possibly saying goodbye to the life he'd built.

"Be prepared for an offer," Ray said. "I'd be shocked if they don't jump at the chance to own JPX Ranch. It checks off almost everything on their list."

"Thanks, Ray." He stared out at the mountains, took in the land, his house in the distance, the other cabins down the way. Why hadn't he thought it was enough? "Go ahead and set up the appointments."

"I will. Hopefully, you'll have a solid contract on one of them soon."

"Yeah, and I'm hoping it's on the other one."

"If they do make you an offer on your ranch, are you mentally prepared to accept it?"

Was he? Jackson's face and raspy voice as they'd ridden around the property all those months before Jackson died rushed back. They'd bonded. Two bachelors—one old, one young—both with a deep connection to this patch of Wyoming. Jackson would be appalled at the thought of his life's work being handed over to strangers.

The bills Wade had tallied, the seriousness of his cash flow problem, came to mind.

"I'm prepared." The words sank like a boulder in his gut. He had to sell—one or the other—soon, or he'd lose it all.

"Good. If you have any questions, call me. I'll let you know when they want to come out."

"Thanks, Ray."

"No problem."

He hung up, tucking the phone back in his pocket.

The day was as bright as could be, but he could feel a charge in the air. Stifling heat. A storm might be brewing.

He'd better take Kit to buy those baby supplies. He might be a bachelor without any plans for a wife and kids, but he was also a friend, and he'd be a real heel if he let Kit down.

Kit and the baby meant more to him than…

He gulped. They might mean the world to him, but who was he kidding? He couldn't be more than Uncle Wade.

Was it enough?

Maybe he'd better make time to pray. Not just about selling the ranch, but about Kit and her baby, too. He had a lot to think about.

The man had done it again. Taken a phone call in the middle of their conversation and left her high and dry, as if whoever was calling was the president of the United States.

Did she have a Don't Mind Me, I'm Invisible sign on her forehead?

And here she'd been all gushy and full of joy because her baby was okay! And Wade had dropped to his knees to kiss her belly and talk to her unborn son. The gesture had been so completely unexpected, so sweet and endearing, she'd almost tugged him back to a standing position to kiss him senseless.

She could *not* kiss Wade.

Even if he was the polar opposite of Cam.

Cam, who'd shown few signs of physical affection. Cam, who'd forgotten their wedding anniversary two years in a row. Cam, who'd looked her in the eye when she'd presented him with the pregnancy test and flatly told her he didn't want the baby and didn't want to share custody, either.

He's dead. Can you really not remember any good things about him?

It was easier remembering the bad. Hanging on to her hurts. But was it good for her?

She reached way back in her memories to when they'd met. He'd had an air about him—a confidence she'd liked. And he'd looked at her like she was something special. Their initial dates had been fun, but then, Cam had been fun…at first. They'd done things—snowboarded, went bowling, played intramural volleyball on Tuesday nights at the university. She'd enjoyed hearing about his family—his father and brother. And they'd fallen into an easy relationship. He wasn't clingy, and neither was she.

But his lack of clinginess had only been a sign she

hadn't recognized. He hadn't been stuck to her like glue because he hadn't really needed her.

For the umpteenth time she wondered why he'd married her. Why?

She'd probably never know.

Her gaze fell on the paper Wade had left on the coffee table. She smoothed it out and, as she read it, her annoyance at him for taking the call vanished.

In his chicken-scratch handwriting, he'd listed a full page of things the baby needed. Diaper cream. A crib. Wipes. Burp cloths. Thermometer. Changing table. On and on it went.

Why did Wade have to be so kind? And gorgeous? And thoughtful?

And off-limits.

She gripped the paper in her hands.

She couldn't fall for him. She'd be in another unfulfilling relationship. He felt sorry for her because of the baby, and he cared for her because he always had—but love? He didn't love her, not the way she needed.

Her relationship with Cam had been bad. If she messed things up by getting romantic with Wade, she'd lose her best friend.

She couldn't handle losing him, too.

She glanced down at her belly, growing bigger by the second. The sooner she left Wade's ranch, the sooner she could adjust to her new life. And he was right. She needed to buy supplies. It was time to get serious about this baby.

"Sorry about that." Wade shut the cabin door behind him.

"Must have been important."

Had she heard his conversation? He should confide

in her about putting his ranch up for sale. Heat rushed up his neck. He wasn't ready. "Nothing major. What do you say we go buy some of the items on the list?"

"Are there any stores around here that carry this stuff?"

"We'll go to the city and find a supercenter. Bound to have some of what you need. Get your shoes on."

"You mean we're going now?" Her forehead wrinkled in adorable consternation. "It's over an hour away."

"Yeah. Why? You have other plans or something?"

"Very funny. You know my only plans involve eating, napping and rocking on the front porch."

"Well, there you go. Looks like you have room in your schedule to shop."

"Fine. Let me put on my comfy shoes."

"I'll run back home, get the truck and pick you up in ten minutes."

After returning home, changing shirts, checking his wallet, and grabbing two bottles of water and a few snacks, he drove back to her cabin. She stood on the porch with her purse over her shoulder.

"Let me help you up," he said.

"I can do it."

"It's a tall step." He escorted her to the passenger side and boosted her up to the seat before shutting the door. Then he loped around to the driver's side. Soon the truck was kicking up dust on the way out.

A tiny smile played on her lips as she stared out her window. Her hand gently massaged her stomach. The image pinched his heart.

She was going to be a great mother.

As he turned onto the main road, his mind wandered back in time. He had snippets of memories of his mom.

Sitting on her lap, watching cartoons together. She'd loved him. He knew she did. He might not remember much, but the feeling of acceptance remained.

And then one day, she'd disappeared.

Just another day. Most of it escaped his memory. He knew he'd been at the babysitter's place while his mother worked. He also remembered worrying when she didn't show up to get him that night. Or the next night. Had she forgotten about him? Stopped loving him? It wasn't long before he'd been sent to his first foster home.

His life hadn't been the same since.

His family ties had been severed that day. He didn't belong to anybody, and nobody belonged to him.

Still, he had friends. Good friends.

He glanced over at Kit. His best friend. Her eyes had closed.

Good. She needed the sleep. He drove the rest of the way trying not to think about his mother, his childhood. He didn't know what tomorrow held for him. The present was all he really had.

"I don't need a wipe warmer. What does it even do?" Kit grimaced at the box Wade held. He'd been trying to convince her to buy things left and right, and she was losing her mind. One tiny baby did not need all this stuff. Or did it? She really didn't know. "How many times have I told you I'm on a budget?"

"You don't want to clean him with a cold wipe, do you?" He inspected the box and read the features out loud. "His little tushie will be frozen."

"Put it back." She scanned the shelves for useful items, like pacifiers, bibs and diaper cream.

Wade pushed the cart forward a few feet and selected something off the shelf.

"What is this?" Taking it from his hands, she gave him her most long-suffering stare. "And why would I need it?"

"It's baby's first alarm clock. Look, it's a frog."

She raised her eyes to the ceiling and prayed for patience. "Wade..." She paused, adjusting her tone to not sound like a hag. "...the baby can't tell time."

"But it's a frog." He held it up and made a puppy dog face.

"I'm sticking to the essentials. A newborn doesn't need an alarm clock."

"Fine." Sighing, he put it back on the shelf.

They strolled through the rest of the aisle, adding anything she needed to the growing pile. He turned to the next one and threw a package of diapers into the cart.

"Wait. I need to check the prices and sizes."

"Sizes? You're telling me diapers aren't one size fits all?"

"They get bigger as the baby does."

He started reading the labels. "What's N? What's 3? How do you know what to buy?" He shook his head in dismay.

"I think N means newborn." She pulled a package off the shelf and read the back. "Yep. The sizes go up from there."

He tossed three packs of newborn diapers into the cart as if he was shooting basketballs.

"I'd better get some bigger ones, too. I've been told babies grow out of everything at the speed of light."

"I'll get 'em." He put a few packages of the larger diapers in the cart. "What's next? Let's go to the clothes. The little guy has to have some style."

Style? The child would likely be spitting up all over himself. And who would see him, anyway? She bit her tongue. At least Wade was enjoying himself. If she had to admit it, she was, too. All of this baby paraphernalia made her son feel real. And this aisle—the diapers and wipes one—smelled like babies. The best smell in the world.

"I'll meet you by the clothes in a minute. I'm grabbing some baby shampoo first."

"I'll go with you." He guided the cart and waited while she decided on shampoo, lotion and creams.

"All set." She turned and felt a sharp pain. "Oh!" She pressed the heel of her hand into her side and almost doubled over.

"What is it? What's wrong?"

"A cramp, I think." She winced, rubbing the spot. Slowly, the throbbing subsided.

"You need to get off your feet." His voice was hard. Before she knew what was happening, he'd swept her into his arms and started carrying her away from the cart.

"Wade! Put me down. I'm fine. I can walk." She lightly slapped his arm, his firm, muscular arm that seemed to have no problem hoisting her pregnant self and carrying her through a crowded shopping center.

"No." He strode down the main aisle to the front, where there was a fast-food sandwich shop. After carefully depositing her in a chair, he went to the counter and bought her a sub and a bottle of water. Then he set them in front of her and took the chair opposite. "Eat."

She took one look at his face, which could have been

carved out of granite, and realized how worried he was about her.

"Wade…" she said softly, covering his hand with hers. "I'm okay. Really."

"You said cramps were bad." The words were clipped. His cheeks were drawn, his eyes sharp with concern.

"This wasn't that type of cramp. It was more like a charley horse in my side. Abdominal cramps are bad." She pointed to her stomach. "The ones gripping your belly. Those are the ones to worry about."

The muscle in his cheek flickered, and he looked to the side and shifted his jaw. Finally, he met her eyes. "I don't like seeing you in pain. The baby… Well, a cramp's a cramp."

His words pounded her heart, and the riot of emotions she'd dealt with all day flooded back. She covered her face with her hands and tried to slow it all down— her thoughts, impressions and whatever was going on with Wade. To have him care about her was so much more than she'd had with Cam.

Then she nodded, trying to figure out how to tell him what she was feeling. She'd never be able to put it in words.

"It means a lot to me. That you care." It sounded so lame. How could she explain?

"Good. Because I do." He visibly relaxed.

"I care about you, too. I don't ever want to see you in pain, either."

"I'm not. You won't."

What did that mean? Either he thought he could avoid pain or hide it from her. Neither was realistic. But then, her growing feelings for him weren't, either. She unscrewed the bottle cap. Took a sip. Unwrapped the veggie sub. When she sank her teeth into the first bite, tears threatened to spill. She was getting too used to his thoughtfulness. When she moved to Casper—and she would be soon—she was going to be the loneliest girl on the planet.

It was time to emotionally distance herself from Wade. If only she knew how…

Chapter Nine

Wade kept one eye on Kit as she mingled with the other ladies Saturday night. Nash and Amy had invited them and some close friends over for a barbecue. The week had passed by quickly. Too quickly. He'd spent most of it harvesting the first cut of hay on the ranch. Cutting, baling, hauling and stacking hay was hot, sweaty, exhausting work. And he'd relished every minute of it. It meant he'd be able to take care of his cattle this winter. Hopefully.

The couple Ray mentioned hadn't visited JPX Ranch yet, but they also hadn't visited Dudley Farms. Ray assured him they'd be out soon.

In the meantime, Kit hadn't mentioned any more cramps and seemed happy spending her days quietly on the ranch. But in the back of his mind, he kept replaying the scene at the shopping center. When she'd doubled over in pain, something inside him had snapped.

He hadn't had that sensation in years—the fear of permanently losing someone he loved. He'd almost forgotten how sharp it hurt, how helpless it made him feel. He never wanted to experience it again.

"Where are you at?" Nash jabbed an elbow into his side. "I just made fun of your hat and you didn't even hear me."

"What's wrong with my hat?" He took off his straw cowboy hat and inspected it. "Looks good to me."

"Yeah, if you want to look like a rodeo wannabe."

"Oh!" Clint and Marshall pointed at him, laughing.

"The only wannabe here is you. You call yourself a barbecue master? The sauce has too much vinegar." Wade loved ribbing the guys. They'd been doing it non-stop for years. He'd always been able to count on them, but he hadn't told them about his financial predicament. He wasn't ready to admit how badly he'd messed up.

"Too much vinegar?" Nash placed his hand against his chest, putting on the wounded show of a lifetime. "Check your taste buds. No one wants candy syrup covering their pork."

He ignored Nash and turned to Marshall. "You ready for the wedding?"

Marshall grinned. "I've been ready since Christmas Eve, when I popped the question."

"Only one week away, my friend. There's still time to change your mind." He slung his arm over Marshall's shoulders and playfully punched his biceps.

"Why would I do that? Ainsley's the best thing that's ever happened to me." He gazed at the group of ladies, lifted his can of Coke to the pretty blonde and nodded. Wade's eyes about popped out of his head. Every woman over there held a baby, including Kit.

"The quadruplets are getting spoiled." Raleigh, Marshall's brother-in-law, beamed a proud smile toward the ladies.

"Yeah, they're growing like weeds. I miss them."

Marshall lived a few hours away from Sweet Dreams. He waved to his sister, Belle, who held one of the quadruplets. She lifted the baby's hand and pretended to wave back.

"I think Belle needs me." Raleigh strode away from the men, and Wade watched him take the baby from Belle. The man kissed the boy's cheek and held him high in the air.

It made Wade think of Kit's little boy and how great it would be to hold him high in the air, too.

He looked at his friends and felt like the odd man out. They'd all found women to share their lives with. None of them had ever thought they'd get married, let alone have kids. But here they were—happy. It was hard to believe he was the only bachelor left.

"I hope Ainsley and I have a bunch of kids, too." Marshall sounded wistful.

A month ago, Wade would have teased him, but now?

He watched the women laugh with each other and coo at the babies. The sight positively tied up his heartstrings. And he didn't think he possessed heartstrings.

He swiveled to face his friends and all three had matching sappy expressions on their faces.

"Okay, what happened to y'all?" One by one, he pointed to Marshall, Nash and Clint. "We used to talk about horses and bull riding and cattle. You're all making goo-goo eyes at a group of women and babies."

The three exchanged amused glances.

Nash clapped his hand on Wade's shoulder. "It's okay, buddy. You'll understand soon."

"What's that supposed to mean?" He jerked away from Nash's touch. Honestly, his friends were starting to get on his nerves. Acting like they were all in on some grand secret.

"We all see how you are with Kit." Nash raised his eyebrows and cocked his head to the side.

"She's my friend. My best friend. That's it." He crossed his arms over his chest.

"It's a good start." Clint's tone was matter-of-fact.

"The woman *is* pregnant and alone." Marshall shrugged and opened his hands to make a point.

"Yeah, and her husband just died and she's moving to Casper."

"So…move with her," Marshall said.

He closed his eyes and counted to five. He was *not* moving to Casper. Why would that even be a suggestion? Were his friends going through some sort of newlywed frenzy?

"I'm not moving. My life is right here." He stamped his foot to make his point. But was it true? He very well could be moving. And soon. He didn't have much say in the matter.

"Won't do you much good if your heart's in Casper." Clint shook his head.

Since when did Clint have so much to say? He'd always been quiet. Didn't stick his nose where it didn't belong—one of his best qualities, in Wade's opinion. A quality the man should pick back up.

Marshall scuffed his boot against the patio stones. "I sure would hate to see you all worked up again if she remarries, though. You were a mess the first go-round."

"I was not all worked up when she married Cam."

The three men pretended to whistle, looking everywhere but at him.

"I wasn't." His voice rose. "And who's to say she'd

get remarried? She'll have enough to deal with. I don't see her adding another husband to the mix."

"She's a beautiful woman. She's young, and she'll have a baby, Wade," Nash said. "Wake up to reality."

A burning sensation flashed through his chest. His stupid friends were stressing him out. Probably trying to give him a stroke.

Clint took a step closer to him. "You've been in love with her for a long time. This is your chance."

Wade shifted his jaw and stared out toward the stables. He hadn't been in love with Kit for a long time. He'd never been in love with her. Wasn't in love now.

He loved her...but not in a romantic, let's-get-married sense.

There was a difference. A big difference. His friends were too thickheaded to see it.

"Land won't keep you warm. It's just a ranch." Clint started making his way to the women, with Marshall and Nash joining him. Wade reluctantly followed them. As Nash put his arm around Amy and made cooing noises to the baby girl in her arms, Wade steered clear of his former friends—the traitors—to stand next to Kit.

She smiled up at him, the freckles on her nose making her look younger than she was. "Isn't he precious? This is Max."

He studied the boy with chubby cheeks, fuzzy hair and big brown eyes. The baby was pretty cute.

"Here." She held Max out to Wade. "Will you hold him for a minute? I have an itch."

"I don't know." He raised his palms and backed up a step. He'd rather scratch whatever itched her than hold a squirming child, although the boy seemed to be quiet.

"Come on. It'll only be a second." She thrust the baby into his arms.

The baby weighed about as much as the injured young fox he'd found in the meadow last fall. But the boy was squishier and more compact. With his hands under the child's armpits, Wade held him out a few inches from his body. What now?

"What are you doing?" Kit straightened. "Haven't you ever held a baby before?"

"No." He tried to hand him back to her, but she wagged her finger, her eyes sparkling. "Oh, no, you need to learn how to hold him. First of all, he's not a grenade ready to detonate. You can keep him close to your body. Tuck him to your chest. Like this." She adjusted the baby, who stared into Wade's eyes as if he was the most fascinating thing he'd ever seen. Wade grinned. To his surprise, the baby smiled back.

"Did you see that?" He widened his eyes. "He smiled at me."

"He's so adorable."

"He is, isn't he?" Wade scrunched his nose at the little fellow, while Kit sidled up next to them and played peekaboo. The baby giggled. Pure joy. "Do that again, Kit."

She did, and Max laughed, his entire body shaking in Wade's arms.

If this was what having a baby was like, he could see why his friends wanted one. He peeked at Kit, who was engrossed in entertaining the baby, and the bottom dropped out of his stomach.

She'd be doing this with her own baby in Casper. Without him.

Someone else would fall in love with her and snatch her up and raise her baby with her.

Could he handle losing her to another man a second time?

When he'd never really handled losing her the first time?

Kit bit into another chocolate chip cookie as Lexi crunched a carrot stick. Amy dropped a handful of potato chips onto a paper plate. Strings of lights overhead added a festive touch to the pole barn awning above where they sat. Belle and Raleigh had gone home to put the quadruplets to bed, and Marshall and Ainsley had left with them. The men were off to the side lighting a fire in the pit. Their guffaws and laughter traveled clear and loud.

All evening Kit had grown more and more comfortable with these women. They'd compared notes on their pregnancies, laughed at the sight of Nash in a Kiss the Cook apron and munched their way through a full spread of food.

She wanted to tell them about the baby's health problems, and she wanted to share the good news that the test indicated he wouldn't have special needs. But she hadn't gotten the guts to do it.

What was she afraid of, anyway?

Pity, for one. And how many times had she confided something painful to a female friend, only to immediately feel an emotional distance? She'd learned the hard way that not everyone could handle the truth.

But…

Did it mean she shouldn't try? She thought of Sandra Bixby. Some women were really good at being there through the tough times. Kit had called Sandra this week and talked for a long time.

"Oh, get this." Amy wiped her greasy fingers on a napkin. "Ruby informed me she wants to name the baby."

Lexi grinned. "What did she come up with?"

"Cinderella if it's a girl, and Kristoff if it's a boy."

"Kristoff?" Lexi asked. "Where did she come up with that?"

"The movie *Frozen*." Kit hadn't taught second grade for years for nothing. "Ruby must love Disney movies."

"Oh, she does." Amy nodded, smiling. "Honestly, I'm surprised she didn't suggest Sven. She adores that reindeer."

"So…are you letting her pick the name?" Lexi teased.

"Uh, no." She shook her head decisively. "It will be a group effort. Kit, have you started a list of names yet?"

She bit her lower lip. "I was waiting."

"For what?"

"Well…" The timing was right. It would be simple to tell them the reason she was waiting. Her palms grew sweaty. "I found out the baby has some health issues. He has a hole in his heart."

"Oh, no!" Lexi's jaw dropped.

"How horrible." Lines creased Amy's forehead.

And before Kit knew what was happening, both women had wrapped their arms around her in a group hug. When they'd hugged it out, they stayed close to Kit.

"The doctor was worried the hole might be caused by a genetic mutation, so they ran a few tests on the baby. Thankfully, I got the results back earlier this week, and they were negative. He still has the hole, but at least he doesn't have special needs, too."

A fat teardrop fell from Amy's eye onto her cheek. "I'm so sorry you're going through this, Kit. If there's anything we can do…" She wiped the tear away. "I'm such a blubbery mess lately—don't mind me."

Lexi reached over and squeezed Kit's hand. "Anything. Anything at all we can do. If you need a ride to the doctor or just need someone to talk to, we're here."

She tried to tamp down the tears pressing against her own eyes and failed. These women had welcomed her without questions or judgment, and now they were offering her so much more than she'd ever given another female friend.

It hit her how stingy she'd been with her friendship over the years. So afraid of getting hurt, she hadn't bothered to show up and try.

"We didn't mean to make you cry." Lexi's lips wobbled and soon she, too, had tears rolling down her cheeks. "I feel so bad for you. You lost your husband, and now your baby has a hole in his heart. It seems really unfair. Your burden is too heavy."

Kit blinked, whisking away the tears and trying to pull herself together. "It isn't too heavy. Don't worry about me. God has held me through all of this, and He won't let me down. I was feeling much worse—depressed, really—the three weeks I had to wait for the test results to come in. Hearing the results were negative was a huge relief. I feel better than I have in a long time."

"Three weeks?" Amy exchanged a horrified glance with Lexi. "You mean to tell me you had to wait three weeks not knowing if your baby had special needs?"

Kit nodded.

They both surrounded her once more and wrapped her in their arms.

"What is going on in here?" Nash stood with his fists planted on his hips. "Why are you all cryin'?"

Kit looked at Amy and Lexi, and all three of them started laughing. And the laughs grew harder and louder until she was afraid they'd gone into full-blown hysteria. She didn't care. It felt so good to laugh and to share her troubles.

"Come on." Nash took Amy's hand and led her toward the bonfire. "You need a marshmallow. I don't like seeing you cry."

"You okay?" Clint slid his arm around Lexi's waist and placed his other hand on her small tummy. She nodded, and they strolled away to the fire, where chairs and bales of hay had been lined up for seats.

Which left Wade. Alone. With her. In all his masculine glory. He took three steps forward. His eyes blazed with intensity. She waited for him to say something. To ask her why she was upset. To try and force her to get off her feet and sit for a while.

He did none of those things.

Face-to-face, under those pretty stringed lights, he cupped her cheeks in his hands. Emotions ran through those blue eyes faster than wild horses pounding across the prairie. Then only one remained. She sucked in a breath.

He'd never looked at her this way before. With need and fire and…more. Her insides warmed, her knees grew weak and anticipation palpitated in the air between them. She could feel his breath as he leaned in. His hands snaked behind her back, and he urged her to him, never breaking eye contact.

When his lips touched hers, she flew back in time, back to when she'd been a little girl and adored him with every ounce of energy she had. When his mouth pressed more firmly, she was reminded she was all woman now. And she gave in to a lifetime of longing and kissed him back.

She spiraled into sensations—the cedarwood scent of his cologne, the hint of lemonade on his lips, the contained muscular strength holding her as if she was valuable, a prize.

She'd waited her entire life for this moment, and she hadn't even known it.

His hands caressed her lower back in circular motions. She touched the back of his neck, sinking her fingers into his cropped hair. The kiss went on until the baby made his presence known.

Wade jerked back. "Did you feel that?"

"Of course I felt it." She kept her arms around his neck. The baby kicked again. His movements were getting stronger. Each little jolt added to her hope of keeping him alive.

Wade shifted his hands and his attention to her belly. Another movement. He flashed her a surprised grin. No words were needed.

His face fell. What went on in that mind of his? He wasn't going to apologize for kissing her, was he?

"A part of me feels like an imposter." He tucked a lock of her hair behind her ear. "Cam should have been here for this. He should have been the one to take you shopping, pamper you, feel the baby kick. I know things were bad and all, but are you missing him?"

Wait…what? One minute he was kissing her with so much emotion her head was still spinning, and now he wanted to talk about her dead husband?

"No, I'm not. He wouldn't have been here for this."

She dropped her hands to her sides. "I told you. He wanted a divorce."

"But the baby…it would have changed his mind."

"Nothing would have changed his mind. Trust me."

Wade's expression softened. "Why did he want a divorce?"

She'd been staying with Wade for almost three weeks. Two weeks ago in Casper, she'd told him Cam wanted a divorce. He hadn't asked for details. Why did he want them now?

"It doesn't matter." She brushed past him, but he caught her arm.

"It does to me."

"Leave it alone." She wanted one night to bask in feeling special. The second she told Wade that Cam had cheated on her not once but three times, he'd wonder why, and he'd come up with the truth.

She hadn't been enough for Cam.

She'd never be enough for Wade, either.

Why would any man blessed enough to be married to Kit throw his marriage away? Wade leaned against the railing on his porch later that night. He couldn't sleep. The stars twinkled brightly above, and every now and then a shooting star would streak through the inky sky. In the distance, coyotes howled.

Things had changed tonight.

He didn't like change. Not this kind, anyway.

He blamed it on his so-called friends. All their talk about families and Kit and her getting remarried had discombobulated him. Was *discombobulated* a word? He didn't know. Or care. Something had shaken him up and left him disoriented.

He'd tried too many new things tonight.

Holding a baby. And liking it.

Seeing Kit surrounded by women he admired. Thinking the three of them laughing and crying and being pregnant looked right.

Watching his buddies pair off with their pregnant wives. Wanting to be paired off with a pregnant wife, too.

He slapped his thigh. That was the problem. He couldn't go on pretending he was right for the role. He didn't have it in him to offer her or any woman forever. Not when forever could be as short as his mother's.

And then he'd gone and kissed her—kissed Kit. He raised his eyes to the highest star and shook his head.

It had been a good kiss.

A real good kiss.

A knock-your-boots-off, never-let-it-end kiss.

He had half a mind to march down the lane and wake her up just to kiss her again.

He could not kiss her again.

Even if she had tasted like chocolate cookies and home. He'd been about to get carried away—and wasn't he a little old to get so caught up in a kiss?—when the baby had kicked. Feeling that little nudge to his abdomen had been about the coolest thing he'd ever experienced.

He dropped his face into his hands. What was he doing?

You've been in love with her for a long time. This is your chance.

Since when had Clint become the expert on Wade's love life?

He didn't have a love life. Wouldn't have one.

Clint was wrong. He hadn't been in love with Kit for a long time, and he wasn't now.

He wasn't in love, period.

He puffed out his cheeks and exhaled. Life had been easier when Kit belonged to Cam. Maybe they were divorcing because they hadn't been compatible. Or they'd grown apart. One of them could have cheated.

Not Kit.

He didn't see her breaking her vows. Loyal to a fault. At times she'd clung to people who weren't good for her, and he'd wanted to tear her away for her own good. But he never had.

He'd been torn away from too many people in his own life to ever insert himself that way in hers. And, if he were brutally honest with himself, she was one of the few people he couldn't lose. He just couldn't.

Jeopardizing their relationship with illusions of love wasn't going to happen no matter what his friends said.

Chapter Ten

She was too aware of him in church Sunday morning. Wade smelled clean and woodsy, and he was wearing dark jeans and a crisp white button-down with the sleeves rolled up. Corded forearms flexed as he held open the hymn book. They sang along with the congregation. His low voice was so inviting, Kit had to discreetly scoot away to create an inch of space between them. She needed to create more than an inch—more like a couple hundred miles. And even that might not be enough.

For hours she'd tried to sleep, only to repeatedly replay his kiss in her mind. Had she been grinning like an idiot in her supercomfortable bed half the night? Yes. And worse, she'd let her mind wander to places it shouldn't go.

Like staying in Sweet Dreams and raising the baby here. On Wade's ranch. With Wade.

Unfortunately, her mind was still stuck in that fantasy, and his presence next to her wasn't helping matters. Had the air-conditioning broken or something? She fanned her face.

"You all right?" Wade whispered.

No, she was not all right. She'd foolishly left herself open to more heartbreak and pain. Wade didn't love her. Sure, he'd been taking care of her. Yeah, last night he'd kissed her. What a kiss…

But a spur-of-the-moment kiss didn't equal love.

And one loveless marriage was enough for her for a lifetime.

"I'm fine, thanks." She wasn't what Wade needed, anyhow. He needed a wife who was fully present. One without a bunch of baggage from her past. Someone fun who challenged him. Someone beautiful and kind. Someone who would make him happy, not disappoint him the way she had Cam.

As much as she loathed the thought of moving in to the apartment in Casper, her move-in date was fast approaching, and her doctors' appointments were less than two weeks away.

She had to get her head out of fantasyland and into reality, where it belonged. Wade's friend Marshall was getting married on Saturday, and Wade was a groomsman. That meant Friday night he'd be at the rehearsal dinner and all day Saturday at the wedding. Marshall and Ainsley had invited her to both. She planned on attending. It would be her last hoorah in Sweet Dreams.

Disappointment made her slump.

She'd come back and visit. After the baby was born and things had settled. She'd been getting better at pushing away worries about his health lately. A big part of that was due to Wade.

It was okay to rely on him as a friend.

It wasn't okay to mentally make him something more.

"In the second book of Corinthians we're told we

have a merciful God, the source of all comfort. As you prepare for a new week, remember His mercy, acknowledge His comfort. Amen." The pastor signaled for them to rise.

Kit placed her program on the seat next to her and pushed her hands against the pew to stand. She was getting more off balance as her belly grew. Wade grasped her elbow and helped her up the rest of the way.

She would miss his touch when she moved. She'd forgotten how a simple touch could make her feel less alone in this world.

Life with Cam had been very lonely.

Her world would be changing soon. New roles, new town, new everything. At least she could rest in the assurance that God would see her through it all.

When the service ended, she and Wade made their way outside to the lawn, where groups of people chatted.

"Do you mind if we skip breakfast at Dottie's this morning?" he asked.

"Not at all. Why?"

"I need to check on a section of fence, and it will take a while."

Disappointment spilled to her toes. She propped up what she hoped was a bright smile. "No problem. I think I'll take a nap. And I might do a little online shopping for the new apartment."

Something flickered in his eyes, but she ignored it. This was what they were doing, right? Reminding each other last night's kiss hadn't meant a thing and they both had their own lives. Apart from each other. With no kissing or commitment allowed.

"Kit!" Amy hustled over with pink cheeks glowing

and dark brown hair swinging behind her. "I talked to my mom this morning, and we want to come down and help you out when you have the baby. We'll stay in a hotel for a few days until you're on your feet."

Amy's eyes sparkled with excitement. This woman—this virtual stranger—wanted to help. And her mother did, too. How amazing was that?

"I would love that." Kit took Amy's hands in hers and squeezed them. "But if it's too much or something comes up, I understand. I'll be fine."

"Nonsense. It will give me a crash course on newborns. And, trust me, you want my mom helping. She knows what she's doing and doesn't get frazzled."

A mom helping her—how bittersweet. She had no memories of her own mother. Aunt Martha had been a nightmare. The foster homes had been fine mostly, but as time wore on and she moved again and again, her heart had crusted over. As much as she'd wanted a mother, she'd given up hope. She'd resigned herself to the fact she was alone. Then Cam came along and she'd thought her circumstances had changed, but they hadn't. Not really.

And now she had two women offering to help her when the baby arrived...

Wade cleared his throat. She'd forgotten he was there. He didn't look happy.

"Sorry. I know you're busy. We can go." She patted his arm, then turned to Amy. "Thanks again. And thank your mom for me."

"I wish you'd stay here for good." Amy hugged her.

"I have to do what's best for the baby." She waved goodbye. Wade put his hand against the small of her back to direct her to the parking lot.

The baby. Best for the baby. An NICU. Good doctors. Proximity to the hospital.

What if the hole healed on its own? Or what if the doctors were able to surgically correct it after she gave birth?

Would she really need to live in Casper?

If the baby's health improved, she could live wherever she wanted. Even Sweet Dreams. What a comforting thought. But could she live near Wade and not fall in love with him? When she was already halfway there?

Wade didn't need to check on fence, and he could have gone to Dottie's Diner with his friends, but he'd chickened out. The more time he spent with the other couples, the more he wanted to be part of one, too. And sitting next to Kit in church this morning had been pure torture.

She'd smelled like tropical flowers. Her warm skin kept brushing his, making him all too aware of her beauty. Now that he knew exactly how she fitted in his arms and how her lips felt against his, he could think of little else. So he'd made an excuse to get away from her, from his friends, from everything.

He needed to create some major distance between himself and Kit.

He steered his truck south to the hundred acres that had started it all. The weather was perfect. Sunny and not too windy.

And while he was driving to inspect fence that didn't need inspecting, Kit was back at the ranch shopping for the apartment he'd been avoiding thinking about. The unsafe apartment he couldn't bear to think of her living in.

He turned up the radio's volume and let the country song chase away his thoughts. Before long he pulled onto the long dirt road leading to the old house, aka the shack. He drove past it to where the pasture began.

Stopping at the gate, he got out and just stood and watched the cattle. Tails flicking, heads bowed to forage the grass.

His cell phone rang, and without checking the caller, he answered.

"The young couple I told you about wants to tour your ranch. Today." Ray Simon sounded excited.

His heart sank. "They haven't checked out Dudley Farms, have they?"

"No. I've pushed it hard. Told their agent you're motivated to sell. They aren't very interested in it. But they definitely want to see JPX Ranch. They can be there in two hours. Are you okay with that?"

Was he okay with selling his home, the inheritance from a man who had given him the rights of a son?

He'd never be okay with it.

But what choice did he have?

"Yeah."

"I'll call their agent and tell them. Hopefully, we'll get an offer soon."

"Got it. I'm out at another property right now."

"That's fine. Their agent can call me with any questions." Ray went over a few more things before hanging up.

Wade slipped his phone back in his pocket and hitched a cowboy boot on the bottom rail of the fence to watch the cattle graze. *How did I get here? How did I go from top of the world, more money than I knew what to do with, to this? I can't believe I might lose JPX.*

If the couple bought JPX Ranch, where would that leave him?

Back to where he'd started. Except with more money in his pocket.

Slowly, he turned and surveyed the land. He would still own this. His original ranch wasn't part of the property for sale. Moving back into the shack would be the ultimate humiliation after finding so much success.

Or he could move to Dudley Farms.

It had been months since he'd been there. He could barely remember the house, since he'd been interested only in the land. He should head up there soon even if the thought of living there, far away from his friends, didn't appeal in the slightest.

Maybe it was better Kit was moving soon. She wouldn't be around to see his fall from grace. With her in another town, he'd forget about the kiss, and he'd figure out how to move forward with or without JPX Ranch. He'd be fine. And so would she. She had Amy and Amy's mom to help her when the baby came. She wouldn't need him anymore.

But he needed her.

Gritting his teeth, he clenched his hands into fists. He'd better get her away from the ranch while the couple toured it or he'd have a lot of explaining to do.

"I've got some good news." Kit scooped coleslaw onto her fork at Roscoe's BBQ late that afternoon. It wasn't really good news, but Wade didn't need to know that. She'd been surprised when he'd shown up this afternoon insisting they go into Sweet Dreams for some shopping and dinner. After smelling all the candles in Loraine's Mercantile, they'd window-shopped on

Main Street. An awkwardness existed between them that hadn't been there before. She figured her news would help distract both of them from the inconvenient feelings surrounding them. "I can move in to the apartment a few days early."

He stared at her for a charged moment, then resumed chewing his pulled-pork sandwich.

"I'm going there Wednesday morning to do a walk-through and to sign the final paperwork. I can move in as early as Friday." She ripped a hunk off her biscuit, but didn't eat it.

"I thought you were going with me to the rehearsal dinner. And what about the wedding on Saturday?"

"I'll still go to both." She was glad he still wanted her to go with him. "I'll move next Monday. It will be nice to spend one more weekend here."

"You can spend more than a weekend, you know."

"I know." She frowned, staring at her plate. "It's time to go, though."

"Line up a few other apartments." He didn't look happy, and the words were gruff. "I'll take you on Wednesday."

"You don't have to go with me."

"I want to. I'll drive." He avoided eye contact. "I've been wanting to check on Dudley Farms, anyhow. We'll swing up on the way back."

"I'd like to see it." She took another bite. "If you don't want to drive to Casper, don't worry about it. I'll be fine going there on my own."

"I'm not leaving you to do this by yourself."

Just the words she'd gotten used to hearing. The ones she relied on from him more than he knew.

He frowned, rubbing his chin. "Will it be too much

for you? Sitting in the truck for hours can't be good for you or the baby."

"It's not as though we'd be driving all day."

He considered it and nodded. "Okay. But if at any point you don't feel right, you let me know and we'll stop and rest. I don't want you overdoing it or getting blood clots in your legs from sitting too long."

Blood clots? She fought the urge to smile. The man got more paranoid every minute. And she didn't mind it at all. It was nice to have him care. She didn't know what she'd do without him to lean on.

Casper already seemed like the loneliest place in the world.

She glanced at his lips and quickly looked away. Her neck grew warm.

His question from last night roared back—*Why did Cam want a divorce?*

Because something was lacking in her that other people had. No one ever chose her, wanted her, and Cam had obviously realized he'd made a mistake.

"And I'm serious about the other apartments, Kit. I don't like the looks of the one you're renting."

She didn't like the looks of it, either. But she didn't have other options. Cam's life insurance would pay for the baby's doctor bills and her living expenses until she found a job. She couldn't blow it all on a fancy apartment. Even if the one she'd lined up did give her the creeps.

"It will be okay." But would it? How many times had she told herself those words? How many times had it *not* been okay? She didn't know what else to do, though. No job equaled no lease unless someone cosigned for it. And she'd never ask Wade to do that.

She excused herself and hurried to the bathroom.

She stared at her reflection in the mirror. Her face had filled out as the pregnancy progressed. The freckles on her nose blended with the tan she'd picked up since moving here. She looked healthier than she had in a long time.

Cam, if you hadn't died, I wouldn't be forced to live in a rat's nest of an apartment.

Closing her eyes, she took a deep breath.

Actually, she'd still be stuck in a crummy apartment. She'd still be alone, desperate for her baby to be okay.

How many times had she stared into a mirror and seen this exact face—the one with hope etched in the forehead—only to shed devastated tears?

She kept telling herself she was over Cam. She kept trying not to be angry at him. He was dead, after all. But the anger flared again and again.

God, please help me to forgive him for real.

Her thoughts went to Wade and the million and one ways he'd taken care of her since she'd arrived. Maybe that was the problem. Wade's natural appealing attributes only highlighted Cam's lack of them.

A soft knock on the door had her scrambling to get herself together.

"Are you all right?" Wade's voice carried through the door.

Was she all right? She didn't know.

"Kit?" His voice grew firm, concerned.

She opened the door. "I'm fine." She moved forward, but he stood his ground, searching her face for... something. She hoped he didn't find whatever he was looking for.

"What's going on with you?" He took her biceps in his hands, caressing them gently.

"Nothing." She tried to smile. Knew she failed.

"Is this about last night? Me kissing you?"

Was it?

Yes.

But not in the way he thought. Wade made her feel cherished, cared for—important—in ways Cam hadn't. Which was worse? Being married to a man who lavished affection on other women? Or getting affection from a man who might not ever want marriage?

"Kit…" He used his talk-to-me tone.

Fine. He wanted her to talk? She'd tell him what she'd been keeping in. Maybe then she could move on from Cam's death and from whatever was going on here. She could slink off to Casper and build a new life.

"I'm not talking in the bathroom." She gave his chest a light shove. He cocked an eyebrow and moved aside for her to go past him.

They returned to the table.

She didn't even pretend to eat. "Last night you wanted to know why Cam asked for a divorce."

His eyes flickered in surprise.

"Our marriage wasn't the stuff of fairy tales and happy endings." She forced herself to maintain eye contact. "It started out fine, like most couples', I suppose. But within a few months, Cam got restless. I liked quiet nights at home. He liked hanging out with his buddies."

She scooted her chair back slightly to rest her hands on her stomach.

"What happened?" Wade asked.

"At first I was hurt. Then I got vocal about his nights out. He didn't like that. The more I wanted him home, the less he stuck around. We pretty much stopped talking to each other."

If she'd made more of an effort with him, would he have stayed faithful?

"He was an idiot." Wade shook his head in disgust.

The corner of her mouth lifted, but she shrugged. "Looking back, I'm not sure why I was so surprised to find out he'd cheated on me."

"He cheated on you?"

She lifted three fingers. "Three times."

His face screwed up as he mulled it over. "Why did you stay?"

"I still wanted it…you know…the perfect family. I thought he'd change."

"But he didn't."

"No, and I couldn't see a different future. So I stayed." Would she have done anything differently? Left him after the first affair? Pushed harder for counseling? Gone out with him instead of staying home? All the options were giving her a headache.

"What happened? You said he asked for a divorce. What changed?"

Her lungs seized up. This was what she'd been avoiding for months. *What changed?*

"I guess he finally realized I didn't make him happy." Saying the words out loud hurt. "He'd found someone who did, and he wanted to be with her." A lump grew in Kit's throat, and she swallowed, but it had lodged in tight.

"Is that what you believe?" His baby blues held no judgment. No pity. Just raw honesty.

She shrugged. *Of course that's what I believe! What*

*else could I think? I bored my husband. Our life didn't
satisfy him. And he wanted out.*

"I'm sorry, Kit. You didn't deserve that."

The lump expanded. She would not cry. She balled
her hands into fists to keep from falling apart.

"Do you still love him?" Wade asked.

Did she? No. What did it say about her? She'd vowed
to love him until death. She'd stopped loving him long
before then. She wasn't going to sugarcoat it with Wade.
He could handle the truth. If he thought less of her, so
be it.

"No, I don't love him. I tried, but I didn't try hard
enough. I haven't loved Cam for a long time."

He nodded and stared into space. "Did you ever love
him?"

"Yes, I did." She'd loved him. He just hadn't loved
her. Not enough, anyhow. And maybe she hadn't loved
him enough, either.

Maybe she wasn't capable of loving anyone enough.

She refused to believe it. That was one lie she would
not buy into. Not today. Not ever. She could love as
fiercely as anyone.

Chapter Eleven

She could not see herself living here.

Kit scrunched her nose at the scratched and chipped laminate countertop in the kitchen of the apartment Wednesday morning. The dark kitchen had worn cabinets, old appliances and pea-green linoleum floors bubbling in spots. A fluorescent light overhead made sizzling sounds and flickered now and then. In the small living room, the carpet was worn and stained. Ditto in the dining area to the right. She wouldn't think about the furniture the apartment came with. The orange-and-brown-plaid couch had seen better days. The faux leather armchair had, too. A hallway led to two small bedrooms and a bathroom with a stained sink and dirty tub.

She pushed away her disgust. For the first time she regretted selling all her furniture. At the time she'd convinced herself she never wanted to see it again. She'd thought it would only bring bad memories.

But this apartment…was one bad memory waiting to happen.

Wade hadn't said a word. His locked jaw and the

muscle flexing in his cheek said it all. He opened the window overlooking the shared balcony. Deafening rap music flooded the room. He slammed it shut with a thud.

"You can't be serious, Kit." His voice trailed off to a low growl.

She wanted to cry, to run screaming from the place, or at the very least, curl into the fetal position until the apartment morphed into something livable. But she held her head high.

"It will be fine." A worse lie had never crossed her lips.

"Let's take this—" he nudged the edge of the couch with the tip of his cowboy boot "—atrocity of furniture out of the equation. It's a bedbug hotel if I've ever seen one. There are too many rough characters out front, it's too noisy and…" He faced her, crossing his arms over his chest. "I can't let you do this."

"You're not letting me do anything." She kept her tone light and breezy, but she was this close to falling into his arms and begging him to take her anywhere but here.

"Where is all your stuff going to fit?" He stepped back, a glazed look of horror in his eyes.

"I don't have any. I thought I told you. I sold it all."

"Why?" He inhaled deeply, made a sour face and appeared ready to gag. Kit didn't blame him. There was an odd smell in this room.

"Easier that way." She hated the memories her old furniture brought up.

"You can't use this furniture. You'll get hepatitis. Or tapeworm. Or both."

"I'll cover it with a sheet." She eyed the couch warily. Wade had a point.

"Kit…don't do this." He reached over and took her hand in his.

She waited for him to say more. Held her breath, hoping he would say the words she wanted to hear. Give her a reason to come up with a new plan for her and the baby. But his silence said it all.

Stupid, really. What did she think? He suddenly had feelings for her? After her confession about Cam's other women and not making him happy? That really clinched it for her, for sure.

Wade's eyes seared into her. And she caught her breath.

I love him.

Of all the terrible places she could have that little revelation, this apartment was the worst.

I love him, and I want him to love me, to say I would make him happy. That I'm enough, I've always been enough for him.

She'd never really been enough for anyone. No one had ever adopted her. She'd been shuffled from home to home. Cam was the first person who'd chosen her. *Her.* And yet the relationship had ended the same— with her not enough.

Her baby would *never* feel that way.

He would feel wanted and important. Every day of his life.

Which was why she would make this nasty apartment work. It was affordable. It allowed her to stay home with him and pay for any treatments he needed. The stinky couch and lumpy mattress on the bed would be a blessing.

"No. No way. We're leaving. End of story." Wade's wide stance and hands on his hips meant business. Didn't he get it? She *had* to make this work. She'd reached the end of her tether.

"I'm out of options, okay, Wade?" She ran her hand over her hair.

"Then I'll cosign and put the money down myself." The muscle in his cheek pulsed.

"I can't let you do that."

"You can. Do you really think it's safe here for you or the baby?" He shook his head. "I can't let you move in to this crime scene waiting to happen. I just can't. You know what happened to my mother. A few years ago, I drove past the address where we lived. It wasn't this town, but it might as well have been. Same run-down neighborhood. Same questionable tenants hanging around. Look at what happened to her."

Kit hung her head. Thinking about Wade's young mother kidnapped and murdered always bothered her. Glancing up, she met his eyes. They pleaded with her.

Okay, Lord, I can't put him through the worry. I won't. But I'm not taking his money, either. If he's generous enough to cosign for me, help me find a better apartment and a way to pay for the rent all year.

"You win," she said softly. "I appreciate you cosigning for me, but I will cover any money that needs to be put down."

His face cleared and he swept his arm to the door. "Let's get out of here and never come back."

"What about my deposit?"

"We'll talk to the landlord on the way out."

An hour later, Kit relaxed as she trailed her finger across the countertop in a bright kitchen with white cabinets, tile floors and white appliances. She would love to bring her baby home to this pretty place. The master bedroom even had a walk-in closet and an attached half bath. Wade had negotiated to get half her deposit back from the other place, which was more than she'd hoped.

"What do you think?" Wade leaned his elbows on the counter. The building was part of a larger complex, and it was tucked back away from the main road.

The rent was more than the other apartment, but, since it was the garden level, not as much as she thought it would be. If she kept her other expenses low, she'd be okay. "Quiet. Roomy. I like it."

"The couches and furniture are in good shape." Wade rapped his knuckles on the counter. "I like that it has covered parking."

"I do, too. I'm putting a deposit down." She snapped a few pictures, then slid the phone back in her purse. She'd need to buy baby furniture. Soon. For the first time, the thought made her smile.

He locked the door on their way out and drove the short distance to the manager's office. As Kit filled out the paperwork, Wade sat stiffly in the chair next to her.

When she finished, she slid the papers to Wade. He scrawled his name on them and handed them back to the manager.

"When can I move in?"

"I'll check both your credit reports now. If they come back okay, you can move in anytime after Friday." The woman scanned them and glanced up at her. "I'll need first and last months' rent today."

Kit reached for her checkbook. A hand on hers had her looking up.

"Are you sure about moving here?" Wade's eyes gleamed. "You can stay on the ranch."

She attempted to smile to reassure him. "I've got doctors' appointments lined up, and I need to get my life together."

"I can take you to the appointments."

Every word out of his mouth was a temptation. *I could stay. Wade would take me to the appointments. Nothing has to change...*

But she loved him.

Which meant everything already had changed. She was just delaying the inevitable.

"It's time for me to get settled." She cared about him too much to flirt with disaster anymore. Her fingers trembled as she wrote out the check and ripped it off. Sliding it to the manager, she couldn't help feeling like a chapter of her life had ended. A good chapter.

Would the next be tragic? Or wonderful?

It was time to find out.

Wade turned into the drive leading to Dudley Farms. He'd taken Kit out to lunch after signing the lease, and they'd driven in silence for over an hour. He didn't know what to think, but whatever it was, he couldn't help feeling his life was slipping through his hands. He'd come this close to telling her he cared too much about her to let her leave. And next thing he knew, he was cosigning for an apartment.

It had been the right thing to do.

He wanted to tell her about having the ranch up for sale, but he would have to admit the truth about his finances. He wasn't ready.

It dumbfounded him how much having money really

did change things. A year ago, he would have taken one look at the filthy apartment, escorted her to his truck and told her he was finding her a new apartment and paying for it himself. He would have found the biggest, brightest, safest, nicest place there was. Somewhere she'd be happy.

Speaking of happy…

He hadn't been able to chase away the thoughts that had been racing around in his head since their conversation Sunday night at Roscoe's BBQ.

Cam had cheated on her.

And she believed it was because she didn't make him happy.

Any man blessed enough to spend even two minutes with Kit would be the happiest man alive.

He tried to shift his attention to the land splayed before him, but he couldn't concentrate. Not with Kit moving in a few days. Not when she'd admitted she'd stopped loving Cam long ago. Not when Wade couldn't bear to think about her not being around. Not with this weight pressing down on his heart.

"It's beautiful." Kit pointed out the window. "No wonder you bought it. I can see the river winding through the land from here. And look at all those pines in the distance. I'm surprised you're willing to sell it."

It was beautiful, and he didn't care. He never should have bought it. It was the source of all his problems right now. If he didn't own it, he could pay for Kit's baby's medical bills and buy her all the baby supplies she'd ever need. He could resume the life he'd enjoyed all these years on JPX Ranch. Instead, his hope was drying up.

The couple who'd toured the ranch last weekend hadn't made an offer on it.

If he could sell one of his properties, he'd have the cash he was accustomed to. There would be no more selling horses and equipment. Paying off the loans and having JPX's income streaming in would allow him to live exactly the way he had before.

Only this time, he wouldn't get greedy. He'd be content with what he had.

God, just give me another chance. Please. Find a buyer.

The truck hit a bump as the main house came into view. The massive log home sat on a hill. He knew it was empty, and he was preparing to drive past it to check the stables, but an SUV was parked out front.

"That's strange. I wonder who's here." He jumped down from the truck and went to the passenger side to help Kit down. Her hand in his was small, delicate. He wanted to hold on to it forever.

He guided her up to the front door. It took a few minutes to find his key. Just when he was inserting the key into the lock, he heard footsteps approach from inside. The door swung open, and a short, balding man with brown eyes and a serious expression appeared. "You'll have to come back. I'm showing the property now."

"Oh, I didn't realize." Wade hadn't expected to see a real estate agent here. "I'm Wade Croft. I own Dudley Farms."

"Joe Selina." His face transformed with a big smile. "My clients are upstairs." Then he addressed Kit. "I'll get out of the way so you can get off your feet, dear."

Wade followed Kit inside.

She turned to him. "Will you point me to the powder room?" He pointed down the hall.

Joe beamed at Wade. "Congratulations."

"What do you mean?" Were the clients he mentioned ready to make an offer? The sheer relief of the thought almost made him stagger.

"The baby. Hard to believe you're willing to sell this place. It's good land to raise a family."

The clicking of footsteps on the staircase in the large foyer had them both looking up. A middle-aged couple, both wearing short-sleeved shirts, jeans and cowboy boots, chatted on the way down.

"Red and Tori, I have a nice surprise for you. The owner of Dudley Farms, Wade Croft, is here with his beautiful bride. He might be able to answer some of those questions from earlier."

His beautiful bride? A wave of longing hit him hard. "Actually, Kit's an old friend visiting from out of town." He shook Red's hand when the man reached the bottom, and greeted Tori. Red asked Wade a few questions about the house, and Wade did his best to answer them.

Kit returned from the bathroom, and Tori zoomed over to her.

"I'm ready to take a short break, Red," Tori said. "Why don't you and Joe check out the barns without me? I'd rather relax a spell here."

"She doesn't care much for stuffy outbuildings on a day like today." Red chuckled.

"I don't mind barns, but you'll want to look at every piece of equipment out there. I know you."

"You say that like it's a bad thing. I've got to know what I'm getting myself into, T." He scratched his chin thoughtfully.

"Yeah, and I reckon you're familiar with every tool and tractor in Wyoming at this point."

"I want to inspect the fields, too." Red eyed Wade for a moment longer than necessary. "You coming with us?"

He wanted to. Wanted to do anything he could to sell this land.

But Kit…

"I'm sorry, but I'd better pass." He glanced over at her, and she waved him off.

"Go, Wade. I'm fine. I'll stay with Tori. Looks like there are some loungers out on the deck. I could use a little time-out from the truck."

"Excuse us a moment." He escorted her to the massive living room, where they could talk in private. "Are you sure? This will take a while. Probably a few hours. We can drive home. I don't want—"

"Go. You might not have this chance again. Who knows? God might have set this meeting up." She patted his arm and smiled.

Had God set this in motion? Did God care about him that much? When Wade so rarely relied on Him? Prayers weren't answered *that* quickly, were they?

"Thank you." He planted a kiss on her temple. "Text me if you need me."

He returned to the foyer. "I'm ready when you are."

Joe and Red grinned, and Tori waved Kit over. "Let's sit on this deck, honey. It's nice and shady. My kids would love it here. They're grown now, but I have a hard time not picturing them young…"

Wade led the way out of the house. "I haven't owned this spread for long, but I'll try to answer any questions you might have."

Red climbed into the passenger seat. "I appreciate it. The house meets Tori's standards. There's no mistaking this is beautiful land. I miss farming. But there are a few things nagging at me."

Wade started the engine, waited for Joe to settle into the back seat, and drove down the long lane to the stables. He didn't like leaving Kit by herself with Tori, even though the woman had seemed nice. He hadn't brought her out here just to abandon her.

Why *had* he brought her out here?

He could have come by himself next week. But more and more, he'd been wanting to tell her the truth about his finances. He was tired of carrying this burden around. Coming out here, seeing the land, well, he needed to decide if he could make a life here. Get closure. Help him accept that if his ranch sold, this might be his new home.

See what she thought about the idea.

After parking the truck, Wade hopped out and described the various outbuildings. They went through each structure, examining everything from tractors to the tack room. As Red peppered Wade with questions, Wade was surprised to have answers for most of them. Maybe he knew more about farming than he'd given himself credit for.

"You okay with riding horseback?" He jerked his thumb to the horses nearby.

"Wouldn't want to see the fields any other way." Red grinned. Joe nodded his approval.

Several minutes later, the three of them headed out. Wade showed Red the river and empty pastures. As he looked around, he was proud to see the ranch held rich natural resources and a charm all its own. Maybe Red would appreciate it and want to buy it.

They moved on to the farmland.

"See, this is what's been nagging me." Red pointed to the weeds and meadow where the crops should have been. "This is fertile ground. I noticed the irrigation equipment. You have water rights. Why aren't there any crops?"

His failure had just been named. He had no choice but to tell Red the truth.

"The irrigation equipment is old and doesn't work. Last summer was dry, if you recall. I bought this land with the intention of farming it. My funds got low, I couldn't afford to repair the equipment and last year's crops never materialized. I opted not to plant seed this year."

Red chewed on the thought.

"It *is* good farmland, though," Joe piped up. "I've got the previous owner's stats in the file."

"Joe here tells me you have another ranch for sale, as well." Red narrowed his eyes. "Why is that?"

He'd thought about his mistake so many times, but until now, he hadn't said it out loud. It was time to own up to it even if it revealed his weakness.

"To buy this property, I had to put my ranch up as collateral."

"Ah." Red's face cleared. "And you need to get the loan taken care of, huh?"

As much as it pained him, he needed to give Red an honest assessment of both properties. "My ranch is on the other side of the Bighorn Mountains. It's near the little town of Sweet Dreams. The price on it is higher, but it's got more to offer. Newly renovated house and cabins. Cattle. Grazing land galore. If you're not sold on Dudley Farms, come out and take a look at JPX Ranch."

"I might. I'll talk to Tori about it. But I have a question for you first."

"Go ahead." He braced himself.

"What do you plan on doing if we buy the land we're on now?"

The future spread out before him so bright, so familiar, it was like the sun suddenly appearing after days of rain. "I'll stick with ranching on JPX. I never should have expanded in the first place. I'm a rancher, not a farmer."

"And if we come out to JPX and love it? What will you do then?"

He could feel his face falling, but he firmed his chin. "I'll move out here and make a go of it."

"You'd be happier on your ranch, wouldn't you?"

"I reckon I would."

"I learned a while back that as long as I'm with Tori, I can be happy anywhere."

The words stung unexpectedly. Lately, any future without Kit didn't appeal, even if the best-case scenario happened and he could keep JPX Ranch.

Had his fear of losing someone he loved made him miss out on something more important?

A wife and family?

He urged the horse into a trot. It wouldn't do any good to think about it now. He'd made his choices. He'd have to live with them.

"Have another doughnut."

Kit happily took one from the box Tori held out. The two of them sat on the back deck, which lined the entire rear of the house. The view before them was breathtaking, with mountains, trees, a river snaking in the distance and meadows for miles.

"I always bring snacks on these adventures." Tori bit into a powdered sugar doughnut and dusted off the crumbs that fell on her shirt. "Junk food is essential for my sanity. Red is meticulous, which is code for *s-l-o-w*."

Kit chuckled. "How long have you been looking for land?"

"Two months. We originally were looking in Montana, but there's something about Wyoming."

"There is, isn't there?" Kit nibbled away at her doughnut and relaxed into the chair. "This is living."

"It is. I could see myself having coffee out here in the summer. Putting a Christmas tree up next to the big stone fireplace. Riding horseback around the property with Red. Hanging out with the kids when they come to visit."

Kit had already explained to Tori about her and Wade's relationship, and Cam dying. Tori had told her about their kids—one married and one a senior in college—and how she and Red had missed farming and ranching for the past five years.

"That friend of yours, he single?"

"Yep." Kit hoped Tori wasn't thinking of setting him up with someone.

"You know, finding a partner in life is important. He seems to really like you."

"We've been friends a long time. He does like me. Just not the way you're implying."

She pursed her lips. "I saw the way he acted with you. Protective. Caring."

"Yeah, that's Wade." She had the strongest urge to stand up and pace. She resisted.

"Are you worried about raising the baby on your own? Sure is a shame your husband passed."

"I would have been raising the baby on my own even if he'd lived." She'd come to terms with it. In some ways, it had kept her from falling apart after Cam's heart attack. "My husband was adamant he wanted a divorce."

"Well, look at me putting my foot in my mouth..." She looked mortified.

"Don't feel bad. I stayed with him too long and for the wrong reasons. It took me until recently to understand that."

"Red drives me batty sometimes, but at the end of the day, he's my best friend."

Kit took another bite of the doughnut. Cam had never been her best friend.

Wade was. Always had been.

"Red's having a difficult time making a decision. He's not one for change."

"Change is hard." Kit finished the rest of the pastry. "I'm struggling with it right now myself."

"Once you're settled and holding that darling baby in your arms, it will all be worth it. You'll see."

"Is that how it was for you? With your kids?"

"Yes. I was surprised at how slow the baby years went by, but the school years? Flew by faster than a tornado. And then the kids were gone. Off living their own lives. Made me appreciate Red even more."

Kit couldn't stand to think that far ahead. If the baby lived, he'd grow up and leave her.

She'd be all alone again.

"We've had our ups and downs. Debt years. Flush years. Sickness. Health. You name it. I wouldn't change a thing, though." Tori stared off into the distance with a gentle smile on her face.

Would Kit have changed a thing about her life? Before finding out she was pregnant, she would have probably said yes. But now? If she hadn't married Cam, or if he'd have left her sooner, she wouldn't have this precious child inside her.

The sounds of footsteps caught her attention. The screen door opened.

"Give us a few days to discuss it, and I'll get back to you," Red said as he shook Wade's hand.

"Well, I guess that's our cue," Kit said to Tori while the men wrapped things up with Joe. "Thanks for keeping me company."

"I enjoyed talking to you, honey. Take care of that baby. And don't worry. It will all work out the way it's supposed to."

Kit wanted to believe it would, but the way life had been going didn't convince her. A few minutes later, she waved goodbye and walked with Wade out to his truck.

As he backed up and pulled away, Kit let her head fall against the headrest. "What nice people."

"They are. I was surprised to see them here. Ray usually tells me when there's a showing." Wade adjusted the air-conditioning with one hand while steering with the other. They passed fields as they drove to the main road.

"Do you think they'll buy it?" She watched an eagle soaring above.

"I'm not sure. He seemed enthusiastic, but he was adamant Tori had to approve."

"She seemed to like it."

"You think so?" He slowed when they drove under the sign hanging from two log posts. Then he took a right and soon they were speeding west toward home.

"I'm glad you came with me. Thank you." He reached over and squeezed her hand.

Her chest expanded. It felt really nice to be appreciated.

As he turned his attention back to the road, she studied his profile. He'd been patient, kind, considerate, selfless and all around wonderful to her since she'd arrived.

Tori had Red.

And Kit wanted Wade.

She loved him.

Simply loved him.

Possible snapshots from the future ran through her mind one by one. Of her and Wade rocking on the front porch. Holding their babies. Riding around the ranch. Church on Sundays with their friends.

None of those snapshots would ever be taken.

Because she and Wade weren't meant to be together.

The only way she'd ever get married again was if the relationship was built on love, commitment and a strong faith in God. Wade didn't love her, showed no signs of wanting commitment and she wasn't sure where his faith in God stood.

In less than a week, she'd be starting a new life, which meant she had to get over Wade Croft.

Chapter Twelve

"We are wearing cowboy boots, right?" Wade asked Marshall at the men's store Thursday afternoon. They were having their final tuxedo fittings for the wedding on Saturday. He was faking a chipper mood for Marshall's sake. Yesterday, after leaving Dudley Farms, he'd wanted to tell Kit the truth about his finances, but she'd been quiet, and before long, asleep.

He hadn't had the heart to wake her up. And the moment passed, and here he was, wondering why keeping it from her was so important. Keeping it from the guys, on the other hand…

"You even have to ask?" Marshall looked disgusted.

"Well, what are these for, then?" Nash held up shiny black shoes.

Marshall hitched his thumb over his shoulder. "As far as I'm concerned, you can leave them here. I'm not wearing them."

"What is this color?" Clint held the bow tie up. His wife had planned Marshall and Ainsley's wedding. "Lexi was adamant it had to be ice blue, not periwinkle, not royal blue, not baby blue. Ice blue. I had to promise to give her the exact description or she was coming along."

Nash took it from him and squinted. "How can you tell what the difference is?"

Wade and Marshall crowded around them. They stared at the tie for several minutes.

"Just take a picture of it and send it to her." Wade slid his arms into the black tuxedo jacket. "It looks like the sky to me, but what do I know?"

"Ainsley will love it, no matter what it's called. Tell Lexi not to worry." Marshall checked out his reflection in one of the three-way mirrors. "What do you think?"

"Looking good, man." Wade clapped his hand on Marshall's shoulder.

Nash whistled. Clint nodded his approval.

When all four of them had their tuxes on, Wade handed the salesclerk his phone. "We need a picture of this. Who would have thought when we met as thirteen-year-olds we'd still be best friends all these years later?"

The clerk took several photos and returned the phone to Wade.

"Who would have thought we'd be living near Sweet Dreams?" Nash slipped the phone into his pocket. "Marsh, you need to move back as soon as Ainsley's done with nursing school."

"We might. We've talked about it." Marshall shot Wade a wicked grin. "Isn't it time you got on it, Wade?"

"Got on what?" He widened his stance. Lately, all he could think about was Kit and the baby and her leaving.

"Claiming your bride."

"We'll lasso you up and force you if necessary." Nash slung his arm over Wade's shoulders. Wade shrugged it off. Lasso him up. As if they could.

"Maybe he's not going to get married," Clint said.

That Clint, he was a good guy.

"And maybe he's too chicken." Nash high-fived Marshall.

"All right. Stop." Wade thrust his palms out. "It's not happening. Although I think it's safe to say I've been thinking things."

"Did you hear that?" Nash elbowed Clint. "He's thinking things."

Wade glowered at Nash, who, thankfully, shut up.

"I'm not as against marriage as I once was." He took off the jacket. "But I'm not in a situation to do anything about it. That's all I'm saying. Don't read too much into it."

"Is it Kit?" Clint asked. "She's mourning her husband, I guess. I hope Lexi would mourn me if I died."

"The marriage wasn't great at the end, so I couldn't say for sure." He wanted to change the subject, to go back to not being in the spotlight. "But I don't think she's pining for him, if that's what you're asking. She's determined to move to Casper. Soon."

"To be close to the hospital, right?" Nash grew serious. "Amy told me about the little guy's heart condition."

Wade nodded.

"Don't assume anything." Marshall undid the tie. "She might be in love with you and you don't know it."

"No one's talking about love." He gulped. Did Kit love him? And why did the thought fill him with so much hope? "I couldn't do anything about it if she did." But if Red made an offer on Dudley Farms… *God, have mercy. Please let me sell it.* Then, and only then, could he explore the feelings he was having about Kit. But all the money in the world couldn't guarantee forever. "What time is the rehearsal dinner again?"

"We're meeting at the church at six tomorrow night, then heading over to Belle and Raleigh's for the rehearsal dinner. Raleigh's having a pig roast."

While Nash jabbered on about how hungry he was, Clint just stared at Wade. Why was he looking at him like that?

When he could take the scrutiny no longer, Wade closed the distance between them. "What? You obviously have something on your mind."

Clint's jaw clenched, but he nodded. "You remember the night I came to your ranch? I'd just told Lexi I was quitting as her ranch manager. I didn't think we could be together."

"I remember." How could he forget it? He'd never seen Clint so distraught. And the next morning, when Clint had been transparent about his feelings, not only about Lexi but about his childhood, it had stuck with Wade.

Clint tilted his head to the side. "You're heading for a bad time if you don't acknowledge what's going on between you and Kit."

"There's nothing—"

"There's something."

Wade ground his teeth together. He could feel the pulse in his temple throb. He refused to say another word.

"Figure out what you want. Then go for it. You'll regret it if you don't."

Marshall and Nash hovered near them.

"You told me the same thing, Wade, six months ago," Marshall said. "It's time to follow your own advice."

"And you would have told me, too, but I was too thickheaded to confide in you guys." Nash grinned.

"I can't have her." His blood pressure was skyrocketing. Wouldn't they just let him be?

Clint exchanged glances with Nash and Marshall.

"I messed up. I bought Dudley Farms, and the crops went bust last year, the equipment is shot, I have no money for seed, I mortgaged my ranch to borrow the money for the property, and I'm up to my ears in bills that I'm dangerously close to not being able to pay."

He took a breath, surprised at how freeing it was to lay it all out there.

"I've been there, man." Clint nodded. "Desperate."

"So have I." Nash rubbed his chin.

"Me, too." Marshall stepped forward. "You need to pray about it."

Prayer. They were always harping on about prayer.

And this time it was such a relief.

"I agree," he said softly.

Three sets of raised eyebrows met him.

"I'm not saying everything's going to turn out all hunky-dory, but I've been talking to the good Lord again." A little, at least.

"Good. We want to see you happy."

"Who says I'm not happy?"

None of them seemed convinced.

"Fine, I'll pray and think about what I want. Now leave me alone."

"If you need money to get you through…" Each man made the offer. He turned each one down.

"I appreciate it. Appreciate you—every one of you. I'll get through this. One of the properties will sell. In the meantime, I'm looking for a buyer for Del Poncho."

"I'll buy Del Poncho. You know I've always loved that horse." Nash seemed serious, not like he was making the offer out of pity.

"Whoa! Wait. You have JPX Ranch up for sale?" Clint asked.

"Yeah."

"But it's…everything to you."

Lately, it hadn't been feeling like everything. Lately, Kit had been feeling more important.

"Yeah, well, things change." He shrugged, trying not to think about losing his ranch.

Marshall rubbed his chin. "When I get back from the honeymoon, I'll come up to Dudley Farms and take a look at the faulty equipment. Maybe I can get it running. Won't help you much this summer, but it would be fixed for next year."

This was why he should have confided in them all sooner. Marshall repaired large machinery for a living. Why hadn't Wade asked him for help last spring when it could have made a difference? No sense kicking himself. He would make better choices from now on.

"I appreciate it, Marshall. And it might not be necessary if the place sells. Concentrate on the wedding. I hope you're packing plenty of sunscreen for the beach."

They all took the hint and started talking about Marshall's honeymoon destination.

Not long after, they split up in the parking lot, saying that they'd see each other the next day for the rehearsal.

Instead of driving home, Wade drove out to the shack. He took long strides to the front door. After unlocking it, he poked around the rooms. Still had mice droppings. Same small rooms and a few pieces of dusty furniture.

Memories of poring over property listings at the tiny table crashed over him. He'd been so sure of himself and his future back then. Nothing would have stopped him, and nothing had. Here he was, years later, and he'd had success.

But whether he lived on JPX Ranch, Dudley Farms or here in the shack, he had no one to share his life with.

Pulling out one of the kitchen chairs, he dusted off the seat and collapsed onto it.

He wanted Kit and the baby. By his side.

But what did he have to give her?

If an offer from Red came in, he'd have money. Land. His name. Security.

It would be enough for most women. However, Kit wasn't most women.

And what if Red did't make the offer? Wade couldn't bear to say goodbye to her and let her move in to the apartment. He wanted to feel the baby kick and help her get to her appointments and hold her hand when she needed it.

He wanted her in his life. All the time. Not just on a come-and-go basis.

But naming this feeling wasn't happening. Because the *L* word made you vulnerable, and sometimes the people you loved disappeared suddenly, leaving you alone and broken.

He'd been alone and broken for a long time.

If he offered Kit protection and a home, but not the emotional part, would it be enough to convince her to take a chance on him?

She double-checked the order for new bedding and towels before finalizing the online purchase. A 70 percent off clearance had proved fruitful. Plans swirled in her mind. She should be happy. She'd have plenty of time to settle into her new home before the appointments with the obstetrician and the cardiologist.

The baby moved, and she smiled at her belly. He was growing stronger every day.

It didn't mean the hole in his heart had gone away, though. He wasn't in the clear. But she'd be the first to admit she'd let down her guard ever since learning he didn't have special needs. Maybe she'd been wrong to enjoy this time. Should she be worrying? He could still die.

She wouldn't think about it.

Life progressed on a day-by-day basis right now. No more long-term planning until after the baby was born. She'd get a plan together then.

She padded to the window. This had been a peaceful interlude. She hated to leave it. She'd miss the ranch, this airy, wonderful cabin and, most of all, Wade.

The box of baby supplies Sandra had sent her stood in the corner. A purple envelope with the greeting card peeked out. She'd forgotten she'd been waiting to open it. But now there was nothing holding her back. Sliding the card out, she studied the front, an illustrated elephant mama with a baby. Very cute.

A note fell out, fluttering to the floor. Carefully, she bent to pick it up. Then she smoothed it open.

Dear Kit,
I hope this card finds you and the baby well. You've been heavy on my heart and in my prayers. It seems so cruel for you to lose your husband at the same time you're having a baby. I can't pretend

to know what you're going through, but I understand loss. I had two miscarriages and a stillborn
child before the Lord blessed us with Greta and
Mark. The only thing that got me through—and
continues to get me through—is knowing I will
see each of my babies in heaven. God is taking
care of them for me, just like He's taking care of
Cam. Hold on to your faith. In the end, it's all
that matters.

Your friend,

Sandra

The card had almost a dozen signatures, all teachers she used to work with. Blurry-eyed, she sat on the
edge of the bed. Cam had been a Christian. A sinner,
too, but who wasn't?

God was taking care of Cam.

A wave of emotion hit her. Did she want God taking care of him? *Lord, I'm tired of holding on to this
anger and guilt. Forgive me for losing control the night
he died, and forgive Cam for causing me so much pain.*

She couldn't get over that Sandra had lost three babies. An ache stole up her torso. How had her friend
been able to go on after those losses? And to maintain
her faith—it blew Kit away.

Sandra had lost children and kept trying to have
them. That was brave.

Could Kit describe herself that way?

Was it brave to be in love with Wade and not tell
him? Was she taking the easy way out by moving next
week?

What did she really want?

She wanted a life side by side with Wade, kids, friends, Sweet Dreams, all of it.

It was probably an unrealistic fantasy. Even if she got it, it would fall apart somehow. She'd try to make him happy, but he'd get tired of evenings rocking on the porch.

She wouldn't be enough for him.

She wrung her hands together.

Were those a bunch of lies? Shouldn't she at least take a chance on having the future she wanted?

She wasn't brave. The thought of telling Wade the truth about how she felt made her want to vomit.

Heat flushed over her skin. The stress must be getting to her.

Wade's knee bounced in double time at supper that night. He wasn't used to feeling so out of sorts. And was he imagining it, or did Kit look pale?

Red and Tori wanted to tour JPX Ranch tomorrow bright and early. He knew they were going to love it. It would solve all his problems, but it was a loss he couldn't bear to contemplate. Moving from his home? Imagining the look on Jackson's face if he could see what Wade had done? His appetite vanished.

He might as well get it over with and tell Kit the truth about his money problems. Tomorrow morning she'd wonder why Tori and Red were here.

He hated admitting he'd failed. Hated it.

"Do you have plans tomorrow for lunch?" he asked. The words he should be saying wouldn't form.

"Not really."

"Want to go back to the river for another picnic?" *Tell her, already!*

Her smile lit her face. "I'd love to."

He couldn't look away from her green eyes. They were tinted with concerns. He could guess what they were. Would the baby be okay? Would she do all right in a new town on her own? Other worries were in there, too, but he couldn't decipher them.

"I've got to be back by five to get ready for the rehearsal. I'd still like for you to come with me if you're up for it."

"Okay." She averted her eyes. "I'll see how I feel."

He lunged for his glass of water again and, in his haste, spilled a few drops. Meals and conversations had never been this uncomfortable in the past. Why couldn't he tell her what was on his mind?

They ate in silence for a while. He managed to choke down a few bites.

"Wade?"

"Yeah?"

"I'm feeling more peace about Cam lately."

Cam? The last person Wade wanted to discuss. His blood still boiled when he thought about how the guy had cheated on her.

She continued. "For a while I had all these regrets, like I should have left him after the first time he cheated. But I can see now I would have lost other things if I'd left."

"You mean the baby?" He leaned back in his chair.

"Yes." She sighed. "You told me I wasn't responsible for Cam's death, and I really didn't believe you."

"You weren't. You yelled at him. People yell at each other every day, and they don't die."

"I know. But I hated him. When he told me he wanted to marry the other woman, I hated them both. My head knows I didn't kill him, but my heart wasn't getting the memo until recently."

"Kit…" He lowered his voice. "Let it go. You never could have anticipated he would die of a heart attack."

He couldn't see her face, but she had an air of defeat about her.

Crossing over to her, he pulled her out of the chair and into his arms.

"Don't do this to yourself. You're the kindest person I know. You would never knowingly hurt anyone."

"I hurt people. I do it all the time." She looked up at him. "I repent, and the next thing I know, I've sinned again."

"We all do. We don't even mean to."

"I prayed about it. I forgave him. And I asked God to forgive me, too."

He held her for a few minutes. "While we're being real, I have something to tell you."

Questions lurked in her eyes.

"I had to put the ranch up for sale."

She wrenched free from his grasp. "Why?"

"I messed up." He stepped to the patio door and eyed the outbuildings in the distance. Then he faced her again. "I couldn't afford Dudley Farms." He explained how he'd taken the loans out, and the series of disasters that had dried up his assets. "Red and Tori are coming out here tomorrow, and maybe God will have mercy on me and they'll buy it."

"Oh, Wade, but then you'd lose it. I know how much you love this ranch."

He clenched his jaw, nodding curtly. "It's better than losing everything. I have to accept the consequences of my poor choice."

"I'm sorry." She sidled up next to him, wound her arms around his waist and laid her head against his chest.

"I am, too. But it will work out." He had to believe it would.

"Wade, you've helped me come to terms with my guilt. I'm returning the favor. You made a business decision, and it didn't work out the way you'd hoped. I don't want you to feel bad. Taking a chance isn't a sin."

He had to take responsibility for this. "You're right, but the reason for me taking the chance *was* a sin. I got greedy. Thought I was invincible. I think I assumed everything I touched would succeed."

He held his breath, searching her eyes for disgust or disappointment.

"Repent and move on. God is our good Father. He loves us and comforts us when we make mistakes. I'm still getting used to the concept." She stepped back, shivering. "Do you mind if I skip the rest of dinner? My nerves must be getting to me. I feel tired."

"No problem. I'll take you over right now."

He helped her into the truck and drove her to the cabin. Part of him hoped she'd change her mind and invite him to sit on the porch with her like she usually did, but she slipped into the cabin with a tiny wave and that was that.

He drove back to the house.

It felt empty.

Lonely.

He'd never felt all that lonely before, so what had changed?

Kit. She'd changed him. And he couldn't go back to the way things were.

He didn't really want to go back to that life. He didn't want to eat alone, or miss feeling the baby kick. Didn't want to be deprived of Kit's conversation, her smile, her easy ways.

He headed straight to his bedroom, threw himself on the king-size bed and turned on a baseball game.

She hadn't judged him for his financial predicament. And she'd made it sound as if all he had to do was repent and he could move forward guilt-free. Her claiming God was a Father who loved and comforted him sounded good. Who wouldn't want some of that? But he'd never had a father. Big Bob at Yearling was the closest thing he'd had, and then Jackson had taken him under his wing.

God, I'm sorry for taking my blessings for granted. For letting my greed get the best of me.

Kit was the best person he knew. Why did bad things happen to good people? *Lord, heal Kit's baby. Let him grow up to be a strong, fine man.*

Wade's mom hadn't deserved to be kidnapped and killed. If she'd lived, his life would have turned out differently. He might not have felt the need to protect his heart so thoroughly.

What did it matter? She *had* been kidnapped and murdered. He'd grown up an orphan. Kit had, too.

He understood how life worked. Could accept that it wasn't fair.

He wanted it to be fair for Kit, though. He'd do about anything to make life fair for her.

Chapter Thirteen

"Best news I've heard in months. Thanks, Ray." Wade had been waiting for news for the past two hours. Red and Tori had toured JPX Ranch all morning with Wade by their side, and he'd been certain they loved it. But they'd shocked him when they'd exchanged glances and told him the ranch was nice but not for them. His heart had sunk like a boulder to the bottom of a lake. Their next words had blown him away. They told him to expect an offer on Dudley Farms within a few hours.

He'd almost collapsed, but he'd willed himself to stay standing as he thanked them, pumped their hands and mentally praised the Lord.

Now here he was, sitting next to Kit after the picnic, his cell phone in hand as Ray confirmed it. Red and Tori were offering him just below asking price for Dudley Farms. His financial crisis would be officially over as soon as the deal closed.

"You're not going to believe this." Wade turned to Kit, who was relaxing on the quilt. A slight breeze teased her hair as she rested on her elbows with her face tipped up to the sky. She looked pale, but content.

"What?"

"I sold Dudley Farms!"

She shot to a seated position, her eyes wide with excitement. "You did? Red and Tori?"

"Yep." He got to his feet and pumped his fist in the air. "Yes!"

She slowly stood up, laughing. And all the thoughts and things he'd been feeling collided into this moment.

He'd sold the land.

He could support Kit and the baby. He finally had something to offer her. And he wasn't going to let the moment slip away.

"Let's watch the water from there." He hitched his head toward the wooden bridge crossing the river. He held his hand out. When she took it, her soft skin and warm touch calmed his nerves. He was doing the right thing.

As they strolled toward the bridge Kit pointed out a pair of small yellow birds darting from tree to tree. She always saw the beauty in nature. He liked that about her.

When they reached the middle of the bridge, they both leaned on the rail.

"It looks shallow," she said. "Does the water usually recede so quickly?"

"Yes. It will be more of a creek by August. Your ankles will get wet and that's about it."

He watched her for a moment as he considered his next words.

"What's going on?" She shifted to face him.

He wasn't surprised. She'd always been able to read him.

He hadn't planned this out enough. What should he do? What should he say?

She stared at him expectantly and the moment stretched to uncomfortable proportions. Finally, he took her hands in his.

"I don't want you to go."

"I know you don't." She looked to the side.

"I want you to stay. Forever."

She jerked, her face all screwed up. "What?"

"I think we should get married."

She blinked. Twice. "Why?"

Why? He racked his brain. *Oh, right.*

"Now that I've sold Dudley Farms, I'll be able to pay off the loans, and I'll have cash left over in the bank. Plenty of it. You won't have to worry about money ever again. I'll give you and the baby my name. I promise I will be faithful. I will be the best husband I can be to you, and I'll be the best father to your son, too."

Her cheeks were flushed. Her eyes darted back and forth.

"Sweet Dreams is perfect for you," he said. "My friends think you're great, and I know you like them. We can make a life together here."

She took a step backward, slipping her hands from his. She looked small, young, fragile—and so much like the girl he'd met all those years ago, it took his breath away.

"You're offering me everything I've ever wanted."

Hope surged through his chest.

"What about love?" she asked quietly.

He couldn't breathe. His lips refused to form the words she wanted to hear.

"You know I care about you." He prayed it would be enough.

"I see. Yes, I know you care about me. But everything you offered? Isn't very much in the end." She met his gaze and held it.

What was she getting at? He massaged his neck absentmindedly.

She placed her hand on his arm. "Thank you, Wade. You're the most generous man I know. I'm floored you care enough to propose. I'd be a fool to turn you down."

He held his breath, waiting for her answer. Hoping…hoping…

"But I love you too much to accept. I'd rather live in poverty with a man who loves me than live in a mansion with a man who doesn't."

She loved him? His heart stopped beating. It was as if someone had dropped him in the ocean and he was floundering, desperately trying to latch on to a life raft. And he was right back to being a scared little kid moving in to his first foster home. He didn't trust love. It hadn't been enough to keep him and his mom together. She'd loved him, too.

She continued. "You're the best friend I've ever had. I want to keep it that way. If I accepted your proposal, I'd resent the fact you don't love me the way I love you. And you would resent me, too."

"I would never resent you."

"You would." Tears swam in her eyes, and her wide smile held so much tenderness. "I can't believe I'm turning you down. You just offered me everything I ever wanted. The perfect family, a ranch, wide-open spaces, financial security, friends. A place to set roots."

"Then say yes." He grabbed her hand and pressed closer to her.

"I want more. I don't want to be your roommate."

He sucked in a breath. More? How much more could he give?

"I had a loveless marriage once." Her voice cracked. "I won't have one again."

"It's not like that." He wanted to explain, to tell her their friendship was deep. They could build a life together. Blood rushed through his veins like the water rushing over the rocks upstream. "It wouldn't be like that."

She gave him a wan smile. "I think we should go back. I'm skipping the rehearsal and dinner. It's for the best."

Why couldn't he say the words she needed to hear? Love was the one thing he couldn't give.

"Fine." He marched ahead, grabbing the picnic supplies and the quilt. They strode in silence back to his truck. He pressed the gas pedal a little too forcefully as he drove away.

Shame crushed his shoulders.

He'd offered her everything. He had nothing else to give. His heart had been out of order since his mother disappeared.

Of all the decisions she'd made in her life, this one had been both the easiest and the hardest. It went against all logic. Her limbs were frozen as Wade opened the door to help her out of the truck. As soon as his hand was on her arm, she sprang into action. She tripped a little on the way to the ground, but he held her steady.

She'd just turned down those strong arms forever.

He tempted her to take it all back. To cling to him, begging for him to ask her again, and, yes, this time she'd agree to marry him, whether he loved her or not.

She wanted to be Mrs. Wade Croft so badly her knees almost buckled.

"I can take it from here." Her voice sounded tight and crackly even to her ears. It couldn't be helped. Only a dozen feet separated her from temptation and common sense.

Please don't say anything. She turned to the cabin. Then disappointment set in as she realized he had no words, anyway. The silence prodded her forward. As soon as she slipped inside, the sound of the truck driving away met her ears. She closed the door, squeezed her eyes shut and stood with her back to it.

Had she just made the worst mistake of her life?

She'd never in a million years guessed he would offer to marry her.

It was so typical of Wade, she was kind of surprised she hadn't anticipated it. He'd always stepped up for her in ways no one else ever did. And he'd stepped up big-time. He'd offered her so much...

She lurched forward, wobbling slightly. The day had been too much. She couldn't make sense of it. Taking it slow, she headed to the bedroom. Had she really said no to his proposal?

He would be faithful. She had no doubt. He was a man of his word and always had been.

His kisses came to mind, along with all the ooey-gooey feelings. She would never forget his hard chest against hers, his powerful arms around her or the tenderness of his lips.

Wouldn't it be worth the disappointment of him not loving her just to have a lifetime of those kisses?

She climbed on top of the bed and stared at the ceiling.

No, it wouldn't. Because every time she'd sit down to dinner, she'd be hoping he'd give her and the baby his entire attention. Every time he came in after a long day, she would want him to wrap her in his arms and kiss her soundly because he loved her and missed her, not because he felt obligated.

Without love, she'd never be the most important part of his life.

But he was already the most important part of hers.

Her heart sliced open. Why hadn't she protected herself the way she'd told herself she would? She should have taken the disgusting hotel room weeks ago and never come back here.

She turned on her side with her hands on her belly. The baby was all that mattered. Her focus had drifted to selfish wants. If her heart was breaking, it was her own fault.

God, I did the right thing, didn't I?

All she could see was Cam's face when she'd shown him the pregnancy test. His eyes had filled with equal parts panic and loathing.

He'd loathed her.

She'd tried to forget the final words he'd said to her after their terrible fight. They rang as clear and hateful as the day he'd said them. *I never loved you. I pitied you.* And he'd slammed out the door. It had been the last time she saw him alive.

He'd never loved her.

He'd taken pity on her.

And Wade was doing the same thing.

She'd been right to turn Wade down. A pity proposal would end the same way her marriage with Cam had—

with bitter regrets, hateful words and not an ounce of friendship left.

Mindlessly, she rubbed her stomach.

Then she sat up.

She hadn't felt the baby in hours. How long had it been? She thought back to when she'd last felt him move. This morning? Breakfast, maybe.

She tried not to panic, but worst-case scenarios popped up over and over in her mind. With shaking fingers, she found the number of the obstetrician in town. She dialed it, pressed through the menu options and was put on hold.

She'd lost her husband and career in Fort Laramie.

She'd lost her shot at her dream life with Wade.

She couldn't lose her baby, too.

"You haven't said more than three words all night, and you look like ten miles of dirt road." Nash set a plate towering with food on the table next to Wade.

Wade glared at him.

Marshall's sister, Belle, had insisted on hosting the rehearsal dinner. The pole barn had been cleaned up and decorated for the event, and at least thirty people milled about. Laughter filled the air. Marshall and Ainsley were standing arm in arm near a group of people in the corner. Their love was so obvious, it almost nauseated him.

That could have been him and Kit.

But he'd blown it.

"What happened?" Nash leaned back, turning to face Wade.

"I sold Dudley Farms."

"That's great news!" He held his hand up for a high five and dropped it when Wade ignored him. "Isn't it?"

"Yep."

"So what's the problem?"

He wasn't having this conversation. He was eating the food, then walking over to the blissful couple and saying goodbye. It was high time he licked his wounds and slunk away like the injured animal he was.

"You might as well fess up." Nash cracked his knuckles. "I'll get it out of you one way or another."

"Leave me alone." He hunched over the plate. His appetite had fled town long ago. Why was he even still here?

"Not until you tell me what has you so worked up."

"What's going on over here?" Clint dropped into the seat next to Wade.

"Someone's having a bad day." Nash arched his eyebrows and pointed to Wade.

"Will you mind your own business?" He should ignore them.

"He sold Dudley Farms. Doesn't look too happy about it."

"You do look...defeated." Clint's low, quiet voice was the final straw.

"Well, maybe I am." He shoved the plate to the side. "I asked Kit to marry me, and she said no. There. Are you happy now?"

Nash and Clint exchanged wide-eyed glances. Wade wanted to wipe his hands down his face, but he wouldn't give them the satisfaction.

"Why'd she say no?" Clint asked.

He balled his hands into fists and rested them on the

table. He clenched and unclenched his jaw. Couldn't these two take the hint?

"Maybe she's shy about getting married again." Nash snapped his fingers.

"She's not shy about marriage." Wade hadn't meant to say anything, but there it was.

"Okay, well, maybe she's not ready. She's got so much on her mind with the baby and all..." Nash scratched the back of his neck. "Those pregnancy hormones are nothing to mess with. Trust me, I know. Every other minute Amy's in tears over something. I don't know what to do. I just hand her an ice cream bar. Sometimes she's grateful, but last night she snapped at me. And then she started crying again..."

"It's not pregnancy hormones," he said through gritted teeth.

"I really thought she liked you." Clint rubbed his chin.

"She does like me." Was he having an allergic reaction to something? His throat felt as if it was swelling up.

"Maybe she's not attracted to you. It happens." Nash shrugged.

He vividly remembered her response when he'd kissed her. "That's not it."

"You sound awfully sure about that." Nash raised an eyebrow.

Wade ignored him.

"Do you know why she turned you down?" Clint asked.

Yes.

"What kind of question is that, Clint?" Nash shook his head. "Like kicking a man while he's down."

As if Nash wasn't doing the same thing. At Clint's crestfallen face, Wade sighed. These were his friends. His best friends. They knew everything about him. He could trust them with this, too.

"I offered her and the baby my name, the ranch, financial security, a lifelong commitment."

Nash and Clint nodded.

"But she wanted love."

Both edged back in their chairs with straight spines.

"And you didn't tell her you loved her?" Nash asked.

Wade shook his head.

"Can't say I blame her," Clint said.

Nash let out a disgusted sigh. "And why didn't you? We all know you love her. It's as plain as the sun rising each morning."

He did love her.

He loved her.

Not as a brother or a friend.

He loved her the way a man loved a woman.

Why hadn't he been able to admit it?

God, I'm scared. Loving means losing, doesn't it?

"You're right. I love her. I couldn't admit it, not even to myself." He dropped his forehead into his hands. He couldn't remember the last time he'd cried. Probably the night he'd been separated from Kit as a kid. But emotions pounded in his chest.

His friends probably thought he was a weak fool. He couldn't bear to look at either of them.

"I've been there, brother." Nash put his hand on Wade's shoulder.

"Me, too." Clint nodded, his eyes full of concern.

Wade took a drink of water to try to loosen the knot in his throat.

"The question you should be asking is what are you going to do about it?" Nash asked.

"I don't know." Here came the part where they told him to rush back home and tell her in no uncertain terms he loved her.

He wasn't up for it.

Clint shifted in his seat. "You didn't pray about the situation, did you?"

No, he hadn't. He'd prayed. Just not about his relationship with Kit.

"It wasn't until I got right with the Lord that I could find my way forward with Amy," Nash said.

"Same here with Lexi." Clint nodded.

"Hasn't it sunk in yet? You're not in control of your life." Clint crossed his arms over his chest.

"Try not to take this the wrong way, man, but things have always come kind of easy to you," Nash said. "You might not have felt like you needed to pray. This isn't one of those times. Get on those knees. Find out God's will."

"How in the world am I supposed to know God's will?" He threw his hands up in the air. "It's not like He's coming down and speaking to me. There's no burning bush on my ranch. I can pray and pray and pray, but how do I really know I've got the answer?"

"The Bible." Clint rapped his knuckles on the table.

"It is the living Word." Nash lifted one shoulder. "You've got to at least try. Pray. Read the Bible. The Holy Spirit will guide you if you ask Him."

"Since when did you become the expert?"

"I've been going to Bible class with Amy." His face reddened. "I'm no expert, though."

"If I tell you I'll pray about it, will you get off my back?" He glared at Nash, then Clint.

Clint held his palms at his chest. "I can't force you to depend on God. Pray or don't. It's your decision."

"But *I* think you should," Nash said.

Wade thought he should, too.

"I'm out of here. I'll see you at the wedding tomorrow." Tipping his hat to them, he stood. After finding Marshall and Ainsley and wishing them well for the night, he strode out to his truck. The sun had dropped low in the sky, leaving streaks of pastel colors.

As he began the drive home, he flicked off the radio and let his thoughts adjust to the silence.

God, I messed up.

He didn't know what to say. It wasn't as if God didn't know all his thoughts, anyhow.

Kit's face earlier, as she'd told him she loved him on the bridge, kept intruding in his mind.

I should have told her the truth. I love her. What do I do now?

The only answer was the sound of the air-conditioning blowing.

Maybe the Bible would have the answers he was looking for. When he got home, he'd dust off the good book and attempt to find out.

He had to do something.

He just hoped it wasn't too late.

Chapter Fourteen

Kit jolted awake. Her skin burned. Why was she so hot? She tried to kick off the covers, but her legs refused to move. The covers weighed a thousand pounds. The clock showed 3:03 a.m. Where was she? The dim room came into view. She was still in the cabin on Wade's ranch. A searing pain in her back made her teeth clench. She forced her legs over the side of the bed, braced her hand under her stomach and hobbled toward the bathroom.

Oh, no, she was going to throw up.

A wave of dizziness stopped the nausea. She groped for something to hold on to, and her hand found the bathroom door handle. Almost there.

Inside, she flicked on the light. A sheen of sweat covered her face. The pain in her back clenched again. She doubled over. What was wrong with her?

Oh, God, not the baby!

Although earlier she'd tried for over an hour, she hadn't gotten through to the doctor's office, and she'd been so tired, she must have fallen asleep. She had to get help. Wade would know what to do.

Her head was spinning. She couldn't straighten. Why wouldn't her feet move?

On her hands and knees, she crawled back to the bedroom to find her phone. The nightstand was a hundred miles away, but she crept to it. Finally, she reached up and grasped the phone.

The exertion made her temperature soar. Her arms no longer supported her, and she fell facedown on the fluffy rug. As she flitted near the edge of consciousness, she forced herself to focus. Somehow, she found Wade's contact and pressed it.

God, I know You're here. Don't let the baby die. Get Wade here now. Please, Lord, save the baby!

Pain drilled through her lower back on the first ring.

"Yeah?" He sounded curt and groggy.

"Help," she whispered. The phone fell out of her hand, and she lay on her side, unable to move.

Nausea threatened once again. She closed her eyes.

"Kit? Is that you? What's wrong?"

She opened her mouth to speak, but no words came out.

Nothing mattered anymore.

Nothing but the baby.

Wade shoved his feet into cowboy boots and sprinted to his truck. He needed to get to Kit. Fast. His truck spit gravel as he tore up the lane to the cabin.

Help. One word. Whispered in desperation.

Fear choked the blood out of his heart.

He couldn't lose her.

He. Could. Not. Lose. Her.

He slammed on the brakes in front of the cabin, unlocked the front door and raced inside. No sign of her in the living area. He looked into her bedroom and almost fell to his knees at the sight of her lying on her side on the rug. Her cheek rested on her arm.

Was she breathing?

He knelt beside her to check her pulse. Her skin was on fire. Quickly, he scooped her into his arms and marched straight out to the truck. He eased the seat back and strapped the seat belt around her. As much as he'd like to call 911 and have medical professionals take over, it wasn't an option. It would take too long for an ambulance to come.

Should he grab her purse? She'd need her insurance card and license. He ran in and spotted it on the table. Five seconds later, he was at the wheel and driving as fast as safely possible. When he reached the road, he looked right, then left. Sweet Dreams didn't have a hospital. He'd have to drive farther, to the nearest city.

Flooring the accelerator, he sped down the road, fear squeezing him from every direction. What would cause her to have a blazing fever and pass out?

Whatever it was, it wasn't good.

Kit was his best friend. The person who mattered most to him.

She couldn't lose the baby. It would destroy her.

Take it all, Lord. Take the ranch, the land, the money—all of it—but let Kit and her baby live.

She was the most precious thing in his life.

She'd always been the most precious thing in his life.

His eyes blurred as he thought back on all the times they'd spent together. The letters she'd sent him every week at Yearling. The late-night calls just because. The visits he'd made to her when she was in college. Their easy laughter and quiet comfort simply being with each other.

And other less fond memories came back, like when she'd told him she was engaged. Or her wedding day—

she'd looked so beautiful. He'd about lost it when she'd said *"I do"* to another man. But he'd wanted her to be happy. It had been hard—no, torture—to pull back on their friendship to let her marriage get off the ground. Then Cam died. And Wade hadn't known how to react to his death.

She'd shown up on his porch as a widow with a baby on the way, and it had scared the snot out of him. Filled him with hope, too. Hope that he'd finally have a chance with her, the woman he'd loved for as long as he could remember. He'd been stupid to think he could protect himself by not telling her he loved her. This pain seared as much, if not more, than the pain of losing his mother.

"I love you, Kit." He reached over and pressed the back of his hand to her cheek. Still way too hot. The fever was soaring, and the fact she was barely conscious took him to bad mental places.

Was she going to die?

Keep it together. Focus on the road. She needs you now.

He slammed the heel of his hand into the steering wheel. He hated not having control.

Once more he was a little boy at the babysitter's, waiting for his mother to come get him. *She's just running late, sugar. Nothing to worry about.*

And the next days had passed in a blur until one day he'd woken up in a foster home. The first of many. And yet he'd clung to the hope his mom would come back for him.

Later, when he'd found out she'd been murdered, he'd shut down. Realizing the finality of it—she would never come get him—set the course for the rest of his life.

He'd put up protective barriers that hadn't protected him at all. He'd convinced himself he could control getting hurt or not by avoiding love. But love couldn't be any more dangerous than whatever was happening right now. He wasn't even married to Kit and the thought of losing her was ripping out his heart.

He'd rather love her and lose her than never have the chance.

The miles fell away and his tension rose higher and higher. He could see things clearly, things he'd never realized were cloudy before.

In all his business deals, he'd been missing out on the one thing that truly would make him happy, would give his life some meaning.

Last night he'd offered Kit a future.

A shabby future.

His throat felt raw. She'd been right to turn him down. She deserved better, more, the world.

If he could do it over, he would bare his soul, tell her the truth—that he needed her more than anything.

The miles sped by and the edge of the city came into view.

"We're almost there, Kitty Cat." He got choked up and had to grind his teeth for a moment before speaking again. "Hang tight."

I can't lose her!

He glanced at her round tummy.

I can't lose the baby, either.

He loved the child like it was his own.

Why was this happening? What if she died? What if she never knew how much he loved her?

He parked the truck and carried her to the emergency room, where the staff whisked her away while a receptionist handed him a clipboard. When he'd filled out the paperwork to the best of his knowledge, he found a seat in the waiting area and slumped in the chair.

All he could do now was pray.

* * *

Kit's eyelashes fluttered. Beeps and lights bombarded her. She moaned. Something was on her arm. Tubes. Why? A gentle touch on her hand made her turn her head.

"Try and stay still, hon." A woman in scrubs adjusted the IV in her arm.

Why was there an IV in her arm? She couldn't remember… She must be in the hospital. What had happened? What day was it? Why—

The baby.

Her hands flew to her stomach.

Still round.

Still there.

"The baby…" Her throat was dry.

"Shh…don't use up your energy."

She'd use up every ounce of her energy to find out if her baby was okay. "Is he alright?"

The nurse's forehead furrowed, and she called over her shoulder for someone to come in. "You still have a high fever," she told Kit. "We're trying to get it down. Try and stay calm."

Why wouldn't they tell her if the baby was okay?

What was happening?

She was losing him, wasn't she? What had she done wrong? Her breaths came in shallow gasps. Hopelessness left a vacuum in her heart. The letter Sandra had written swam through her mind. She'd lost babies. *God is taking care of them. Hold on to your faith. In the end, it's all that matters.*

Kit didn't want God to take care of the baby for her. She wanted to raise him herself!

Two other people in scrubs entered and talked with

the nurse in hushed voices. She couldn't make out what they were saying.

Where was Wade? He'd make it all better. He'd explain to her what was going on. He'd get them to talk to her. Slightly lifting her head, she tried to see across the room, but the nurse pressed her back. She felt funny, like her limbs were made of taffy.

Wade wasn't in here. And why would he be? She remembered his proposal, remembered turning him down. He must have driven her here, though.

He'd always stepped up and done his duty where she was concerned. Was that why he'd asked her to marry him? Was she his duty?

"Don't move. We need you to stay as still as possible for the baby's sake."

For the baby's sake… It meant her son was still alive, right?

"Is he—"

"Just relax." The nurse patted her hand while someone fiddled with the IV. "The doctor is coming soon. Rest."

Rest? She didn't want to rest. She wanted them to save her baby.

Her eyelids felt so heavy. She'd close them for a moment. Just a moment. The seconds before she'd called Wade earlier bombarded her. She'd been in bed. Hot, so hot. Crawling to the bathroom. The cramps…

"Save my baby." The words came out scratchy. Had she even said them? Or was she in a dream?

"I'll get you some ice chips," the nurse said. "They'll make you feel better."

Kit reached for her, wanting her to wait, to stay and answer her questions, but her hand grabbed air. Too late.

The story of her life.

Too late.

Always just a little too late.

Too late to save her marriage. Too late to save Cam.

Too late to beg Wade to hold her and never let her go.

He'd offered her everything she'd ever wanted. His name, his home, his protection, his money. Safety. Belonging.

Security.

And like the idiot she was, she'd turned it all down. If she could go back… *Yes. Say yes, Kit.*

She stopped fighting the grogginess. Maybe if she slept, she'd dream about Wade, and this time she'd accept his proposal. This time she'd say yes to what she'd always wanted.

But even in her half-awake state, she knew it was a fantasy. Saying yes wouldn't change reality.

She loved Wade. And he didn't love her back.

Her love wasn't enough for him.

Some things never changed.

Wade jerked awake. Was Kit okay? His neck had a crick from him slumping in the waiting room chair. Sunlight brightened the area. He checked his watch. After eight thirty. He must have drifted off.

He rubbed his neck and crossed to the reception desk.

"Any word on Kit McAllistor?" He took in the other people sitting nearby. Most of them had the same bleary-eyed fear he couldn't shake. It had been hours since the staff whisked Kit away. Surely they knew something by now?

"I'm sorry, sir. I'm not authorized to say." Her compassionate eyes darted back to the computer screen.

He had a bad feeling about this. "I'm getting a coffee and will be right back. You'll let me know when I can see her?"

"Of course." Her sympathetic smile didn't put him at ease. "The cafeteria is down the hall. Vending machines are in the opposite direction."

He could barely lift his boots as he made his way to the cafeteria. Doctors and nurses passed by in their scrubs and lab coats. Beeps and muted conversations filtered to the hall from the rooms he passed. A double door up ahead swung open, revealing the cafeteria. He poured a large black coffee, paid for it and returned to the waiting area.

For all his talk with Clint and Nash about seeking God's will and praying, he had yet to open his Bible and actually do it. Wade set the coffee on an end table, dropped into a chair and pulled out his phone.

Fear roped around his heart for Kit. For the baby. But he scrolled through until finding a Bible app.

Okay, God, now what?

The app opened to a Bible verse. It was from John. He skimmed through it. Then read it again. *"In the world ye shall have tribulation."* Great.

But God overcame the world.

He frowned, trying to decipher what it meant in this situation.

He moved on to the Psalm Dottie used to read to them at night when he lived at Yearling. *"The Lord is my shepherd..."*

The valley of the shadow of death—yep. That described this situation. He read it again, carefully, pausing to grasp each phrase.

He sat back in the chair, mindlessly reached for the coffee and took a drink. Still hot.

I've been so stupid, thinking I was so smart.

Clint and Nash were right. He'd never been in control. He thought about all the years he'd avoided church and ignored God.

I'm sorry, Lord. I didn't thank You or appreciate all You've blessed me with. I was arrogant. Thought I'd done it all myself. Didn't give You credit at all.

Hanging his head, Wade felt the full weight of his sin claw through his body.

Forgive me, Lord. Forgive me.

He wiped his face with his hands, surprised at the emotions coming to the surface. Jesus had died for him. Out of love. The ultimate love. The ultimate sacrifice.

God, I'd do the same for Kit. Please let her live. Please! Save her. Save the baby. I'm begging You.

He couldn't bear to live in a world without her in it. She'd been his rock, his stability, the anchor in his life for so many years. He couldn't stand the thought of not seeing her cute freckles, not listening to her tinkly laugh, not rocking in chairs on the porch as they appreciated the beauty of Wyoming.

The world would be a bleak, dark place without her in it.

He thought of Jackson leaving him his entire estate. All because the old man had no wife, no family, no kids.

Wade didn't want to end up the same. He wanted to create a legacy. With Kit beside him.

Peace spread from his heart to his mind.

I've finally made it, Kit. Choked up, he tilted his head and looked to the ceiling. She'd asked him when he would know he'd made it. The moment had come. And all he wanted to do was hold her hand and tell her.

God, I'm trusting You. But if my prayers aren't enough, I'm getting some help.

He dialed Marshall. "Hey, man, I'm at the hospital

about an hour and a half away from Sweet Dreams.
Kit's in trouble. I don't know what's wrong with her or
how the baby is at this point, but there's a good chance
I won't be able to make it to the wedding."

"I'm sorry, man. Don't worry about the wedding. Just
stay there and take care of Kit. Hey, I had to miss Nash's
wedding because Belle was having the quadruplets."

"Thanks, Marshall. I hate to do this to you. Will you
ask everyone to pray for her and the little guy? I'm calling Clint and Nash now."

"Sure thing. We'll be praying for Kit and the baby.
And for you."

He couldn't speak for a moment. His friends were
too good to him.

"I hope today is everything you've dreamed of,
Marsh."

"If it ends with Ainsley as my wife, it will be. Keep
us posted." He hung up.

Wade called Nash and Clint and explained the situation. They promised to pray, too, and told him they'd
check in now and then for updates.

He tossed the coffee cup in the trash and returned
to his seat. What if Kit had taken a turn for the worse?

What if she lost the baby?

*God, let them both live. If You'll give me another
chance, I'll never let her go. I'll tell her in no uncertain
terms how much she means to me. I'll put a ring on her
finger and break every speed limit to get to a church.*

I need her, God.

I need her.

Chapter Fifteen

Gentle pressure on the inside of Kit's wrist made her eyelashes flutter. Muffled voices filled her groggy head, but only snippets made sense. Words like *pulse* and *temperature* and *blood pressure* were familiar. Other words? Not so much. She opened her eyes. Two concerned faces stared at her.

"You're awake." A nurse smiled.

She didn't know what to think. The events of the night were there, front and center, in her mind. But calm had overcome the earlier panic. She had the overwhelming feeling she'd be okay no matter what.

God, my Father, I trust You.

A strap covered her belly and cords led to a machine next to her. She couldn't see the display. A fetal monitor. The fact it was still hooked up filled her with hope.

Lord, my baby is so precious to me. And I know he is to You, too. Whatever happens, give me a strength like Sandra's to hold on to my faith.

"Please—" she reached for the nurse "—tell me if the baby made it."

A kick in her abdomen made her cover her mouth.

He was alive! Tears streamed from her eyes. He kicked again, and she laughed and cried at the same time, rubbing her belly.

"I felt him," she said to the nurse. "He's in there. He's okay."

The nurse gave her a tender smile. "He's strong. We've been monitoring him since we brought you in. It was touch and go for both of you for a while, but we're glad to have you back."

"What happened?" She hugged both arms around her stomach as best as she could.

"You arrived unconscious with a high fever. We tried to get your temperature down, but your body wasn't co-operating." The nurse motioned for a worker to get Kit something to drink.

"Do they know what's wrong? And did it hurt the baby?"

"I'll get the doctor. She'll explain everything." The nurse finished checking her vital signs and left the room.

Kit relaxed into the pillow. *Thank You, God! Thank You for saving my baby. And me. Your grace astounds me.*

"Hi, Kit, I'm Dr. Patel." The doctor's dark brown eyes and light brown skin contrasted with her black hair. Her smile lit her pretty face. "You have pyelone-phritis—a severe kidney infection—and I'm happy to report you and your baby have passed through the most critical phase."

"So he'll be okay? Did you know he has a hole in his heart?" She massaged her tummy.

"No, I didn't know that. I don't think the infection would affect it. We'll send you down for an ultrasound later, but from the monitor, he seems to be doing fine."

Once more, relief poured through her. *Thank You, God. Thank You.*

"We're keeping you here for a few days. Expect lots of fluids, antibiotics and medicine to combat the fever." The doctor asked her a few questions and answered hers. "Are you hungry? The staff can bring you breakfast. I'll be back to check on you later."

A man in scrubs set two cups in front of her. "I brought you an ice water and a lemon-lime soda. Are you hungry?"

"No, but I need to see someone. My friend Wade Croft... If he's still here, will you bring him in?"

"I'll check. Be right back."

As soon as he left, she took a drink of the lemon-lime soda. Sweet cold perfection. It refreshed her parched throat. Her hand shook as she set it back on the tray.

Was Wade still here? She assumed he'd brought her to the hospital last night, but she didn't remember anything after calling him. How else could she have gotten here? Of course Wade had driven.

But wait...today was Marshall's wedding. The clock on the wall said it was almost eleven.

Where was she, anyhow? Sweet Dreams didn't have a hospital. What town was she in?

It didn't matter, because every hospital was over an hour from Sweet Dreams. Which meant by now Wade would be back at the ranch getting into his tux for the wedding.

She couldn't wait to thank him.

He'd saved her and the baby.

She wanted to do more than thank him. She had to tell him more. Needed to tell him more.

He might not love her the way she loved him, but she couldn't let another day go by without him knowing how important he was to her.

Wade had been her safety net for as long as she could

remember. He hadn't asked for the job. Maybe he didn't even want it. But if it wasn't for Wade, she'd be adrift.

She could not do life without him.

She took another drink of the soda as jumbled Bible verses came to mind. God promised to never leave her or forsake her. God loved her. She knew it as surely as she knew she didn't deserve it.

A sense of calm whisked away the nervous energy. *God, You've always been with me. I'll never be alone.*

When Wade came back—tonight, tomorrow, whenever—and if she got the courage to spell out everything— her feelings, her admiration, her love—would she be able to get through to him? Or had the trauma of his childhood killed any prospect of a real love and life together?

"She's asking for you." The receptionist tapped Wade's shoulder. Exhausted, he glanced up, registering that Kit must be okay if she was asking to see him.

She's alive! Thank You, God. Thank You.

"The baby?" he asked.

"I'm not at liberty to say." She turned and went back to the desk.

If Kit had lost the baby...

He couldn't bear the thought. The child he'd felt kicking had to live. He just had to.

Stiffly, he stood and went to find the room number the receptionist had given him. He had so much to say and no idea how to say it.

How could he adequately tell her everything in his heart?

He strode down the hall, ignoring the beeps and antiseptic smells. He'd gotten this far. He'd be here for her. He would hold her hand if the baby hadn't made it. He'd take care of her.

No matter what, he'd do whatever it took to make Kit understand the depth of his feelings.

Pausing in front of her door, he hauled his shoulders back, sent up a quick prayer for the right words and knocked.

Kit's eyes opened and grew wide. "You're here." She sounded breathless.

He covered the distance between them and sat in the chair next to her bed. Taking her hand in his, he caressed it, kissing the back of it.

"Of course I'm here. Where else would I be?" He kept his voice low. Flushed cheeks stood out in her pale face. "Tell me, Kitty Cat, did the baby… Is he okay?"

Her smile lit her eyes as she nodded. "He's fine. I'm having an ultrasound this afternoon, but the doctor thinks he'll be okay. He's been kicking ever since I woke up."

Emotion welled and Wade had to clench his teeth together and avert his eyes. The baby was okay. *You are a good God. Thank You.*

"Why aren't you at the wedding?"

The wedding? Did this woman have any idea how terrified he'd been of losing her?

"I would never leave your side, Kit." He stared into her eyes. "I was so scared. Scared of losing you. Scared of losing the baby."

Hope made her eyes shine greener than ever.

He pressed his lips to the back of her hand again.

"I was, too," she said. "When I felt him kick… It was the best feeling in the world."

"I can imagine." He attempted a smile. "Knowing you two are okay—well, that's the best feeling in the world for me. I've done a lot of thinking over the past twenty-four hours. And I realized a few things."

Her forehead wrinkled, but she didn't speak.

"I've been a big scaredy-cat, running away from the most important thing in my life. You." He waited for the choked-up feeling to subside. "It was easier for me to add to my ranch than it was for me to acknowledge reality. I've loved you since the day I met you. It started out innocent, and, as we grew older, I fought it tooth and nail every step of the way. I didn't want to open myself up to that kind of hurt. You and I both know what it's like to lose our loved ones. But the fact is I love you. Not as a foster brother. Not as a friend. I love you the way a man loves a woman. You mean more to me than a thousand ranches ever could. You could never be my roommate. You're my soul mate, Kit."

She stared at him, her mouth gaping open.

He continued. "I know this is a shock. I'm not trying to freak you out or anything, but I also can't wait another minute without telling you how I feel. I love your compassion, your sassy comebacks, your freckles, your smile. I love that you've always known what's most important—God and family—and you've never made any bones about wanting both. I love sitting on the porch with you, rocking and talking, or just sitting and watching the beauty of the land. I love your baby. Yes, your baby. I love your child like he's my own."

A river of tears ran down her cheeks, and he reached over and brushed them away with his thumb.

"Don't cry, Kit. I never want to make you cry."

"I'm not crying because I'm sad." She wiped her eyes. "I just never expected to hear those words from you."

He blew out a breath. "Until yesterday, I didn't expect to admit them. You make me human, Kit. Without you, I'd be lost, thinking a ranch would fulfill me."

"You've always been human, Wade. You're the most

giving person I know. I've been able to rely on you. No one else has ever offered me true security. But you? You've never let me down."

"You've always been my anchor."

"We can be each other's anchor—how does that sound?"

He squeezed her hand. "It sounds meant to be."

He had more to say. Including the things that made him squirm.

"Yesterday, when I proposed, I was a fool." He ducked his head. "I thought I could have it both ways—you and the baby without admitting my feelings for you. I didn't even want to admit them to myself. And I'm sorry, Kit. It was an insult. I hope you can forgive me."

"Hey," she said. He glanced up. "It wasn't an insult. It was the kindest gesture—"

"No, it wasn't. It was cowardly."

"It was generous. I'm used to feeling unwanted."

"I hope you never feel that way again. To me, you're the most important woman alive." He shifted his jaw. "I'm sorry. My offer was shabby. I don't blame you for turning me down."

"Oh, I didn't mean it like that… I'm botching this." She shook her head and rested it against the pillows. "Wade?"

"Yes?"

"Did you mean it? About loving me? And the baby?"

"More than anything."

"Why don't you ask me to marry you again?"

Kit held her breath as she watched the emotions playing across his face. He'd stayed! And he loved her! When he'd said he loved the baby like he was his own, she'd almost dissolved into a sobbing mess.

All the wonderful things he'd said…and he meant them. He did.

Wade rose from the chair, his blue eyes gleaming, then got down on one knee and took her hand in his.

"Kit McAllistor. My best friend. The girl who took me under her wing and never let me go. You are the love of my life. I don't want to spend a single minute without you. I want to take care of you. I want a ranch full of your babies. Please have mercy on this cowboy. Say you'll marry me."

A fleck of fear in his eyes made her heart skip a beat. She could barely grasp the wonders of the past hour. She was alive. The baby was alive. And Wade truly loved her and wanted to marry her—for real.

"Wade Croft. My best friend. The boy who protected me and never made me feel inferior. The man I cherish. You are the love of my life. You're the one who cared enough to cook for me, to drive me hours away to check out my living arrangements and not let me live in the worst apartment on earth. You offered me everything, and I want to give you the world in return. Yes, I will marry you. I want to have a ranch full of your babies, starting with this little one."

She placed her hand on her stomach, and he covered it with his. Then he leaned over, gently took her into his arms and whispered in her ear, "I love you. It's my mission to make you happy."

"Do you know what would make me happy?"

"What?"

"Kiss me and you'll get an idea."

His eyes darkened as a grin spread across his face.

"Gladly." He bent and claimed her lips with his.

This was what she'd been waiting for her entire life. She sank into his embrace, her pulse quickening as his mouth moved against hers. She tasted his need, his fears and a future full of love. In return, she poured her own need, hopes and desires into the kiss.

"Do you think it was always meant to be?" She traced his cheek with her finger.

"God works in mysterious ways." He kissed her lips once more. "Now tell me what happened to make you so sick. No one would fill me in on what was happening."

The poor man. She thought he already knew... "Well, apparently I have a severe kidney infection. Don't ask me to tell you the clinical name. I can't pronounce it. Anyway, it caused the fever and nausea and whatnot. They couldn't get the fever down until now."

"That was too close. I could have lost you." He sat back in the chair, scooting it as near as possible to the bed.

"All I could think of was the baby."

He held her hand and she got lost in his eyes.

"My friend—you know, the one who sent the baby items?—she wrote me a letter about losing three of her babies and having to trust God with their care. Believe it or not, it comforted me. Not right away. But as I woke sporadically, I felt this peace that no matter what happened, I would be okay, God would take care of us."

"I admire your faith. I never gave God credit for all my blessings. I guess it took almost losing you to make me realize how much I need Him."

"I do, too. I need Him every day."

"Kit?"

"Yes?"

"I made it."

"What?" What was he talking about? She tried to figure out what he meant, but couldn't.

"You asked me a while back when I'd know if I made

it. I did. I have enough. I have more than enough. It's time to focus on what's really important."

A rush of emotion hit her.

"You're what's really important." His voice was low and it sent a shiver down her spine.

"You mean it, don't you?"

"Yes. I don't want a single day going by without you being crystal clear how I feel about you. I love you. I thank God for you."

"I guess it's official."

"What?" His eyebrows formed a V.

"We both got our wishes from all those years ago. Except I'll never have the perfect family. It doesn't exist. I want to spend my life perfectly imperfect with you."

"Let's set the wedding date."

She laughed. "Speaking of weddings…shouldn't you head to Marshall's? I'm going to be stuck in the hospital for a few days. Why don't you go celebrate with him?"

"I'm not leaving your side."

She gave him a fake glare. "I'll probably be sleeping, anyhow."

"I'll consider going to the reception." He sighed. "After the ultrasound. I want to be there to hold your hand."

"Oh, Wade, that's why I love you."

"I'll be by your side for it all. The good. The bad. You can count on me. You can lean on me."

"I always have."

Epilogue

"They should have been here by now." Kit angled her neck to look down the front hallway.

"They'll get here. Don't worry. The snow isn't too bad." Wade looked around his house, now truly a home. "They'll make kickoff."

Wade and Kit had invited their friends to JPX Ranch for some Sunday football. Clint, Lexi and their baby, Clara, had already arrived, and the rest of the crew would be here any minute. The aroma of taco meat hung in the air, making Wade's stomach growl.

"Oh, where is my head? I forgot to change Jackson into his football outfit." Kit wiggled her fingers, indicating he should hand the baby over.

Wade cradled little Jackson to his chest and gave Kit puppy eyes. "But he's all snuggled in."

"I'll give him right back." Her eyes teased.

She was radiant. His. He still couldn't believe how quickly his life had changed since he'd proposed. It had taken them only a month to pull off a small wedding attended by their closest friends. The reception had been intimate, elegant and at Lexi's reception hall, the Department Store, like all their friends' weddings. A few months later his and Kit's pride and joy, Jackson, had arrived, at seven pounds and five ounces.

Every day felt like a new beginning with Kit as his wife. Jackson was developing like any other four-month-old baby. The sweet tyke had Wade wrapped around his finger and didn't even know it.

"Do you mind if I join you? Clara is getting fussy." Lexi held the wiggly two-month-old.

"Of course not. Wade ordered matching gliders for the baby's room. We can chat in there."

Wade and Clint watched the women walk down the hall to the nursery he'd set up in one of the spare bedrooms.

"Any word from Nash?" Clint checked his watch. "The game's starting soon."

"They're probably exhausted. Colten's only a month old, and if he's anything like Jackson was when we brought him home, he's up all night."

Clint rubbed his eyes and yawned. "Yeah, Clara gets up every three hours. I know you'll probably rib me for this, but I like getting up with her. She's so tiny and cute."

"I'm not ribbing you, man. I hold Jackson every chance I get." Wade grinned.

"Did you hear back from the doctor about the hole in his heart?"

"Yeah, and it's good news, considering. They're running more tests and will be checking it when he turns six months, but the doctor thinks there's a strong chance the hole will close up on its own. If not, he'll have to have surgery. We've been assured this type of operation is routine."

"That's great, and in the meantime, we'll keep praying for his heart to heal."

A knock on the door got Wade to his feet. He hurried to the front entrance. Nash, Amy and Ruby, with Colten all bundled up in his carrier, were on the porch.

"It's about time you got here."

"Uncle Wade!" Ruby held her arms up, and he tossed her in the air.

"You're lighter than a feather, Ruby. Did you come to cheer on the team?"

She pulled a face. "I brought coloring books. I don't like football."

Voices and footsteps sounded on the porch.

"What's this about you not liking football?" Marshall asked, appearing in the doorway.

"Uncle Marshall!"

"You made it." Wade slapped him on the back and ushered him and Ainsley inside.

"I guess the gang's all here."

"The way it should be."

Colten let out a tiny cry. Amy lifted him out of his carrier.

"Ladies, Kit and Lexi are in the nursery. Feel free to join them."

Ainsley and Amy hugged, then took Colten down the hall, with Ruby leading the way.

The men all headed to the living room. Snow was falling outside and the football game would begin in ten minutes.

"This reminds me of the day we met." Wade tapped his chin. "Except for the snow."

"All we need are bunk beds." Nash grinned.

"And a hole in my sneaker." Clint pointed to his shoe.

"And a chip on my shoulder." Marshall pretended to brush lint off his shoulder.

"And here we are. Best friends. Married. With families. Living the dream."

"I couldn't ask for more." Wade closed his eyes and counted his blessings. He'd been given a lifetime of them. He truly was a blessed man.

* * * * *

HER LAST CHANCE COWBOY

Tina Radcliffe

This final book in the Big Heart Ranch series
is dedicated to the staff and children of
Big Oak Ranch. Big Oak Ranch is a Christian home
located in Alabama for children needing a chance.
Find out more about them at www.bigoak.org.

Thank you to Tim at ARCpoint Labs for taking time
to answer my numerous questions on DNA testing.
All errors are my own.

A great deal of appreciation goes to my wonderful
agent, Jessica Alvarez, for partnering with me
on this series. Thank you, as well, to my editor,
Dina Davis, who helped ensure that this last book of
the Big Heart series was as heartfelt as the first.

Casting all your care upon him; for he careth for you.
—*1 Peter* 5:7

Chapter One

Trouble.

Tripp Walker sensed it the moment he drove around the bend. He hit the brakes as he came upon the beat-up silver Honda parked awkwardly on the shoulder of the two-lane road that led to Big Heart Ranch. Dangerous place to park, which no doubt meant the vehicle was disabled.

His gaze shot toward the sky to assess the weather. Several hours ago, a tornado watch had been issued for Osage County, Oklahoma. Conditions were ripe for dangerous storms and even a tornado. By the time Tripp finished his business in Pawhuska and passed through the small town of Timber, the watch had changed to a warning, meaning a tornado had been sighted.

Overhead, the angry gray clouds tinged with green crowded closer, making the threat of the first tornado of May all the more real.

When a ping hit the windshield and frozen pellets began to descend, Tripp made a split-second decision. Despite his need to get back to the ranch and out of the dangerous weather, he couldn't ignore the disabled

Honda. He parked a safe distance from the vehicle and flipped on his pickup's emergency flashers.

Pulling up the collar of his denim jacket, Tripp reached for his cowboy hat before he got out. He inhaled. The air smelled like a storm was imminent. *The smell of the ugly*, some folks called it. Rain and ozone mixed together.

Hail continued to fall fast enough to form shallow puddles of white as he headed to the Honda and rapped his knuckles on the driver's-side window.

The tinted window inched down a fraction and a woman's big brown eyes met his gaze. She stared for a moment, no doubt taken aback by the scar that ran down the left side of his face, stopping right beneath his eye. After eighteen years, he was used to people staring.

"Ma'am, do you need assistance? Is everything okay?" he asked.

"Okay? Not lately," she replied with a sigh.

"What's wrong with your car?"

"Apparently, I ran out of gas."

His glance swept the Honda, from the cracked windshield on the passenger side to the temporary tags hanging in the rear window. Colorado. Well, that explained the funny way the woman talked. Definitely not an Okie. But it didn't explain why she was driving around in this weather. "Didn't you hear the news of the tornado warning on your radio?"

"The radio is dead and my cell is off to save battery life." The window inched down a little more and her gaze followed his to the dark sky. "Has a tornado been sighted?" she asked.

"Funnel cloud south of here." Tripp frowned and turned back to the woman, whose face registered alarm.

"Why aren't there any sirens?" she asked.

"Too far off the beaten track. The only thing up this road is Big Heart Ranch."

"That's where we're going."

He barely had time to register the word *we* when a little girl, about five or six years old, poked her head into the front seat. She pushed back a riot of orange curls and grinned up at him. "We want to go to the ranch and see horses, Mr. Cowboy."

Tripp bit back a smile, his good humor fading fast as he realized the child was in the path of a tornado. "I'll take you to Big Heart Ranch."

"And who are you?" the woman asked, her gaze assessing.

"Tripp Walker. I'm the equine manager at Big Heart," he said, annoyance mounting. "Ma'am, we need to hurry."

The driver's-side door opened and a petite dark-haired woman stepped out. She opened the back seat passenger door. "I'm Hannah Vincent. This is my daughter, Clementine." The child sat in a booster seat and stared up at him while clutching a pink stuffed horse. She was dressed in clean pink jeans and a pink patterned long-sleeved shirt. Clearly, the kid had a penchant for that color.

"Come on, baby, we're going to the ranch." Hannah unbuckled the straps and pulled her daughter into her arms.

"Horses?" the little girl asked.

"Shh," Hannah said. "We can discuss that later."

Tripp glanced at Hannah's left hand. No ring. Though his head tried to stop him, his gut moved quickly to judgment. *Plain irresponsible.* Who ran out of gas in the middle of a tornado?

Irritation continued to brew as he ran a hand over the scar on his face and worked to control the emotions he'd so carefully learned to stuff years ago. He'd spent a lifetime paying for the sins of an irresponsible single mother. Now the memories all came rushing back.

Hannah faced him with Clementine in her arms. "Is everything okay?" she asked.

"Just dandy." Tripp turned and headed to the truck. He held the passenger door open. Hannah lifted Clementine into the cab and then put her foot on the truck's running board. When she reached for something to hang on to, he took her arm and guided her into the truck.

"Thank you," Hannah said.

He offered a curt nod.

She pulled Clementine onto her lap and inched nearer to her side of the vehicle as he went around to the driver's side.

Once he got in, Tripp gripped the steering wheel and turned his head a fraction to meet Hannah's dark eyes.

With that tumble of wavy chocolate-brown hair that touched her shoulders, and a face devoid of makeup, she seemed harmless. But he knew only too well how deceiving looks could be. As if sensing his annoyance, Hannah moved even closer to the door.

They headed down the ranch drive toward a split-log archway with the words Big Heart Ranch burned into a hanging sign. He stopped the truck in front of a drop-arm barrier that kept unauthorized visitors out and put his key card in the reader slot.

"Is this the ranch?" Clementine asked as the arm lifted.

"It is," he said.

The child's orange corkscrew curls bounced when she turned to look out each of the pickup's windows. "Where are the horses?"

"They're in the barn because of the storm. You'll get to see them before you leave."

"Oh, thank you, Mr. Cowboy." She rewarded him with a huge grin. The kid had a smile that could warm even the most frozen hearts.

When his cell phone rang, Tripp pressed a button on the dashboard. "Walker."

"Looks like the funnel cloud jumped past us. Storm moving in. A big one," the mature female voice on the speakerphone said.

"Thanks, Rue. I'm bringing guests to the admin building."

"Guests?"

"A Hannah Vincent. She ran out of gas on her way to see the Maxwells."

The sound of papers shuffling could be heard. "The receptionist is out until Monday, but I'm looking at the appointment list she left and I don't see a Hannah Vincent. Is she here to see all of them?"

Tripp turned to Hannah, and she nodded.

"That's right, Rue."

"Well, no worries. I'll find them and we can sort it out." She chuckled. "Just get out of that weather."

"Yes, ma'am." Once again, Tripp looked at his passenger. "You have an appointment at Big Heart Ranch, right?"

"Not exactly," Hannah said.

"Not exactly?" Tripp exhaled and held back a biting retort. Though the tension in the cab was palpable, he focused on driving, staring straight ahead out the window where fat drops of rain began to splash on the glass as he approached the administration building.

His job was to manage the horses. It would be good to remember that. Hannah Vincent was Lucy Maxwell's problem now.

Tripp pulled the truck into a parking lot and led them out of the rain and into the brick building. "This way." He opened the door to a small conference room where Rue Butterfield sat with a cup of coffee watching the news. The gray-haired physician and retired army general turned to offer their guests a welcoming smile. "Welcome to Big Heart Ranch."

"I hope I'm not…" Hannah began. She pushed back rain-dampened hair from her face.

"You're not." Rue stood. "Big Heart Ranch aims to be a refuge in the storm. Literally." She chuckled and held out a hand in greeting. "I'm Dr. Rue Butterfield."

"Hannah Vincent. This is Clementine."

"Clementine!" Rue grinned. "Now isn't that a unique name?"

"It's 'cause of my hair," the little girl said. "It's orange."

Tripp bit back a smile when Clementine shook her head back and forth, causing the bright curls to move with the motion.

"Your hair is quite lovely and I am certainly pleased to meet you, Miss Clementine." Rue offered a hand in greeting. "I'm Miss Rue."

"Rue. That's a nice name, too." Clementine shook Rue's hand and smiled, obviously delighted by the grown-up gesture. "Mr. Cowboy is going to show me horses."

Rue lifted her gaze to Tripp. "Oh, are you, Mr. Cowboy?"

He knelt down next to the little girl. "You can call me Mr. Tripp."

"Mr. Tripp." She scrunched up her face and looked hard at him. "You are a cowboy, right?"

"Yes, ma'am."

"Do cowboys keep their promises?" Clementine asked.

"Always." He stood and turned his attention to the television screen on the wall. "What's going on with the storm?" he asked Rue.

"Funnel touched down on Route 66. No damage reported. Looks like we're safe. For now, only thunderstorms."

"I like rain," Clementine said.

"So do I." Rue smiled at the little girl and then turned to Hannah. "You're here to see the Maxwells?"

"Yes."

"Did they know you were coming?"

"Um, no." Hannah adjusted the purse on her shoulder and clasped her hands together. "This was sort of spontaneous. I drove straight from Denver."

"That's a long drive," Rue returned.

"Yes. Thirteen hours."

"We paid our respects," Clementine interjected.

Rue's eyes rounded, reflecting confusion and surprise at the comment. "How did you say you know the Maxwells?"

"I'm a relative."

Rue blinked. "I wasn't aware that they had any living relatives."

"Neither was I… I mean, until recently," Hannah stammered, her attention on Clementine.

"So how is it you're related to the Maxwells, dear?"

Tripp kept his eyes on Hannah Vincent. She took a deep breath and looked up. Her gaze moved from Rue to him.

"If you don't mind, I thought I'd discuss it with the Maxwells," Hannah continued.

"Of course. I don't mean to pry."

Hannah offered a hesitant and awkward nod.

Rue glanced at Tripp and he returned her searching expression with a slight shake of his head. If she wanted answers, she was looking in the wrong direction. He didn't have a clue and he didn't want to know, either.

"How about a cup of coffee?" Rue asked Hannah. She picked up her own mug from the table and smiled. "Fresh pot."

"May I please have a glass of water?" Hannah asked.

"Certainly. We've got chocolate muffins in the break room. Our Emma is quite the baker." She cocked her head toward Clementine. "Would that be okay for…?"

"Yes. Thank you very much," Hannah returned.

"Come help me, Tripp," Rue said.

He narrowed his eyes at the good doctor, but she ignored him and started down the hall. When they entered the kitchenette, Tripp released a breath. "I smell a scam."

"Oh, don't be so cynical." She paused. "Colorado is where their parents died, and where the kids went into foster care."

"Okay, so why didn't she call and schedule an appointment? Why surprise them on a Friday afternoon?" he asked.

"I have no idea."

"I've known the Maxwells for eight years. I was their first employee. If they had family, I would have heard about it by now." Tripp began to pace back and forth across the tiled floor as he continued to mull the situation.

Rue shrugged and reached for two glasses from the cupboard. "They'll be here shortly, and I guess we'll find out."

Find out? He didn't want to find out. This entire situation made him uneasy. Tripp pulled off his cowboy hat and ran a hand through his short hair. All he wanted to do was go back to the stables and be left alone.

He froze at the sound of the big glass door of the admin building opening and then closing with a whoosh and a dull thud. Boots echoed on the tile floor, along with soft murmuring. The Maxwells had arrived.

It was like the still before a tornado, and after thirty-four years in Oklahoma, he knew better than to stand in the path of a storm minutes before everything was getting ready to break loose.

Hannah swallowed hard as she faced the Maxwell siblings seated across the conference table from her.

Lucy, Travis and Emma in person. All dark-haired with dark eyes and generous mouths accustomed to smiling. And they were smiling now, which was a good sign. The Maxwells were accompanied by their spouses.

Jack Harris, Lucy's husband, was an attorney. Emma Maxwell Norman's husband, Zach, a former navy SEAL, sat next to his wife. The man looked like he could break her in two with his pinky.

Travis sat holding hands with his wife, AJ, a pretty blonde in a denim jacket who'd entered the room with a straw cowboy hat on her head. She was clearly very pregnant.

Though Rue was entertaining Clementine in another room, they'd asked Tripp Walker to stay. The man was just like family, Lucy Maxwell Harris, the oldest, had said. Pretty scary family, in her opinion. He wasn't smiling and hadn't since she'd met him, except when he was speaking to Clementine.

The man baffled her. He'd been nothing but a gentleman when he had rescued them. And when she'd struggled to climb into the cab of his truck, the cowboy had held her arm and easily helped her. His touch was surprisingly gentle for such a big and disapproving man.

Right now, the cowboy's cool blue eyes were nearly ice as they pinned her. Hannah tugged her sweater close against the chill in the room and looked away.

A tiny niggle of excitement churned inside of her. Excitement even Tripp Walker's less than warm welcome couldn't dispel.

She'd started over many times in the last seven years, but this was different. For once, she wasn't hiding or running away from something. No, for the first time in her life she was slipping from the shadows into the light and searching for her future.

And maybe she had found it.

This could very well be her family sitting around the table. Except they all sat on one side while she sat on the other.

She silently prayed for help and grasped for a scripture to cling to. Her grandmother may have been misguided in many ways, but when Hannah was growing up she'd made certain they both were in the pew every Sunday.

Casting all your care upon Him; for He careth for you.

Yes. That would work.

Lucy cleared her throat and smiled. "I have to admit we're all shocked to find out we have a relative. Travis, Emma and I went into foster care after our parents died because we were told we had no family." She pushed her short dark cap of hair back and folded her hands on the table.

"Are you related to our mom's cousin? She's the one who adopted us," Emma, the youngest Maxwell, asked.

"I believe I'm related to your father. Jake Maxwell."

Travis grinned and leaned forward in his chair. "You're related to Dad? Really? How?"

Hannah hesitated, then met his gaze. "I think Jake Maxwell was my father."

Travis's grin faded away at the same instant that Lucy's jaw sagged. She turned to Emma, whose eyes were round with shock.

The silence in the room was even louder than Hannah expected. She let her gaze slide to Tripp. Stormy blue eyes met hers before he looked away.

Hannah held her hands tightly in her lap and willed her heart to slow down. She tried to relax her clenched jaw. In the last ten minutes, she'd destroyed years of orthodontic alignment.

"Do you have proof? A birth certificate maybe?" Lucy asked.

"My birth certificate says my mother is Anne Bryant and the name of my father is noted as *declined*."

The siblings looked at each other. Hannah could practically read their minds. They were doing the math. But she had already done that in Colorado and knew only too well that she was a year younger than Emma.

"I'm confused," Lucy said.

"Believe me, I am, as well," Hannah said. "I was

born twenty-nine years ago last month. My mother died when I was too young to ask who *declined* was, and my grandmother wouldn't discuss my father." Hannah took a deep breath. "Clementine and I were in Denver for my grandmother's funeral. Until the reading of the will, I thought she was my only living relative."

"We're so sorry for your loss," Lucy said gently. "We know what it's like to lose everything. But what led you to think…" She gestured with a hand.

"I inherited a chest of my mother's things after she passed." Hannah paused for a calming breath. Again, she reminded herself that she hadn't done anything wrong. "There was a Bible with photos of my mother and Jake Maxwell tucked inside."

"Surely there's more than one Jake Maxwell in all the world," Lucy said.

"I compared the photos to the Denver Public Library microfiche files with your father's obituary photo. That's also what led me to Big Heart Ranch."

Lucy grimaced and nodded.

"Could we see the photos you have?" Travis asked.

"Yes. Of course. They're in the trunk of my car."

The eldest Maxwell's gaze moved out the window to the pasture of tall grass in the distance. Then she slowly turned back to face Hannah. "I want to be sensitive to you, but this still doesn't prove that he's your father."

Hannah stared down at her tightly clasped hands for moments, recalling the letters she'd read over and over again.

Dearest Anne, you are on my mind constantly…

She raised her head to face the Maxwells. "There are also dated letters from Jake to Anne that indicate a very close relationship."

Lucy's face paled as she released a soft, anguished sigh and covered her mouth with a hand.

"I'm sorry," Hannah murmured.

"There's nothing for you to be sorry about," Travis said. "This has to be as difficult for you as it is for all of us."

"We could do a DNA test. Couldn't we?" Emma asked while looking at Jack Harris for a response.

The attorney reached out to hold Lucy's hand. "Sure, but as I recall, without paternal or maternal DNA, the results won't be absolutely conclusive, though they will show if you're family."

"I think we should talk to a lab and find out how to proceed," Emma returned.

"This is a lot to take in, Em," Lucy said. "That Dad had a relationship outside of his marriage."

"Four years before they died," Travis murmured.

Emma turned to her siblings. "We can't begin to presume to interpret the past. I don't think we should even try. I say we deal with facts. Hannah is here and for her peace of mind and ours we should find out if we are indeed family." She offered Hannah a sad smile.

Travis, too, offered a sympathetic nod. "All of our lives are affected if it's true."

Lucy met Hannah's gaze. "I have to be clear. The ranch is a charity. The land was given to us by our mother's cousin. The woman who adopted us. Big Heart Ranch is a sanctuary for orphaned, abused and neglected children. This ranch is our life mission, but we have no inheritance. Nothing."

Hannah's gut clenched at the words. Inheritance? If only they knew she'd already walked away from one. What she longed for was to find her place in this world.

"I'm here for the same answers you want," Hannah murmured. "Period."

Once again, an uncomfortable silence filled the room.

"Where are you staying?" Lucy asked.

"I saw a motel on the way in."

"The Rooster Motel?" A horrified look crossed Lucy's face. "Oh, you don't want to stay there. We have a nice bed-and-breakfast in Timber."

"That's not really in our budget, but thank you," Hannah said without looking at any of them.

"Well then, I'd like to invite you to stay at Big Heart Ranch, at the very least until we can figure all of this out," Lucy said while she looked to her siblings for confirmation.

Hannah held her head high. "I don't do charity."

"Of course not. We can always use help on the ranch," Emma said.

"What about Clementine?" Hannah asked.

"There is a licensed daycare at the ranch now," Lucy said. "How old is she?"

"Clementine is five. Almost six."

"It's May. Isn't she enrolled in school?" Emma asked.

"We've moved around a lot," Hannah said. There was no point sharing further details. Her past had nothing to do with the Maxwells other than when it intersected with theirs.

Emma frowned. "I handle childcare at the ranch and I can tell you that kindergarten is mandatory in Oklahoma."

"It's not in Texas, Kansas and Missouri."

"You certainly have traveled," Emma murmured.

Traveled. Hannah nearly laughed out loud. Not quite.

She had been running from her grandmother's reach for nearly seven years. Staying one step ahead of the wealthy woman who insinuated that she could take Clementine away from Hannah if she so desired.

"I'm sure we have some area you could contribute to on Big Heart Ranch."

"What's your background?" Lucy asked.

"Recently, I've been a bookkeeper, cashier and mostly a cook."

"All useful skills." Travis shook his head. "Can you ride?"

"Yes, absolutely. I have an extensive background with horses. I've been riding since I was a kid. I worked in children's camps and equine clinics when I was a teenager and in college." Hannah paused and swallowed. "However, there's something you should know."

"What's that?" he asked.

"I'm pregnant." Hannah sat straight and proudly. Yes, she was a single mother whose husband had left her not once, but twice. But she refused to give in to the whispers of shame fueled by her grandmother that had dogged her for the past seven years.

"Congratulations," Travis said. He grinned like a preening peacock as he put his arm around his wife. "AJ and I have a baby due in August." He glanced over at Emma. "And Emma and Zach are expecting a baby in December."

"That's wonderful," Hannah said.

Emma chimed in, "When is your baby due?"

"Late December."

"Congratulations," Emma added, her face lighting up with genuine pleasure. "Oh, my, we're due at the same time."

"I'll add my congratulations, too," Lucy said. "As you can see, we love babies around here. Your…um, partner is with you in Oklahoma?"

"I'm recently divorced." She cleared her throat and once again focused on her hands, running her thumb over a ragged hangnail. Recently divorced because once he'd found out she wasn't going to be a wealthy woman, he'd walked away.

An awkward silence stretched before Lucy cleared her throat.

"You do understand what we do here at the ranch, right?" Lucy asked.

"Not exactly," Hannah admitted.

"We create a new normal for the children who come to live with us at Big Heart Ranch. We have two ranches here, the boys' ranch and the girls' ranch. The children are placed in a real house with house parents, not a dormitory. Though they aren't a biological family, they are a family of the heart. A forever family. Our children have daily devotionals, lessons, homework and chores, just like any other child."

Lucy looked to Travis. "We have been promising Tripp an admin to do the paperwork, scheduling and ordering supplies for about two years now, haven't we?"

Travis nodded with enthusiasm. He turned to Tripp, but the equine manager's face remained stony. The blue eyes flickered and his jaw twitched, though he didn't utter a word.

"We'd still have to run a background and fingerprint check," Emma chimed in. "It's ranch policy."

"Would you consider staying?" Lucy asked.

"I don't know…" Hannah murmured with a glance at Tripp Walker.

"Tripp?" Emma nudged the silent cowboy.

"If the Maxwells welcome you, then so do I." The words were a slow drawl, his gaze cautious, revealing nothing to indicate he'd changed his opinion about her.

Hannah was silent. So what if the horse manager didn't like her? This wasn't about her. She wouldn't knee-jerk and make a decision based on pride. Clementine and her unborn child deserved to be around family, if that's what the Maxwells really were.

"Thank you. I'll stay…for now."

She glanced around the table for a moment. Did she dare to hope that Big Heart Ranch might be the end of the road? A place where she and her children would be welcomed unconditionally? Or would she always be searching for home?

It's in Your hands now, Lord, she silently prayed.

Chapter Two

Disoriented, Hannah sat up in bed. Something was off. Normally, she woke to the spring scents of hyacinths, daffodils and lilac that floated into her furnished apartment from the florist shop downstairs.

Her searching gaze landed on Clementine, who slept soundlessly in the next bed, cuddled into a softly faded multicolored quilt with her pink stuffed horse clutched to her chest.

Hannah blinked against the dappled sunlight sneaking into the room through the blinds and realized she was in a guest bunkhouse at Big Heart Ranch. Today was Saturday. She yawned as Friday's events came back to her.

"This is it," Rue Butterfield had announced when they arrived at the bunkhouse yesterday afternoon.

Hannah had enough money for one night at the Rooster before they'd have to head back to Missouri. Staying at Big Heart Ranch was an answer to prayer.

"This is where we're staying?" Hannah had asked Rue. The bunkhouse was a rustic log cabin cottage with six bunks, a small living room and a kitchen area. It was several paychecks nicer than her place above the floral shop in Dripping Falls. Yet, her grandmother would have been appalled.

"Yes," Rue had answered. "This is the guest bunkhouse."

Hannah had glanced across the room at a neatly made-up bed. "Who else lives here?"

"That would be me. I stay when I'm needed and, with summer coming up, that will be most of the time." She paused. "Oh, and Dutch will bring up your car and your bags. He put gas in your Honda."

"Dutch?"

"Dutch Stevens. Senior wrangler. Can't miss him. He's bowlegged and has a silver handlebar mustache."

"Please tell him thank you. And thank you. For all this." She had waved a hand around the room.

"You're family, dear." Rue smiled.

At that moment, something like shame had clawed at Hannah. *Family.* As far as she could tell, she might be the illegitimate daughter of Jake Maxwell. Family or not, she'd certainly put a pause and a huge question mark into everyone at Big Heart Ranch's thoughts yesterday.

Hannah glanced at the clock. It read 7:00 a.m. She wiped the sleep from her eyes and looked over at the two battered suitcases that the wrangler had brought to the cabin yesterday. Nearly everything she owned had been shoved into those bags or into a cardboard box in the trunk of her car when she'd left Missouri for her grandmother's funeral in Colorado.

She stared at the ceiling and considered the wisdom of leaving her job as a short-order cook at the all-night diner. The pay was regular and Clementine slept in the manager's office during her shift, saving Hannah a fortune in childcare expenses.

It wasn't the career she'd planned on, but there was no point in looking back. She'd learned long ago that the only thing certain in life was that she had to live with her choices. Big Heart Ranch it was. For now.

Just as Hannah swung her legs over the side of the bed, the strong waft of bacon, eggs and fried potatoes hit her full force. With one hand on her stomach and the other covering her mouth, she quietly headed to the restroom.

Morning sickness. She splashed cold water on her face and stood over the sink taking slow breaths, willing her stomach to calm down.

"What am I doing here, Lord? I hope this was Your nudge and not another mess up for You to get me out of."

Patting her face dry with a towel, Hannah brushed her teeth before coming out to the main area again.

"Morning, Momma." Clementine sat on the edge of her bunk, biting her lower lip as she concentrated on buttoning up her blouse.

"Well, look at you. No nagging you to get out of bed today."

Clementine raised her head and smiled, brown eyes sparkling. "Miss Rue said to get ready. Mr. Tripp is coming by to take me to see the horses after breakfast."

Hannah eased down next to her daughter on the bed and pulled a hairbrush from her purse. "Let me fix your hair."

"I have a twisty." Clementine held up a nylon hair tie.

"Good, because the snarls have taken over. I'll brush it thoroughly tonight," Hannah said as she pulled the springy orange curls into a ponytail.

"Thank you, Momma."

Rue popped her head around the corner. "Breakfast is ready. I made eggs, bacon and my special home fries."

"Toast would be good." Hannah swallowed, praying she wouldn't retch. "But you don't have to cook for us."

"I was making breakfast anyhow."

"Coffee?" Rue asked once Hannah had changed into jeans and a T-shirt and was seated at the table nibbling toast.

"Water is fine. I'll get it." She stood and moved to the sink. The coffee smelled wonderful, and she'd kill for a mugful, but that would wait until she could get decaf.

"What a good eater," Rue said to Clementine as she sat down at the table and picked up her coffee.

"She's filling her reserve tank," Hannah said.

The five-year-old scooped up another forkful of eggs and shoveled it into her mouth like a starving trucker.

"Whoa, Clemmie. Slow down there, good buddy," Hannah said.

"This is really good, Momma," Clementine said.

"Please don't talk with your mouth full." She put the water on the table and slid into the chair next to her daughter.

"Yes, Momma," Clementine said over a mouthful of eggs.

Hannah looked across the table at Rue Butterfield. The woman's serene smile said that all was well with the world. It was as if Hannah and Clementine belonged in this kitchen, at this moment. There was a peace in the room that Hannah hadn't experienced in a long time.

"This was very nice of you, Rue. I'm not accustomed to someone cooking for me."

"Mind if I ask how far along you are, dear?"

Hannah froze. "How did you know?"

"The morning sickness, and you turned positively green when you laid eyes on the bacon." Rue smiled. "I'd have never noticed otherwise."

"I'm eight weeks." Hannah placed a hand to her stomach. "I can barely zip up my jeans."

"You're slim as can be."

A knock at the door interrupted the conversation and had all heads turning. "Come on in," Rue called.

Tripp opened the door and removed his hat. The lean cowboy stood in the threshold surrounded by the morning sunlight. The man had to be at least six foot five. An inch or so more and he'd hit his head on that low doorway. He ducked as he entered the kitchen. The man had a thick head full of toffee-colored hair, trimmed short and neat.

When Tripp turned a bit more, Hannah noted that with his stubbled shadow and strong jawline, he was almost perfectly handsome. The scar running down his face only added to his rugged and dangerous appeal.

Appeal in general, she corrected herself. Not appealing to her. Nope. Things only became complicated when there was a man in her life.

She placed a protective hand on her abdomen when Tripp's frosty blue eyes assessed Hannah with an expression she couldn't define. It seemed the man was constantly sizing her up and each time she fell short.

"Coffee, Tripp?" Rue asked.

He held up a hand. "I'm good, thanks."

"Horses. Horses. Horses," Clementine chanted. She jumped up from her chair.

"Hold it right there," Hannah said. "Clear your place setting and thank Miss Rue for breakfast."

"Thank you, Miss Rue." Clementine put her silverware on her plate, turned to the sink and stopped. "I can't reach the sink."

Before Hannah could even get out of her seat, Tripp had gently lifted the little girl to the stainless steel sink.

"Thank you." Clementine giggled.

Tripp turned to Hannah as he lowered her daughter to the floor. "Ready to go?"

"Yes. Let me get our sweaters."

"Does she have any other shoes besides sneakers?" Tripp asked.

"Oh, I didn't even think… Clemmie, go put on your cowboy boots."

Clementine nodded and raced from the room, happy to return wearing her scuffed Western boots. The pint-sized show-off did a little jig of a dance ending with a small, "Ta-da!"

"You're a real cowgirl, aren't you?" Tripp said with a wide grin.

Hannah nearly fell over at the smile that lifted the corners of the cranky cowboy's mouth. It was a genuine smile that transformed the stone-etched face into swoon-worthy. For a fleeting moment, Hannah longed to make Tripp Walker smile again.

Then she remembered that believing in white knights who came with happy endings was how she'd gotten derailed in the first place.

Hannah followed Tripp and Clementine out the door. She couldn't keep up with his long strides, but her daughter skipped and jumped across the yard to the stables, splashing in a few mud puddles on the way, with joy shining on her face.

Tripp stood at the entrance of the big building, allowing them to enter the stables first. Hannah stopped and met his gaze. "Thank you for keeping your word. That's a novelty in my world."

"I'm sorry to hear that." His eyes skimmed over her. "You said you're comfortable around horses, right?"

"It's been a long time, but yes."

"How long is a long time?"

When she paused to think, a rope of melancholy tugged at her. There were very few things from her past that pulled at her heart. Her horse was one of those. But when she'd walked away from her grandmother, she'd walked away from everything her money could buy. "It's been more than seven years. A beautiful mare named Sage."

"What happened?"

"That's a story for another day." She stepped into the building, her boots echoing on the floor. The place was abuzz with activity. "Why are things so busy on a Saturday?"

He shrugged. "The usual. Lessons are scheduled Monday through Saturday. Most of the kids and staff sign up for recreational rides, as well."

She offered a small nod.

"I manage the equestrian center located on each ranch. We house over twenty ranch horses, plus those owned by the staff."

"That's a lot of horses and a lot of work," Hannah said. Her grandmother hired a team of grooms for her stables.

"The kids muck and groom as part of their daily chores."

"I'm sure that's helpful, but someone has to manage

the entire program, including veterinarian visits, feed, supplies and the day-to-day issues."

He stared at her, a flicker of surprise crossing his face.

"I worked for the manager at an equine clinic long ago," she admitted. "Which may come in handy as your assistant."

"So you said." He paused. "That starts on Monday." Tripp offered a dismissive nod, before he turned to her daughter. "Miss Clementine, would you like to ride today?"

"Oh, yes, please, Mr. Tripp. I've never been on a real horse." She cocked her head and pursed her mouth for a moment. "Do you have any pink horses?"

"We don't, but I have a nice horse named Grace who would like to be your friend."

"Okay."

Once again, Clementine's short legs skipped to catch up to Tripp. Hannah's jaw nearly dropped when her daughter put her little hand in Tripp's and followed him. Clementine was friendly by nature, but this...this was unusual.

As she followed, Hannah spotted the tack room next to an office with glass windows all around. The sign on the door read Tripp Walker, Manager. They stopped at the last stall on the left where a chalkboard on the outside of the stall had Grace printed in white letters.

"Do you want to introduce yourself and Clementine to Grace while I grab some equipment?" Tripp asked.

"Oh, yes. Sure," Hannah returned.

"Mommy," Clementine whispered. "I'm really going to ride a horse?"

"You are." Hannah knelt down next to her daughter.

"It's very important that you follow all of Mr. Walker's instructions today."

Clementine gave a solemn nod and then frowned. "His name is Mr. Tripp, Momma."

"Mr. Tripp." Hannah barely resisted rolling her eyes. "I'm going to lift you up so you can pet the horse's nose. Talk to her and say hello. Be very gentle."

Clementine reached toward Grace without hesitation. She stroked the animal's chestnut nose, her fingers lingering on the white patch of her forehead. "Hi, Miss Grace. My name is Clementine," she soothed, like an old pro.

The animal gave a nicker and nudged at Clementine's hand.

Clementine's eyes popped wide, and she giggled. "Momma, she likes me."

"Why wouldn't she?" Tripp asked from behind them. He held a saddle, a blanket and a currycomb. "Come on, we'll get Grace ready to ride and I'll take you both for a little walk."

"Oh, I hate to take you away from your work," Hannah said. "I can do that."

He looked at her and seemed to be searching for a response. "Sometimes, I like to be taken away from my work."

"We've already imposed," Hannah protested.

Tripp cleared his throat. "Ma'am, there's a liability issue here."

"But I'm about to be an employee." She paused. "At least temporarily."

"Monday. After you fill out the paperwork and such on Monday, you'll be official and all."

Hannah swallowed and stepped back. "So I have to trust you with my daughter for now?"

"Yes, ma'am. You can watch from outside the corral."

Could she trust Tripp Walker with that which was most precious to her? Clementine was the reason she'd been on the run for the past nearly seven years. Leaving Colorado, she knew that their running had come to an end and that eventually, she'd have to trust someone. Maybe Big Heart Ranch was the place to start. After all, this ranch was all about trust and second chances, wasn't it?

She met Tripp Walker's steady gaze and nodded. "Okay."

Tripp lifted a grinning Clementine from the saddle and set her on the ground in the stables.

"How'd the ride go?" Rue asked as she entered the building.

"This little cowgirl is a natural," he said.

"I expected as much." Rue turned to Hannah. "I've got some friends to visit over at the chicken coop. Mrs. Carmody and the rest of the girls. I thought Clementine might like to join me. Would that be all right with you, Hannah?"

"I, um…" Hannah blinked, eyes wide, obviously caught off guard.

"Oh, yes. Please, Momma. It will be all right. I'll be good." Clementine's brown eyes begged as loud as her entreaty.

Tripp narrowed his gaze. The single mother didn't like to be separated from her baby. Had he misjudged her? Time would tell.

Hannah nodded and offered Rue a shaky smile. "Sure, okay."

When Tripp led Grace to her stall, Hannah followed. She cleared her throat. "I'll untack the horse. It's the least I can do, and clearly, Grace is no threat."

He glanced from Grace to Hannah and nodded his approval. "Let me know if you need anything." Tripp turned and headed to his office. "I've got to make a few calls."

Tripp settled into his desk chair and stared at his cell phone. He wrestled the merits of an idea brewing in the back of his mind and finally punched in the number.

A moment later, the sound of boots pounding through the stables could be heard. Dutch Stevens planted himself outside Tripp's office and knocked on the open door with his fist. The old cowboy pushed his ancient straw cowboy hat to the back of his head and stroked his gray mustache. "I need some help outside."

"Give me a minute."

"A minute? I don't have a minute. I've got a mean horse you bought who's trying to bust out of the trailer. What I need is another hand."

Though Tripp stood and kicked the office door closed with the toe of his boot, he could still hear Dutch griping through the glass as his cell connected.

"Hello?" the raspy voice on the phone said into Tripp's ear.

"Slats, this is Walker over at Big Heart Ranch. I need a favor."

"Guess I owe you a few, don't I?" Slats Milburn returned.

"I need a discreet background check."

"I'm always discreet."

"Good to know." He took a deep breath. "The name is Hannah Vincent."

Tripp swiveled his chair in time to see Hannah and Dutch talking outside Grace's stall. His trouble radar began to sound when Hannah tossed her sweater onto a wall peg and followed Dutch outside.

A moment later, a loud crash and bang of metal filled the stables, echoing over the noise of the riders and horses. Staff and children raced down the center aisle and poured into the sunlight to see what was going on.

"I gotta go. I'll text you the details." Tripp dropped the phone on his desk and wove past people crowded in the stable doorway.

Outside in the gravel parking area, Hannah Vincent lay on the ground with her posterior in a mud puddle while Dutch struggled to lead a rambunctious horse to the corral. Tripp stepped up to the horse, whose ears were snapped forward, his head up and the whites of his eyes bright as he whinnied in protest.

"What happened?" Tripp demanded.

Dutch grimaced. "Rowdy here kicked open the trailer same time I was opening the door. Horse exploded out of there. Door flew open and Miss Hannah went flying."

Hannah blinked and sat up. She shoved her dark hair from her eyes and brushed red dirt from her hands. "Sorry, I wasn't much help, Dutch."

"Aw, not your fault."

Tripp moved to Hannah's side, belatedly remembering that the woman was pregnant. When he did, it was a punch to his gut. "What were you thinking?" The words came out sharper than he intended.

"I said I'm fine," she answered.

Tripp and Dutch stood over Hannah, each offering a hand and helping her to her feet.

Dutch chuckled. "Never seen anyone go flying like that before."

"Yeah. We'll talk about that later," Tripp growled. He moved near the excited horse and spoke in soothing tones before he moved closer and started scratching and petting around the withers. As the horse stilled, Tripp rubbed him between the eyes. "It's going to be okay, buddy."

Tripp handed the horse off to a wrangler and turned back to Hannah.

"Got a few scratches on your arm, Hannah," Dutch said. The old cowboy grimaced, his eyes filled with concern. "That's my fault. I'm sorry."

She raised her arms and sure enough, gravel and dirt were embedded in scratches on the backside of her right forearm. Tripp cringed at the sight. She'd gotten hurt on his watch.

"I'm okay," Hannah repeated firmly. She slapped at her backside and straightened her blouse.

"We'll let Rue decide that," Tripp said. "She's the staff doctor. For now, we can clean it up and put on a little antiseptic ointment." He gave a curt nod toward the stables.

"Your concern is overwhelming," Hannah murmured drily as she followed him.

"Rinse your arm in the sink over there." Tripp cocked his head to the right. "Then come into my office. I have a first aid kit."

Minutes later, Hannah sat in Tripp's office staring at the wall as she held her arm up.

"What's that?" she asked.

He removed the cover from the antibiotic ointment and glanced up at the wall. She was staring at the poster for the 100-Day Mustang Challenge.

"Just what it says. One hundred days to gentle, halter break, saddle train, and build trust with a horse."

"Do you get to keep the horse when you're done?"

"Nope. End of the hundred days there's big grand finale competition and the animals are auctioned off by the Bureau of Land Management."

"So what's the point?"

"It's for a good cause. Re-homing mustangs, raising money to start the process all over again."

"All good, but that's it?" Hannah said.

"Braggin' rights. To say you've done it."

"And have you? Done it before?"

"No time." He shrugged. "Been on my bucket list for a while."

"What's the prize money for something like that?" she asked.

"This year, fifty grand."

Her eyes rounded. "That could buy a lot of buckets."

"Lift your arm," he said.

She complied, and he examined the abrasion. When he shifted his gaze sideways, he could see her long lashes resting on her flushed cheeks. Hannah's full mouth was set in a tight line as he applied the ointment. Tripp worked to gentle his touch, reminding himself it didn't matter how long her lashes were or how smooth her skin.

Except, the truth was, something about Hannah Vincent made him think about and feel things he hadn't considered in a long time. He quickly gave himself a reality check. Hannah's character was still under question. If the woman had secrets, Slats would find out exactly what they were.

Tripp's gaze wandered to the sweet curve of Hannah's neck. He glanced away, praying that Slats would be quick with his research.

And what if Hannah is as innocent as she appears? Tripp shot back at the errant thought, telling himself that the truth was, beautiful women didn't look twice at scarred men. They went for the pretty guys like Travis.

He wrapped Hannah's arm with gauze and taped the edges before stepping clear and putting plenty of space between them. "All done. Rue can check your arm when she and Clementine get back."

Hannah raised her arm and assessed his work. "Thank you."

"No problem," he said with a quick glance. Before he was able to look away, she met his gaze.

"Why do you keep looking at me like I'm a particularly annoying bug on your windshield?" she asked quietly.

"Didn't notice that I was." He sat down in his chair and put the ointment in the first aid kit, feigning nonchalance at her challenge.

"I'm not planning to sue you for a little scratch on my arm, so you can relax."

He was silent, knowing that she was spoiling for a fight.

"You've got something on your mind," Hannah continued. "You have since I arrived." She eyed him up and down. "You don't look like someone who plays games, so maybe you should just spit it out."

Tripp leaned back in his chair and crossed his arms. He prided himself on being a man of few words, but the woman was a burr under his saddle and for the first time in a long time, he couldn't keep his mouth shut.

"I keep asking myself what was so important that you had to risk yourself and your daughter in a storm yesterday and how a smart woman like yourself ran out of gas."

"I bought the car in Denver. Turns out the gas gauge sticks at times. Usually at the wrong times. Like Friday."

He gave a slow, considering nod.

"As for the other…do you have family?" She didn't wait for a response but plowed right ahead. "I found out forty-eight hours ago that I might. That was enough to put me on I-70 at noon on a Thursday headed to Oklahoma. Believe it or not, and I imagine you will choose not to, I was unaware that I was in the path of a tornado."

Tripp didn't know what to say to the outburst. But it didn't matter because Hannah Vincent wasn't done yet.

"It's clear you're determined to think the worst of me, Mr. Walker. It's a good thing I don't answer to you."

"You will," he murmured. "Come Monday."

When her face paled, remorse poked him in the chest. Now he'd gone and done it. Acted like a mule.

Why was this particular woman so good at pushing buttons he didn't even know he still had available to push? He stood and cleared his throat. "Excuse me. I've got work to do." Tripp felt her gaze staring him down as he left the office, but he had to get out of there before he shoved both of his boots in his mouth and discovered a perfect fit.

Chapter Three

Hannah slipped from her seat in a back row pew of the Timber Community Church the minute Pastor Parr dismissed the service. She'd barely taken a step when she ran into a wall of muscle and her Bible fell from her hands to the carpeted floor of the chapel. Stunned, she found herself inches from Tripp Walker as he scooped up the good book and offered it to her.

Accepting the tome from the lean cowboy, she stepped back and brushed an imaginary wrinkle from her simple cap sleeve lavender dress while avoiding eye contact. She would not notice his clean-shaven face, nor how blue his eyes were in that teal chambray shirt and navy tie.

"Thank you," she murmured. Without another word, she hurried past him to the church nursery hall to fetch Clementine.

Eyes on the room numbers, Hannah walked slowly down the long hall until she found Clementine's class. In the doorway of the next classroom, Lucy Maxwell Harris stood with a baby in her arms, herding three identical children into the hall. The triplets waved construction paper with colorful paintings and all jabbered at the same time.

Lucy looked up and her gaze met Hannah's. Her face lit up, and she seemed genuinely pleased at the encounter. "Hannah! Good to see you."

Hannah smiled at the unexpected welcome.

"How's your arm? I heard about Rowdy."

"A scratch. I've been upgraded from critical to a small bandage."

"That's good," Lucy returned.

"This is your family?" Hannah asked, eager to change the subject.

"It is." Lucy put a hand on the heads of each of the tow-headed children, one at a time. "Dub, Eva and Ann. They're seven now." Then she smiled down at the dark-haired baby with the sweet curls. "This is Daniel."

"Your family is precious." The words couldn't be any truer. Love radiated from the children's faces to their mother. "How old is Daniel?"

"Five months old this week." Lucy pressed a soft kiss to the infant's forehead. "Born on Christmas."

A Christmas baby. Like Hannah's baby would be, perhaps.

"Would you and your daughter like to join us for lunch?" Lucy asked. "Emma cooks on Sundays."

"I, um… That's very generous of you." Hannah stumbled over her words, surprised at the offer. "Clementine and I have plans. But thank you."

They did have plans, though in truth, until she could prove she was family she was an outsider and didn't want to be an interloper, as well. Besides, Tripp might be there and she'd had her quota of disapproving glances for the week.

"Where are we going, Momma?" Clementine asked once they were in the car headed to downtown Timber.

"It's Sunday, sweetie."

Clementine's eyes lit up.

The very least she could do for her daughter was maintain some semblance of routine over the last few weeks since they left Missouri. Sundays were for church and a special meal together. They'd kept that tradition while in Colorado and would continue here in Oklahoma.

"Pancakes?" Clementine asked with a hopeful lift of her brows.

"Whatever my girl wants." When they stopped at a light, Hannah reached into the back seat to straighten the pink bow in her daughter's hair.

"With whipped cream?"

"Of course."

Hannah passed the Timber Diner on Main Street and searched for a parking spot, finally pulling in outside the Timber Daily Gazette, which was closed.

A smiling server met them as they slid into a booth in the diner. "Coffee, ma'am?" the young woman asked.

"Decaf, please."

The server placed crayons and a paper placemat to color in front of Clementine. "And for you, miss?"

"Strawberry pancakes with whipped cream, please," Clementine said.

Hannah glanced around as her daughter examined the crayons. The view from the booth was limited. *We could have sat at a table.* The thought made her smile. No more hiding from whatever private detective her grandmother had hired. She was free.

"What did you do in Sunday school class, Clemmie?"

"I showed you my picture." Her daughter concentrated on coloring without looking up.

"Yes, and it's a beautiful picture of a pink horse and a house."

"No, Momma. That's Big Heart Ranch where my pink horse lives and so do I. Forever and ever."

Forever and ever. But only if the DNA test showed they were Maxwells.

She looked up and met the gaze of a tall, thin cowboy she didn't recognize. At least not from Big Heart Ranch. He stared first at her and then at Clementine. When the man realized she was looking back, he eased from the counter stool and headed out the door. Hannah shivered, offering up self-talk. *Nothing to worry about. Those days are gone. Just a coincidence our gazes met.*

When their server slid their plates in front of them, Hannah released the worrisome thoughts and took Clementine's hand for a mealtime prayer.

Hannah placed her napkin on her lap and tried to relax as her daughter dug right in.

"Good pancakes," Clementine mumbled.

"Sweetie, don't talk while you're chewing." She reached for a napkin and swiped at the whipped cream on her daughter's face.

Outside the window, budding tree branches reached for the Oklahoma blue sky where the spring sun peeked out from the clouds.

The clatter of silverware hitting the floor had Hannah turning her head back to the table. Clementine squirmed off the bench to retrieve a fork from the ground. She stood and pointed with the utensil. "Look, Momma. Mr. Tripp."

Hannah cringed as several patrons turned at the outburst. "Oh, sweetie, put down that fork. It's not polite to point."

Timber, Oklahoma, wasn't a big town, yet it still seemed odd that she wasn't able to go a day without running into Tripp Walker. Hannah dared to look up to confirm her daughter's comment. Yes, the cowboy's dusty boots were taking him across the room toward their booth. He'd changed into Levi's and a plaid Western shirt, but failed to look any less handsome and intimidating.

"Made it to church and to town, so I guess that means your car is still doing okay," Tripp said.

"Yes. Thank you for…" She raised her bandaged arm. "You know."

He pushed his hat to the back of his head with a finger and nodded.

"Did you eat pancakes, too, Mr. Tripp?" Clementine asked.

Hannah shot her daughter the *behave yourself* glance, willing the child not to embarrass her further.

"I did. I always have pancakes on Sunday," he returned. "Just like you are."

Clementine's face lit up at the words.

"You don't have family dinner with the Maxwells?" Hannah asked. The words were out of her mouth before she could take them back. What was she thinking asking such a personal question? It was none of her business, nor her matter to consider.

"Nothing better than a little alone time one day a week," he said without further explanation.

"You don't spend Sundays with family?" Oh, she was really on a roll now. Her mouth was clearly in gear and bypassing her brain. And did she imagine it, or did he tense at the question?

Tripp stared out the window. "No, ma'am." The cowboy blinked and his gaze returned to the table, moving from Hannah to Clementine. "I wanted to apologize for being a bit harsh yesterday."

"I, um…" Hannah nearly fell out of her seat at the unexpected admission. A suitable response failed her.

Tripp tipped his hat and turned. "You two have a nice day."

"Bye, Mr. Tripp," Clementine murmured between bites.

"Bye, Miss Clementine," he said as his long strides carried him away as quickly as he had appeared.

What just happened? Hannah sat back and did a mental play-by-play of the situation while her daughter finished off her meal, but minutes later, she still remained confused by the cowboy's hot and cold attitude.

When Clementine inched a pudgy finger onto her plate to wipe up the remaining syrup, Hannah flagged down the server as she passed by their booth.

"Ma'am, do you need more coffee?" the young woman asked.

"No, thank you. We're done, and my daughter gives your pancakes a thumbs-up."

"That's what we like to hear." The server grinned as she picked up their dishes.

"May I have the check?" Hannah asked.

"Oh, Mr. Walker paid for your meal and left me a generous tip." She smiled. "Y'all have a blessed Sunday."

Stunned, Hannah tried to wrap her mind around the fact that Tripp Walker paid for their brunch as she pulled a wet wipe from her purse and washed Clementine's sticky fingers.

"Mommy, I'm clean," Clementine declared.

"So you are, Clemmie."

Confused, Hannah glanced up and down the sidewalk for the cowboy as they headed to their car. She didn't know what to make of the gesture. Did he think she needed a handout? She'd taken care of herself and her daughter for many years.

It was time to put Mr. Tripp Walker in his place. Hannah Vincent didn't need help, nor did she want any handouts.

"This is the day that the Lord has made," Tripp said as he unlocked the door to his office on Monday morning and turned on the lights.

Sunday's sermon had been about compassion and second chances. Apparently, the good Lord thought he needed to review. And He was right. Tripp repented while kneeling in the pew and followed through with an apology to Hannah at the diner.

Though he still wasn't thrilled about working in proximity with Hannah Vincent, he'd manage until further notice or Slats provided him with information that changed the situation.

Tripp grimaced, not certain contacting the private investigator was a wise move or fell in line with Pastor Parr's sermon goals. It was a little late for regrets, he reminded himself while absently rubbing his hand over the scar on his face. Slats informed him yesterday as they crossed paths outside the diner that he was on the job. Tripp could only pray that Hannah came up smelling like an Oklahoma rose.

He glanced at the clock and then his cramped office. Dutch had helped him move a desk and computer into the room for Hannah. It was in the opposite corner from his own desk and faced the window.

That way she could see into the stables…at least, that was his rationalization of the situation. In truth, he didn't need to be staring at the woman eight hours a day even if she did have long eyelashes and a pretty face. Not that he'd ever admit that to anyone but his horse.

Tripp turned at a knock on the door.

Hannah stood in the doorway looking like someone stole her puppy. "Sorry I'm late. It was Clementine's first day in daycare."

"First day? Like, ever? Or just here at the ranch?"

"Ever, except for the church nursery on Sundays. We've always been together."

"What about when you worked?"

"I always found a way to keep her with me."

"Overprotective?"

"Yes."

"So how's she doing?"

Hannah bit her lip. "Clementine is fine. It's her mother who's having adjustment issues."

"You can check on her during the day, if that will help."

Her eyes rounded with cautious hope. "That would be okay with you?"

He nodded. "Of course."

"Thank you."

They stood awkwardly for a few seconds before he remembered what he was supposed to do.

"That's your desk," he finally said. "I've put your tentative schedule on top. When I'm here, you're here.

That means basically we work one Saturday a month. The staff alternate working Saturdays. Chores are scheduled for Sunday, but everyone is expected to be in church. Those are ranch rules."

Hannah offered a short nod as she stepped hesitantly into the office, put her purse in the bottom desk drawer and sat down. She turned to him. "Mr. Walker, thank you for picking up our tab yesterday, but it was wholly unnecessary."

Her expression tacked the word *unwanted* onto the end of her spiel.

"I'm not looking for handouts," she continued.

"First, I'm Tripp. Not Mr. Walker." He tipped back his tan cowboy hat on his head and then crossed his arms. "Second, there's no need to get offended. I was paying it forward."

"Paying it forward?"

"Yeah. Don't overthink the situation."

She opened her mouth and then closed it again.

"Did you complete the paperwork at human resources?" he asked.

"Yes. They fingerprinted me, and I have my security pass for the gate. I'm ready to go, pending the results of the background check."

"Your temporary password and login information are on that paper on the desk. You have an appointment with Iris, Lucy's admin, over at the administration building this afternoon. She'll walk you through the programs we use on the ranch, payroll, vendor orders and scheduling."

"Oh, I thought you would..."

"You don't want me teaching you anything that has

to do with a computer. I type with two fingers and I barely speak the language."

Hannah nodded.

"I'll show you around the boys' ranch stables today and tomorrow we'll go over to the girls' ranch."

"'Scuse me, Tripp. Got a problem with Rowdy again. He's holding his hoof off the ground, and he won't let me near him."

He looked to Hannah. "We can do the tour later."

"Of course."

Rowdy, again. The horse was a stout nine-year-old Sorrel gelding with a flaxen mane and long, flowing flaxen tail. Perfect for the riding program...or so he'd thought. Besides the horse's fear of trailers, clearly something had happened since Tripp first saw the horse and now. Rowdy moved back with each step Tripp made toward him.

"Easy, boy. Easy."

When he got close enough to touch him, Tripp ran a hand over his withers, slowly massaging back and forth, until the horse was relaxed. Finally, he eased his hand toward the animal's affected leg, inching closer, slowly and patiently. He moved toward the horse's ankle, gaining trust until Rowdy was willing to let him hold his foot and examine the hoof.

"Stone in here. I'm guessing he came over to us like that. It's festered. He'll need the vet and the farrier."

"They don't call him the horse whisperer for nothing," Dutch said with a nod to Hannah.

"That's what they call him?" Hannah asked.

"Yep."

"Don't listen to that horse whisperer malarkey. What

I do is called common sense," Tripp said as he strode past them toward the stables.

"Where are you going?" Dutch hollered after him.

"To call the vet."

Hannah walked up and down the equine center looking into stalls as Tripp talked to the vet. By the time his conversation was completed and he was back at his desk, she had moved into the office, sat at her desk and logged into the computer.

"The sign-up deadline for that mustang competition is coming up," she murmured.

Tripp looked up from his calendar. "What?" A glance at Hannah's computer screen told him she was searching the 100-Day Mustang Challenge site. The woman was a bulldog with a bone.

"You know." Hannah pointed to the poster on the wall.

"I told you. I have a full-time commitment to the ranch." He didn't even attempt to hold the annoyance from his voice.

"I'll help you."

"You?" He shook his head at her offer. "And what makes you think you can help me enough that I'll have time to train a mustang?"

"I looked at your schedule on the wall outside. There isn't anything on that list that I can't do."

"You're pregnant."

"Pregnant is not a terminal disease, and I don't need to ride a horse to help you. I saw that ute out there. That'll work. I mentioned that I have an extensive background with horses. I worked in children's camps and equine clinics when I was a teenager and when I was in college."

"So you keep saying." Tripp narrowed his eyes as he tried to figure the woman out. "What exactly did you go to college for?"

"Business administration with a minor in accounting."

"Why?"

"My grandmother was paying."

He continued to stare. The woman was a puzzle. "Why aren't you working as a bookkeeper or accountant then?"

"Because childcare is expensive."

"College isn't?"

"I've already explained that."

Tripp frowned. Yeah, and his gut told him something was not right with Hannah's explanation. Hopefully, Slats would be able to sort it out.

"Let me get this straight. A woman with a degree in business, who works as a cook, is telling me how to run my equine facility and the mustang challenge?"

"Who told you I work as a cook?"

"You mentioned it during your meeting with the Maxwells last Friday."

"Oh." Hannah exhaled. "My point is that I think you should consider doing the 100-Day Mustang Challenge."

"Why?"

"Is that the only word you know?"

"Maybe so." He shrugged.

"You should enter because you can do it and because the purse is fifty thousand dollars."

"Money isn't high on my priority list."

"That's why you have that poster on the wall?"

"I like the idea of rehoming the animal." He gave

a slow shake of his head. "But you and I working together? It'd never work. We rub each other the wrong way."

Hannah's brows shot up and her eyes rounded. "That's your issue, not mine. And in case you haven't noticed, we're already working together."

A knock on the door had both of them turning to see Travis Maxwell. "What are you two talking about?"

"The 100-Day Mustang Challenge," Hannah said.

"*We* weren't talking. She was."

"You finally going to do it, Tripp?" Travis offered an enthusiastic grin.

"One of these days," he groused. Because he sure wasn't going to let a bossy thing like Hannah Vincent push him into anything.

"Why not now?" Travis asked.

"'Cause I don't have anything to prove. I train horses all the time."

"Tripp, you're not going to stay with us forever. I know that. This might be a good way to get your name out there and get you on your way to your own horse training facility. You used to talk about doing that all the time."

Tripp frowned, his mind taking a cautious detour to consider Travis's words. *Used to* was a long time ago. What had happened to his dreams along the way?

"I don't know," Tripp finally said.

"Come on. I know I could talk Lucy into the idea. Let Big Heart Ranch help you. You've helped us. You worked for us when we could barely pay you."

"Where would we put a wild horse?"

"We'll clear the old barn and set up a dedicated round pen for training."

"And the prize money?" Tripp asked.

Travis raised his hands. "Hey, that's all yours. The ranch is a charity. We won't touch your winnings."

Silence stretched for moments as Tripp battled with the idea of change. The *terrifying* idea of change. His life was a steady, predictable ride right now. Why look for trouble?

"I'll think about it," he finally said.

"Think hard. When the door opens, you have to walk through. Big Heart Ranch didn't get to be where it is without us stepping out in faith."

Tripp cleared his throat, eager to change the topic. He met Travis's gaze head-on. "Did you have something on your mind when you stopped by?"

"I came to tell Hannah that Lucy scheduled an appointment with the lab in Tulsa for them two weeks from now. Soonest she could fit it in. Lucy's schedule is tight this time of year."

"Why can't you or Emma go to the lab with her?" Tripp asked.

"I can't go because female-to-female DNA comparison yields a more accurate result. Emma can't go because Lucy is a helicopter sister. She still thinks she's in charge of me and Emma."

"I guess so," Tripp murmured.

"Thank you," Hannah said. When Travis left, she turned to Tripp again. "That was a confirmation."

"A what?"

"A confirmation. You know, a sign that you should enter the challenge."

Tripp looked her up and down. The woman was a sassy thing for a stranger who'd only arrived a few days ago.

"You don't even know if you'll be here in one hundred days," he returned.

Though her eyes said she was dumbstruck by his bold statement, her mouth kept moving. "You don't believe I'm related to the Maxwells, do you?"

Tripp raised both hands. "I don't know what to believe." Though he tried not to judge, there was a part of him that had already stamped the woman's card and dismissed her.

"I am, and I'm willing to stick around to find out if it will help Clementine."

"Help Clementine?"

Hannah offered a shrug. "We could use a little nest egg to start over."

"The prize money?"

"Sure. Why not? If I make it possible for you to train, maybe it would be worth some of the purse." The flush of her cheeks told him that her words were all bravado.

"What makes you think I'm going to win?" Tripp asked.

"I've seen you with the horses." She paused. "I know a winner when I see one."

He nearly laughed aloud. "So what kind of split are we talking about here?" he asked.

"Fifty-fifty."

Tripp released a scoffing sound. "In your dreams, lady. I'm the trainer and I'm paying for fees and feed and everything else out of my pocket."

"Sixty-forty?"

"More like seventy-thirty, and you have a deal." The words slipped from his mouth before he could take them back. What was he thinking, making a pact with a pregnant single mother who might very well prove to be a seasoned con artist? His mouth hadn't run off on him in years. Yet here he was, with his good sense galloping away.

"I, um..."

Despite his misstep, Hannah seemed reluctant to commit, and that stuck in his craw. Was she having second thoughts about his ability to win the challenge?

"What's the problem?" he asked. "Your bravado seems to be fading the closer it gets to the chute."

"Seventy-thirty?" She shook her head in disagreement.

"Are you telling me that you couldn't start over with fifteen thousand dollars? If you can't, then you're doing it all wrong, my friend."

"We aren't friends," Hannah said. Then she stood and walked over to his desk. She offered him her hand, and he stared at it for a moment before accepting the handshake.

"Deal," she said.

Tripp stared at her small hand in his.

The day had started off like any other. In a heartbeat, everything was sideways. He'd agreed to the 100-Day Mustang Challenge and was seriously thinking about a future that didn't include the Maxwells.

Was he ready to move on from Big Heart to start his own business? The thought left him as nervous as a heifer about to give birth. Tripp offered a silent prayer, knowing this was going to take a real step of faith and no doubt bigger boots than he had on.

Chapter Four

❦

"I don't understand why Clementine couldn't come with us," Hannah said. About now, she was feeling like her daughter on the downside of a temper tantrum. Being stuck in a truck cab with Tripp Walker for three hours and seven minutes one way might be the reason.

She stared out the passenger window of Tripp's pickup at the Oklahoma countryside. Today the view had easily earned the name Green Country. Only minutes ago, cedar elm and bald cypress trees graced the emerald green lawns of residential properties they passed when they detoured from the highway to a small town for beverages and a rest stop.

Tripp adjusted his sunglasses and rolled down his window a bit to let in the morning breeze. "The Bureau of Land Management station in Pauls Valley is not a place for children."

"If this is because of that incident with the feed yesterday, I said it was an accident. We've had a discussion about going into the stalls alone," Hannah protested. "Clementine understands."

Tripp held up a hand. "Not insulting your child,

Momma. She's as smart as a dozen five-year-olds put together. Most kids are naturally curious. Your daughter is all that ratcheted up to Mach four."

Hannah grudgingly admitted that even though he'd only known Clementine a week, his assessment was spot-on.

He shot her a sideways glance. "You didn't have to come with me."

"Of course I did. This is my future. I'm so excited I could barely sleep last night."

"Then try to relax. Clementine is having a great time with Lucy's triplets."

"Lucy has four children already."

"She loves kids. More importantly, everyone loves Clementine."

"They do?" Hannah's spirits lifted at the unexpected words.

"Yeah. You haven't noticed? Your daughter brings out a smile wherever she goes."

"Thank you," Hannah said softly. She glanced at the cowboy out of the corner of her eye. "That was a really nice thing to say."

"Wasn't trying to be nice. Those are the facts." Tripp offered his usual shrug as he checked both ways before easing back onto Interstate 35. When the truck hit a bump, the empty horse trailer behind them rattled. "Besides, six hours round-trip is no fun for a kid."

Hannah conceded that he was right on that count as well, though being without her daughter for this long was new territory and a bit scary. Maybe she was a helicopter mother, but for good reason. She'd been raised by a series of nannies and a judgmental grandmother. Hannah was determined Clementine would know her mother and feel unconditionally loved at all times.

After the first hour, Hannah got used to the silence that stretched between her and Tripp in the truck, and she relaxed. He apparently liked it quiet as much as she did. The radio was off and whenever she sneaked a peek at his profile, she found him focused on the road as if thinking very hard.

What was going on in the man's head? It was hard to say, and she'd already figured out that he wasn't going to give her more words than absolutely necessary.

She peeked at his profile again. With his hat tipped back and his eyes locked on the road, he seemed unnecessarily attractive. Perhaps more so because he had little regard for superficial things like appearances.

"I hope we find a good horse," Hannah finally spoke into the silent truck cab.

"Yeah, except that's not how it works. You get what you get."

"What do you mean? I thought we'd be able to pick the horse we spend one hundred days training."

"Not unless we participate in the auction." He shook his head. "And that's not going to happen. Doesn't make sense to spend money bidding on a horse that's going to be auctioned off again in one hundred days. Nope. We'll do things like everyone else. What we get is what we train. That's the real challenge."

"That certainly doesn't seem fair."

"It's not about fair." He shot her a quick look. "And I'm guessing by now you realize life isn't fair."

She pulled her denim jacket close and frowned. "It doesn't mean I have to like it."

"This challenge is all about the big picture. Come September, the horses will be adopted."

Cocking her head, she turned to look at him. "How many is that, exactly?"

"Close to three thousand."

Hannah leaned back against the seat. "I had no idea."

"There are about sixty thousand horses being held in Bureau of Land Management facilities across the United States."

Stunned, Hannah opened her mouth and closed it again.

"Truth is, I'm glad you lassoed me into this challenge. It's about time I gave back."

"Really?"

"Yeah." Once again, he looked at her. "Don't read anything into that."

"No. Of course not." Hannah directed her gaze out the window at the highway signs. *Chickasha. Anadarko. Shawnee. Seminole.*

"Native American names," she murmured.

"What?" His gaze followed hers to the signs. "Yeah. Chickasha, Shawnee and Seminole are tribal names. Anadarko is headquarters for a good many tribal nations."

"Have you lived around here all your life?"

Tripp nodded. "Rumor has it that my great-grandfather on my mother's side was from the Osage Nation."

"Rumor?"

"I don't have any family left to verify that information."

"Oh. I'm so sorry." She lifted a hand in gesture. "I was just making conversation. I didn't mean any offense."

"Why would I be offended?"

"I just thought… Never mind." Hannah paused. "I don't have any family, either."

"No one at all?"

"No," she said. "My grandmother raised me."

"And you drove all the way here from Colorado."

Hannah stiffened at the question. How many times did she have to explain before he believed her? "Actually, I drove all the way from Missouri by way of Colorado. They're holding my job in case I decide to come back."

"I guess you were pretty good if they're holding your job. What did you do? Some kind of cook, right?"

"Yes. I was the head cook at a very popular twenty-four-hour diner in Dripping Falls, Missouri." She glanced at him. "And yes, I am a really good cook. Plus, I was in great demand during tax season for my mathematical skills."

He said nothing for minutes, clearly not impressed by her résumé. Yes, right, she wasn't, either. She had graduated from an Ivy League school at the top of her class so she could be a short-order cook. A total waste of time, energy and tuition.

"Dripping Falls," Tripp mused. "Population three thousand and twenty on a good day. Two stoplights and a one-way street around the center of town."

"How could you possibly know that?" Hannah asked. She was dismayed that he'd been checking on her.

"I caught a glimpse of your paperwork. Got curious and looked it up." He spared her a glance, clearly holding back a smile. "Seriously? Dripping Falls?"

"Despite the name, it's a very nice town."

He nodded as though considering her words. "You're a jill-of-all-trades, aren't you?"

"I suppose that's one way of looking at it. I have a

daughter to consider so I'll do whatever I have to do to make ends meet for her."

"Her daddy?"

"You certainly ask a lot of questions," Hannah shot back.

"Just making conversation. I guess that's a sore subject."

"Not at all. I have nothing to hide." She fiddled with the brass snap on her jacket. "Clementine doesn't really know her daddy well. His loss."

"That I can agree with," Tripp murmured.

A half a mile down the road, he turned on his signal and nodded his head toward the right.

Hannah read the sign at the entrance. Bureau of Land Management Horse and Burro Adoption Center. "This facility doesn't look like much," she observed.

"Twelve pastures and four hundred acres of land. They've got six hundred animals they're holding before they're moved east or west to adoption centers. Lots of controversy about the land and the animals that roam wild and free. But we're not getting into that today."

She glanced around. Several other rigs with trailers were parked in the facility parking area and a line of people had formed outside a small building.

"What do we do now?" Hannah asked.

"Pick up our registration packet over there and then they'll pull our horse for us."

"That's it?"

"That's it. I registered us for the challenge online."

"Us?" She blinked at the comment.

"Both of our names are on those forms." Tripp eased the truck into a parking spot and turned off the engine.

"I don't have any credentials."

"You were added as the assistant trainer, based on my recommendation."

"You don't even know me."

"Nope." He met her gaze before he jumped down from the cab. "So you better not prove me wrong and ruin my reputation."

"Yes, sir." Hannah carefully eased down from the truck before Tripp could come around and assist her.

Once Tripp locked the truck and headed toward the registration area, Hannah realized she'd have to walk twice as fast to keep up with his long strides.

The line moved quickly. They picked up their paperwork and moved over to the main corral where at least forty horses raced around the giant metal circular pen, grunting and whinnying. A few rambunctious ones kicked at the pole fencing and the sound of hooves hitting metal rang into the morning air. Beautiful animals, strong and filled with pride, waited restlessly for their futures to be decided.

Hannah stared at the sight for a long minute while Tripp handed his receipt with the horse's number to the cowboy manning the loading chute.

"You got a good one," the cowboy said with a laugh. "We nicknamed her Calamity Jane." He pointed to an animal with a copper-red coat and dark brown-and-copper mane, about fourteen hands, who edged closer to the gate latch. "That's her. Five-year-old sorrel mare. Good-natured animal."

"Calamity Jane? Why's that?" Hannah asked.

"Oh, she's smart. Too smart. Couple of times she tried to jump the fence."

"That's a ten-foot fence," Tripp said.

"*Tried* being the operative word." He chuckled. "Failing that, she got her mouth on the gate latch during the night. Given a little more time, I do believe she might have opened the pen."

"Calamity Jane," Tripp murmured with a smile.

"Yeah, she's something special." The cowboy nodded. "Back your rig up and we'll get her loaded."

Hannah guided Tripp with hand signals as he steered the trailer until the entire rig was backed up to the loading chute. She raised her palms, and the vehicle stopped.

Tripp got out, jumped the fence and unlatched the trailer, opening the doors wide before he jumped back out of the chute and away from the horses.

Hannah's gaze followed the cowboy in the holding pen as he encouraged Jane toward the narrow chute.

"Ya!" the cowboy called out, urging Calamity Jane toward the trailer.

For a moment the horse stopped as if in slow motion and turned to the left, the chocolate eyes searching. When her gaze connected with Hannah's, the mare moved closer to the fence. Hannah raised her hand, flat palm up. She was far enough back to stay safe, but her gesture caught the horse's attention. Jane sniffed curiously.

"Well, I'll be," the cowboy murmured. "I've never seen anything like that from these mustangs."

The horse blinked and then shook her head, tossing her mane back and forth as if breaking a spell.

"Ya. In you go," the cowboy said from his perch on the fence. The sound of hooves on the trailer floor told them Calamity Jane was tucked inside.

Tripp jumped forward to close the gate and latch everything securely. "Thanks," he said with a nod to the cowboy.

"Let me know how it goes," the cowboy said. "I

meant what I said. I really have the feeling you've got something special there."

Something special. Hannah shivered. Exactly what she'd been praying for. A horse who needed her as much as she needed it.

"What are your plans?" Hannah turned to Tripp as she fastened her seat belt.

"Plans?" He adjusted his hat and put on his sunglasses.

"Training plans."

Tripp shrugged. "Ask the horse. I just show up. The rest is up to her."

"No. You can't mean that. You're a trainer. I imagine you've trained dozens of animals."

"More than dozens and generally, they trained me," he murmured with a lift of his brow.

"How can I help?"

"You can do all the administrative chores so I can train this horse. That's the deal."

"You put me down as co-trainer."

"Hannah, that was honorary. The challenge was your idea and I'm giving credit where credit is due. You're enabling me to train. Assistant trainer aside, I don't want to see you in the same pen or stall with that horse, ever."

"That's not your business…" She clamped her mouth shut before she could finish and allow an opening for Tripp to give her one of his lectures.

"You're pregnant. Don't do anything that could compromise your or your baby's health. That horse is wild and unpredictable, and you're not taking risks on my watch."

She offered a tortured sigh. Apparently, lecturing was on today's menu anyhow.

"I'm not going to ride." Hannah took a deep breath and crossed her arms. She had no intention of doing anything that would put this pregnancy at risk. At the same time, she wasn't going to let anyone, including her enigmatic boss, tell her what to do.

"You heard me. My stable. My rules."

"What exactly does that mean? You want me to sit at a desk all day?"

"It means you're going to do what you signed on for. Keep the books, manage the schedule, order the supplies and answer the phone."

If Hannah bit her tongue any harder she was pretty sure she'd draw blood. But she'd learned a long time ago that it was a waste of time to go through when you could go around. If there was a way around the stubborn cowboy, well, she was just the gal to find that road.

Tripp downed the last of his coffee and opened the door of the bunkhouse.

May had turned to June in the blink of an eye, bringing with it warm temperatures and sunshine. At nearly six, the sun had managed to paint the sky in gold and burnt umber as it stretched sleepy fingers toward daylight.

He stepped out to the gravel yard, enjoying the quiet. When he turned the corner, a lone figure stood silhouetted at Calamity Jane's fence. Murmured words had the mare leaning closer.

Hannah.

She reached a hand through the fence to stroke the horse's mane.

Unbelievable. They brought Jane home on Tuesday and here it was Wednesday. Less than twenty-four hours and already she had bonded with the mare. Somehow between yesterday and this morning, Jane had figured out that touch was a good thing. Tripp wasn't certain who should be applauded: Hannah or the horse.

As Tripp got closer, Jane's ears perked, and she whinnied as if warning Hannah of his approach. Two females in cahoots. Just perfect.

Hannah whirled around to face him, pushing her dark waves back. "Did you see that?"

He was dumbstruck at the sweet expression she gave him. A smile lit up her face all the way to her brown eyes, which fairly sparkled with happiness.

Tripp caught himself before he stumbled.

"Did you bring her a treat?" he asked.

Hannah laughed. "Excuse me. I do not bribe horses. Jane happens to appreciate me just the way I am."

"Is that so?" Tripp moved closer, resting his arms on a rung of the high pen fence. Jane raced around the circle, kicking up dirt and sand, the tilt of her head proud. There wasn't a more awesome sight to behold on all of Big Heart Ranch.

Overhead, a hawk circled in the clear powder blue sky, doing a lazy dip before he landed on the branches of a mighty elm tree.

"What are you going to do today?" Hannah asked, her voice eager and enthusiastic.

"I'll let her run the pen, get her used to me. Just like yesterday. She's committed to ignoring me. I'm committed to not letting her."

Hannah smiled. "She's watching you right now."

"Yeah. That's exactly what I want. She's a little jealous of all the attention I'm not giving her at this moment."

"Most trainers would force her to bend to their will."

"That's how either the horse or the trainer gets hurt.

Though it's not my place to be critical, there are many right and wrong ways to train a horse." He paused. "I'll stick with what works for me."

"Can I help?"

Tripp kept his voice low, his eyes on Jane. "Are we going to have this same discussion every day?"

"There has to be something I can do."

"There is. May not seem like much, but having you in the office frees me up so I can take my time out here with our friend." He turned and met Hannah's gaze. "You are vital to the success of this challenge."

"Vital. That sounds very important." Her tone said she was being sarcastic again.

"Yeah. You do your job, and I'll do mine."

"Tripp, look." Hannah's attention was focused on the pen behind him.

He turned back in time to see the horse mouthing the gate latch and nearly opening it wide. Tripp chuckled. "I wouldn't have believed that if I hadn't seen it."

Pulling a bandana from his pocket, he tied the gate near the bottom. "This will do for now. I'll have Dutch add an extra latch."

"I wish Clementine could have seen that," Hannah said.

"Where is she?"

"Rue is going to bring her to daycare this morning. The doctor is going to do eye exams in the childcare classrooms today."

"You talked to Clementine about the horses, especially this one, right?"

"We had a chat, and she repeated the rules back to me."

He nodded. "The local vet, Trent Blaylock, will be by at nine or so this morning to check on a few issues. If you could follow him around with Dutch, I'd appreciate it. I'd like to work with Jane without interruptions around that time."

"Of course."

"All you have to do is make note of his recommendations and leave your notes on my desk. Trent is easy to work with."

"Will do." She paused. "Lucy asked me to help with a church fund-raiser she's working on."

"Okay?"

"That means I have to go to a meeting Friday morning. It's at the chow hall."

"Fine by me."

"Thank you. But, um, where is the chow hall again?"

"Here at the boys' ranch, right next to the administration building. It's the cafeteria."

"Got it."

Tripp left Hannah at the corral and headed to the stables. Flipping on the lights to his office, he sat down at his desk and blinked. He was a tidy man but things were tidier than usual. Hannah had left paperwork with sticky notes indicating his signature was needed. The May accounts had all been checked and verified and were ready to close out with checks sent.

A pang of guilt stabbed at him. He needed to call and tell Slats to back off. Except the cowboy was in Texas this week for a rodeo and probably not picking up his phone.

Still, he could leave a message.

Tripp looked around to be sure Hannah hadn't slipped into the stables.

He hit auto dial and to his surprise, the cowboy picked up.

"Slats, this is Tripp Walker."

"I was going to call you today."

"Yeah, well, I want to cancel that request. You know the one."

"There's something you ought to know first."

"Whatever it is, I don't want to know."

The woman worked for him; if there was something he needed to know, he'd find out himself. Hiring Slats had been a bad idea and for the first time in years, Tripp knew that he was dipping into dangerous territory. You hang around in low places, you become a low place.

He looked up when Hannah quietly stepped into the room and moved to her desk.

"Bill me and I'll drop a check in the mail."

Tripp didn't give Slats a chance to respond. He hit the end button, stood and tucked his phone in the back pocket of his jeans.

"I'll be with Jane if anything comes up."

"Yes, sir."

"*Sir* isn't necessary."

Hannah didn't look up from the spreadsheet on the computer screen. "My grandmother had her issues, but she taught me proper respect for my elders."

First Dutch and now Hannah. "I'm not that old," Tripp grumbled under his breath as he headed to Jane's pen. The sorrel mare followed Tripp around for two hours, stopping when he stopped and changing direction at his pleasure.

He put a light blanket on her back and she barely reacted. If he didn't know this horse was from the Bureau of Land Management he'd have never believed the fact. The horse was a lover, longing for affection and giving back the same.

"Whoa," he said with a pat to the mare's bare backside. "Good job, Jane."

Tripp looked up in time to see Dutch walking back to the stables alongside Rowdy.

"How's Rowdy doing?"

"Vet says he's ready to ride."

"Great, and how's he behaving?"

"Settled down some. I think this fella's going to fit right in."

"Great. Until we're sure of his temperament, keep him scheduled with the certified instructors only."

"You sure that's necessary?" Dutch asked.

"Something's not right yet," Tripp said. "Be careful with him. Jane here is less twitchy than Rowdy, and that's not a good sign."

"Will do, boss."

"Dutch, don't forget I need an extra latch for this gate."

"On my list. I'll be going to town this afternoon. Need anything else?"

"Check with Travis before you go."

"I already did. Won't be any flies on me today. Between you and Travis, I'm working from can to can't." Dutch paused then looked pointedly at Tripp before glancing around.

"Something on your mind?" Tripp asked.

Dutch stepped closer to the pen. "I'm not privy to all the information like you are, but I hear tell Hannah might be a Maxwell."

"How'd you squirrel that information?"

"I pestered Rue until she finally let it slip." Dutch shrugged. "I'd have to be half-dead and living under a rock not to figure something was up around this place. You getting an assistant and all was the kicker."

Tripp faced the weathered cowboy. "Did you just insult me?"

"Nope, just stating the facts. You're not exactly a social being, so you getting an assistant and signing up for the hundred-day challenge, well, it sure seemed the world must have been knocked off kilter a bit."

When Tripp offered a death stare, the weathered wrangler raised his hands.

"I tells it like I sees it."

"Lucy and Travis have been promising me an assistant for a long time. That's no secret." Tripp grabbed his lead rope from the fence and wrapped it up.

"And the challenge?" Dutch persisted.

"You don't expect me to stay here at Big Heart for the rest of my life, do you?"

"Why not? That's my plan. I figured it was yours, too."

Tripp stared at him. Did everyone think he was a fixture here at Big Heart? A man without dreams of his own? He shook his head. Maybe he'd done that to himself, put his dreams on the back burner because it was safer that way.

"I'm not a hundred years old, Dutch," he finally muttered. The words *like you* hung in the air between them.

The old cowboy frowned. "No need to be disparaging."

"You asked." Tripp checked Jane's feed bucket.

"So that's all you know about Hannah?" Dutch asked.

Tripp wordlessly stared him down. Dutch knew good and well that Tripp wouldn't tell him anything, even if he did know something. The wrangler couldn't keep a secret to save himself.

"That's what I figured you'd say," Dutch muttered.

"Everything go okay with the vet?" Tripp asked.

"Hannah and Trent are still in your office, jabbering."

"Jabbering?"

"Yeah. Don't know about what, but it looks serious. Those two are getting along like long-lost friends."

Tripp stepped into the stables. Sure enough, through the glass windows of his office he could see that Hannah seemed to be lecturing the vet. Trent nodded thoughtfully as though he hung on her every word.

Suddenly Trent smiled and offered Hannah a quick hug.

A strange emotion wrapped itself around Tripp. If he had any interest in Hannah, he might have suspected it was jealousy. Except that was a crazy notion. The last thing he needed in his life was a woman. If he did, it sure wouldn't be Hannah Vincent.

Not only was she trouble, but she was an opinionated, bossy woman. A single mother with more baggage than he had time to deal with and more on the way.

The vet met his gaze as he exited the offices. "Hey, Tripp. I don't know where you got Hannah, but she's a keeper."

Tripp nodded. A keeper? Confused, he turned.

When Hannah's gaze connected with his, her lips curved into a smile. A pink blush warmed her cheeks, and for the second time that morning he was hit with a jolt in his midsection. He quickly looked away.

"Looked like you and Trent hit it off," Tripp said as he sat down and fiddled with the papers on his desk.

"We did. He's a nice guy. Turns out we know a few of the same people. In Colorado, no less." A musing smile lit up her face.

"Trent's father is an Oklahoma senator," Tripp said, trying to connect the dots between Hannah and the blue blood family.

"I know," she said.

Dutch stuck his head in the door. "I'm headed into town now."

"Oh, Dutch, may I go with you? I got an email the supplies I ordered are in."

"Surely. I'll meet you at the ranch truck."

She turned and looked at Tripp. "I'll have the vet visit notes typed up and on your desk as soon as I get back."

"This afternoon is fine." Tripp glanced at the clock. "What about your lunch break?"

"Oh, I'll have a yogurt when I get back."

"Aren't you supposed to be eating for two?"

She frowned. "You're an obstetrician in your spare time?"

"Have you been to one lately?"

"It's on my list." She cocked her head and gave him a slow assessment. "Burr under your saddle?"

"Not that I know of."

She opened the bottom drawer of her desk and reached for her purse. "Maybe you're right about lunch. Today's the meat loaf special at the diner. I'll take Dutch with me."

"Great," Tripp muttered as she left. He'd been so rushed he hadn't even packed a lunch today, and he was pretty sure he'd memorized the contents of the mini-fridge. Opening the door, he stared. An apple and a jar of crunchy peanut butter stared back at him.

If he had more sense, he would have offered to take Dutch and Hannah out to eat himself. He reached for the apple. No one ever accused Tripp Walker of having too much sense.

Chapter Five

Hannah slid into a chair at the table in the chow hall on Friday morning. The combination cafeteria and gathering room for special events had enough long laminated picnic-like tables and chairs for the entire ranch. The walls were covered with framed, enlarged photographs of ranch events. Hannah spotted Tripp in more than one picture, always with the horses and the ranch children. Her heart did a little leap at the rare smile that had been captured in one particular photo. The man related to four-legged animals and kids. Adults, not so much. Why was that?

She glanced at the big schoolhouse clock and paced back and forth, becoming more and more nervous.

"Hannah! You're early."

Hannah turned at the oldest Maxwell's voice. Lucy's administrative assistant, Iris, trailed behind, talking on her cell phone while writing on a clipboard. Both wore red T-shirts bearing the Big Heart Ranch logo. "So glad you're here," Lucy continued.

"I'm happy to help, though I don't know what I can do." *And I have no clue why you would want me to help.*

"We need some fresh ideas and you're part of the brainstorming process," Lucy said, clearly reading her mind. She put a folder on a table and sat down. Iris placed a legal pad next to Lucy and slipped into a chair.

"Sorry I'm late," Emma Maxwell Norman called as she pushed through the glass doors. "Meeting with the twins' teacher. They've been fighting over a boy in class."

Lucy chuckled. "And so it begins."

"Not funny, Luce. They're three—that's too young for relationship issues. Zach is going to have to deal with this tonight." Emma frowned and sat down next to Hannah. "Hey, Hannah. How's Clementine liking the childcare program?"

"I think it's safe to say she loves it. She gets up early every morning to get ready. The program challenges her and she talks nonstop about all her new friends."

"I'm so glad to hear that," Emma said. "The reports I've heard have been glowing. Clementine is very bright." She leaned closer. "Probably gifted, and she loves the interaction. The teachers adore her."

"Thanks for sharing that." Hannah smiled. "In truth, it makes it so much easier for me to leave her when I know she wants to be there."

"Of course. Trust me. It's hard for all of us." She met Hannah's gaze. "What do you think about your new boss?"

Hannah mulled the question for a moment, not sure how to answer.

Emma chuckled. "That wasn't a trick question."

"He's always prepared," Hannah finally said.

Once again, Emma laughed. "Isn't that, like, the Boy Scout motto?"

"I don't mean any offense," Hannah backpedaled. "I'm very appreciative of the opportunity, but it's been a challenge to figure out Tripp."

"Yes. Welcome to our world," Emma said.

"How long have you and Lucy known him?"

"Eight years," Lucy piped in. "He was our first employee, followed by Dutch soon after. We started the ranch with six children and two heifers."

"Where is Tripp from?"

"Are you kidding? That drawl of his is pure Texoma." Lucy laughed. "Which reminds me, how's that horse challenge coming along?"

"Calamity Jane is very responsive. I have no doubts Tripp will win."

"Wonderful."

Emma glanced at her watch and then looked at her sister. "Who else is coming?"

"AJ was going to participate," Lucy said. "But she had an obstetrician appointment."

"Here I am," AJ called as she waddled into the room with a hand to her lower back. "I rescheduled."

"Was that wise?" Emma asked. "You look like you're ready to pop."

"I'm sure she means that in a good way," Lucy said.

"I'm fine," AJ said as she eased herself down to a bench. "I have two months left, and this baby is doing calisthenics already. They've checked me for gestational diabetes but everything is fine. Travis Junior is simply going to be a big kid."

"Football player," Lucy said.

"Yes. Naturally, Travis says OSU, but I'm pulling for crimson and cream. University of Oklahoma all the way."

Hannah listened to the friendly exchange, amused. She had only met AJ Maxwell, Travis's wife, once, but the spunky blonde ranch foreman was seven months pregnant and still out doing chores while driving the ranch all-terrain vehicle. She'd seen AJ's name on the schedule for fence checking just this week. Hannah would have to find a subtle way to bring that information into the next conversation with her stubborn boss. Though subtle probably wasn't going to work. The man needed a two-by-four wake-up call that she wasn't a fragile flower, nor a stick of dynamite ready to explode.

Lucy's gaze moved from Hannah's loose denim shirt to AJ's maternity top to Emma's baggy white oxford boyfriend shirt. She smiled and turned to Iris. "Okay, I don't know how this slipped past me. Could you check into staff maternity shirts?"

"I'm on it," the admin said as she scribbled on her clipboard once again.

"Good morning, ladies," Rue said as she strolled into the room with a travel mug of coffee in her hand. "What have you wrangled me into this time, Lucy?"

"Nothing dangerous. I promise," Lucy said.

"This from the woman who organizes scavenger hunts on the summer trail rides."

"This idea is much safer and there are no children involved. I'm trying to encourage more female members of the staff to get on board with the Pawhuska Orphanage outreach that the Timber Community Church does each year. Summer is our give back time. The guys took over the rodeo at the end of summer, but we need something targeted to involve women of all ages."

"What did you have in mind, Luce?" Emma asked.

"It seems like we've done everything. I'm out of new ideas."

"Auctioning picnic baskets went well last year," Emma said.

"Then how about we auction off something even more intriguing. A bachelor, perhaps?" Rue suggested.

Lucy shook her head. "That leaves out our married women and we've had a spurt in those the last few years."

Rue eyed the women on the other side of the table over her mug. "True enough. I heard that sweet wrangler AJ hired, Josee Queen, is engaged."

"She is. He proposed just last night," AJ confirmed. "Marrying that nice vet, Trent Blaylock, thanks to our Hannah."

"Hannah? Are you a matchmaker?" Lucy asked with a smile.

Hannah's face warmed as all eyes turned to her. "No. The match has been in progress for months apparently. Trent asked, and I gave him a little advice on how to pop the question."

"It worked," Rue said. "Well played."

"What about you, Rue? Any plans to settle down?" AJ asked.

The doctor's eyes rounded. "I thought I was settled down. I'm retired after thirty years of being married to the army, aren't I?" She grinned. "Why would I want to complicate things?"

"I always sort of thought that you and Dutch might get hitched someday," AJ added with a conspiratorial wink.

Rue released an unladylike snort. "In the words of Dutch Stevens, if it ain't broke, don't fix it."

"You've never wanted to marry?" Emma asked.

Rue closed her eyes and opened them, glancing around the table. "I must be hallucinating. For a moment I thought we were at the Timber Big Hair Emporium slinging gossip like Aqua Net hairspray."

When AJ burst into a fit of giggles, Hannah put a hand to her mouth to suppress her own laughter. This was more fun than she'd had in a long time.

"Point well taken, Rue." Lucy held up a hand and chuckled. "Back to church business."

Emma wiped her eyes and took a deep breath. "What do you think about doing something along with the summer church picnic this year? The Sunday of Fourth of July weekend? Attendance is high with lots of tourists in town."

"Sounds like a great way to bring in donations for the orphanage," Rue said.

"We could do a fun run. Five kilometer," Lucy said.

"I'm sorry, but I do not run," Rue said. "At this stage in my life, trust me, if I'm running, I'm being chased."

AJ rolled her eyes. "I agree. Y'all can run if you like, but I cannot see myself even waddling five kilometers in this heat."

"How about an old-fashioned cakewalk?" Hannah asked. "Anyone with a spatula and a recipe can participate, and there's no real exercise involved."

All heads turned to her and she swallowed.

"Oh, my, this is a wonderful idea," Lucy said.

"How exactly does a cakewalk work?" Emma asked.

"We did them in my home church in Denver when I was growing up," Hannah said. "The cakes are on display before the event starts. Numbers are taped to the ground to form a circle. Tickets to participate are sold."

She looked around to be sure everyone was following her explanation.

"Everyone who purchased a ticket starts walking on the numbered squares while the band plays music. When they stop playing music, you stop on a numbered square. A number is drawn from a hat and whoever is on that number gets to pick the cake of their choice and is out of the game."

"Does that mean some people don't get a cake?" AJ asked.

"Yes," Hannah said. "Usually there are consolation prizes offered."

"I like it!" Rue said. "We could do this in the church meeting hall. It would keep the cakes cool and we can easily tape numbers to the floor. In fact, I'm sure Dutch and some of his buddies will play music for us."

"Dutch plays an instrument?" Hannah asked.

"He plays a mean fiddle," Rue said. "His band will be playing at the Spring Social again this year."

"Spring Social?" Hannah asked.

"It's a town party with music and food, held the Friday night before the Fourth of July weekend celebrations," Rue said. "Long-standing tradition around here."

"Since the town of Timber is so supportive of Big Heart Ranch, we encourage staff support of the social, the rodeo and the parade," Lucy said. "So we hope to see you at as many events as you can get to."

"I see," Hannah said. Her stomach churned. She'd had a lifetime of being social.

Lucy turned to her administrative assistant. "Iris, what do you think about the idea? Will it bring in the younger women, as well?"

Iris nodded. "I like the cakewalk idea, but maybe

it would add to the fun if the baker shares the dessert with the winner of their cake."

"But what if someone other than your fella picks your cake?" Emma asked. "You'd have to have dessert with them."

Lucy laughed. "Oh, the fun is in accidentally-on-purpose letting your fella find out which cake is yours. That obligates them to buy a ticket and play."

Rue burst out laughing. "Oh, Lucy, I like how you think. You're going to make quite a few menfolk squirm."

"And empty their wallets," Emma said.

"Occasionally, it's nice to have the upper hand," Lucy said with a serene smile.

"I'm in," Emma said. "Competition. Cake. What's not to like?"

"Oh, so am I," AJ said. "Hannah, this is a fabulous idea."

Hannah blinked as she realized what her idea had morphed into. Sharing her cake with someone? Suddenly her fabulous idea didn't seem quite so fabulous.

"We can have some fun prize drawings for those who enter their cake and ask the local businesses for contributions," Lucy added.

"I can handle that," AJ said. "It's hard to say no to an expectant woman, and I don't mind using my condition for the church."

"And I'm pretty good with graphic design," Iris said. "I can get some posters for the local businesses and see if the Timber Daily Gazette will give the church a discount in the Sunday paper."

"Great," Lucy said with a satisfied grin. "I'll notify

Pastor Parr and I think the rest of the prep can be done by email."

"Isn't this all coming together nicely?" Emma said as she helped AJ to stand.

"It is," AJ added.

"I'm so glad you're on this committee, Hannah," Lucy said.

Hannah stared at her for a moment. Despite the fact that she'd disrupted their lives with her claims, the Maxwells treated her like she was one of them, with or without a DNA confirmation.

"Thank you, Lucy."

"Did I give you the number of the obstetrician in Pawhuska?" Lucy asked.

"Yes." Hannah grabbed her purse and stood. "I have an appointment scheduled."

"Great. AJ's baby shower is coming up. I hope you'll help us with that, as well. We'll have one for you and Emma in the fall," Lucy said.

"I'd be honored to help." She paused and glanced around. "But I don't even know if I'll be here in the fall."

Lucy looked up from her folder and got to her feet. "Why not? Clementine has started school. You have to settle somewhere. Why not Big Heart Ranch? You fit right in."

"I doubt that Big Heart Ranch will notice if I stay or leave," she said quietly as everyone else left the chow hall.

"Oh, that's not true. All of us will notice, especially Tripp."

"Tripp?" Hannah froze at the comment.

"Yes. I've seen the difference in him since you've been here."

Hannah stared at the eldest Maxwell, unsure of what to say.

"The man purposely avoids conversation." Lucy smiled. "It's like a game around here. Who can get the most words out of Tripp Walker? But lately, well, he's had a lot to say."

"I'm sure he does." Hannah grimaced. "My presence has irritated him from day one. For some reason, Tripp really doesn't like me much."

"Not true." Lucy shook her head as she, too, stood. "We have weekly staff meetings. You've been here two weeks, and he speaks highly of you."

"Really?"

"Yes. You know, Tripp is like all men who don't know how to express their feelings. They bark to protect us from finding out they're really a softie inside."

Hannah blinked. "I… I don't know what to say to that, Lucy."

"No response is required. Just keep in mind that maybe, just maybe, you're right where God wants you to be and the good Lord doesn't need any DNA test to tell you that."

"And here I thought things were going so well," Tripp said. He stomped into the stables with Dutch and Hannah following. "We've gone three weeks without any problems. Made it clear to another Friday, even."

"It's my fault, boss."

Tripp turned to Dutch, who now stood outside of the equine office. "Hannah is pregnant." He ground the words out. "You couldn't find anyone else to help you with the fences?"

"It isn't a terminal disease," Hannah murmured.

Dutch wiped his face with a red bandana and grimaced. When the old cowboy looked to Hannah, she stepped forward. Hands on hips, she shoved her dark waves off her shoulder and got right in Tripp's face. Fire lit her eyes as she met his gaze.

"Don't blame Dutch. It isn't his fault and I won't have him thrown under the bus for my actions. I told him it was okay for me to help and practically twisted his arm to let me assist."

Stunned, Tripp opened his mouth and closed it again. His quiet assistant had morphed into a raging spitfire.

"AJ is pregnant and so is Emma," Hannah continued. "They're still on the schedule. And for the record, I was simply helping. I rode in the ute."

He took a calming breath. "Your job is in the equine center. We've already had this discussion."

"I was all caught up in the office. Even the stable chores were completed."

"You can't play internet solitaire like everyone else?" he asked.

"You pay me for eight hours, so I work eight hours." She waved a hand at the office. "This is a bit under-challenging for my skill set."

"This is your job."

"I'm not going to collect my share of the winnings for doing nothing. That's not how I operate. If I don't earn the money, then I don't want the money."

Tripp shrugged. "I'm happy to take your share."

"That's not what I said. I intend to earn my share."

Dutch pulled off his straw cowboy hat and then slapped it back on as he looked from Hannah to Tripp. "Whoo-ee. You two are as much fun as being caught in a thunderstorm in your long johns." He turned on his heel.

"Where are you going?" Tripp asked.

"It's Friday afternoon. I'm a free man in two hours. I'm gonna go seek shelter until this particular storm passes."

Rue stepped into the stables as Dutch stomped out, her arms filled with a large crystal vase of flowers. Her gaze followed Dutch as she approached the office. "Everything all right in here?"

"Fine," Tripp said at the same time as Hannah.

"Sounds like it," she said. "These are for your assistant."

"Me?" A pleased smile curved Hannah's lips. She took the vase and brought it to her desk before plucking the card from the center.

"Lovely flowers, aren't they?" Rue said to Tripp.

Tripp glanced at the arrangement and scowled. He didn't know much about flowers, but they looked impressive and expensive. "Yeah. *Lovely.*"

"Trent Blaylock sent them."

"Trent? Why would the vet be sending Hannah flowers?"

Rue offered a secret little smile before she turned to leave. "Maybe you should ask her."

Tripp stared through the glass at Hannah, trying to figure out why the woman kept vexing him at every turn.

When his desk phone rang, Hannah picked it up. "Big Heart Ranch Equine Center. Hannah speaking." She nodded. "Sure. Let me ask Tripp."

She stepped out of the office with the portable phone in her hand. "Lucy wants to know if you can meet with her and the architect regarding the addition to the girls' ranch equine center on Monday."

"I thought you and Lucy were going to Tulsa for that lab testing Monday."

"She had to cancel," Hannah said.

Tripp resisted the urge to growl. Nothing was going right today, and now Lucy was messing with his calendar.

"What do you want me to tell Lucy?" Hannah asked quietly.

"Tell her I'm headed to the admin building now." He glanced at the flowers again. "Nice flowers."

"Thank you."

Tripp stomped to the administration building and straight past Iris Banner who manned the front desk, stuffing flyers into envelopes.

"Morning, Tripp."

"Morning." He kept moving down the hall, stopping in the doorway of Lucy's office. As always, he paused cautiously on the threshold before entering. Lucy's office had the distinction of looking like an Oklahoma twister just hit. It had gotten better since her husband hired Iris to help out. But not much.

"You can come in," she called from behind her desk.

He took a hesitant step into the dimly lit room. "I'm never sure if it's safe."

"It's before the F1 hits you have to worry. Not after."

"That's your story."

Lucy stood and stepped from around her desk. She cleared a stack of papers from a chair and gestured for him to sit.

"This is where you greet ranch guests?" Tripp asked.

"Give me some credit, Tripp. I use our very professional conference room for guests and business associates."

Tripp crossed his arms and frowned.

"We have established that you woke up on the wrong side of the bed." She sat down again and picked up a mug. "Will coffee help?"

"I'm good."

Lucy arched a brow as if to contradict that statement. "To what do I owe this pleasure?"

"Why did you cancel the DNA testing?"

"Is there a rush?"

"Hannah Vincent claims to be your half sister."

"That and two dollars will get you a pecan muffin at the Timber Diner. I don't understand the problem."

"What if she's not?"

She shrugged. "Then Hannah is an employee of Big Heart Ranch, like everyone else."

"Lucy, it seems to me you aren't taking this seriously. As I recall, you were pretty broken up the day she arrived."

"I was shocked. As was Hannah."

"What's changed?"

"I've had time to think and pray about the situation. Knee-jerking is never a good idea."

"I don't know. Going with my gut has served me well."

"What exactly is your gut telling you?"

He released a breath. "That maybe she's scamming the ranch."

"Tripp, I am the director of a children's ranch. Sixty children call Big Heart Ranch their forever home. Do you honestly think I wouldn't have Hannah checked out even more than the usual candidates?"

"So we're on the same page?"

"Not exactly. My page says cautious and yours says cynical and distrustful."

"Same thing."

"Not really. I've been where Hannah is. When I met Jack, you'll recall he was the in-house counsel for his aunt's foundation. The foundation that supports Big Heart Ranch. He thought we were snake oil salesmen."

Tripp nodded, recalling that day nearly two years ago.

"In addition to the regular background check, I've asked Jack to dig a little deeper."

"Slats Milburn says he found something."

Lucy's eyes rounded, and she shook her head. "Tell me you did not ask that slimy detective to snoop around in our business."

"I'm afraid I can't tell you that. What I can tell you is that I hired him and then fired him."

"You hired him, why? Because you thought I wasn't able to handle the situation?"

"When was the last time someone showed up at the ranch claiming to be your kin?"

This time Lucy groaned and rubbed the middle of her forehead with two fingers.

"I wasn't thinking," Tripp said. "We can agree on that. That's why I fired him before I even got a report."

"Then how do you know he has information?"

"He told me so, but I hung up on him."

"Maybe you better at least find out what the man has to say."

Tripp pushed his hat to the back of his head and grimaced. "I was afraid you'd say that."

"Please?"

"I'll do it." He met Lucy's gaze. "You don't believe she's Jake's daughter, do you?"

"It doesn't matter what I believe. What matters is that we are slow to judge and quick to love."

"Lucy, that doesn't answer my question."

The oldest Maxwell released a breath. "I've combed through those letters of Hannah's, and it's all about perspective. The way I see things, my father did have a relationship with Hannah's mother, but I believe they were very close friends. I don't read anything more than that into any of those missives. Hannah sees what she wants to see in those letters. Maybe what she needs to see."

"Are you going to tell her that?"

"I don't think that's necessary. Eventually, she's going to figure that out for herself. When she does, it's our job to support her."

"You've obviously got something planned here."

"Actually, I don't. Hannah is a good person, and she's looking for what everyone at Big Heart Ranch is looking for. A second chance. Family. Unconditional love."

When Lucy met his gaze, he didn't like what he saw. "You got a second chance, Tripp. So did I. Does Hannah Vincent deserve anything less?"

"That's all fine and dandy, and it's plenty clear that you're a much nicer person than I am. But you have to tell her, eventually. Get the DNA testing done and all."

"I will. But can it hurt to put this off a little bit longer?"

"I don't know, Lucy. It might hurt more for her to go on thinking she's a Maxwell."

"I'd like Hannah to realize that she's safe here. Safe from whatever it is she's been running from." She looked him in the eye. "I think it's clear something has kept her off the grid and working far below her potential for the last few years."

Tripp was silent at the words. Lucy was right. Hannah had been on the run, with Clementine never leaving her sight.

"Look, Tripp, I'm giving Hannah the benefit of the doubt. But I'm also doing what's right for the ranch. I believe the good Lord sent her to Big Heart Ranch for a reason."

"A reason?"

"Maybe it's just that Hannah, Clementine and Hannah's unborn child need a family. This ranch is all about finding forever homes."

"I don't know," he grumbled.

"What have you got against Hannah Vincent?"

"Lucy, you believe in the good in everyone. I admire you for that. But I can't be that trusting."

"Why not, Tripp?"

Tripp rubbed the scar on his face. "I'm not going there. You're going to have to take my word on this." He looked away, shoving back memories of another single mother who was cavalier about her child and her pregnancy. "Trust has to be earned."

Chapter Six

Hannah opened the tailgate of the pickup truck and reached for one of the boxes of supplies stacked on the sidewalk outside the feed and tack store.

"Hold it right there, little momma," Dutch Stevens called out. He strode outside and stepped between her and the boxes. "You trying to get me in trouble with the boss?"

"This is becoming beyond ridiculous," Hannah muttered. "The West would not have been settled if homesteading women sat around doing nothing. Why, they had babies one day and were out baling hay the next."

"Yep."

"Ranch women are the unsung heroes of the West, in my opinion," Hannah continued. She was on a roll now and couldn't stop if she tried. All her frustration from the last few weeks bubbled over.

"You're preaching to the choir. Maybe you should take that up with Tripp."

Hannah groaned. "Take it up with Marshal Dillon? No, he doesn't listen to Miss Kitty. You should talk to him."

"Are you calling me Festus?"

"Dutch," she pleaded. "I need help."

The cowboy shook his head adamantly. "Hey, this ain't my circus. You may like living life dangerously, going toe-to-toe with the man, but not me. These are my golden years and I plan to cruise on autopilot straight to retirement. I am not looking for problems."

"Your golden years?"

"Yes, ma'am."

He chuckled as he lifted a box into the truck bed. "Pretty funny when you think about it."

"What's funny?"

"A little thing like you getting in Tripp's face on Friday. The man is at least six foot five."

"I'm glad I can entertain you." Hannah glanced down the street in time to see a tall, rail-thin cowboy get out of a rusty truck. The man narrowed his eyes and stared at her before he turned and started down the sidewalk toward the diner. "Dutch, who is that cowboy?"

"Slats Milburn."

"Who is Slats Milburn?"

Dutch heaved another box up and slid it into the bed of the pickup with a grunt. "Washed-up rodeo clown."

"What does a washed-up rodeo clown do for a living?"

"A little wrangling here and there. Odd jobs. Security. You know, watching herds and lots of such stuff."

"Such stuff?"

The wrangler leaned closer and did a quick look around. "Slats is the guy you call if you need to check something out," he said in hushed tones.

"Check something out?"

"You know, investigate your sister's new boyfriend,

or locate your missing cattle. He's kind of sketchy, but he gets the job done. Slats is the guy who found AJ's horse when it was stolen. Though you didn't hear that from me."

"Seriously?" Hannah shivered as the man disappeared from sight.

"Somebody's gotta do it." Dutch dusted off his hands and wiped his forehead with his sleeve. He shot a quick glance at the sky before slamming the tailgate of the pickup shut. "Monday morning and it's already ninety degrees and nary a cloud in sight. Not a breeze to be found, neither. The only thing moving around here are the flies."

"Is it always this hot in mid-June?" Hannah asked.

"Depends on how fickle Mother Nature is feeling." He tossed his keys in the air. "Ready to go?"

Hannah nodded as Dutch stepped around the truck and plucked a flyer from the windshield before he got in the cab.

"What's this?" she asked, turning over the colorful paper on the seat between them.

"Timber Fourth of July rodeo is coming right up."

"Is anyone from Big Heart Ranch participating?" she asked Dutch.

"Oh, probably some of our young college-aged wranglers, but not the Maxwells. Travis had the good sense to retire after he nearly killed himself last year. And everyone else either has a bun in the oven or they're too busy with their own families and the ranch."

Dutch raised a palm to thank and acknowledge the truck behind him that waited as he backed out of the parking spot.

"What about Tripp?" Hannah asked.

"Oh, he never competes anymore. Used to, though, and he was good."

"Why not?"

"Tripp isn't about competition. Not an adrenaline junkie like most cowboys."

"He's doing the 100-Day Challenge," Hannah countered. "That's pretty competitive."

The cowboy turned left at the intersection of Main and Cedar Avenue and headed out of town. "That's just training them so they'll get adopted. Our Tripp is a bit of an animal activist. Lucy and Emma advocate for the children of Big Heart. Travis for the cows. AJ for the bison. And Rue looks out for those crazy chickens. Our Tripp advocates for every horse and donkey in a fifty-mile radius."

"How long has he been training horses?"

"No idea. Tripp Walker is a man of mystery. Showed up eight years ago when the ranch was getting started. Maybe you should ask him."

"Me?"

"He talks to you more than I've ever seen him talk to anyone outside of the Maxwells. While you're at it, could you ask him to share his prize-winning chili recipe? Been trying to get that for years."

"Tripp has a prize-winning chili recipe?"

"Yep, he's won every year since they started the competition at the ranch rodeo."

"Wait, there's a rodeo in Timber *and* at the ranch?"

"Missy, you're going to have to try to keep up." Dutch frowned, his bushy gray eyebrows nearly coming together.

"The Timber rodeo is part of the town's Fourth of

July celebration. Mostly for the tourists. Our rodeo is for kids."

"Oh." She offered a nod.

Dutch looked at her and frowned. "No, you don't get it. This is huge. We have a full-on barbecue and chili cook-off with the rodeo. It's the end of summer for the kids visiting from the Pawhuska Orphanage, and all the children who graduated and left the ranch return. It's huge, I tell you. Huge. One of two times they open the ranch to the public. The other being Christmas."

"Wow. I had no idea." Hannah paused. "But you said Tripp isn't into competition."

"That's right. But he is into cooking. Whoo-ee can that man cook. He cooks and wins. No competition about it."

"Tripp cooks." She said the words with stunned disbelief.

"As I recall, AJ said the same thing. She found out what I'm talking about at Thanksgiving." Dutch laughed. "No one's ever mentioned this before?"

"That's a factoid I would not have forgotten."

"He's like some kind of gourmet. Why, the entire staff holds their breath at the holidays, waiting to find out what Tripp is going to bring. The man makes your taste buds roll over and beg for more."

Hannah blinked. "Tripp Walker?"

Dutch chuckled. "Sure enough. He has a big old cookbook held together by rubber bands and he has his own set of knives. Keeps them with his Bible. Man could easily have his own show on that cooking channel."

Hannah cocked her head and looked at him. "Are you pulling my leg?"

"Ask anyone. He's got these spinach lasagna roll-ups that melt in your mouth." A grin split Dutch's face. "It gets better. Tripp is a vegetarian."

"A vegetarian equine manager on a cattle and bison ranch who is a gourmet cook and wins the chili cook-off. Do I have that right?"

"Sure do." He smacked his lips. "Mmm, mmm. That's how good his chili is. Vegetarian chili and the man always wins." Dutch shot her a quick glance. "Wait a minute. You said you cook. Have you got a winning chili recipe in your back pocket?"

Hannah hesitated. "You know, I just might."

"Think about entering. There's a small cash prize, and they throw in some fancy pots and pans, oh, and dinner at the Oklahoma Rose."

"How small a cash prize?"

"I do believe it was one hundred dollars last year. But there's a fifty-dollar entry fee. The entry goes toward the orphanage in Pawhuska. They send the kids back at the end of summer with something for the facility. Last year it was a big-screen television."

Hannah pondered the idea for two seconds. "How do I sign up?"

"Iris over at the admin office will collect your money." Dutch laughed and slapped the steering wheel with his palm. "This is gonna be fun."

Hannah smiled serenely. She'd walked many roads in life and worn many hats, but the fact was she could cook. That was the reason the Dripping Falls Diner had called twice since she left, wanting to know when she was coming back.

If circumstances were different, she could work in any fine dining restaurant, but she chose to slide under the radar for Clementine. To protect her daughter.

"What kind of chili do you make?" Dutch asked.

"I can't tell you that." She turned back to the old

cowboy. "Don't you tell him that I'm considering entering the contest."

"My lips are sealed. But if you're looking for someone to taste-test, I'm your man."

They rode in silence for moments. Finally, Dutch chuckled and shot her a glance. His eyes sparkled with mirth. "You sure you're up to this?"

"Excuse me? What's the big deal?"

"Tripp has an entire posse cheering him on."

"A posse?"

"Yep. People come out of the woodwork to watch him prepare his chili. They all pray for a sample before the judging."

Hannah stared at Dutch. "Tripp Walker?"

"Why do you keep asking me that?"

"I've been working with the man for nearly five weeks now and as far as I can tell, he's reclusive. I can't believe he'd be willing to be in the public eye."

"Tripp has a soft spot for orphans. He'll put up with a whole lot of attention if it will benefit orphans or horses. Maybe you should ask him about the stuff he does for the kids. Stuff he thinks no one knows about."

Hannah shook her head. "No. Haven't you heard anything I said? Tripp and I don't do well with conversation. I'm certainly not going to ask about his secrets."

"You two communicate. You just go at it like you're old married folk." He released a loud snort.

"That's not true at all," Hannah insisted.

"Sure it is. I think you like arguing with him."

Dutch approached the Big Heart Ranch security gate, rolled down his window and held out his electronic badge. When the arm slowly raised, he drove in and then turned left into the equine center parking area.

"I'm not about to let the man run over me," Hannah huffed. "And just because no one has ever dared to challenge him before doesn't mean I won't."

Laughter spilled from the wrangler as he turned off the engine and got out of the truck.

"What's so funny?" Hannah asked.

"Not a thing. Not a single thing." He grinned. "You know what, Hannah? You're all right. I hope you stick around."

"The Dutch seal of approval?" Hannah smiled at the cowboy, finding herself inordinately pleased with the words. Could it be she was really fitting in at Big Heart Ranch?

"You betcha." He nodded toward the truck bed. "Leave those boxes for now. I've got one of our college kids working with me for the summer. He's going to take care of them."

"What are you going to do next?"

"Got an appointment with Rowdy. I've been giving our resident troublemaker saddle time each day, getting him ready to be put in the schedule. Think I'll give him a little ride before the kids start showing up for lessons."

"I'm in the office if you need anything."

The sounds of a busy stable drifted into the open equine office as Hannah answered emails and checked inventory. Every now and then Dutch could be heard as he took long minutes grooming the gelding.

"Easy, boy," he murmured. "Don't you be pulling faces at me. I'm the boss here."

"Everything, okay, Dutch?" Hannah called.

"Aw, he's fine," Dutch called out. "We're friends, ain't we, Rowdy?"

When things got quiet, Hannah glanced at the clock.

Nearly noon. Everyone was off grabbing lunch. The only sound was Dutch arguing with Rowdy.

An ominous chill raced over Hannah.

She got up and stood outside Rowdy's stall, debating whether she should say something. But the only words that came to mind were admonitions to use care. Dutch was an experienced horseman who wouldn't appreciate her interference any more than she would have appreciated his. Hannah bit her lip and kept her mouth shut.

The old cowboy eased the saddle on Rowdy and began to adjust the cinch. "Stand back. I can't say I trust this horse yet and the boss will cut off my mustache if he finds out it was my fault you got hurt."

"Hand me those grooming tools and I'll put them away," Hannah said.

When Dutch handed her a soft brush and currycomb, she headed to the tack room. A heartbeat later, Rowdy's agitated whinny filled the morning silence.

"What's got into you, boy?" Dutch said. "Whoa, Rowdy."

A loud bang echoed through the stables, followed by a reverberating thud.

"Dutch? Everything okay?"

Hannah raced back into the center aisle of the stables to Rowdy's stall. Dutch Stevens lay slumped against the wood slats. Panic slammed through her at the sight of his pale face, eyes closed. Her heartbeat pounded in her ears as she yelled his name. "Dutch!"

Ears flat, Rowdy ducked his head and shook his mane.

Without thinking, Hannah pulled open the stall door and stayed behind the gate, releasing Rowdy. The horse whinnied and danced, then burst out of the stall into the center arena of the stables, dragging his lead rope on the ground.

When the horse was clear, Hannah stepped into the stall. Kneeling in the hay, she slid her fingers to Dutch's neck and the carotid artery.

Her shaking fingers were rewarded with a pulse. His breaths were shallow, though, and he remained unconscious.

A cursory check with her fingers revealed what seemed to be a small cut to the back of his head. Hannah grimaced at the amount of blood that covered her hand.

"Dutch, can you hear me?" She pulled her bandana from her pocket and applied pressure to the site while continuing to assess the cowboy.

"What can we do to help, Hannah?"

Hannah looked up at the voice, relieved to see Josee Queen and Tanya Starnes. Travis's lead wranglers leaned over the stall, their worried gazes moving from the agitated horse to the man on the ground.

"Call 9-1-1, and then get Rowdy into the corral. Keep the children out of here."

"Yes, ma'am," Tanya said with a nod.

"Whoa, boy. Easy," Josee murmured as she picked up Rowdy's lead rope.

Concerned staff rushed into the stables, offering assistance once Rowdy was outside.

Hannah kept her hand firmly on Dutch's wound as she yelled to another wrangler. "Someone please go and find Rue and Tripp."

Eyes fixed on the weathered cowboy, Hannah bit back tears and offered a silent prayer. *Take care of Dutch, Lord.*

* * *

The door to the bunkhouse creaked and opened. Hannah turned from her position leaning against the porch post. Rue Butterfield was silhouetted by the light of the kitchen.

"Is Clementine still sleeping?"

"Yes. Your daughter can sleep through anything."

"A blessing," Hannah murmured.

"Yes." Rue stepped onto the dark porch. "Honey, are you okay?"

Hannah nodded and gripped the railing. "I just can't stop thinking about Dutch." Every time she closed her eyes she saw the cowboy crumpled in the stall.

"The hospital tells me it's a few bruised ribs, a laceration to this head and a slight concussion."

"There was so much blood."

"Looked worse than it was. Those head wounds bleed heavily, so they stitched it up. Fortunately, that old cowboy has a hard head."

Hannah swallowed. "I've never been more scared."

"Yet, you responded like a pro. I'm so proud of you."

"Thank you, Rue." She frowned. "You're sure Dutch will be okay?"

"He'll be fine. I'd stay at the hospital but it might interfere with all the attention he's getting. Right now he's being waited on by a cute nurse who's doing neuro checks on him every hour and monitoring his IV antibiotics. Dutch is in cowboy paradise."

Hannah smiled.

"And trust me, he's going to milk this as best he can. It's not going to help that AJ will make him her special blackberry pie. Emma is no doubt right now whipping up chocolate muffins. Lucy can't cook so she'll go into Pawhuska for cookies from her favorite bakery."

"Dutch is well loved," Hannah murmured.

"Yes. That old codger is one of a kind." Rue offered a tender smile.

"What's Dutch's favorite cake?"

"Ha! You, too?"

"It'll be good practice for the cakewalk."

"All right then, German chocolate for sure." The older woman nodded as she settled into a rocking chair. "He'll love that, though he'll likely not be able to get his swelled head through a door anytime soon."

"I can live with that," Hannah said. She turned to Rue. "Are you spending the night here?"

"If you don't mind?"

"Mind? No. Clementine and I love having you for a roommate."

"That's good because the summer has begun at Big Heart Ranch. Children from the orphanage are bussed in daily for vacation Bible study. The trail ride schedule is up and the ranch buddy plan is in full swing. I'm on call 24/7 from now until the end of August."

"I noticed how busy the stables have gotten."

"Busy is an understatement. But I wouldn't have it any other way."

Hannah glanced back inside the bunkhouse. "Would you mind keeping an ear out for Clementine? I'm going to take a walk."

"Sure. Take your time."

"Momma?" As if on cue, Clementine appeared at the door, her pink pony clutched under her arm. She rubbed her eyes with her fingers.

"I thought you were sleeping, sweetie," Hannah said.

"Can I have a glass of water?"

"May I?"

"May I?" Clementine repeated.

When Hannah stood, Rue put a hand on her arm. "Take your walk. I have this."

"You're sure?"

Rue nodded as she reached for the screen door. "It's a glass of water, dear. Go. We'll be fine."

Hannah strolled across the grass toward the gravel and dirt road. Ahead of her, the sun had dipped behind the old barn and now the only thing that remained was a soft pink glow against the velvety black sky. Reaching down, Hannah spotted a dandelion. She plucked the yellow flower and twirled it between her fingers.

With a low whistle, she called Jane and was rewarded by the soft thud of hooves pounding across the red dirt and hay as the horse moved across the pen in the dark. Hannah opened the barn door and turned on the switch that would illuminate the circular pen with a soft pink glow. Overhead, the mercury lamp sizzled.

From behind the fence, Jane offered Hannah a welcoming snuffle.

"Hey, girl, how you doing tonight?"

The horse nodded her head in response and nudged her nose through the fence in greeting. Hannah rubbed the mare's satin neck and stared deep into her dark chocolate eyes.

"You're going to win, Jane."

Jane nickered.

"Are you ready to practice?" Without waiting for a response, Hannah walked around the outside of the fence in a complete circle with Jane following on the inside.

Hannah stopped.

Jane stopped.

Hannah changed direction and the horse did the same.

"Good girl. Now let's walk backward." Hannah stepped back and so did Jane."

They repeated the process over and over again until Hannah stopped to reward Jane with a nose rub.

"Good girl."

"What are you doing?"

Hannah tensed and whirled around to face Tripp. "A little protected contact training. You'll note that I am not in the pen."

"So I see." He glanced at Jane. "You two have done this before."

"A time or two."

"I knew something was going on. Never have seen a horse so willing to follow."

"She's an amazing horse." Hannah turned to Jane and smiled.

"You're falling in love with this mare," Tripp said after a minute.

"Maybe," Hannah murmured, turning back to Jane.

"Not a good idea, Hannah. She's going to auction after the challenge."

"It can't hurt anything to love her."

"As long as you can let go," he said softly. He, too, turned to Jane. "She sure likes getting attention from both of us."

"Hasn't hurt anything. I think it only ensures she's going to be a winner." Hannah smiled. "Besides, I'm not really training her. Just following up on what you've already done."

"Don't sell yourself short. I was watching for quite a while."

Hannah smiled to herself.

"Have you been inside the pen?"

She glanced at him. "I promised I wouldn't."

Tripp seemed to relax at her words. He stood next to Hannah, loped his arms over a rail of the fence and stared out into the night. Before them the sky stretched far and wide, unobscured by buildings. A thin band of crimson from the departing sunset continued to backlight the darkness.

"Red sky," Tripp observed.

"You can almost smell the rain coming in. The air is heavy with loam," Hannah agreed.

"We could use a good storm, though Travis won't be too happy."

"Travis?"

"AJ and Emma are out of commission for trail rides this year. So he's replacing them. Three days under the stars with the ranch children. Rain can make things mighty uncomfortable."

An easy silence stretched between them as they stood enjoying the evening. The sound of frogs and crickets could be heard from the pond. A barn owl hooted in the distance.

"You saved Dutch's life today," Tripp said.

"I did exactly what you would have done."

"Maybe so. But you didn't panic. You were calm. Directed the staff and kept the children out of the way." He shook his head.

She shrugged. "Like I said. You would have reacted exactly the same."

"Still, pretty impressive."

"For a pregnant woman?" she asked quietly.

"Touché," he returned.

"What will happen to Rowdy?"

"I suspect our Rowdy is claustrophobic. The trailer episode and now in the stall. I'll start by grooming him outside to help his stress and break his response patterns."

"You'll have time to work with Rowdy and train Jane?"

Tripp gestured with a hand. "This is my life."

"I'll do what I can to help more."

"Help more? Is that possible?"

"I can muck stalls. I asked my doctor. He said no riding, of course, but anything that I'm used to doing I can do. With reasonable caution."

Tripp eyed her. "You mucked stalls in Mudville?"

"*Dripping Falls.* And no, but I scrubbed the kitchen on my hands and knees." She met his gaze. "I'll be careful."

"We can talk about it."

Hannah exhaled. *We can talk about it* translated to *topic dismissed.* Would he dismiss her if she was a Maxwell? "Lucy and I go to Tulsa for the DNA testing on Wednesday," she said.

He nodded but said nothing.

"We should have the results in forty-eight hours."

Once again, he didn't respond but continued to keep his attention focused on the mare who moved gracefully around the pen.

"Listen, I want to apologize," Tripp murmured.

"For what?" she asked.

"Come on, you know for what."

"There are so many things. You're going to have to be specific."

A tenuous smile touched his lips. "I've been a bit harsh."

"Yes. You have been. Why is that?"

"I'd say I jumped to conclusions."

"That's *what*. I asked why."

"Hard to explain."

"I've got all night."

"Yeah," he said with a nod. "It might take that long."

She stared at his profile in the soft light. His strong nose and firm lips. Once again, she was impressed by how the scar running down his face only added to his character.

"What happened to your face?" Hannah dared to ask, surprised at her own boldness.

Tripp swallowed and blinked slowly. "My mother pushed me through a window."

Hannah worked hard not to gasp. "How old were you?"

"Sixteen. She was so strung out, she didn't know what she was doing."

"But your mother?" Hannah could barely say the words. "Where is she?"

"She died giving birth. A drug baby. Didn't make it past his first few days." The words were void of emotion.

"I'm so sorry."

"I'm not asking for pity, Hannah."

"Good thing I wasn't offering any." She took a deep breath as she tried to make sense of his tragic admission.

The urge to reach out and touch Tripp Walker was strong. Unable to resist, Hannah reached up and gently touched the scarred side of his face.

Tripp stiffened. Then he covered her hand with his and turned to face her. In that moment, something flickered in his eyes and his gaze almost became tender.

Hannah's chest tightened, and she nearly forgot how to breathe.

Then he released her hand and stepped away, his gaze returning to the mare.

"Mothers are supposed to protect their children," Hannah said, her voice shaky.

"Doesn't always work like that." He nodded toward the brick houses in the distance. Home to the children of Big Heart Ranch. "That's what this place is all about."

Hannah nodded.

"You've been protecting Clementine. Hiding out," he said. Not a question, but a statement.

"Yes." Hannah released a sigh. She was so weary of the sad story of her life.

Tripp faced her again and leaned close. Close enough that she could see the dark circle around the amazing blue of his eyes and smell the scent of horse, hay and man. His gaze skimmed her face as though searching for something. Then he stuffed his hands in his pockets.

"It's getting late," he murmured.

"Yes. It is."

"Good night, Hannah."

"Good night, Tripp."

The cowboy walked away, leaving Hannah trying to figure out what just happened. They'd passed some sort of milestone in their relationship, but she didn't know if she should be pleased or terrified.

Hannah turned to Jane. The wild mustang was much easier to figure out.

Chapter Seven

Something was off. Hannah felt it in the air when she got up in the morning and struggled into her jeans. She was entering her second trimester, and it was about time to break out the maternity clothes that announced to the world that she was a single and pregnant mother.

The good news was she could eat bacon again. Morning sickness had passed.

An envelope addressed to Hannah in Rue's handwriting was propped on the kitchen counter next to the empty cake plate that had held a German chocolate cake a week ago. She slid the notepaper from the envelope.

"Dutch ate the entire cake and says thank you. He also says if your chili is as good as your cake you're going to give Tripp a run for the prize money."

So much for keeping her entering the chili cook-off a secret. Hannah smiled. The old cowboy was supposed to be back at work next week. She missed one of her favorite curmudgeons.

The week had been strange enough as it was without Dutch. Tripp seemed to be avoiding her since their late-night conversation at Jane's corral. Fine, the horse whisperer didn't do well with people. There was no doubt that she had terrified the man. If only he knew that he scared her, too.

Hannah couldn't explain her behavior that night. It was unlike her and she had no defense, except that unless she was arguing with the man, being around Tripp made her all fluttery and nervous at the same time. Arguing was safer, because the rest of the time, she longed to take away the sadness in his eyes. Saving Tripp Walker wasn't her place. She had enough of her own issues to deal with.

"Ready, Clemmie?" Hannah asked her daughter.

"We're early, Momma. The clock hands aren't where they're supposed to be."

"Clementine, sometimes we have to change our routine and that's okay. Momma has a lot of work to do today because it's Friday and the end of the month."

"Friday means that it's almost time for pancake Sunday again. Right?" Clementine said. She hopped from her seat and carried her empty oatmeal bowl to the sink.

Hannah rinsed the bowl and placed it in the dishwasher.

"Right, Momma?"

"Right," Hannah said.

As she answered, she suddenly realized what today was, besides Friday. *Today is the day.*

Hannah glanced at the calendar and shivered. It had been forty-eight hours since she and Lucy had gone to Tulsa for the DNA lab work.

"Where's Miss Rue?" Clementine asked.

"She's out on a trail ride. She'll be back tonight."

"I miss her," Clementine said.

"Me, too. Now go brush your teeth and I'll grab your backpack."

"Yes, Momma."

Hannah picked up the pink backpack from the foot of Clementine's bed. She carefully tidied the quilt and smoothed her daughter's pillow. Glancing around, she noted all the little touches that served to make the bunkhouse feel like home.

Clementine's drawings were tacked to the bulletin board. A bouquet of black-eyed Susan mixed with daisy fleabane picked in the ranch pasture sat on the table between her bed and Clementine's. Propped on Clementine's bureau was a paper menu from the Timber Diner that the five-year-old liked to peruse on Saturday nights before she went to bed, even though she always ordered strawberry pancakes.

Was this their forever home or only another stop on the way? Hannah couldn't shake the ominous feeling that crowded her, dogging her steps as she locked the bunkhouse door and walked to the childcare building while holding her daughter's hand. Once she dropped Clementine off, she started in the direction of the equine center.

The air was thick with the humidity. Low clouds had lingered all week, trapping the world in a dismal gray blanket with either a threat or a promise of rain, depending on your perspective. Hannah preferred sunshine to this gloom.

The light was on in the equine building and the repetitive sound of shovels mucking stalls could be heard as she walked to the office. Nose buried in his laptop, Tripp didn't even look up when she walked in.

"Lucy wants to meet with you at the admin building around nine if that works for you."

Good morning to you, too, Tripp.

"Okay," she said.

Hannah kept her eye on the clock as she worked through the monthly ordering. "I'm ready to send out the feed order for July," she said. "Anything special you wanted to add before I hit Send?"

"No. I'm good."

The only sound in the office was the loud tick of the second hand on the industrial wall clock. It was five minutes to nine. Hannah turned off the monitor. At the last minute, she grabbed her purse from the desk drawer. Just in case.

"I guess I'll get going," she murmured.

Tripp merely nodded.

Hannah counted her steps as she walked along the sidewalk to the administration building.

"Fifty-seven."

Why was she nervous? Jake Maxwell had to be her father. What other explanation could there be for the letters to her mother?

"Ninety-six."

What if he's not? What then?

She stood outside the admin building, staring at the double glass doors.

Then I'll start over. I know how to start over.

Hannah opened the door and stepped inside. Her boots echoed on the tile floor as she walked up to the reception desk. Iris met her gaze.

Was that pity in her eyes?

"Good morning, Hannah." Lucy's admin put a smile on her face. "Is it still dreary out there?"

"Uh, yes, still gray."

"We certainly could use the rain," Iris continued.

"Rain," Hannah murmured, trying to focus. She glanced up at the clock. "I have a nine o'clock appointment with Lucy."

"Yes. Of course. Head on back to the conference room. She's expecting you."

When she entered, Lucy greeted her with a smile. "Hannah." Emma was also in the room. Both stood when she entered and both wore awkward smiles on their faces.

"I hope you don't mind that baby Daniel is here." Lucy waved a hand toward the portable play yard in the back of the room.

"No. Of course not."

Lucy picked up the landline on the table. "Iris, hold all our calls. I'd like no interruptions."

Hannah swallowed back the dread. "DNA results?"

Emma glanced at Lucy, who nodded and shuffled through the files in front of her. "Hannah, I've given this a lot of thought and prayer. I believe our father was a very close friend to your mother. Unfortunately, we, like you, have very few physical memories." She paused and met Hannah's gaze.

Hannah heard everything in Lucy's pained expression and bowed her head before the words reached her ears.

"The results are back on the DNA test. They show no match."

No match.

No family. No plan. No resources.

Nothing.

Nausea choked Hannah. Her heart pounded against

her temples and for a moment darkness swallowed her. She gripped the chair arms, willing herself not to pass out. "I should leave."

"Leave?"

She reached for her purse. "Leave Big Heart Ranch. I'm so embarrassed."

"There's nothing to be embarrassed about," Emma said. Anguish laced her words. "I think we can conclude that your mother and my father must have been very close friends who communicated during a difficult time in her life."

"And I jumped to conclusions because I needed to believe…" Hannah couldn't say the words aloud. *I needed to believe that I was connected to someone. That I had a family. That I mattered to someone.*

"That's not what I'm saying," Emma said. "Jake and Anne's friendship brought you to Big Heart Ranch. You have to believe that you're here for a reason. I do."

"Exactly," Lucy said. "Please, Hannah, we're here for you." Lucy reached out to touch her hand. "We don't want you to leave."

Hannah swallowed. "I need to think."

"Sure. Absolutely," Lucy said. "Take the rest of the day off if you need to."

Clementine. She had to find her daughter.

The sky opened up as she walked back to the child-care building. Rain soaked her, drowning her tears.

"Here, take this umbrella for Clementine," her daughter's teacher said.

Hannah carried Clementine to the Honda parked behind the bunkhouse before she dashed into the cottage to collect a change of clothes for her and Clementine. She opened her bureau and shoved her hand to the back and pulled out an envelope filled with crisp bills. All her paychecks from the ranch that she had cashed and squirreled away for the future. A future she was unsure of, but a future far from this particular moment in time.

Hannah looked at the scribbled tally on the outside of the envelope.

It wouldn't get them far. Back to Missouri and then they'd have to find another furnished apartment and a reliable vehicle.

Maybe she should have taken the offer from her grandmother's estate. Then she wouldn't have to have a backup plan.

No. That money came with too many strings. She could never do that to Clementine or her baby.

"But Momma. Today is watercolor paint day," Clementine said when Hannah returned to the Honda and checked the straps on the booster seat.

"I'll buy you some paints today. Let's take a ride and get ice cream for lunch and pancakes for dinner." She just needed a little time to think and plan. Everything would be fine. It was always fine once she had a plan.

The little car made a funny noise before the engine finally turned over. Hannah released a breath. The windshield wipers slapped an even rhythm as the rain beat down on the windows.

Miles down the road, on the outskirts of Timber, the car began to sputter. Hannah revved the engine. That helped for a moment, but relief was short-lived when minutes later the Honda coughed and choked in earnest.

"Don't die on me now, baby," she muttered as she pulled the vehicle off the road. Another shudder and the vehicle gasped its last breath.

Hannah slapped her palm against the steering wheel of the Honda.

"Momma, is everything okay?"

"Just fine, sweetie." She fumbled in her purse for the ranch cell phone Tripp insisted that she keep with her at all times.

No. She wasn't going to call Tripp. She could handle this. She'd handled the last seven years without Tripp Walker saving her. Hannah nearly laughed out loud at the idea of Tripp being her knight in shining armor.

The man would give her a lecture about being an irresponsible mother before he'd do any saving.

"Momma, I'm hungry."

Hannah checked the time on the phone. "I guess you usually get a morning snack around now at school."

"Uh-huh."

"Let me see what I have in my bag." Hannah foraged around the tote bag she'd grabbed and pulled out a box of animal crackers. "Will this do?"

"Oh, yes, please." Clementine reached forward and took the box. "My favorite. Thank you."

While Clementine ate and drew pictures in the condensation in the back seat window, Hannah took out her worn Bible. She flipped the pages, reading underlined verses.

"Momma, what are you doing?"

"Preserving my sanity." She knew only too well that her daughter was going to ask another dozen questions before something else distracted her.

"Momma, are you talking to yourself?"

Hannah raised her head from the pages. "I'm talking to God, Clemmie."

"What's He saying?"

"Right now I'm doing all the talking."

"My teacher says you have to be silent sometimes so you can hear God."

She released a long sigh and couldn't help but smile at the words. "That's right."

Wiping the fog from her window, she peeked outside. The rain had stopped while they sat in the vehicle. Hannah rolled down the window a few inches and let the cleansing breeze, ripe with the sweet fragrance of grass and plants, fill the car.

"Are we going to stay here all day?" Clemmie asked.

"No. We are definitely not going to stay here all day." Hannah met her daughter's expectant gaze in the rearview mirror. The five-year-old's expression clearly asked, *What's the plan?*

"See if you can find a camel in that box, okay?"

Hannah closed her own eyes for a moment. When she opened them, a flash of red and blue lights in the rearview mirror caught her attention. Hannah turned around to see a Timber police vehicle approaching. Her stomach did a complete drop to the floor.

"Are we in trouble?" Clementine pushed her springy curls away from her face and turned around in her booster seat.

"No, sweetie. The nice policeman is here to help us." *Because this day can't possibly get any better*, she silently added.

The officer got out of his vehicle and approached. A middle-aged man with salt-and-pepper hair, he wore a gray Stetson with his dark gray uniform.

"Ma'am, is there a problem?"

"My vehicle died."

"I'll call the Timber Garage. In the meantime, may I see your license and registration?"

"Certainly, officer." Hannah rummaged in her purse and handed over the paperwork and her license.

He glanced from her license to her. "Missouri?"

"I'm temporarily staying at Big Heart Ranch."

"That so? Haven't had the pleasure." He offered a hand. "I'm Chief Daniels."

"Hannah Vincent and—"

"I'm Clementine," her daughter piped in.

"Pleased to meet you." The man grinned as he peeked into the back seat to look at Clemmie. "I've got a few grandchildren about her age." He nodded toward his cruiser. "It'll take a moment to run this information."

A few minutes later Chief Daniels approached the Honda again. "Ma'am, I'm going to need you to step out of the vehicle."

Hannah swallowed as adrenaline shot her heart rate into overdrive. "My daughter, too?"

"No, ma'am. Your daughter can stay in the car while you and I chat."

She opened the door and stepped outside. "Ma'am, I need you to keep your hands where I can see them."

"Yes, sir." Hannah folded her hands as if in prayer.

"Are you aware this vehicle is stolen?"

"What?"

"Plates and VIN match up to a vehicle stolen from Oklahoma City six months ago."

"I have a bill of sale from a used car dealer in Denver."

"Do you have that paper with you?"

"Yes. Of course. I have all the paperwork the dealer

gave me." A fat drop of rain plopped onto her face. Hannah brushed it away with the back of her hand.

Chief Daniels glanced up at the sky where dark clouds had gathered. "Tell you what. I'm going to take you down to the station and we'll sort it all out in the comfort of our brand-new climate-controlled building in downtown Timber."

"Is that necessary? I told you I work at Big Heart Ranch."

"Just until all this is straightened out." Chief Daniels opened Clementine's door.

"Momma, are we going to ride in the police car?"

"Yes, Clementine. Our car is broken so the nice police chief is going to give us a ride."

"Yippee," Clementine said as she unfastened her booster seat and leaped into her mother's arms.

"This wasn't the plan I hoped for, Lord," Hannah said under her breath as she scooped up Clemmie.

Overhead, thunder cracked and a streak of light shot across the sky like a bottle rocket.

"Fine," she muttered, closing her mouth.

"Seriously, Chief? You arrested a single mother and a five-year-old?"

"Now calm down, Tripp. I didn't exactly arrest them. Took her statement and Ms. Vincent asked me to call you."

Tripp glanced around the stainless steel and tile office. "Where are they?"

"They're in the interrogation room. I gave the little girl milk and cookies and her momma is reading back issues of *Cowboy* magazine."

"Why are you holding her?"

"She's driving a stolen vehicle. Well, not exactly driving. That thing is held together with two rubber bands and a paper clip. We towed it to our impound lot." Chief Daniels frowned. "I'll have to check on the protocol, but you know, with a child involved in this situation, I may need to call social services."

Tripp winced, his gut taking a hit at the words. *Not Clementine.* No way was that going to happen.

"Is that necessary? Hannah is my assistant at the ranch."

"She is?"

"Fact is we're friends. Closer than friends."

Chief Daniels blinked and his eyes popped. "You are?"

"Yes, sir. We're, uh… She and I are…" He took off his cowboy hat, slapped it back on and cleared his throat as he worked desperately to find a way around the situation without digging himself any deeper. "Close," Tripp repeated.

A grin of pure surprise split the chief's face. "Well, I'll be. Why didn't you say so? Wait until I tell the missus." Chief Daniels shook his head again. "Sure are closemouthed about your personal life. I suppose we can dispense with calling social services under the circumstances."

Relief ripped through Tripp. "Thank you. Hannah and Clementine live at Big Heart Ranch."

"I can remand her to your custody then while I turn the vehicle over to the Denver Police. I've taken a full report. She claims she paid cash for the vehicle right before she drove out here." He met Tripp's gaze. "That true?"

"Doesn't she have a bill of sale?"

"Yeah, but I called over to Denver. Can't find any trace of the dealer. They admit he could have been there, but the lot is empty. Nothing but cement and an empty building."

"Hannah arrived in late May. Been at the ranch all this time. Lucy hired her and did a complete background check."

"That makes two of us. She's clean. Not even a traffic ticket." Chief Daniels scratched his head. "Though I should ticket her for not getting the car registered. She's been here six weeks."

"The car wasn't worth registering."

"Just the same."

"Come on, Chief. Cut her some slack. Hannah drove here straight from her grandmother's funeral in Colorado with a tank of gas, her little girl, and not much more than that."

"Fine. Fine. This is an election year. And I guess I do owe Big Heart Ranch a few favors for making me look good by breaking up that horse thieving ring last year." He smiled. "And Mrs. Daniels does like happy endings. Can't wait to give her a call."

Tripp squirmed at the words. "So can she go?"

"Sure, don't have to tell you she shouldn't leave town, in case the Denver Police have questions. For now, we'll consider this poor judgment." He clucked his tongue. "Shame she's out what she paid for the vehicle. But at least she's not in jail. Next time you might consider helping your little woman with her vehicle purchasing decisions."

Tripp nearly choked. *Little woman*. Hannah would have something to say about that term.

"How soon until you can release her?" Tripp asked.

"Now works for me." Chief Daniels walked down to a small room with a two-way window on the outside. He opened the door. "Ms. Vincent, your... Tripp Walker is here."

Hannah jumped up, her gaze shifting to him with relief. If only she looked that glad to see him all the time.

"Mr. Tripp," Clementine cried. "We got to ride in a police car with the lights and sirens."

Tripp ran a hand over his face. "Really, Chief?" he muttered.

"The little girl asked for all the bells and whistles. I was happy to oblige."

"Are we leaving?" Clementine asked, her gaze going from Tripp to Chief Daniels.

The chief nodded as he handed Hannah a sheaf of paperwork. "Sorry for the inconvenience, ma'am. Here's a copy of your paperwork, just in case."

When they stepped into the central area of the station, Hannah glanced at the stack of her belongings on the station floor, along with Clementine's booster seat. "Thank you for getting my stuff from the Honda, Chief Daniels."

She reached for a box, but Tripp intercepted and grabbed everything in two hands.

"Clementine, can you take your backpack?" he asked the little girl.

"Yes, Mr. Tripp." Clementine smiled as she followed him through the double doors and out of the police station. "They have the best cookies there," she said with one last glance through the glass.

Hannah settled Clementine into the back seat of the truck while Tripp placed her belongings in the flatbed.

"Well, that was fun," Hannah said as she stepped up on the running board and into the pickup.

Tripp fastened his seat belt and turned to her. "Hannah, I don't think you understand the implications of what just happened."

Hannah stared at him like he was a two-headed cow. "Excuse me?" She glanced in the back seat and lowered her voice. "I was there. I understand completely. And it hasn't escaped me that I was ripped off a thousand dollars by a con man and arrested for my troubles."

"You weren't arrested." Tripp shook his head. "Be grateful for that. Employees have been terminated at Big Heart Ranch for less."

"Are you telling me I'm going to be fired?"

"It's possible. If anyone gets wind of this."

"I happen to have an impeccable job record up to now." Panic flashed through her eyes. "And he didn't officially arrest me."

"That's because he thinks you and I are…" Tripp swallowed. "He thinks we're…"

Hannah's eyes rounded. "You told him I'm your what?"

"I didn't exactly tell him anything. I just didn't correct his assumptions."

Hannah groaned and rubbed her forehead, pushing her hair off her shoulders.

"Look, I can think of a lot worse things than having Chief Daniels assume that—"

"Oh, really?" Hannah asked. "Neither of us can even say the words out loud. That's how horrified we both are by those assumptions."

"*Horrified* is kind of harsh. I'm a little embarrassed."

"I embarrass you?"

"No. I didn't say that."

"Sure you did." Hannah shook her head. "But it hardly matters. Having people think I'm… That you and I are…" She stumbled over her words. "All I can tell you is that I'm used to people sneering first and asking questions later. Being a single mother seems to be a free-for-all for everyone to voice their opinions and judge me. And they do."

"I think it's possible you're exaggerating. Besides, no one is judging you at Big Heart Ranch."

"Right. Like you never judged me."

He opened his mouth and closed it again, not willing to risk a lightning strike for denying her charge.

"You probably ought to know that the chief had been considering calling social services."

Hannah gasped. "You probably should have told me that right away." Her dark eyes pleaded with him. "Why would he do that?"

"Just doing his job. I told him it wasn't necessary, and he agreed when I alluded to…"

"Yes. I get it."

"Chances are that's the end of the whole thing," Tripp said, hoping he sounded upbeat.

"That's not how it works in my world," Hannah muttered.

They drove in silence for several miles before Tripp checked his rearview mirror. Clementine had fallen asleep. The little girl's pumpkin-colored tresses were a wild and frizzy disarray from the weather. His heart melted.

He had never considered the possibility of having a family, but today, something changed and he realized that having the chief think he and Hannah were... Well, it wasn't the end of the world.

"Where were you going when the Honda broke down?" he asked.

"I was going to fill up with gas and head back to Dripping Falls. They're holding my job for me."

"Why?"

"You know why. You knew before I went to see Lucy, didn't you?"

"So when the going gets tough, Hannah Vincent packs her bags," Tripp said.

"That is not true. I move to keep Clementine safe."

"She's safe here."

"Tripp, I've made a fool of myself."

"Only a handful of people know why you came to Big Heart Ranch, and they're the people who care about you. Truth is, everyone likes you and Clementine."

"I don't know about that," she murmured.

"I do."

Tripp turned to Hannah and saw the battle going on in her head reflected on her face.

"So your plan is to pluck Clementine from her friends at Big Heart and take her back to Mudville without looking back?"

"Dripping Falls."

"Whatever."

Once again, she massaged her forehead. "I generally have a plan. This time everything caught me by surprise."

"What about Calamity Jane? You're on the challenge agreement as assistant trainer."

She released a bitter laugh. "Assistant trainer of a horse I don't get to train."

"Be that as it may, you agreed."

Hannah was silent.

"I don't want to pull out the paperwork, but you and I had an agreement. I can't train Jane without your help, and you have a legal responsibility to help me."

"I never signed any legal documents."

"We shook on it. A gentleman's good faith agreement. That's legal around these parts. They used to hang a man for breaking an agreement."

"Why am I not surprised? This is the most convoluted state I have ever stepped foot in."

He continued, ignoring her rant. The more he talked, the more important keeping Hannah at Big Heart Ranch seemed and he wasn't quite sure why.

"Lucy has an ugly mustard-colored Honda she holds on to for sentiment. I'll have Dutch take it in for an oil change and you can drive it."

Hannah shot up in the seat, outrage splashed all over her face. "No. Absolutely not." When Clementine stirred in the back seat, she lowered her voice again. "I don't need handouts or charity. I can do it myself or I can do without."

Tripp shrugged. "Life is all about handouts. One way or another, you can't always do it all yourself."

"Sure, I can."

"You're missing the point. The hard part is learning to play on the team. Clementine deserves that."

"You do it all yourself. You don't need anyone." She slid him a pointed glance. "I'd hardly call Tripp Walker a team player."

He grimaced at her words. Trust Hannah to find the buttons to push. "Maybe we both need a lesson in team sports."

"Maybe."

Hannah turned to the window. Her chocolate-brown hair was all wavy and full from the rain and provided a curtain between them, hiding her face and her emotions.

"You okay?" he asked.

"I was so sure that Jake Maxwell…" She took a deep breath. "I'm weary. It's battle after battle and I'm always taking two steps forward and one step back. I'm just tired, Tripp."

Tripp longed to pull the car over, take her in his arms and tell her it would be all right. But Hannah would be the first to tell him that *all right* was a fairy tale, and he hadn't believed in fairy tales in a long time, either.

"I told you. You don't have to do it all alone. Let your friends help you."

"I'm not used to having friends."

"Yeah. I get that. But you've been here six weeks now. It's time you accept the fact that we like having you around."

She turned in her seat and searched his face. "Are we friends?" The words were barely a whisper.

"Yeah, we are."

As Tripp stared into her sad eyes, he realized he didn't want Hannah and Clementine to leave. He swallowed hard at the revelation, shoving it to the back of his mind to examine at another time.

Tripp dropped Hannah and Clementine off at the bunkhouse and brought her box of stuff from the Honda inside for her.

When he turned to leave, Clementine put her hand in his and tugged. "Mr. Tripp, how will we get to the parade next week if our car is gone?"

He knelt down next to her and gently tugged an or-

352 Her Last Chance Cowboy

ange corkscrew curl. "No worries, little pumpkin. I'm taking you."

Clementine threw her arms around his neck. "Oh, thank you, Mr. Tripp, for saving us."

Tripp didn't dare look up and meet Hannah's gaze. He knew what she thought about Clementine's admission. Instead, he stepped out the back door and pulled out his phone as he headed back to the pickup.

"Slats, this is Tripp Walker. I want to know what you found on Hannah Vincent."

"That's going to cost."

Tripp grit his teeth. He knew what was coming. "I already paid you."

"That was weeks ago. The price of information is fluid, and it so happens that it just went up." The cowboy chuckled. "I'll need twice what you paid me."

"Fine. I'll look for you at the Timber Rodeo."

"Sorry, I've got bigger fish to fry. I'll let you know when I'm back in town."

Tripp disconnected the call. Slats was going to gouge him good. Didn't matter. He needed to know if there were any more surprises before Hannah got herself into any more trouble.

Chapter Eight

"No, thank you." Hannah opened a kitchen drawer and searched through the papers. She pulled out the drawer itself, just in case something had fallen behind. "I think the Spring Social is a fine idea. You two go and have fun. I'm not interested."

"Now, Hannah, don't you want to hear me play the fiddle?" Dutch asked.

"Hmm?" She turned and met Dutch's gaze. The bow-legged wrangler was all spruced up in a starched white Western shirt with pearl buttons. He wore a silver trophy buckle with his black Levi's.

Hannah smiled and reached out to straighten his black-and-turquoise bolo necktie. "You look so handsome."

The cowboy blushed bright crimson and shook his head. "There's no talking sense to her. I'm gonna wait in the truck."

Hannah glanced around the room and then stepped to the other side of the kitchen to inspect the small stack of cookbooks that she had brought along from Missouri. She carefully flipped through the pages of each book.

"Emma and Lucy have a babysitter who is happy to watch Clementine, too," Rue said. "You have plenty of time to get ready. It doesn't start until dusk. Dutch and I are going early so I can help him set up. His ribs are still sore."

"Poor Dutch." Hannah raised her head. Rue also wore a white Western shirt, hers paired with a long denim skirt and square-toed brown boots with a wing design. Silver and turquoise bangle bracelets adorned her wrists.

"Rue, you look amazing as well. Love those boots. What do you call them?"

"Ariat. They're about a couple hundred years old, like me. What about the parade tomorrow?" Rue asked, undeterred by the flattery.

"Clementine has already wheedled Tripp into taking us to the parade. We'll be there." *Whether I like it or not*, she mentally added.

"I hate leaving you all alone."

"I'm not alone. My daughter is here."

"That little girl fell asleep in the middle of dinner," Rue said. "Why, her face was nearly in the spaghetti." The older woman's face softened and she offered a musing smile, her affection for the five-year-old obvious.

"Kindergarten is tough work," Hannah said with a laugh. She placed her hand on Rue's arm. "Please, stop worrying about me. I'd be absolutely miserable at a dance. I've never been one for that sort of thing."

Hannah had her fill of parties growing up. Debutante balls, soirees, and receptions were the norm at her grandmother's sprawling estate. Unlike her granddaughter, the CEO of Bryant Oil thrived on the constant social events.

She smiled as she glanced down at her T-shirt, cut-offs and flip-flops. It had been a long time since she'd worn a designer dress or had her hair and nails done and she didn't miss any of that world.

A knock at the back door had both Rue and Hannah turning.

Tripp Walker stood on the porch with his hat in his hand.

"Come on in, Tripp," Rue said.

The cowboy stepped inside, wearing his usual work uniform of faded Levi's and a plaid Western shirt rolled up to the elbows.

"Tripp isn't going to the social, either." Hannah stated the obvious. She left off the fact that she was somewhat relieved to know that he wasn't going to be dancing with all of Timber's beautiful buckle bunnies and cowgirls.

"Tripp not going to the social is a given," Rue said.

"Excuse me?" The cowboy stood in the doorway, eyes wide. "Am I in some kind of trouble?"

"Not yet," Rue said. She smiled up at him. "I had a nice chat with Chief Daniels when I was in town today. He told me the oddest thing. That you two are—"

"Don't believe everything you hear," Hannah interrupted with an adamant shake of her head.

Tripp did a double take from Hannah to Rue as panic galloped across his face. "You didn't tell anyone, did you, Rue?" he asked. "Like Dutch?"

"No, but the chief is probably going to take care of that."

"Perfect," Tripp muttered.

Rue glanced at her watch. "I'll see you two later."

She offered a two-finger salute as she slipped past Tripp and out the door.

"Don't stay out too late," Hannah called after the older woman.

"Very funny, dear."

"You think she's serious?" Tripp asked as he stepped farther into the kitchen.

"About Chief Daniels? I don't know the man. You tell me."

"This is a small town, Hannah. Gossip spreads like butter on warm biscuits."

She shrugged. "Sometimes all you can do is nod and smile and let the gossip roll on past."

"That's your plan?"

"No more." She held up a hand. "I'm done with crisis intervention for a while. Could we postpone any further meltdowns until after the holiday?"

"Fine by me, so long as the grapevine doesn't have us married by Monday."

Hannah laughed. "If we are, I promise you'll be the first to know."

"You aren't taking this very seriously," he said.

"I do take this seriously, Tripp. And I haven't thanked you for coming down to the police station. Only a real friend would do that." She looked up at him. "You were willing to let people think that you and I…you know… to protect Clementine. Don't think I don't appreciate that. I do."

He nodded.

Silence filled the space between them. "May I offer you a soda?" Hannah asked, hoping to move past the awkward moment.

"Well, sure. Why not? What do you have?" Tripp asked.

"Root beer and root beer. It's my favorite."

"I'll have a root beer, please."

"Good choice." Hannah opened the refrigerator and grabbed two glass-bottled longnecks, doing her best not to chuckle. As she closed the door, Trent Blaylock and Josee Queen's save-the-date card slid down the refrigerator to the floor.

Tripp and Hannah reached for the paper at the same time.

"I got it," Tripp said as their fingers touched. He handed her the card without meeting her eyes.

"Thank you." She offered him the bottle and stepped back.

Tripp twisted off the cap and took a long pull. Hannah stared, fascinated. Something about Tripp always seemed to fascinate her.

She needed to learn to be un-fascinated ASAP because Tripp Walker was a dead end. He'd made it clear how he felt about her on too many occasions, despite their fake relationship.

When Hannah struggled with the cap on her own root beer, Tripp slipped the bottle from her fingers and twisted off the cap.

"Thank you," she murmured, holding the cold bottle to her heated face.

"So you're not going to the social tonight?" Tripp asked.

"Small talk with strangers is not my idea of fun," she said.

"Mine, either."

He rubbed his calloused thumb over the top of the bottle and met her gaze. "Mind if I ask you something?"

"I'm an open book."

"Yeah. Nice try, but I do have a question."

Hannah offered him a long, tortured sigh. "Please, go ahead."

"Why did Trent Blaylock send you flowers?"

"That was weeks ago." She took a sip of the soda and relished the cool liquid.

"Yep. Weeks ago."

"I gave him relationship advice, and he was grateful. He and Josee are now engaged."

Tripp frowned. Clearly, that was not the answer he expected.

"I never asked why you stopped by," Hannah said.

"I came to return something." He pulled a small, rolled-up spiral-bound notebook out of his back pocket.

Hannah inhaled sharply and her face lit up. "My recipe book! I've been looking for it all week." She put her root beer on the table and reached for the notebook. "Thank you so much. Where did you find it?"

"It was under the front passenger seat. I found it when I cleaned the truck."

"It must have fallen out of my purse."

"You've got some pretty interesting recipes in there." He leaned back against the cupboard and crossed his legs, looking as comfortable as can be, and took another swig.

"You looked in my personal notebook," Hannah said.

"How else would I find the owner?"

Hannah flipped through the pages. "My name isn't in here."

"There's a folded menu from the Dripping Falls

Diner at the corner of Central and Fir Streets tucked in the back."

"Oh."

"Are those secret recipes?" he asked.

"They're my best recipes. My famous chili recipe is in there."

"I missed that." He reached for the notebook. "Let me see."

Hannah held it away from him. "No way. I'm entering that in the…" She slapped a hand over her mouth. "Oops."

"You're entering the chili cook-off?" He grinned like he'd just heard a joke. When he did, Hannah realized he had a small dimple in his right cheek.

She looked away and held her notebook close to her chest. "Yes. I am. Don't sound so surprised. I do cook for a living."

"Why didn't you mention that you entered?"

"It wasn't a secret."

"Then why didn't you mention it?"

"Dutch knew. Besides, it's four weeks away. I wanted to wait until closer to the competition for more impact."

Tripp chuckled. "You like competition. Admit it."

"Maybe I do." She smiled and met his gaze. "I heard that you've won the contest every year since it started."

"That might be an exaggeration since this is only the third year they've held the contest."

"Yes, but you did win. Correct?"

Tripp shrugged. "Yeah, okay, I won."

"What kind of chili are you making this year?" she asked.

He stared her down. "I can't tell you that."

"Does it bother you that I've entered the competition?"

"Bother me?" He shook his head. "Nope." Tripp opened the cupboard under the sink and put his bottle in the recycle bin. "Entry fee is pretty stiff, though. Fifty bucks."

"I already paid."

"Sounds like you're getting serious about this," he said.

"Fifty bucks is plenty to get serious about, but I don't play unless I'm going to win."

Tripp laughed. "A little full of yourself, aren't you?"

"Not at all. Where'd your prize-winning recipe come from, anyhow?" she asked.

"When I was a kid I got a job bussing tables at a diner in Oklahoma City. The owner said he used to be a Michelin-star chef. Who knew if he really was?" Tripp shrugged. "But he could cook and the old guy taught me everything he knew. Passed many of his best recipes on to me."

"That's a cool story, but I can't believe you were a kid when you started. How old were you?"

Tripp nodded. "Sixteen. I had just left home after... you know. I looked older than my age and I didn't get paid or anything. He gave me all the food I could eat and a place to sleep. Didn't ask questions, either."

Hannah's heart tightened at his words. "You and I have more in common than I would have thought," she said.

"Because we both ran away from home?"

She studied the floor tile for a minute before meeting his gaze. "How did you figure that out?"

"Wasn't all that difficult to connect the dots. You said

that your grandmother put you through college, yet you showed up at Big Heart Ranch in a disreputable car that held the sum total of your life in a cardboard box, and your last job was in a diner in—"

She raised a hand to stop him. "It's Dripping Falls."

"Yeah, that's it." He met her gaze. "Why have you been running, Hannah?"

Sucking in a breath, she swallowed. All this time, and she hadn't talked to anyone about her grandmother's betrayal. Maybe it was time. Time to at least release a little of the pain of the past. After all, her grandmother couldn't hurt her anymore.

"My grandmother disowned me and started making noises about taking Clementine."

"Why?"

"Because I broke her rules." Hannah took a deep breath. "She had an inordinate number of rules. I ran off and got married after college. My grandmother said he was no-good. She was right. And the sad part is—" Hannah ran a hand over her blossoming abdomen "—I gave him a second chance and she was still right."

"Guess you won't make that mistake again."

She narrowed her gaze, offended at the cavalier comment. "This happens to be my life. It isn't funny."

"Didn't say it was, but the fact is, we either laugh or cry. The choice is yours. I've made plenty of mistakes. Some two or three times."

"Are you saying I'm in good company?"

"I'll let you figure that out for yourself. But there's no use bemoaning our past or the people in our past that did us a disservice. It's all about what you do today." He glanced around, noting the cake flour and mixing bowls on the counter. "So what *are* you doing?"

"Prep work for Sunday's cakes. You know. The cake-walk at the church."

"Cakes. Plural?"

"I've picked up a few custom orders."

"From who?"

"It's a secret."

"In case you haven't noticed, I'm sort of known for keeping my mouth shut."

"Okay, but you cannot tell anyone. I'm baking for Lucy because she claims she can't bake. And for Rue, because she says she's retired and absolutely refuses to bake." Hannah smiled. "It's a little surprising what a woman will pay for a cake."

"Does that mean you're making three cakes? Which one is Hannah Vincent entering in the cakewalk?"

"You'll have to try to figure that out yourself."

"I will."

She smiled. "No, you won't."

"We'll see." He glanced at the clock. "I gotta go. There are a few hours of daylight left. Jane is waiting for a ride and I promised her we'd work on our special routine."

"You have a special routine?"

"Yeah. Didn't you read the judging criteria?"

Hannah didn't bother to resist the urge to roll her eyes. "I guess I forgot since I wasn't actually training her."

"You're like a dog with a bone, aren't you?" he observed.

She crossed her arms and tossed him a few daggers.

"As far as I can tell, we'll nail full points for the handling portion. Jane is cooperative as a kitten. The judges come around with clipboards to evaluate the horse's demeanor and responsiveness with the trainer."

"Maneuvers, leading and riding. I saw that on the list."

"Uh-huh, and if we make it to the top ten finalists, then we start from scratch in the finals competition with more compulsory maneuvers and a freestyle performance."

"I can't see Tripp Walker doing a hotshot performance in an arena wearing a silk fringed shirt and chaps."

He laughed. "That makes two of us. For the record, I'm riding bareback without a bridle."

Her jaw sagged. "Jane's going to tolerate that?"

"Yep. You can stop by the corral sometime and watch. But stay back. Jane's partial to you and she'll want to cozy up to her favorite trainer instead of doing her job if she sees you." He chuckled at the admission. "You've spoiled that horse with your daily visits to love on her."

Hannah smiled at his admission. Was Jane really partial to her?

Her gaze met Tripp's and held for a moment. A warmth crept up her neck at the tiny spark of tenderness she saw in his eyes. It was like that night outside Jane's pen. A memory she cherished, in spite of herself.

As if he was thinking the same thing, Tripp's pupils rounded with concern before he broke the connection and quickly turned to the door.

"I'll be by early to pick up you and Clementine. Bring water and your patriotic spirit," he said in a no-nonsense tone as he pushed open the screen door.

"Yes, sir," she called after him. *And I won't even think about waxing sentimental about Tripp Walker.*

"Mr. Tripp, you won my momma's cake!" Clementine announced. She stood on the picnic table bench in a pretty red, white and blue dress with her orange hair pulled into a ponytail, blowing on a stars-and-stripes pinwheel.

"Yes, I did, Pumpkin," Tripp said with a smile for his favorite five-year-old.

Hannah eyed him as he held the cake in one hand and plastic cutlery and paper plates in the other. He placed everything on the picnic table.

"How did you know that was mine?" she asked.

"A brilliant deduction."

He stared down at her, struck by how downright irresistible she was in a blue patterned cotton sundress, with her dark hair pulled back from her face into a high ponytail. Hannah Vincent was the complete package: smart, pretty and she didn't hesitate to speak her mind. She'd be a handful for most men.

He blinked, surprised at the thought.

"Momma, look. Miss Rue is coming. May I go in the church for face painting now? She'll watch me."

"Miss Rue may be busy eating cake," Hannah said as she helped her daughter jump down to the grassy ground beneath the beech tree.

"Dutch refuses to cut the cake right now," Rue said as she stepped up to the table. "He's already put it in a cooler in his truck before anyone can ask for a sample."

Hannah chuckled. "Are you serious?"

"Totally. He's flummoxed and proud as can be about that cake." She winked at Hannah.

"What kind of cake did you bake, Rue?" Tripp asked.

"Well, um, I…" She turned to Hannah.

"That's hummingbird cake, isn't it, Rue?" Hannah said.

"Why, yes. That's right, dear. That is definitely a hummingbird cake."

"Do you use coconut in yours?" he asked.

When Rue shot Hannah another panicked look, he burst out laughing.

"Very funny," Rue replied. "To be perfectly clear, since we are at a church gathering, I never once said I baked it. I said I'd entered a cake. That's all."

Tripp offered a slow nod of acknowledgment, doing his very best not to laugh again.

"May I go with Miss Rue, Momma?" Clementine's brown eyes pleaded with her mother.

"I'm delighted to watch Clementine for a bit. You two enjoy your dessert."

The older woman offered him a bemused smile with a twinkle in her eye that said she had the inside track on something. Tripp didn't want to go there. Not today. Things were going too well.

"Thank you, Rue," Hannah said.

"Mind if I sit down?" Tripp asked as Clementine skipped away.

"Oh, yes. Sure." Hannah quickly scooted clear to the other end of the table.

"Think you moved far enough down there?" he asked as he straddled the picnic bench.

Hannah opened her mouth and then closed it. "I was being polite."

"Ah. Right. Polite."

"So how did you know this was my cake?" she asked.

"I saw the one you made for Dutch when he was recovering. You used the same cake plate."

"Oh, very clever."

"I have my moments." Tripp eyed the pristine white double-layer cake. "That cake looks professional."

Hannah's brows shot up. "Is that a compliment?"

"Sure is. I'm wondering how you got that fancy decorating on the frosting."

"I used an offset spatula to make the striped pattern on the sides and top."

"Nice. Who taught you how to do that?" he asked.

"A friend of my grandmother's. Kind of like your chef friend."

When he opened his mouth to ask another question, she held up a hand and nodded toward the table. "Could we cut the cake? Or do you want to take yours home, too?"

"I'm all for sharing." He inspected the plate in front of him. "What kind is it?"

Hannah's mouth dropped open. "Didn't you read the description before you picked it?"

"Nope. I got here late because one of the chickens got out. Barely had time to enter. I slapped down my money and when I found myself on a winning number, I picked the cake that I knew was safe. Yours."

Hannah's eyes rounded. "Safe?"

He crossed his arms. "Let me tell you a story."

"Okay."

"Last year I entered the picnic basket auction and mine was won by Estelle, Pastor Parr's mother-in-law." He glanced around. "Nice lady, but the woman is a gabber. Talked nonstop for two hours and asked me so many questions that I had hives by the time we were done with lunch."

Hannah smiled. "I'm not sure if I should be flattered or insulted."

"Don't read too much into it." He met her gaze. "Why weren't you at the cakewalk?"

She looked away. "I was a little nervous about the whole thing. To tell you the truth, I nearly pulled my cake from the fund-raiser."

"Why?"

"Oh, you know."

He stared at her for a moment as she twisted her hands and looked anywhere but at him. Then he understood. "Not excited about sharing cake and chatting with a stranger?"

"Correct," she murmured.

"Another reason I picked your cake."

She smiled. "Thank you, Tripp."

"Win-win for both of us." He paused. "By the way, I ran into Chief Daniels's wife as I was leaving the church hall and she congratulated me."

"What for?"

"She didn't say, but I think she was talking about you and me and our supposed relationship."

"Well, we do have a relationship. With a mustang and a 100-Day Challenge."

He nodded a greeting to the couple that walked past the picnic bench and offered Tripp and Hannah a smile. "I guess that means you haven't noticed folks walking by our table and grinning."

"This is a church picnic. There is nothing unusual about smiling people here."

"If you say so."

She stared at him for a minute before her eyes widened and a pained expression crossed her face. "Oh, I didn't even think. Is this whole situation putting a damper on your social calendar?"

"My what?"

"You know, dating."

Tripp nearly burst out laughing at the idea that he had a social calendar.

"Maybe you should let me worry about my social calendar." He shook his head. "Are we going to have cake or what?" He slid the paper plates and forks across the table. "What kind of cake did you say that is?"

"Lemon with lemon curd filling."

Tripp slowly turned the cake plate, inspecting from all angles. "Cream cheese frosting?"

Hannah made a face and scoffed. "Hardly. It's whipped mascarpone."

"Impressive."

"Thanks. I hope the cake was worth the price of the ticket."

"More than worth it."

"Exactly how much did you pay for that ticket?" she asked.

"You don't want to know. Needless to say, I won't be eating pancakes at the Timber Diner anytime soon."

"All for a good cause. Dutch says you have a few pet projects of your own for the orphanage."

"Dutch talks too much."

She pulled a cake knife and server, two fancy dessert plates, cutlery and cloth napkins from her tote bag.

"You came prepared. Is that china?" he asked.

"Yes. They're flea market finds. My one weakness.

But I keep moving around, so I can't collect more than fits in the trunk of my car."

"How'd you get from Missouri to Colorado anyhow?"

"I drove an old Subaru wagon whose engine caught on fire outside of Denver."

"Not real good with vehicles, are you?"

Hannah sigh. "I have other talents."

He raised the dish and turned it over. "Excellent taste."

"A cowboy with discriminating china opinions?"

"I like a nice plate as much as the next cowboy."

"Good to know." Hannah cut the cake and slid a piece onto a dish, then pushed it across the table to Tripp. "Oh, I brought lemonade." She pulled out a thermos and plastic glasses.

"You thought of everything." He brought a forkful of cake to his mouth and paused midtaste, stunned at the flavors on his tongue. "Hannah," he said.

"Is anything wrong?"

"Are you kidding? This tastes like more."

"Excuse me?"

"*More.* That means that your cake tastes like second helpings will be in order."

"Oh, I'm so glad."

He scooped up another piece, savoring it before slowly swallowing. When he looked up, Hannah was watching him.

"You really like it?" she asked.

"Hannah, I know horses and I know cooking. This is a masterpiece."

"A masterpiece?" She blinked and stared at him.

The way she beamed at his compliment and hesitantly smiled beneath his gaze caused a jolt of awareness to hit him. On the outside, Hannah was in your face, but inside, she was as insecure and shy as he was.

He took another bite. "Sour cream?"

Hannah blinked. "Um, what?"

"Sour cream. That's what makes the cake so moist."

"Yes." She grinned. "Yes. That's right."

"Would you consider sharing recipes?" Tripp asked.

"What do you have to offer?" She cocked her head and frowned. "I heard you don't bake."

"Not true. Baking is personal. I don't share my baking with just anyone." He picked up the last crumb of lemon curd from his plate and popped it in his mouth.

"Yet, you offered to share recipes with me?" Hannah asked.

"You're clearly a discriminating baker. I'd consider it an honor."

"Oh?" She cocked her head as if assessing his words. "So you'd share your best cake recipe if I shared mine?"

"I'll have to give that some thought," Tripp said.

"Seriously? You said my cake was a masterpiece."

"Hey, all of my cakes are my best, though I think this lemon cake might beat me in competition."

"Really?"

"Yeah, but I do have a secret carrot cake recipe that makes folks swoon. I hardly ever make it because it makes women get crazy ideas. Like I might be getting serious or something. Carrot cake doesn't say love, it says friendship."

Hannah gestured with her fork. "You know, not many people understand the language of food."

"Never thought of it that way, but you're right," Tripp said.

"And clearly," she continued, "red velvet cake is the language of love."

He looked at her. Really looked at her, realizing he'd underestimated the little baker.

"More cake?" Hannah asked.

"Oh, yeah."

Hannah crinkled her nose and flinched as she put another slice on his plate.

"Sunburn?" Tripp peered at the pink skin across the bridge of her nose.

"Yes. That was a long parade yesterday."

"Every year the Fourth of July parade gets a little longer. But it was a good time, wasn't it?"

Hannah offered a musing smile. "The best. I took a dozen pictures of Clementine on your shoulders waving her flag and laughing so hard she was near tears."

Tripp grinned. Hannah and Clementine made it fun. Once or twice he'd grabbed Hannah's hand to pull her through the crowd of tourists visiting for the holidays and she'd laugh as the three of them jockeyed for a better viewing spot along the sidewalk. A tiny place in Tripp's heart that had been closed for a long time seemed to open up yesterday.

Despite the side glances and meaningful smiles of those that he'd known for a long time, Tripp realized that there were a lot worse things in life than folks thinking he had a ready-made family.

Chapter Nine

"Why are you mucking? Aren't you supposed to be off this morning?" Tripp asked.

Hannah jumped at the words, surprised to hear Tripp outside the stall. She yanked the bandana covering her mouth and nose down and turned around. "Yes. Just like you're supposed to be on a conference call."

"I'm done. Took less time than I figured."

"Have you ever noticed that you always seem to show up when I least expect it?" she asked.

"That's my job." He frowned. "But you didn't answer my question."

"I had to cancel my doctor appointment." She picked through the shavings with the rake and dumped the unwanted stuff into the wheelbarrow. "I checked the schedule and one of the kids assigned to muck is out sick with poison ivy."

"Why?" He pointedly looked at her.

"I told you why. Poison ivy. Apparently, it's all over him." She glanced up at the row of ceiling fans. Though they continued a nonstop rhythm, the air seemed without movement in the huge facility. "Whew. Hot today, isn't it?"

"Hannah, why did you cancel your appointment? If you needed a ride, why didn't you just say so?" He swatted at a fly, growing more annoyed by the minute.

"Tripp, you've got back-to-back conference calls this morning." She swiped at her forehead with a sleeve.

"I can easily reschedule the rest of them if you need a ride."

"No way." She grabbed the wheelbarrow and backed out of the stall, nearly running Tripp over in the process.

"Hey, careful there, and I am trying to talk to you," he protested.

"Keep talking. I can hear you," she said over her shoulder. "I just need to dump this load. Did you forget that I'm supposed to be freeing up your time so you can work with Jane?"

"Hannah, we're six weeks from Fort Worth. Jane and I are doing just fine."

She stopped for a moment and looked at him. "July has absolutely flown by, hasn't it?"

Tripp's long strides had him moving ahead of the wheelbarrow and standing between her and the path to the mulch pile. "Call and un-cancel your appointment. I'll meet you at the truck in ten minutes."

Hannah released the handles and let the wheelbarrow go, then stared him down. "Ten minutes?" She grimaced and glanced down at herself. "I have to shower. I stink."

"Okay. Fifteen."

Thirty minutes later, Tripp guided the pickup truck past the sign announcing that they were entering the city limits of Pawhuska. "So where are we going?" he asked.

"The clinic off Main Street. You can drop me off."

She pulled her still-damp hair into a ponytail and fastened it high on her head.

He shrugged. "I don't have anything else to do and I've recently been upgraded to your significant other by the new teller at the Timber Bank, so I may as well go with you."

Hannah whirled around in her seat. "Significant other? What did you say to that?"

"Not a thing. Sometimes the best response is no response." He shrugged. "I'm kind of getting used to it. Besides, I don't mind being significant and I guess I'm already other."

"The only significant other I've ever had in my life turned out to be insignificant."

"Clementine's father?" he asked.

"Exactly."

"He's not in the picture?"

"Only when he smells money."

When Tripp raised his brows in question, she took a deep breath. Sharing was never easy, but Tripp deserved to know.

"He disappeared before Clementine was born as soon as he realized that I didn't have a penny to my name. After seven years of random drive-bys, he showed up again a few months ago. I'd always let him know where I was, in case he wanted to man up and be a father. I thought he deserved a second chance because of Clementine. It turned out that he had somehow found out about my grandmother's failing health, something I was not aware of, and determined that my financial situation would change. He was wrong." She let out a breath. "I did the best thing for all concerned and cut him loose."

"I'm sorry, Hannah."

"There's nothing to be sorry about. I hung on all those years because I didn't want to admit my grandmother had been right. But she was. The man gladly relinquished parental rights in return for not having to pay back child support."

He met her gaze, and she knew what was coming. "Are you still in love with him?" Tripp asked.

"When we met, I was in love with love." Hannah paused. "I'm no longer a woman who believes in happy endings and that love conquers all."

She shook her head. "Enough fairy-tale talk. The doctor awaits."

Tripp came around to the passenger side and offered a hand to assist her as she stepped from the truck. His touch was gentle as he held her arm.

A gal could get used to being treated like she was special, but Hannah knew better than to read more into it than the fact that Tripp Walker was always a cowboy gentleman.

"Maybe you should go grab a cup of coffee. There's that place on Kihekah Avenue," she said.

"Nope. I'm coming with you. You shouldn't have to do everything all by yourself. Friends support each other."

"Okay," she murmured. "But don't say I didn't warn you."

He held the door of the office to the large obstetrical practice open and let her lead the way. Inside the spacious waiting room, no less than fifteen pregnant women sat on the padded chairs in various stages of discomfort.

Tripp's eyes rounded and he did a very genuine deerin-headlights impression. "Why are there so many pregnant women here?" he whispered.

"Think of this as a cattle station for expectant women."

"I guess so."

Every eye in the room was on the tall, lean cowboy who entered and stood awkwardly behind Hannah as she checked in. By the time she turned to find a seat, they were blatantly staring at the only man in the room.

"Ladies," Tripp said with a nod as he took off his hat.

He sat down next to Hannah and casually picked up a magazine. Flipping through the glossy pages, his eyes rounded and he blinked with surprise.

Hannah glanced over to see what he was reading. *Modern Childbirth* magazine. She bit back a laugh when he grimaced and quickly closed the periodical, placing it back on the table.

"Mrs. Vincent?" A nurse in pink scrubs with a clipboard called Hannah's name.

Tripp glanced around the room as if looking for Mrs. Vincent.

Hannah gathered her purse and stood. "Tripp, that's me. I have to go in now."

"You're Mrs. Vincent?"

"Yes," she whispered. "You knew that."

He chuckled. "I never put two and two together before. Mrs. Vincent sounds like your grandmother."

"No. Her name was Bryant."

"Sir, do you want to come in with Hannah?" the nurse asked.

"Sure," he said with an enthusiastic grin.

"I don't know if that's a good idea, Tripp," Hannah said quietly.

He took her arm. "Hey, we're buddies, right? I got this, Hannah."

"If you say so."

"First door on the left, sir. I'm going to weigh our patient first."

Hannah waited until Tripp was out of sight before she took off her shoes, removed her earrings and watch and gingerly approached the industrial scale. The device clanged rudely as she stepped onto the black pad. She frowned as she got off the scales and entered the examination room.

"How'd it go?" Tripp asked.

"How do you think it went?" Hannah grumbled. "I'm the size of two hippos and a small elephant."

"Aw, you are not."

"I am, too. Stop being nice."

"Whoa. I've heard about those hormones from Jack Harris," he muttered. Tripp stood and walked around the room, inspecting the framed medical certificates on the wall. When he got to the wall behind him, he jerked his head back. "What is that?"

Hannah turned to see what he was referring to. "Those are a series of photos depicting the birthing process."

"With no warning label? That's just wrong. At least *National Geographic* warns the reader."

"This is a medical office." She looked at him and narrowed her gaze. "Are you okay?"

Tripp's color had paled. "I, um…"

The nurse came back in the room and grabbed the blood pressure cuff. Her gazed moved from Tripp to Hannah. "Is he okay?"

"No, he's not." Hannah placed a hand on his arm.

"He's leaving to grab a cup of coffee." She squeezed his bicep. "Right now."

"That sounds like a very good idea," the nurse said. "Should I get him a wheelchair?"

Tripp held up a hand. "Not necessary. I got this."

"At least he tried," the nurse said. "Most of them don't even try." She smiled wistfully at Tripp's retreating form. "He's one of the good guys."

Hannah stared at the nurse. She was right. Tripp was one of the good guys.

After her appointment, Hannah found Tripp pacing back and forth across the lobby with his hat in his hands. As if sensing her presence, he looked up.

"I don't know what happened to me," he said. A pained expression crossed his face. "I deliver cattle and horses all the time. But this was different. I just sort of lost it."

"It's okay, Tripp. Here, I brought you a present." She handed him a small snapshot.

"What is this?"

"My ultrasound photo. This is the baby."

"Ultrasound. We do those for horses, you know."

"Yes, I do know. Babies are different. They grow up and want an allowance and eventually ask for the keys to your car."

Tripp was oblivious to her joking words. He continued to stare, mesmerized, at the photo, turning it around to different angles. "Look at that. You can see the little fingers and toes and all."

Hannah grimaced. "Ooh, ouch. The baby just kicked me."

"What?"

Hannah took his palm and placed it on her abdomen. "Feel that?" She had his full attention now.

Tripp's gaze met hers and the blue eyes widened. "*I felt that*. The baby kicked. Unbelievable."

"Oh, it's believable at 3:00 a.m. Trust me." She hooked her arm through his. "Now, do you mind if I pick up my prenatal vitamins at the drugstore before we head back to Timber?"

"Not a problem. I canceled everything for the morning."

"That means tomorrow will be even busier."

"It's fine. I never take any time off and you haven't since you arrived on Big Heart Ranch."

They pushed through the glass doors of the clinic and started down the street.

"Look," Hannah said. She nodded to the left. They stood in front of a small infant and children's shop. A white crib with pink polka-dot decor had been set up in the window. Small bubbles of joy released in Hannah's heart. For the first time in a long time, she was excited instead of worried about her upcoming delivery.

"Pink polka dots?" Tripp scoffed. "What if you have a dirt-loving cowboy?"

Hannah leaned close. "I'll let you in on a secret. I'm having a little cowgirl and she's going to love pink and dirt."

"I thought you didn't want to know."

"No one told me. I just know."

"You just know, huh? Have you thought about names?"

"Yes. Anne. After my mother."

"That's really nice, Hannah." A soft smile crossed

his face. "Really nice." He glanced at the sign on the shop's door. "Do you want to go in?"

"Could we?"

"Sure, why not?"

"You really don't mind going in there?"

"This looks a whole lot easier than that doctor's office." He reached for the door. Musical chimes sang a nursery rhyme as they entered the shop.

"Hello there. How may I assist you?" the young clerk asked.

"Oh, we're only looking," Hannah said.

"When is your baby due?" The woman's gaze went from Tripp to Hannah.

"December," Hannah said.

"Your first?"

"This is number two," Tripp answered. "Pretty exciting, huh?"

"Yes. Congratulations." The clerk smiled and handed them pink-and-blue lollipops with the store name on a clear cellophane wrapper. "Let me know if I can help with anything."

When she walked away, Hannah dared to look up at Tripp.

He shrugged and offered a sheepish grin. "Sorry. I opened my mouth and it came out, and then I got carried away."

Hannah laughed. "Don't apologize to me. I'm fine with it, as long as you don't mind being accused of being the baby daddy."

"I've been accused of worse." He glanced at a neat stack of blankets. "These are kind of thin—what are they for?"

"Receiving blankets. You swaddle the baby with them."

"Swaddle?"

"Wrap them tightly. It's comforting for the baby."

"Swaddle. Got it." He nodded to another item on the shelf. "And this?"

"Thermal carrier."

"To keep the baby warm? Seems a little small."

Hannah broke out in giggles, which brought a look from the clerk. "No, it's to keep the baby's bottle warm."

"Right. That makes sense." He turned and inspected a shelf of infant T-shirts. "What have you gotten for the new baby?"

"Nothing. Not yet. I don't even know where I'll be in December."

"What do you mean, nothing? Your baby is coming, Hannah." Tripp seemed genuinely distressed with her answer.

"I have plenty of time. The only thing I'm certain of is that I'll be at Big Heart Ranch until the 100-Day Mustang Challenge is completed."

"And then what? You don't have to leave the ranch, you know."

"I can't live in a bunkhouse with a baby and a five-year-old forever. I need a place of my own. I don't want to have to move twice."

"Clementine will have started first grade by early September," he said. "That's coming right up."

"I know, Tripp. I know. Try to understand that a part of me just doesn't want to think about all the decisions I have to make just yet." She tugged on his arm. "Come on. Let's go. I have to get my prescription."

He held the door for her as they left the shop and

stepped out onto the sidewalk. "Mind if I run an errand while you get your vitamins?" he asked.

"Of course not."

He handed over his key fob. "I'll meet you at the truck."

"You can meet me all you want, but I'm never going to be able to get into that truck." She patted her abdomen. "At least not without help."

He chuckled. "There's a bench on the sidewalk where we parked. I'll meet you there."

"Okay."

Hannah stood in line to pick up her prescription. On the way out, she heard her name called and looked around. Standing next to the candy aisle was AJ Maxwell.

"AJ! What are you up to?"

"Ogling chocolate I'm not supposed to have while my husband is bringing the truck around."

"You're due any day now, right?"

"Yes. Travis is helping me run errands. I'm no longer allowed to drive."

"The doctor won't let you drive?"

"No. Travis won't let me drive."

Hannah chuckled at the words.

AJ rubbed a hand over her stomach. "I sure hope this baby is punctual. I'm ready to have my body back."

"I hear you." Hannah laughed.

"What are you doing?"

"My car died, so Tripp took me to the doctor."

"Oh, my. That is so sweet. Someone told me you two were close."

Hannah held up a hand and shook her head. "No,

it's not like that. I know there's sort of a rumor going around about us, but we're just friends."

"Oh, yes. I understand. Tripp and I are friends, too. He was one of the most welcoming and supportive people at the ranch when I showed up." AJ smiled. "But he looks at you a tad bit different than he looks at his other friends."

"Tripp only looks at me like he wants to give me a piece of his mind." Hannah released an awkward laugh. "And then he generally does."

The blonde gave a slow shake of her head. "Not true, Hannah. Maybe you should open your eyes. That cowboy is smitten." AJ glanced at her watch. "Uh-oh, I promised to be outside."

"See you back at the ranch," Hannah said, still dumbfounded by the other woman's remarks.

"Yes." AJ reached out to catch Hannah in a hug. "Good to see you."

Hannah paid for her vitamins and headed out of the store, still pondering AJ's words. The morning sunshine was already blinding and hot. Hannah slipped on her sunglasses and looked down the street. There was Tripp, waiting on the bench under a store canopy.

He stood and smiled when he saw her.

Smitten?

"How come I beat you back to the truck?" he asked.

"I ran into AJ. We were chatting. She and Travis are running errands today."

"You all right? You sound odd," he asked as he helped her into the truck.

"I'm fine." Hannah glanced into the back seat of the cab as she fastened her seat belt. She did a double take. The entire back seat was filled with pink polka-dot shopping bags. "Tripp, what is that?"

He grinned and looked at her. There was a glint of humor in his eyes. "I had so much fun at that baby shop, I went back and picked up a few things."

A few things? Hannah was stunned silent. It was all she could do to close her gaping mouth.

"What do you think?" Tripp asked.

"What are they for?"

He looked at her like she was a few heifers short of a herd. "*For your baby.* You said a girl, right?"

She nodded numbly.

"Don't worry. That clerk said to keep the tags and you can return anything that doesn't work for little baby Anne."

Hannah stared at him.

"Hot in here." He started the truck. "Let's get that air conditioner cranked up."

"Thank you," she murmured.

Tripp turned at her words and peered closely, blue eyes filled with concern. "Hey, there. Are you sure you're okay?"

"I'm speechless."

"I'm sure it's only temporary." He chuckled. "By the time we're home, you'll be back to giving me what for."

An unfamiliar ache welled up inside of Hannah.

Home. By the time they were home.

She stared at his strong profile, knowing that she was very much in danger of forgetting that she didn't believe in happy endings and losing her heart to this stubborn, unpredictable and generous cowboy anyhow.

"What do you think?" Tripp asked. The sun had begun its slow descent as he turned from the center of the pen toward Hannah. She had been sitting on a folding chair under a tree for hours while he went through the steps of the judging routine with Jane.

"I'm impressed." She stood and stretched before walking up to the pen. "You said Jane was having issues with the side pass and pivot. I thought she ran through everything like a pro."

"You think she's weak in any area?"

"Tripp, honestly, this horse is amazing and so is her trainer. Aren't you going to show me your freestyle performance?"

"It's getting late and I've kept you from your daughter long enough."

"Jane has to get used to an audience," Hannah countered.

"I've been running through it with the music and all with the kids watching over at the girls' ranch. They have a better sound system there. Jane can handle an audience. And we have it nailed down to the three and a half minutes required."

"I'm sorry I missed that."

"It's a not fancy show like some of those trainers will have, but it's a solid performance that will demonstrate this horse is special. Maybe I'll get a judge who favors simplicity over grandstanding."

Tripp opened the gate and locked it behind himself. "Did I remember to tell you that Lucy's sending me to a two-day conference in Tulsa next week? You're going to be in charge."

"Only twice already and it's on the calendar."

"Did I? Well, the big alumni barbecue and rodeo will be over by then."

"And the chili cook-off, too," she said with a grin.

"My point here is that things will have returned to normal. Whatever that is."

"You're only gone for two days and a night. I can handle it."

"You're also five months pregnant."

"Don't start that again. I've been here since late May. Surely you trust me by now."

"Not about trust. I trust you, Hannah. You know that."

Jane whinnied loudly as if to tell them to stop bickering.

"Look at her," Hannah said. Awe laced her voice. "It's horse ballet," she whispered.

They were silent for a few moments. In the pen Jane danced across the dirt, her copper mane flying as she showed off, enjoying the audience.

Tripp turned and leaned back against the fence, his eyes on Hannah.

"She's so lovely," she murmured.

"Yeah," he agreed, his attention focused on the woman next to him. A soft breeze fluttered the trees overhead. Instead of the usual humidity, tonight the temperature had dropped a tad as though Mother Nature was as tired of summer as everyone else.

When Hannah's hair blew into her face, he was unable to resist leaning closer to gently brush the strands from her cheek. Their gazes met and held, and somehow Tripp closed the distance between them.

Hannah's lashes fluttered downward as he bent his head until his lips grazed hers, hesitantly until he realized she was kissing him back. Then Tripp was helpless to do anything but take her in his arms and deepen the kiss until he was lost in the sweetness and rightness of the moment. It was as if his whole life he'd been waiting for that kiss and this woman.

It was Hannah who stepped out of his arms. He watched her closely, but she just stood there. Her eyes were round, and she held her fingers to her mouth as if she was as stunned as he was.

What just happened? Why is my heart ramming up against my ribs and my breath catching in my throat?

Tripp opened his mouth to say something, but he didn't know what to say. It wasn't like he had a mental saddlebag filled with things to say to a woman after he kissed her. Fact was, his saddlebag was pretty much empty. Apparently, his mind was, too. Yet, there was no way he wished it hadn't happened.

"I'm not sure if I should apologize or say thank you," he finally said.

Hannah finally blinked and looked at him. "I don't know what to say to that."

"Not much to say," he admitted.

Tripp's phone began to buzz, and the sound startled him, pulling him out of his reverie.

"Mine's buzzing, too," Hannah said.

"That can't be good," Tripp said as he pulled his phone out of his pocket.

"AJ," Hannah said, glancing at the screen of her cell. "She had a boy."

"Travis Jake Maxwell." Tripp grinned and shook his head.

"Oh, my, this is so wonderful."

"Yep, and I'm guessing that kid will be as funny-looking as his parents."

"I heard Travis was on the cover of *Tulsa Now* magazine a while back. Gosh, and AJ looks like a model. Their baby is going to be beautiful."

"I was kidding, Hannah." He shook his head. "The irony here is that Travis was burned so badly in the past, he was dead set against relationships. Until AJ came along. He fell hard and fast."

"I suppose you can't plan for everything, can you?" she said softly without looking at him.

"No. I guess not."

When the breeze blew Hannah's hair again, Tripp clenched his hands at his sides. She nodded toward the bunkhouse.

"Rue is watching Clementine. I better go."

"Yeah." He nodded.

Hannah turned from him and then stopped and pivoted right back around. "Don't apologize," she said with a determined look in her eye. "That was a very good kiss."

His lips twitched as she walked away. Yeah, she was right. It was a very good kiss. Behind him, Jane nickered. When Tripp didn't turn, she bumped into the fence and nearly knocked off his hat with a nudge from her nose. He finally turned and met the mare's velvet brown eyes.

Tripp released a long breath. "Yeah, I know. She likes us. Now all we have to do is find a way to make her stay."

Chapter Ten

❧

"Did you ever smell anything so amazing?"

Hannah turned at Tripp's voice. She'd been trying to ignore his presence in the small exhibitor tent to her left for the last few hours. Though the tent canopy was down on that side, she still caught glimpses of him and found herself thinking about that kiss last night.

She'd lost sleep over that kiss. Well, she certainly did not intend to lose the Big Heart Ranch chili competition over it. Maybe that was his strategy.

It wasn't going to work.

"Hey, anyone home over there?" he persisted.

"Were you speaking to me?" Hannah asked. She lifted the side flap on her tented booth and glanced over at him ever so nonchalantly. The man looked like Clint Eastwood in an apron. Tall and lean and all cowboy, minus the cowboy hat today. And apparently cooking brought out the best in him because he was grinning as he stirred a giant cast-iron pot.

"Who else would I be talking to?" he asked. "My competitor on the left is Mrs. Hagwood, the retired town librarian, and she's profoundly deaf. I have to keep going over to her tent to tell her that her phone is ringing."

"Good for her. No interruptions while she's cooking."

"I guess." Tripp shrugged. "But you still didn't answer my question."

He carefully wiped the edge of his pot with a paper towel. Hannah inched closer to look at his tent. The place was immaculate. She frowned as she glanced around her slightly disorganized cooking table, strewn with spices and over to the corner of the tent, where Clementine sat on the ground coloring in a book. Well, she was a free spirit. Nothing wrong with that.

She looked back at Tripp somewhat confused. "I'm sorry, could you repeat the question?"

"Never mind. It was rhetorical."

"I see." Hannah inhaled deeply. The chili cook-off was into its third hour, enough time to allow the enticing blend of sausage, beef, tomatoes and spices to mingle and create a potent aroma. "It really smells amazing now that everyone's chili is simmering, doesn't it?"

He stared at her and chuckled.

"What?"

"Nothing. Inside joke." He nodded toward the stove. "Ever cooked on a camp stove before?"

"I have not and I must admit that there has been a bit of a learning curve."

"Hi, Mr. Tripp," Clementine called. She peeked around Hannah and waved.

"Clementine. I didn't know you were there. What are you doing?"

"Coloring." She looked at her mother. "Momma, I'm hungry."

"She can have some of my chili," Tripp called.

"Or we can borrow your mini-me and take her for

hot dogs and curly fries," Dutch said as he approached her booth with Rue.

"Hot dogs," Clementine said. Her eyes lit up.

Hannah frowned at the exchange.

"Dear, let us take Clementine," Rue said.

"Please, Momma," Clementine pleaded.

"Dutch and I will take good care of her," Rue continued. "We're on our way to find something to eat right now."

"Rue, you're always helping me out. I don't want to take advantage of you."

"Think of us as honorary grandparents. We get to wind her up and tire her out. Then we give her back to you. It's a wonderful arrangement."

"Yeah, and we're real good at it," Dutch said.

"If you're sure," Hannah said.

"Very sure. Are there any special stops we should make along the way?" Rue asked.

"Clementine wants to watch Dub Harris in the greased pig competition and she wants to ride a burro."

"I do believe we can handle that," Dutch said.

Hannah glanced at her watch. "I didn't think about the time factor when I signed up for this. It's pretty much an all-afternoon event." She sighed. "I was in a rush to sign up so I could beat Tripp."

"Understandable," Dutch said with a glance over at Tripp.

"We'll be back later to see who wins," Rue said.

"To see me win," Hannah added.

"I heard that," Tripp called. "My chili is ready for tasting. Is yours?"

Hannah grabbed the wooden spoon and stirred her own velvety mixture. "Mine is, as well."

Next door, Tripp positioned a mason jar in a prominent position near his cutlery and napkins.

"What's he doing over there?" Hannah whispered to Dutch.

"A little side fund-raising. That's a donation jar to raise money for the Pawhuska Orphanage."

"I thought the chili was free. Take a scorecard, sample chili and turn it in," Hannah said.

"Sure, it's free. They pay money to get in the gate. Tripp there is utilizing a little free enterprise. Hit 'em hard and hit 'em fast while their taste buds are dancing."

"Two can play at that game," Hannah said. "I need you to go to my bunkhouse and bring me the two Texas sheet cakes that are on the counter."

"You made cakes?"

"I was going to just put them on the buffet table but I can see I've been approaching this all wrong."

"Let's see who raises more money for the orphanage," Dutch said with a grin.

"Exactly."

"How much are you going to charge for each piece?"

"I'm not going to charge. I'm going to take donations." She nodded to her left. "Just like he's doing."

"Yee-haw. Let the games begin."

With the appearance of the cake, Hannah was suddenly so busy she almost didn't have time to think about Tripp being next door. The line to her tent rivaled Tripp's line. After scooping up chili samples, she continued to cut cakes.

Yet, despite being busy, she was aware of him and caught herself peeking a glance over at the other tent watching him interact with his friends and neighbors and offer a greeting and a smile. This was a Tripp that wasn't seen very often, she was certain. He liked people much more than he let on and enjoyed their approval.

Occasionally, his gaze met hers and he'd smile, and her heart would catch and she'd forget what she was doing.

"Hannah," Tripp called out hours later.

"What?" She pulled off her plastic gloves and grabbed a bottle of water. Turning toward his tent, she met the blue eyes assessing her with respect and a hint of something else she couldn't put her finger on. *Interest?*

"They're announcing the cook-off winners over at the main podium. We can hear it from here."

"Oh, that means we're done." Hannah leaned against the table with relief and glanced around her. The chili was nearly gone and all that remained of the cake was crumbs. Hannah absently swiped her finger along an empty sheet cake tray and tasted bits of delicate chocolate cake. Absolutely delicious, even if she was a bit biased.

She looked over at Tripp's tent. He was neatly stacking up his kettles and utensils.

"Your pot is empty?" she asked.

"Uh-huh. They cleaned me out. But I saved you a cup of chili. Want to trade?"

"Yes. I'm starving. And, of course, I want to taste your prize-winning chili."

"You want to try to figure out the ingredients," Tripp said.

Hannah bit back a laugh. "That, too."

Tripp pulled off his apron and closed the distance between the booths. He offered her a paper cup with a spoon and glanced around her tent. "Any cake left?" he asked hopefully.

"No, sorry."

"That's a shame."

She scooped up a sample of her chili and handed it to him before she took the cup he offered. "Mine is not vegetarian."

He shrugged. "It's okay. I'll work around it."

Hannah dug her spoon into his chili and lifted it to her mouth. "*Oh, this is good.* This is very good."

"Yeah?" He laughed. "Maybe you could try not to sound so surprised."

She tasted again and frowned, closing her eyes for a moment as she separated the flavors in her mind.

"You're frowning."

"No, I'm analyzing. Is that sweet potato in there? And do I taste a bit of cumin?"

"Right on all counts."

"Black beans and lentils," she added.

"Well done, chef."

"What kind of chilies?"

"Ancho, pasilla and arbol." He paused. "And maybe a hint of chipotle."

"Oh, Tripp, this is a winner. I'd really like the recipe."

"We can negotiate." He raised his brows. "When you bake another cake."

She chuckled at his response.

Overhead, a microphone screeched and squealed. "Big Heart Ranch's own Tripp Walker wins the chili cook-off. Second place goes to Hannah Vincent, also of Big Heart Ranch."

"Congratulations," Hannah said with a slight bow of deference. "Well deserved."

"Second place is pretty good for your first year," Tripp said.

"I am not a sore loser. In fact, I am delighted to have had the opportunity to compete against you." Hannah grabbed the glass jar and started counting the cake donations.

"That's the spirit. How much money do you have in that jar?"

"Give me a minute." She finished counting the change and dumped it all back in. "Two thousand and fifty-one dollars and ten cents."

Tripp's jaw sagged. "What? You're kidding me, right?"

"No. I'm serious."

"How many pieces of cake were there?"

"Fifty-six."

His eyes rounded. "You charged thirty-six dollars for each piece of cake?"

Hannah blinked. "That was some impressive math. But no, I took donations, just like you. AJ was right—people do open up their pocketbooks for the pregnant lady."

She handed the jar to Tripp.

"Why are you giving it to me?"

"It's for the Pawhuska Orphanage. I trust you'll get this to the appropriate parties."

"Hannah, that was unbelievably cool of you to do that."

"I happen to be an unbelievably cool person. It's taken you three months to figure that out?" She nodded toward his donation jar. "How much did you rake in with your chili samples?"

"Couple hundred bucks." He frowned. "Maybe I should bake cakes," he said.

"Your chili also won a hundred bucks and that will go to the orphanage."

"Two thousand dollars?" he repeated.

She nodded. "You won the pots and pans and the gift certificate to the Oklahoma Rose. Not a bad haul."

"I'm particular about the tools of my trade. I always give the ones I win back. They've been trying to give away those skillets for three years now."

Hannah laughed at the notion.

"Is Clementine still with Rue and Dutch?" he asked.

"No. She's sleeping." Hannah pointed to the blanket pallet on the floor of the tent. "They claim they wore her out. Although I suspect she wore them out."

She began to collect her own pots and utensils.

"The cook-off was a lot more fun than usual," Tripp said, giving her a meaningful glance. "We should compete more often."

Hannah smiled. "Should we?"

"Yeah. I don't know many people who take their horses and their cooking as seriously as I do."

"Did you just compliment me?"

He granted her a rare full-on smile. "You know, I might have."

She was silent, pondering his words as she cleaned up the booth. "Will you keep an eye on Clementine while I run this stuff up to the bunkhouse?"

"Happy to. Are you coming back for the fireworks later? There's rumor of a s'mores booth."

"That sounds wonderful. But I've been on my feet all day. I'm exhausted. And my daughter is a lightweight like me."

"Sure," he said with a nod. "I'm not much of a s'mores fella anyhow. If I can't have Hannah Vincent's cake, I'd rather go hungry."

"I guess there's some baking in my future. It's good to keep the boss happy."

"Now don't feel like you have to do it on my account."

She laughed as she collected trash from the tent and

walked it over to a receptacle. "Will someone be breaking down the tent and collecting the camp stoves?"

"Yeah. There's a crew that will do all that."

"Then I'm done here. I'll be right back." She grabbed the rolling cart she'd borrowed from the chow hall and put everything on the shelves.

The day had begun to slow down. The rodeo was over and families were moving toward home. They'd come back in a few hours for fireworks at the pond or watch them while sitting on blankets on their lawns.

The bunkhouse was quiet. Rue would be back in her apartment in Timber tonight, now that the summer was over. Hannah put the leftover chili and sour cream and cheese in the fridge and dumped the dirty dishes and pans on the counter.

Heading back to the tent, she opened the back door. Across the grass strode Tripp with Clementine in his arms. The little girl was still asleep.

The picture they made of the tall cowboy, his face partially covered by his hat and her little girl nestled in his arms, plucked at her heartstrings.

She held open the screen door for him. "You didn't have to."

"Sure, I did. It's okay to let your friends help you."

Yes, but there was a price to pay for getting accustomed to Tripp Walker helping her all the time. She'd get used to it, maybe even expect it, and that wasn't a good idea when she had plans to head back to Dripping Falls next month.

"You can put her on this bunk."

"That little girl needs pink boots," Tripp murmured as he laid her down on the bed.

"Little girls grow out of boots much too quickly for that."

Hannah pulled off Clementine's boots and socks and tucked her beneath the sheet.

She went back into the kitchen where Tripp waited. "Thank you."

He stared at her and she was only too aware of the chili stain on her shirt and the blobs of sour cream on her pants. Her hair was a lopsided sagging ponytail now, and she smelled like pork sausage and tomato sauce.

"Yes, I know I look like I've been slinging chili for eight hours."

"Nope. I was thinking you look lovely."

Hannah blinked and leaned against the counters, speechless. She nervously tucked a loose strand of hair back behind her ear.

"Why are you surprised?" he asked.

"I, um, my physical appearance is just not something I've ever thought much about."

"And yet, you are a beautiful woman. Inside and out."

"Thank you," she murmured.

"I'm glad you came to Big Heart Ranch. Your strength and Godliness is an inspiration to everyone."

"Where did that come from?" Hannah asked.

"I don't know. I've been watching you all day today and it sort of hit me. You give two hundred percent to everything you do and you do it selflessly." A small smile touched his face. "Five months pregnant and you've been on your feet all day serving chili, *and* you raised a small fortune for the Pawhuska Orphanage."

"Oh, that's only because I was trying to beat you."

Tripp smiled before he crossed the room. He gently took her face in his hands and pressed a soft kiss to her forehead like she was cherished and precious. "Thank you, Hannah."

And then he was gone and Hannah was left staring

at the door, her heart pounding as she realized she'd fallen in love with Tripp Walker.

"Cold, rainy and plain disagreeable," Dutch muttered as he stomped into the stables and parked himself outside the office door.

Hannah turned at Dutch's words.

"What's wrong?" she asked.

"Don't ever get old. That's all I'm gonna say. Though for the record, I'm not just old, I'm two years older than dirt. This weather makes everything ache."

"Well, go on home, then," she said.

"Naw, it's Friday. I'll see the day out."

Hannah finished filling out the September supply list and turned off her computer. Dutch was right. It had been a miserable few days of weather with nonstop rain. But the horses loved the moisture and the drop in temperatures that came with the end of summer.

September was days away, along with the 100-Day Challenge finale. She planned to go to Fort Worth, Texas, to cheer Tripp and Jane on with Clementine, Lucy, Travis and Dutch. Hannah glanced at the calendar, counting down the days. When it was over, she'd have to make some serious decisions about her future.

But not today. Today, despite the weather, everything was just fine in her world. If she had any more days like today, she would be inclined to stay.

She stood and stretched before stepping out of the office to find Dutch. The wrangler stood in the center aisle, untacking a horse.

"Dutch, I keep telling you. Go home," she said. "Everything is done here. It's almost Friday quitting time anyhow."

"Naw, I can't. I promised Tripp I'd keep an eye on

you while he was gone." Dutch froze with a saddle in his hands. He closed his eyes and scrunched them tight and then opened them. "You didn't hear that."

"He doesn't trust me." Hannah's heart fell flat at Dutch's words. Things had been going so well while Tripp was in Tulsa. She'd been buoyed with confidence at the thought that he left her in charge.

"No, Hannah." Dutch tossed the saddle onto the stall hook. "That's not it. Maybe when you first got here. But not now."

The heat of embarrassment warmed her face. She was humiliated in front of Dutch and becoming more annoyed with each passing moment. What a fool she had been, yet again believing that Tripp trusted her. He'd told her no less than three times that he was going out of town. In return, she'd assured him all would be well in his absence.

She thought they had an understanding.

"I should have known it was too good to be true," Hannah murmured.

"Now stop that. Did you ever think that maybe our Tripp asked me to keep an eye out because he cares about you? Come on now, you're pushing six months pregnant."

"I'm not mad at you, Dutch. You're caught in the middle."

"Go ahead and be mad at me. I should have told him no."

"The subject is closed," she said. "I'm going to go spend some time with Jane." She grabbed her rain slicker from the hook outside the office and strode past Dutch.

"Outside the pen, right?"

"Now you sound just like Tripp," she called over her shoulder.

"That was plain rude, Missy."

"Yes, well, it is what it is."

"Don't be shooting the messenger. I'm only doing my job."

Hannah shrugged into her slicker and pulled the hood up, tucking her hair inside. She spared a glance at the gray sky overhead. The steady rain had stopped and had turned into an annoying drizzle. Wiping the moisture from her face, she called Jane.

The horse trotted to the fence and offered a welcoming whinny.

"Good to see you, too, sweet girl." She rubbed Jane's mane and offered her an apple from lunch. "Come on, let's get some walking in."

Together they walked around the pen, stopping at intervals until Hannah was tired out. "Sorry, Jane. I'm a slacker, I know. This whole pregnancy thing has me winded faster."

Hannah climbed to the top rung on the fence, leaned in and put her arms around Jane. She rested her head upon Jane's neck and inhaled, finding the peace that she always did with the mare.

"What are you doing?"

Startled, Hannah nearly lost her balance.

The next thing she knew, she'd been grabbed under the arms and set on the ground.

Tripp was back.

Hannah slowly turned to face him. "Jane needed some love," she murmured. *And I did, too*, she silently added.

"Don't ever let me see you on that fence like that again," he thundered. Tripp was angry. Steam was practically coming out of his ears. He was mad enough that Jane whinnied and raised her head in alarm.

In a heartbeat, her joy at seeing him again was replaced by confusion. He stared at her as if he didn't know her. Didn't want to know her.

Tripp Walker apparently ran hot and cold. Was this the same man who had kissed her so tenderly just a few days ago?

His eyes were a stormy blue. He stood straight and unyielding, rigid with irritation. Rain dripped from the brim of his hat as he pinned her with his gaze.

"You're scaring Jane," Hannah said. She folded her arms across her chest and stepped right into Tripp's personal space, unwilling to let him know that he scared her, as well.

"Jane is a wild mustang and what you just did was reckless. You have a child and a baby to think about, Hannah."

"I think we established weeks ago that Jane isn't like other horses. Jane is special. And I think we also established that I am a responsible adult who would never put her child in danger."

Dutch was suddenly at her side. "My fault, boss. This whole thing is completely my fault."

"Dutch, stop that," Hannah said. "I take full credit for what I did. You had nothing to do with this."

Tripp looked at them both, then as suddenly as he'd stormed in, turned on his heels and headed into the stables without so much as a backward glance.

"He's in a mood," Dutch said.

"Tripp around?"

Both Hannah and Dutch turned at the voice. It was the tall, thin cowboy she'd seen in Timber. There was something menacing about the man. Hannah instinctively stepped back.

"Slats Milburn," Dutch echoed. "What are you doing here? How'd you get past the front gate?"

"Someone going out let me in."

"Well, that was a mistake," Dutch said. "Any business you have should be done in the admin building."

Slats nodded to Hannah. "You must be Hannah Vincent."

She ignored the hand he offered.

"Slats Milburn. I've heard a lot about you," he continued.

"That's unfortunate," Hannah murmured. She turned away and stood at the fence. Why did she have the feeling that things were about to implode?

"What are you doing here?" Dutch demanded.

"I've got business with your equine manager."

"No way does Tripp have business with you. I would have heard."

"Guess you weren't privy to this information. I'm here to meet with him because he said he was ready to settle up."

"Dutch, show him into my office," Tripp called from the doorway of the stables."

"Yes, sir, boss."

When Dutch rejoined her at the fence, Hannah asked, "What's going on, Dutch? Why was he here?"

"You got me. I don't have a clue. He closed the office door. Shot me a *mind your own business* look." Dutch shook his head. "Something ain't right, Hannah."

Hannah shoved her hands into her pockets as the rain began to fall in earnest. She shivered. Dutch was correct. Something was not right.

Chapter Eleven

❧

"*You're an heiress.*"

Hannah swiveled around in her desk chair, stunned by the accusation. It wasn't so much the words but the delivery. Tripp Walker might as well have accused her of being a horse thief for all the hostility that laced his words.

He stood in the doorway of the office looking larger than life and just as formidable. She hadn't seen the man since he'd voiced his displeasure with her on Friday. He'd even avoided her at church.

This morning he stepped in and closed the door behind him before he sat down. His face was a stony mask, revealing nothing. There was a calm about him that frightened her.

"Who told you that?" Hannah gripped the arms of the desk chair and braced herself for the storm that was no doubt coming. She'd lived through worse, she reminded herself.

"Dorothy Lee Bryant was your grandmother."

"Yes." She said the word slowly.

"Dorothy Lee Bryant of Bryant Oil," he stated, his voice flat and cold.

"I know who she is. She raised me."

"Why didn't you tell me?"

"I mentioned it the first day I arrived at Big Heart Ranch when I spoke with all the Maxwells." She scrambled, her mind searching. "At the obstetrician's office, too. Remember? I said my grandmother's last name was Bryant."

"Hannah, you never made it clear that you are the sole heir to the Bryant fortune. I would have remembered if my employee told me that her grandmother was one of the richest women in the country." He crossed his arms over his chest. "Why did you hide such important information?"

"I didn't hide anything. It wasn't relevant because I had already walked away seven years ago." She stared at him. Clearly, he'd missed his calling. Tripp would have made an excellent defense attorney.

"You may have walked away, but that doesn't alter the fact that you are Hannah Bryant."

"No. I'm Hannah Vincent. And why does it matter so much? I stopped being Hannah Bryant a very long time ago." She met his gaze, searching for something that told her the Tripp she knew was still there, somewhere.

He looked past her as if she wasn't in the room. "Everything you've said has been twisted tales and lies."

"That isn't true at all." She stared at him, trying to figure out where this hostility was coming from.

"Where did you say you went to college?" he asked.

"What does that matter?"

"You said you worked in equine clinics when you were a kid and when you were in college."

"I didn't lie, if that's what you're asking."

"You worked with thoroughbreds. In rich folk's stables."

"I worked with horses."

"And who taught you to bake those fancy cakes?"

"You're blowing this out of proportion, Tripp. I said it was a friend of my grandmother. Eric Frombeau taught me to bake cakes."

He blinked, processing the information. "That chef on television who bakes for movie stars?"

"Chefs on television have friends, too." She gestured with a hand. "What's your point, Tripp?"

"I'm a fool, that's my point. I marveled at how much we had in common. But we don't have anything in common. Nothing at all, do we?"

"Tripp, it was you who judged me the moment you saw me in that disreputable Honda in the middle of a storm on the side of the road. I've been honest about everything."

"You never said you were an heiress."

Hannah felt her own anger beginning to rise. "*Stop saying that.* I didn't mention who my grandmother was because she was not part of my life."

"Your life? You walked away from your life and you're pretending to be someone else."

The irony of the situation didn't fail to slap her in the face and it stung.

"That's sort of like the pot calling the kettle black, isn't it? You walked away from your life as well, didn't you?" She offered a bitter laugh. "I walked away from my grandmother's life to find my life." Hannah sighed, suddenly weary. "I thought you of all people would understand. I thought you knew me. Apparently, I was wrong."

"Nothing you say makes sense, Hannah. Your grandmother was a powerful woman. She could have found you and Clementine if she wanted to."

"Yes. I'm sure she could have. So I stayed off the grid and under the radar at all times. I moved a lot. Dripping Falls is the longest I've lived anywhere. I lived there for six months before I came here." She released a slow breath. "And maybe I didn't share more because I was ashamed."

"Your grandmother really threatened to take Clementine?"

"The threat was unspoken. But it was real. She took me away from my mother after I was born, and I always knew she would take Clementine if she so desired."

He seemed caught off guard by that bit of information and for a moment, silence stretched between them, with only the noises of the stable that drifted through the glass, breaking the tension in the room.

"You never told me that about your mother."

"Maybe because I was ashamed about that, too. I should have fought harder to find my mother before she died." Hannah stared at Tripp as the pieces of the puzzle began to fit together. Suddenly, she realized how he found out about her grandmother. "That man. Did you hire that Slats person?"

Tripp grimaced. "Yes."

His answer was like a physical blow, and Hannah flinched at the pain. "He shared information about my past with you." She paused. "I thought we were…close. I trusted you and I would have answered any question you asked. But you didn't ask. You went behind my back."

Emotion flashed in his eyes before he answered.

Hannah felt some relief that perhaps, finally, her words were getting through to him.

"It wasn't like that, Hannah. I hired him a long time ago. When you first arrived. And then I fired him. He called and told me that he had information about you. I was concerned that it could compromise Clementine, so I agreed to hear him out."

"This is why you were so angry on Friday."

"Yes. That and seeing you with Jane."

"What exactly did he tell you?" Hannah asked.

"He said you inherited a fortune from your grandmother. That you could buy and sell Big Heart Ranch if you wanted to."

"That's not a secret. I hope you didn't pay him too much for that."

"Is it true?"

"It's absolutely true. But what he didn't tell you is that I turned it down. I walked away. That's not my money." She shook her head. "All I ever wanted was my grandmother's attention and unconditional love. The same thing my mother wanted."

He stared at her. "I don't know who you are anymore."

She met his gaze. "Funny, because that's exactly how I feel about you."

"None of this makes sense. You could take care of your children with that money."

"Bryant Oil is not my money. Even if I wanted to claim the estate, my grandmother's will has strings attached in order to control my life even from the grave."

"What strings?"

"Where I live, how Clementine is to be schooled, a

prenuptial agreement if I marry again and a dozen more clauses in the will."

"Doesn't change the fact that you're a majority shareholder in Bryant Oil now." He shook his head. "One newspaper article called you the runaway heiress."

"Fake news, and I'm sure that sold a lot of newspapers." She shrugged. "Actually, there is very little about me available online. I've stayed out of the spotlight since I left for college."

"Hard to know what to believe," he murmured.

"Yet, you were willing to believe Slats and what you read online over what I have been telling you for the last fifteen weeks." She rubbed her forehead. "What the papers don't say is that I relinquished any claim on the estate. A team of attorneys and the board of directors of Bryant Oil will run her company. Once the official paperwork is signed, then I'm out of the picture."

"You're going to tell me that you drove a broken-down Honda and lived from hand-to-mouth on purpose when you had a bank account you could have tapped into at any time?"

"I want my daughter to grow up with trust and with unconditional love. Not a love based on rules or financial payoffs. I want her to know there is a God out there who loves her unconditionally, as well. The money has never mattered." Hannah took a deep breath. "My grandmother's money has destroyed my life at every turn."

Hannah stood and paced back and forth, trying to contain the emotions that threatened to erupt. Finally, she stopped and stared out the office window at the stables. She had trusted Tripp Walker with her heart and soul and secrets. He'd let her down, like everyone else.

Rejected by one man because she didn't have a fortune and by another because she did.

Suddenly, she was angry. Angrier than she'd been in a long time, because anger didn't come easily to Hannah. She was annoyed and irritated on a regular basis. Especially with Tripp. But never truly angry. She always found a way to see around the issue and back off before she reached a boiling point.

But now…now she was mad enough to do something stupid and that meant it was time to back off and walk away. She pulled her purse out of the bottom drawer and turned to face him.

"You've made yourself judge and juror and found me guilty. The truth is that the only thing I've ever been guilty of is believing in happy endings when clearly since birth, my life has been nothing but betrayals."

She stepped toward the door.

"Where are you going now?"

"I quit."

"We leave for Fort Worth on Thursday. You can't quit until then. We have an agreement." Though he said the words, the fight seemed to have gone out of Tripp.

"Our agreement was broken when you chose to believe Slats over me." She opened the door. "I'll be in Fort Worth for Jane. Because she deserves it. Then I'm leaving."

"That's your specialty, isn't it, Hannah? Leaving?" he murmured.

Her steps slowed at his words. "Maybe so, and maybe someday I'll regret this, but I don't think so."

Hannah kept walking until she was out of the stables and into the sunshine.

"Well, now you've gone and done it," she heard Dutch grumble as she left.

She walked past Jane's pen, her gaze lingering on the copper horse. The mare nickered as if calling out.

"I can't, Jane. I can't. I have to keep moving or I'll never make it to the bunkhouse without breaking down."

Hannah clenched her jaw, fighting off the ache deep in her soul. Jane accepted her unconditionally, and in return, she loved that horse with her whole heart. Now she had to leave her. As if her heart wasn't broken into enough pieces already. Head down, Hannah sniffed and kept walking.

Rue was in the doorway of the bunkhouse with a box in her arms when Hannah arrived.

"Oh, hi there, Hannah. I'm just dragging more of my stuff back to my apartment." She hitched the box higher in her arms. "What are you doing home so early?"

"I…" Hannah stumbled over a response.

Rue peered closer. "Oh, Hannah, is everything all right?"

"No," Hannah said. "Everything is perfectly awful."

"Is there anything I can do?"

"I don't think there's anything anyone can do, Rue." She put her hand on the older woman's arm. "Some days I just have to wonder how I could have so thoroughly and completely missed God. It's like I had my eyes closed when He put up the road signs."

"We all experience that, dear. Trust me." She smiled sadly. "This too shall pass."

"That's normally what I would have said." Hannah released a sad sigh. "But I don't think there's anything about this that's going to pass anytime soon."

* * *

"You planning to be like this the whole ride to Fort Worth? If so, it's gonna be the longest five hours of my life," Dutch said.

"Like what?" Tripp scowled and gripped the steering wheel all the harder as he focused on the road and the precious cargo in the horse trailer.

"Like you're waiting to slug someone, that's what." Dutch jammed his hat on his head and crossed his arms. "I tell you, I've had fun before, and this ain't it."

"Why is it you're riding with me, anyhow?" Tripp asked.

"Because Hannah is acting even ornerier than you are and she flat refused to ride with you. Lucy ordered me to. Since she signs my checks, here I sit."

"Great. Just absolutely perfect," Tripp growled.

When Dutch reached out to turn on the radio, Tripp's arm shot out to stop him.

"I'm not listening to that *cry in your beer, miss my horse, my girlfriend doesn't love me* music," he said, instantly irritated.

"We can listen to something else," Dutch said.

"Quiet is good," Tripp returned.

"No, quiet just gives you more time inside your head and I'm not too sure that's a good place for anyone right now."

There was silence for the next few miles before Tripp finally shot a glance at Dutch. "The breadcrumbs were all there," he said.

"Huh? The what?"

"Hannah. I chose to see what I wanted to see." He shook his head. Like Hannah and the letters from Jake

Maxwell to her mother. Hannah saw what she needed to see because she desperately needed a family.

He'd seen Hannah as a scheming, irresponsible single mother because that's what he needed to see to once again justify his rotten childhood. Of course, he chose to ignore all the little things along the way that said she wasn't at all what he'd labeled her.

"Aww, get over yerself, will you?" Dutch remarked.

Tripp jerked back at the words. "Excuse me?"

"You're mad at Hannah because it turns out she's not a grifter. Is that about right?"

"No," he started. "No. I didn't say that."

"Sure you did." Dutch snorted. "I didn't notice you speaking up when everyone thought you and she were an item."

"I did that for Clementine."

"Yeah, right. I'm pretty sure you were okay with things when you thought you were the one saving her. When you got to be the hero."

"What's that supposed to mean?"

"Just what I said. You're copacetic if you're the one wearing the cape. Looks to me like you're plum scared because the tables are turned."

"Now you're just insulting me for no good reason."

Dutch kept talking without pause.

"I think you got a whiff of that, which is what's eating you up. Ever think that maybe Hannah and Clementine are saving you?"

Tripp gripped the steering wheel, debating whether he should let the old cowboy walk the rest of the way to Fort Worth. The idea held merit, but Lucy would kill him.

"You listening to me?"

"I don't have much choice, do I?" Tripp asked.

Dutch kept talking. "I think your problem is now you think Hannah is too good for you because of her money."

Tripp glanced over at the old wrangler. "How did you know about the money?"

"Same as you. I tracked down Slats and he told me everything for a small nominal fee."

"You paid him?"

"Sure I did. I'm emotionally invested in Hannah and Clementine. Unlike you, I care about what's going to happen to them even if that slimy cowboy charged me half my paycheck."

He paused. "Rue made you do it, didn't she?"

"That, too. Doesn't matter, I was willing. More than willing."

"By the way, I do care," Tripp added.

"Then act like it. This ain't all about you and your feelings."

Tripp swallowed the ugly truth that Dutch Stevens, of all people, was right.

What could he possibly offer someone like Hannah? She had so much potential, and now that she was no longer hiding, the whole world was hers to grab. She might decide she wanted to be an heiress after all.

Why would she need him in her life?

He was protecting himself from what couldn't possibly end well.

Tripp inhaled and exhaled slowly.

Besides, they had nothing in common, he told himself. Nothing to build a future on. Nothing.

"It's your differences that make a relationship interesting. Not your similarities," Dutch said. "Not much fun to fall in love with a clone of yourself." The old cowboy shot him a look that said that was a particularly unpleasant thought.

Tripp stared at him. Was the crotchety wrangler reading his mind? And who said anything about love?

"What are you looking at?" Dutch asked. "You don't get to be my age without learning a thing or two." He shrugged. "Why do you think Rue and I get along so well?"

Tripp wasn't going to touch that one. He stared out the window for minutes before responding.

"You don't understand, Dutch. That woman is way out of my league. The pitiful part is that I've spent the last three months thinking she was a gold digger. Fighting my feelings and being judgmental because I thought she had a shady history. What a joke. Even worse, what does that say about my judgment?"

"A tad off the mark, I'll give you that. But then you've always been somewhat skewed and cynical in your outlook when it comes to grown-up type people."

"Skewed and cynical? That's not true."

"Sure, it is. You give kids and horses a second chance. You'll go out on a limb to trust them and offer unconditional love. Anyone else? They cross you once and you write them off."

Dutch shook his head. "And cynical?" He laughed. "You wouldn't see a silver lining if it wrapped itself around your big head and tugged."

Tripp turned and glared.

"I'm just saying."

"Don't hold back. Tell me what you really think."

"What I think is that all you young bucks are the same. You get run over by love and you struggle to stand, looking around, trying to figure out what hit you without a clue that what you need to do is grovel and get it over with."

"I'm not in love with Hannah," Tripp roared.

"Whatever you say." Dutch chuckled, unperturbed by the fact that Tripp was now fuming.

"Look, we have a long ride ahead of us and I don't want to spend it talking about Hannah," Tripp said.

"Fine by me. But you and me both know you're gonna be thinking about her all the way down I-35 South."

Tripp took a deep breath and shook his head, knowing the old wrangler was right and hating it.

Chapter Twelve

"What's wrong with Jane?" Dutch asked as he dragged a bale of hay into the stall.

Tripp stepped into the stall and did a quick assessment, running a gentle hand over her flank and abdomen and then inspecting her legs. "Doesn't seem to be a physical ailment, but something is definitely off," Tripp said. "I'm just not sure what."

"What do you mean, you're not sure?" Dutch prodded. "You're the horse whisperer."

"Be that as it may, I don't know what's wrong. Jane flat refuses to budge." He stepped out of the stall. "She was fine at Big Heart Ranch and she's not fine now. That's all I know for sure."

"Did she hurt herself in the trailer?"

"That doesn't appear to be the case."

"That mare has got her face in the corner. That's not good," Dutch said with a frown.

"Thanks for the valuable input, there, pal." Tripp's gaze moved to the center aisle. He glanced around the backstage area of the Fort Worth arena, which was lined on both sides with stalls. The place was huge, with over two thousand horse stalls total in the multiple arenas. The facility was used for public events in the auditoriums and had an impressive livestock complex and multiple arenas. Underground tunnels connected the equestrian facilities.

Today, the place was busy with cowboys, staff and even the media. There was a buzz of excitement in the air. This was it. The finals. The culmination of everything he'd work for. Could he deliver?

The judges were at the other end of the center aisle right now, but it wouldn't be long before they were right in his face.

"Maybe it's because she's used to being turned out 24/7," Dutch mused. "Or maybe she's just plum mad at you."

"Why would she be mad at me?"

"I can think of a dozen reasons," Dutch muttered.

"She's not mad at me, but I've got to do something before those judges come around with their little clipboards. I could lose forty points before this even begins, and then I'm out of it. One small misstep and we may as well go home. One hundred days of training circling the drain."

The horse had been eating, drinking and eliminating without a problem. Tripp glanced at Jane again, suddenly realizing that Dutch might not be too off the mark.

No, Jane wasn't mad at him. She missed Hannah. Leaving Big Heart Ranch and coming to this strange environment had only intensified the mare's feelings of loss.

Tripp swallowed hard because he knew his next decision meant laying down his pride and doing what was best for the horse. Truth be told, he still wasn't sure eating his hat would save them today, but he had to try.

"What are we going to do?" Dutch asked as he spread the hay around the stall.

"I need Hannah," Tripp admitted. "Right away."

"Hannah ain't even here yet and even if I do find her she's so mad at you I'd be spitting in the wind asking her to help you out. She might be so inclined to give me a piece of her mind, and I guarantee she's real good at that."

Tripp did a double take. "Wait a minute. Why isn't Hannah here yet? I saw her packing up the truck at Big Heart Ranch with Travis and Lucy as we pulled out. They should have been minutes behind us."

Dutch stepped out of the stall and dusted himself off. "They had a flat tire outside of Ardmore. Put them behind schedule."

"Call and make sure they're okay? Would you?"

"I already talked to them an hour ago."

"Dutch, for once can you not argue with me and just call and make sure Hannah is okay?"

"For a man who dismissed the woman a few days ago, you're sure riled up," Dutch scoffed. "Maybe you oughta just quit taking the long way around the barn and apologize to her."

Tripp narrowed his gaze and pulled out his own phone. "Never mind. I'll call Travis myself."

"Hold on. No need." Dutch nodded straight ahead. "Look there. Coming toward us."

Tripp glanced down the long hall, finally spotting Travis and Lucy weaving in and out of the crowd. They were all smiles as they approached. Hannah lagged behind, her gaze on anything but him. He knew he deserved that. He'd been a pigheaded fool, blind to anything but his own feelings.

"Well, would you look at that? Seems to me she don't look much like an heiress today, does she?" Dutch asked quietly. "She just looks like Hannah."

Tripp shook his head. Okay, fine. Dutch was right. She did just look like Hannah and he was glad to see her. The dark hair floated around her shoulders in waves and she wore a loose maternity blouse with jeans and cowboy boots. Hannah was so trim, you'd have to look twice to notice she was actually pregnant.

But he knew it, and he had a picture of baby Anne sitting on his desk in the bunkhouse.

"Hey, Tripp," Lucy said. "This is so exciting."

"Thanks for coming," Tripp said.

"Are you kidding?" Travis said. "Wouldn't miss this. I'm so excited you're finally going after your dreams."

Was he? Tripp considered the words for a minute. His dreams. This competition was about Jane and Hannah. Yeah, he'd win this for them.

"Thanks, Travis." He turned to Hannah. "May I talk to you? It's about Jane."

"Jane?" Concern filled Hannah's eyes. She looked to Travis and Lucy.

"We'll go find our seats," Travis said. "Come on, Luce."

"What's going on?" Hannah said.

"I need help with Jane. Do you suppose that you and I can put aside our differences for that mare?"

"What's wrong with her?"

Tripp's gaze followed Hannah's as she glanced behind him, searching the stalls for the mare. He could see Jane, and the animal's ears twitched as though she was listening.

"I can't get her to budge from that stall. She misses you. I've got about five minutes until I'm out of the competition before it even begins."

"I didn't mean to upset her. I couldn't bear the thought of her being auctioned off, so I've stayed away the last few days. Kept Clementine away, as well."

Tripp raised a palm. "I get that. No judging here. I just need your help." He glanced down the center of the stable area. "Those fellas with the clipboards are getting closer."

Hannah hesitated, her gaze going from Tripp to the stall.

"Please," he said. "For Jane."

She crossed her arms. "As I recall, you said that you don't want me near her."

"Hannah, I may have been a bit overprotective."

"You think?"

She wasn't going to make this easy, and he was running out of time.

"I was wrong," he said.

"Yes, you were."

Tripp shot a nervous glance down the walkway. "If you could go and talk to Jane… Just go to her stall and talk to her. That mare will do anything for you. I think we both know that."

A determined expression crossed Hannah's face, and she stood straight and proud, meeting his gaze. "Okay, but we do this my way this time, Tripp. I mean it. My way."

"Whatever you say." Tripp nodded and stepped aside as Hannah walked to Jane's stall.

"Jane," Hannah called. "Hey, there, sweet girl."

The mare shook her head, snuffled and offered a low snort as if to say she heard but she wasn't going to forgive that easily.

"I'm sorry, Jane. Please turn around," Hannah cooed.

Jane shook her head, then finally nickered and moved, as if considering Hannah's words. A moment later, she slowly stepped in a semicircle until she faced center aisle. Her head dipped over the stall gate to inspect Hannah.

"Aw, she sure loves you, Hannah," Dutch said.

"Grab that stool," Tripp said to Dutch.

"Got it, boss."

Tripp placed the stool outside the stall and helped Hannah to step up. She put her arms around the mare's neck and buried her nose in Jane's mane. The horse held very still as Hannah smoothed her mane and ran a hand over her withers.

He wanted to tell her to be careful, but he kept his mouth shut. Her way, she said.

"Oh, sweet girl, how I've missed you." Then she carefully stepped off the stool and opened the gate. "Come on now, Jane, let's get going."

She handed the lead rope to Tripp and moved aside as Jane walked out of the stall.

The rush of relief slammed into Tripp. "Thank you," he murmured.

"I didn't do it for you. I did it for Jane. This is her time to shine. She's worked hard for this, and she deserves a good home and a family that will love her. If winning this competition will do that, then I'll do whatever you need."

Tripp swallowed the lump in his throat. He'd given

Hannah nothing but trouble from the day they'd met, yet here she was, helping him out when his back was against the wall.

Hannah met his gaze. "I'll stay down here until she's tacked up. Just to be sure and send a few pictures to Clementine and Rue." She looked at him. "Are you ready to go into that arena?"

"I've done everything I know to do with that horse up to this point. I'm as ready as I'll ever be."

Hannah put her hand on his arm. "You got this, Tripp. I believe in you."

Tripp stood there for a moment, stunned by the generosity of the woman in front of him and wishing things could be different between them.

"Thank you, Hannah."

She nodded and turned away.

"Only a fool would let her go," Dutch muttered. "Go on and win that competition and then get your saddle back home and fix this mess."

Tripp opened his mouth and then closed it again. There was nothing to say. Dutch was right. Again.

First Jane. And then he'd have the daunting task of making things right with Hannah. He'd stepped in a lot of cow patties lately, and cleaning things up would take some time.

Day one hundred.

Hannah stood in the aisle of the arena, looking over the crowd in the grandstands. They'd really made it to day one hundred of the challenge. Who would have thought that her journey from Missouri would take her to this moment?

She was honored to be in this historic arena. Despite

what had happened between her and Tripp, she was glad to see this through and be able to close the door on this chapter of her life. And she was glad she could be here to help Jane.

Above her, the flags of Texas and the United States waved. She scanned the arena, taking in everything, trying to capture every sight, sound and scent from today. Memories to tuck away, because soon enough, she'd be far, far away from this arena and from Big Heart Ranch. All of this would be a memory. A memory of the horse and the man she'd loved and lost.

The day was filled with mixed emotions. There was no doubt in her mind that Tripp would at least take Jane to the final ten. After that, she was going to lose the mare that she had grown to love. This moment was oh so bittersweet.

She'd gone back and forth on attending today, until Lucy pulled a guilt trip on her. The family needed to support Tripp and Emma wasn't feeling well. She had reservations about the Big Heart Ranch equine manager, but at the very least, Jane deserved the support. So Hannah had gotten in the truck to drive here with Travis and Lucy, while Rue kept Clementine for the day.

Now she was glad she'd come. Being here provided one more opportunity to see the beloved mare and would bring Hannah closure. She'd stayed away the last few days, hoping to make their final parting easier. It wasn't easier. Every second that she inched nearer to losing the horse she'd grown to love, her heart ached more.

The air smelled like hay, sawdust, horses and popcorn. Cowboys and cowgirls in tight Levi's, crisply starched Western shirts and cowboy hats stood around chatting, all eyes on the center of the arena, anticipating the action which would soon begin. Hannah walked down the rows of the grandstand to the bright blue seating area where Travis and Lucy waited. Around her, the crowd was settling in, preparing for the event, and the excitement in the arena was undeniably contagious.

"How'd it go?" Travis asked. He stood so she could sit on the other side of Lucy.

"Jane will be fine."

Music blared from the overhead speakers and the crowd got to their feet when a mounted rider carrying the US flag entered the arena and stopped in the center for the singing of the national anthem.

When they sat down, Hannah pointed to the white arena gate. "Look. I see them at the gate. They're going to be up first."

Overhead, the announcer confirmed Hannah's words. "Ladies and gentlemen, competitor number twenty-one, Tripp Walker from Big Heart Ranch in Timber, Oklahoma, riding Calamity Jane."

The gate opened and out rode Tripp and Jane. Completely in synch, they trotted around the entire arena before they began the required maneuvers. The audience was still as if sensing that they were witness to something special.

"They're looking really good," Travis said. "Jane is making smooth transitions, maneuvering like she's been doing this her whole life. Far as I can tell, they haven't missed a thing on technical."

"Very nice work," the announcer added, as though he could hear Travis's words. Cheers and applause said the fans in the stands agreed. "This could be as close to perfect tens as we're going to see today. What a way to start the afternoon, folks."

"They received high numbers. It's all going to depend on the rest of the rides," Hannah said.

"How many horses are competing?" Lucy asked after they'd watched a number of horses and trainers.

"One hundred, and the competition has been spread over two days," Hannah said. "Tripp and Jane are in the last batch. We should find out the standings soon. But as of the last rider they were in the top ten."

"Here are the top ten finalists for our final round." The moment the announcer said the words the arena fell silent.

When Tripp's name was called, Travis launched from his seat, pumping his fist and hollering, "Woo-hoo!"

"I knew they'd make it," Hannah yelled. "I knew it." She was unable to contain a wide grin of pure joy. Tripp Walker might be relationship challenged, but he lacked nothing in the equine department. The man deserved a win today. So did that horse.

"What's next?" Lucy asked. "This is so exciting."

"Four minutes to set up and four minutes to perform. They'll do the required maneuvers and then the freestyle performance," Travis said.

"Gosh, I can barely sit here," Lucy said. "My knees are knocking."

Hannah released the breath she was holding and nodded. She was on the edge of her seat herself as one by one, the ten trainers completed their program. Each performance seemed more amazing than the next, making it more unbelievable that the horses were actually wild one hundred days ago.

When Tripp and Jane came out into the arena, they

stopped in the center. Tripp's gaze scanned the crowd until it met hers. He tipped his hat, then patted Jane on the neck and whispered something to her.

Hannah's heart fluttered at the gesture.

"Why, he did that just for you," Lucy murmured. "That was so sweet, Hannah. He's acknowledging you."

A warmth crept up Hannah's neck at Lucy's words.

As promised, Tripp and Jane did a bareback routine that left the audience in the grandstands on their feet begging for more. Clearly, the team was a crowd favorite, and the applause was deafening.

The performances continued until all ten trainers lined up with their horses in the middle of the arena as the winners were called.

"First place goes to Tripp Walker and Calamity Jane."

The arena exploded with noise. Hannah jumped to her feet, screaming as loud as anyone in the stands. Lucy grabbed Hannah and hugged her, while Travis continued to whistle, hoot and holler.

When the horse and rider did a victory ride around the arena, galloping the perimeter, Hannah stood with the crowd.

Tripp waved at the cheering arena. Then he dismounted and wrapped his arms around Jane's neck in a tender showing. He turned and once again searched the stands for Hannah, and when their gazes met, he offered a thumbs-up.

Yes, they'd done it. Tamed a wild horse in one hundred days. Hannah put a hand to her chest where her heart trotted out of control.

Who would have thought? It was only May that she'd

challenged Tripp and they'd begun verbally sparring until he'd finally agreed.

Hannah closed her eyes for a moment, savoring today's memories. He won. She was so proud of him.

Cameras flashed at the presentation of the check and all attention in the arena remained focused on the winners.

"Isn't the auction next?" Lucy asked.

Hannah nodded. She swallowed hard. Jane was going to be auctioned off. The mare with the velvet eyes. Her special girl would be gone.

Travis met Hannah's gaze, concern in his eyes. "We don't have to stay for that. Let's head back to Timber. We'll stop and congratulate Tripp first, then maybe find a Sonic drive-through and celebrate with cherry limeades."

"I like how you think, Trav," Lucy said. She squeezed Hannah's hand.

"Thanks, Travis," Hannah said. "Why don't I meet you two at the truck? I want to call and check on Clementine."

"Sure," Travis said.

She'd call Clementine and Rue and give them the good news, because she couldn't bear to see Jane again and know that the mare wasn't going back to Big Heart Ranch.

Her heart ached. She'd lost it all.

The man, the horse and the family.

Chapter Thirteen

"But Momma, I don't want to leave." Clementine choked the words out on a heartfelt sob.

"Clementine, it's going to be all right, sweetie." Hannah dropped to the mattress next to the five-year-old, her heart aching along with her daughter's.

"No. It's not all right. I don't want to go. Big Heart Ranch is my forever home, Momma."

"Oh, Clemmie. I wish…" Hannah didn't know what she wished and anything she said would only make her daughter break out in a fresh round of tears. Her little face was bright red with the effort and the orange curls had given up and formed a frizzy halo around her head.

The problem was Hannah wasn't sure everything was going to be all right. She wasn't sure of anything anymore and she was fresh out of plans.

Her daughter remained inconsolable. Her wet and noisy sobs gave way to soft hiccups as Hannah rubbed her back. Finally, after several minutes, Clementine fell asleep.

Hannah took a deep breath. She longed to fall apart

but simply didn't have the luxury of a meltdown. So she'd stay strong for her daughter.

"Everything okay?" Rue asked as she knocked gently on the screen door. "I heard her crying."

Hannah eased up from the bed, went to the kitchen and unlocked the door. "She's asleep now. I'm sure she was overtired. I let her stay up late last night when I got back from Fort Worth and then we got up early for church."

"Poor baby," Rue said as she stepped into the kitchen. "What got her started?"

"I pulled out the suitcases."

"Oh." For the first time, Rue seemed without a quick response.

"I should have known better."

"Clementine doesn't want to leave." Rue stated the obvious.

"Would you like a cup of tea?" Hannah asked. "I sure could use one."

"Yes, please." Rue sat down at the table. "Although you understand, I'm about to dive right into your business."

Hannah smiled as she turned the burner on under the kettle and grabbed two mugs from the cupboard. She was going to miss Rue Butterfield. "Thanks for the warning."

"I don't understand how you can think about leaving. You won the competition."

"Tripp won."

"He never would have done that without you, dear. He never could have done it without you."

"It doesn't change things, Rue." The kettle began to

whistle, and Hannah poured water into both mugs before sliding the tea box across the table.

"Hannah, Big Heart Ranch is your family. You don't leave family."

"The DNA test said otherwise. I am not family. I don't know what I am."

Rue clucked her tongue. "Don't let anyone hear you say that. Big Heart Ranch is all about family and DNA has nothing to do with the families that fill this place with love."

"You're right, I'm sorry. It's just that it's too awkward to be around…" She glanced over at her daughter to be sure she was asleep. "You-know-who, when he believes that I misrepresented myself."

"Honey, don't you get it? You-know-who loves you. He feels like the ground shifted beneath him and he doesn't know the rules anymore. That's why he lashed out."

"I can't fix this, Rue." Hannah dipped her tea bag into the water. "The next move is his, and until he works things out in his head, there's nothing I can do."

"He's a man, so, unfortunately, that may take a little longer. They tend to be as confused as a cow in a parking lot when it comes to women."

"I don't have the kind of time required for him to figure things out," Hannah said. "I'm not even sure I want him to figure things out."

"Oh, the way I see it, you have all the time in the world." She sipped her tea. "Why, this is about the prettiest season in Oklahoma. Although Emma would argue it was Christmas." She glanced outside where the redbud had begun to change to color, their royal reddish-purple leaves shimmering in the breeze.

"I've lived many places. They're all pretty."

"Not as pretty as Big Heart Ranch." Rue smiled her trademark serene smile. "There is no place on God's earth like Big Heart Ranch, dear."

Hannah didn't know what to say to that because deep in her heart she suspected that Rue was right.

"You know, Clementine is counting on enrolling in kindergarten at the Christian school in Timber, just like her hero, Dub."

"Yes. I'm aware." Another hurdle they'd have to overcome. Convincing Clementine there were other heroes in the world.

"Look, how about if Clementine spends the night with me? She and I will go check on the chickens, and then we'll eat cupcakes, watch some very G-rated movies and paint our nails. A girls' night."

Hannah leaned closer. "You're going to bake?"

"I said eat cupcakes. I bought packaged ones."

"I don't know, Rue, Clementine spent yesterday with you."

"So what? Don't even think about denying me time with my honorary grandchild. Especially when you're telling me you're going to leave." She shot Hannah a stern look. "Besides, you need some alone time to think and maybe she needs a break, too. This is a lot for a five-year-old to try to process."

"Rue."

"Don't *Rue* me. I'll let her get a nap in and then I'll be back around dinnertime to borrow her for the night."

"Thank you."

"No thank-you needed. Now tell me about the finals in Fort Worth."

"Oh, Tripp and Jane were amazing. Never in a million years would anyone guess that Jane had been a wild horse one hundred days ago."

"Calamity Jane won." Rue released a sigh. "Imagine that."

"You should have seen them in the arena. Tripp rode bareback in the finals freestyle round." Hannah pulled out her phone and scrolled through the pictures.

"Look at that!" Rue exclaimed. "Amazing."

Hannah nodded.

"Success with wild mustangs is based on the relationship and Tripp understands that. Relationships are based on trust, consistency and respect. Always those three."

"Yes, and that's the same with human relationships, isn't it?" Hannah asked.

"But our Tripp hasn't had much experience with relationships. Personal ones. Like a man and a woman."

"Surely he's dated before. I mean he's how old?"

"Thirty-four, I believe. Maybe he has. But not much. In the eight years here on the ranch, he's never dated."

"What? I don't understand. Why not?"

"I suspect it has something to do with his past and I also believe our Tripp sees his scar as a disfigurement." Rue offered a wry smile. "Of course, I'm a family practitioner, not a psychiatrist. So what do I know?"

"Not dating. That doesn't make any sense. He's a very handsome man, and he has so much to offer a woman." Hannah blinked. "Why, he cooks, too."

"I didn't say it made any sense. I'm simply telling you how I see the situation."

Hannah sipped her tea and then met her friend's gaze. "And why is it you're telling me this?"

"Because I'm hoping you'll find it in your heart to give him a second chance."

"Oh, Rue, that was low."

"I'm willing to stoop low if you'll rethink this leaving idea." She put her hand on Hannah's. "You and Clementine are far too dear to me to let you go without a bit of a fight. Especially when I can clearly see your happiness is close enough to pluck from the tree."

"If only it was that easy."

"It is that easy. Pray about it, would you?"

Hannah walked Rue out when she left and then sank into the rocker with her tea in hand. The trees rustled with the wind and for a moment, Hannah imagined she heard Jane. A slow tear slipped from her eye and she quickly wiped it away with the back of her hand. Tears were a waste of time. She'd learned that a long time ago. She'd trust in God and put one foot in front of the other.

Casting all your care upon him; for he careth for you.

"What have I learned from all this?" Tripp leaned on the rake and caught his breath. "Don't want things you can't have." He wiped the sweat from his face with his shirtsleeve and shook his head.

"Are you talking to yourself?"

Tripp jumped and turned around to face Travis Maxwell. The pretty-faced cowboy had a smile on his face. Why was he so happy?

As far as Tripp could tell, things were exceptionally lousy in the world.

"Did you need something?" he grumbled.

"Yeah, I'm trying to figure out why you're mucking stalls. That's not your job. You're the equine manager," Travis said.

"Mucking stalls is the best way that I know of to get thinking time in."

He glanced behind Travis and noted Lucy and Emma bringing up the rear guard. "What is this?" he asked. "An intervention?"

"It may as well be," Lucy said.

"Hannah is leaving," Emma said. She pushed in front of Travis, crossed her arms over her pregnant abdomen and shot him her steely-eyed glare. "What are you going to do about it?"

The youngest Maxwell clearly had a burr under her saddle today. Tripp looked her up and down.

"How is Hannah leaving? She doesn't even have a car. Does she think she can call an Uber or something?" He nearly laughed aloud. Then he realized they were serious.

"Dutch is taking her to the bus station in Pawhuska tomorrow," Lucy said. "You know I'm completely against interfering in your business, Tripp, but you have to do something. You're the only one who can make Hannah stay."

Tripp stared at Lucy as his mind took off like a galloping horse.

Dutch? Why would he do that? Hannah and Clementine belong on Big Heart Ranch. He made a mental note to fire the old wrangler.

He glanced at his watch and handed the rake to Travis. "Here, you finish." Tripp headed toward the exit. "Oh, and lock up my office when you're done."

"Me?"

"Yeah. I blame you for this."

"What? Why?" Travis called.

"You hired Dutch."

He strode out of the stables and across the yard to the bunkhouse he used in the summer months. It was a good thing he hadn't moved back to his apartment in town yet because he was running out of time.

Fortunately, he had a plan. Trouble was he'd been pondering said plan since he got back from Fort Worth last night and so far he hadn't found the courage to put it into motion.

It was now or never. Time to cowboy-up because you only got one chance at a second chance.

He had this. The horse was in the pen. The cake was on the counter and the check was in his wallet. All he had to do was shower and grovel.

He could do that. Right?

Tripp swallowed the fear edging in and walked faster.

It took him ten minutes to shower and dress, collect everything and head over to Hannah's bunkhouse. He had to slow down some so the cake wouldn't flip over and land in the dirt.

"You got this," he repeated over and over. "Grovel and give it your best shot and the rest, well, it's in the good Lord's hands."

His fingers trembled as he knocked on the door.

"Tripp?" Hannah blinked with confusion when she appeared at the screen. "Is there something—?"

"Yes. I brought your check."

She opened the screen door and held it open. "You brought a cake, as well. Come on in."

"Yeah, I was testing out a new recipe." He thrust the cake, tucked neatly in a plastic carrier, into her hands.

"Thank you." Hannah placed the cake on the table. She still looked confused but confused trumped hostile.

"It doesn't sound like you're still mad at me," he said, then nearly slapped himself. What a stupid thing to say.

"I'm annoyed and irritated. Does that count?"

"I like a challenge," he murmured.

"Excuse me?"

Tripp kept talking, counting on the fact that his feet were too big to get them both in at one time.

"I brought your check. Did I mention that yet?"

"My check? Oh, the check from the 100-Day Challenge. The seventy-thirty deal we shook on. The agreement that I broke." She met his gaze. "That check."

"Jane was trained by the time you quit and you only quit because I was a donkey." He pulled the check from his wallet and handed it to her. "It's yours fair and square."

"Thank you." She looked at him. "Do you mind if I sit down? Things have been a little overwhelming lately and my center of gravity is off, as well."

"You all right?" He quickly pulled out a chair for her.

"Fine." She eased into the chair.

"What about the cake?" he asked.

"Cake?" She started to rise. "You want cake now?"

"Sit down. I know where everything is." He grabbed Hannah's two mismatched china plates from the cupboard and opened the drawer for napkins, forks and a server. "Could you take off the cover for me?"

"Sure. I can do that. This must be a very special cake." She depressed the tabs and lifted the cover. Then she released a small gasp. "Red velvet."

"Yeah." He sliced the cake and slid a piece over to

her before cutting a sliver for himself. "Food love language," he said.

"I remember." Hannah bit her lip as a pained expression filled her eyes. "Tripp, I don't know what to say."

"There's nothing for you to say. I need to do the talking."

Hannah nodded, and he wasn't sure if she was going to cry or throw something at him.

"I was wrong, Hannah. Completely. I've been overprotective because every time I saw you around a horse I saw my past and how I couldn't save my brother or my mother."

"Oh, Tripp."

He held up a hand. "No. I'm not here for your sympathy, empathy or pity. I'm here to apologize. Let me do that before my brain figures out what I'm doing and I run the other direction."

She nodded.

"Hannah, you were right, I did judge you. I apologize for that, too. I was falling in love with you from day one. The more you made me feel, the more I backpedaled. After all, who was I to love you?"

He met her gaze, finding comfort in the warm brown eyes. "Once I found out you were an heiress, well, that blew everything out of the water."

She sighed. "It's more than a little disturbing that you think I am that shallow and that you think so little of yourself."

He looked away for a moment. It took every bit of courage inside him to meet her gaze once again and allow her to see him raw and vulnerable. "I'm afraid, Hannah. I haven't been this afraid since I was sixteen and walked away from home."

"What are you saying?" Hannah asked. Her expression said that she needed to hear it all. That this was not the time to be economical with his words.

"I'm saying that I should have come to you to ask about your past." He swallowed. "I don't want to have a whatever-maybe relationship with you. I love you and I love Clementine."

She ran a hand through her dark tresses, tangling them into an adorable mess as she most likely battled the same fears he had. "You don't know what you're getting yourself into. I have so much baggage."

"We both have a lot of baggage. I thought maybe we could use our winnings to find a little starter ranch that would have room for you and me and Clementine and the baby and all the baggage."

Hannah laughed.

He reached out and touched her hand. When she didn't pull away, he was buoyed with hope and continued. "I went after the 100-Day Challenge thanks to you. You made me dream a dream that I hadn't even considered chasing. I thought dreams were for other people."

"Tripp, there was never any doubt that you'd win."

"Hannah, I'm nothing but doubts." He stood and tugged her hand. "Come on. I want to show you something."

"Where are we going?"

"Outside." He led her across the yard and the gravel toward the old barn. The scent of hay being baled in the north pasture filled the air.

"What was that?" Hannah turned her head to listen.

As they rounded the corner, the circular pen came into view. Calamity Jane walked toward them, nickering in welcome.

"Jane," Hannah breathed, her voice laced with wonder. "I'd run to that fence, but I'm afraid my running days are over for a few months."

Tripp took her elbow and walked with her to the fence where the mare welcomed her.

"Jane, my sweet girl, it's really you."

"Go ahead, you can climb up on that rail. I'll hold you. Jane wants some loving."

"Thank you, Tripp." She climbed to the first rung, and Tripp's hands held her steady as she hugged Jane. For moments, she murmured endearments to the mare. When she got back on the ground her eyes were moist with unshed tears.

Hannah turned to face him. "Jane says I should marry you."

"Aw, you don't have to marry me because I brought Jane home."

"Tripp Walker, look at me."

"Yes, ma'am." He obeyed and prayed she couldn't tell he was scared to death.

"I love you," Hannah murmured. She lifted her hand and caressed his scar. "I'd love you even if you hadn't brought Jane back to Big Heart Ranch. Now, I just love you more."

Tripp bent his head and whispered, "I love you, too" against her lips, before he wrapped her in his arms for a long, lingering kiss.

Behind them, Jane nudged Tripp's shoulder and nickered in complete agreement.

Epilogue

A year made all the difference in the world. A year ago she arrived at Big Heart Ranch.

Jane nickered and Hannah looked up to see Dutch lead Clementine around the circular pen on the mare's back. Now six years old, almost seven, Clementine wore a pink riding helmet and pink cowboy boots, both birthday gifts from her new daddy, Tripp.

Nestled in Hannah's arms, baby Anne scrunched up her little face and stirred.

Overhead, a robin's egg blue sky was dotted with fluffy cotton clouds. Hannah inhaled when the warm spring breeze stirred the air, bringing with it the scent of Oklahoma red clay, grass and the fragrance of dozens of lilac trees that had been planted years ago on Big Heart Ranch.

Could life get any better than this?

She turned at the sound of boots crunching on gravel. *Tripp.*

Her husband was back from Tulsa, and she offered him a welcoming smile.

Tripp closed the distance between them, wrapping

his arm around her shoulder and pulling her close, his lips warm upon hers.

"I missed my girls," he murmured.

"We missed you, too," Hannah breathed.

"Daddy Tripp!" Clementine called out. "Look, I'm riding almost by myself."

"You'll be ready for the rodeo by summer," he said.

Clementine beamed beneath his praise. "Did you bring me something?" she asked.

"Well, of course. I found those pink hair clips you wanted."

"Oh, thank you."

"Did you bring me something?" Dutch called.

"You bet. Twelve bags of feed. They're still in the truck."

"You're just too generous, boss," the wrangler grumbled as he helped Clementine down from the mare.

Tripp met his wife's gaze and reached into his back pocket. "I brought you something, too."

"What's that?"

He pulled a neatly folded paper out of his back pocket and handed it to her.

Hannah's hand shook as she unfolded the paper.

"They agreed to our offer," Tripp said. "I got the call on my way home and stopped at the real estate office in Timber."

"The ranch and the house?"

"Yeah. They're expediting closing, so the Walker family can be in our new home in two weeks."

Hannah's breath caught, and she leaned against Tripp. "Our own place," she said.

"So what do you think about heading down to Pauls Valley to get a horse for this year's 100-Day Challenge?"

Her eyes widened.

"Fact is, there's no reason why we can't get two horses this year, right? One for each of us."

She nearly gasped at the words. "Really? That's a wonderful idea. I mean, as long as you don't mind if I beat you in the competition."

Tripp released a laugh, his blue eyes twinkling with amusement. "Dream on, Mrs. Walker."

She met his gaze.

"Oh, it's really happening, Tripp."

"Yeah. And the best part is that our place is right down the road from Big Heart Ranch."

Hannah nodded. Yes. She'd always be part of the ranch that gave her a second chance.

"So what's next?" she asked Tripp.

"I'll get you to sign the paperwork as co-owner of Walker Equine."

"Co-owner. I like that."

He kissed her forehead. "Me, too."

Hannah glanced at her watch. "We better head over to the chow hall. That meeting is in five minutes."

A small cry from baby Anne had their immediate attention.

"Your daughter is awake," Hannah said.

"Do you want me to hold her?" he asked.

"Yes, please. But let me warn you. She's been a real squiggle bug today."

"That's because she misses her daddy."

The five-month-old looked up at her father with adoring eyes. He took the baby from Hannah's arms and cradled her against his chest like he'd been doing it all his life. He'd taken so quickly to fatherhood that Rue had dubbed him the baby whisperer.

"What's this meeting about?" Tripp asked.

"It's time to get ready for another year of events at Big Heart Ranch."

Clementine led the way to the chow hall. Just steps ahead of them, she skipped and sang a little song to herself.

Tripp opened the big glass doors for them and then stepped inside where Lucy, Emma and Travis stood at the front of the room preparing for the meeting.

Emma's husband, Zach, walked back and forth, gently rocking five-month-old Zachary Steven Norman. His twin girls, Elizabeth and Rachel, followed him while chattering nonstop.

Across the room, Jack Harris sat at a table feeding eighteen-month-old Daniel, while triplets Ann, Eva and Dub colored with crayons at the table.

The double doors opened again, and AJ Maxwell walked in with Rue and Dutch. AJ carried little Barbara Ellin in her arms. The baby was now nine months old and, as predicted, with her golden curls and bright blue eyes, looked like she belonged on the cover of a parenting magazine.

"Momma, may I go sit with Dub and his sisters?" Clementine asked.

"Okay, but you have to be very quiet during the meeting."

"Yes, Momma."

Planning for another year at Big Heart Ranch included the staff Thanksgiving dinner, the Holiday Roundup, another summer of trail rides, vacation Bible school and the summer rodeo.

All of this would be part of Hannah's life for many

years to come. Her children would grow up taking part in this ranch that healed so many hearts.

It didn't escape Hannah that Jake Maxwell had somehow managed to lead her to this place over thirty years ago by writing letters to her mother.

Hannah sighed and reached for her husband's hand.

"I love you," Tripp mouthed.

"I love you, too," she whispered. Her heart was full as she smiled at the cowboy she loved so very much.

By the grace of God, she had been blessed with a second chance that took her to Timber, Oklahoma, and Big Heart Ranch. Home to the people who would be her forever family.

Hannah had been wrong; love did heal all things.

* * * * *

WE HOPE YOU ENJOYED
THIS BOOK FROM

LOVE INSPIRED

INSPIRATIONAL ROMANCE

Uplifting stories of faith, forgiveness and hope.

Fall in love with stories where faith helps
guide you through life's challenges, and discover
the promise of a new beginning.

6 NEW BOOKS AVAILABLE EVERY MONTH!

LOVE INSPIRED

INSPIRATIONAL ROMANCE

UPLIFTING STORIES OF FAITH, FORGIVENESS AND HOPE.

Join our social communities to connect with other readers who share your love!

Sign up for the Love Inspired newsletter at **LoveInspired.com** to be the first to find out about upcoming titles, special promotions and exclusive content.

CONNECT WITH US AT:

f Facebook.com/LoveInspiredBooks

🐦 Twitter.com/LoveInspiredBks

Facebook.com/groups/HarlequinConnection

LISOCIAL2020